THE
LAST ORPHAN

STERLING R. WALKER

The Last Orphan
©2014 Sterling R. Walker

Cover by Jessica Bartlett and Nathaniel Walker
Model: Kelly Furr

Disclaimer: All characters appearing in this work are
fictitious. Any resemblance to real persons living or dead
is purely coincidental.

Printed in the United States of America

ISBN 13: 9780990019046
ISBN 10: 0990019047

PART I
BANGKOK

ONE
COMPLICATIONS

SOMETHIN' IS WRONG!

The thought was subliminal, but insistent enough to wake Blaze Smith out of a sound sleep. He sat up and looked around. It was still pitch dark where he'd been sleeping beneath the bower of the gnarled, multi-trunked Banyan tree, stretched out on the grass, but he sensed something had changed in the past few minutes.

"Shima?"

There was no answer.

Blaze's wide-awake concern was ratcheted up to heart-pounding fear. He sprang to his feet. "Shima?"

He knew there was only one place his crewmate He-shima Oryang could be—factory number six. She wasn't supposed to go near it until after the Interstellar Peace-keepers Patrol raided the illegal factory, arrested the criminals who ran the place, and liberated the children who were forced to labor there as slaves.

The ISPP captain's orders to Blaze and Shima were clear. "Look, we've got a job to do here. I know you want to find your niece, Oryang, but this raid could potentially turn ugly, and you could get killed—or get someone else killed—and I can't let that happen. I don't

1

have enough officers to send someone to babysit you, so I'll say this one last time—*stay here* and *keep quiet.*"

What part of 'stay here' didn't you understand, Shima? Blaze took off running.

The field of weeds sloped upward for one hundred meters until it reached a high plateau where a razor-wire fence surrounded factory number six, overlooking the Chao Phraya River. He ascended the riverbank as fast as he could in the darkness.

Blaze thought of many things in hindsight as he ran. First, the earcom lying in the grass where he and Shima had been sitting. *That might come in handy right about now so I could call for help!*

He remembered the binoculars also lying in the grass. *I could've used those to take a look at the scene before runnin' right up to the fence and possibly gettin' myself shot!*

There was the loaded G30 Excalibur compact pistol in the right-hand cargo pocket of his jeans. *I'll use it only if I have to.* It sounded good in theory, but Blaze didn't know if he had the courage to use the gun on another person, even in self-defense.

The engineer's thoughts turned to the technical—the tiny personal transmitter attached to the skin of his left bicep like a leech. *Captain York'll know I'm on the move, and he's gonna be furious!* Blaze realized the ISPP team preparing to raid the factory would register his transmitter on their scanners and avoid shooting him, although the armed factory guard would do the opposite and kill him on sight.

So stay out of sight, he advised himself, running as fast as his tall, lanky, nonathletic frame could carry him. As he approached the crest of the riverbank where the land leveled out, he realized the sky seemed brighter because the spotlights were turned on over the only gate in the razor-wire fence, which faced the river.

Blaze knew why the lights were on because he'd witnessed it the night before—*a prisoner exchange*. Older girls would be taken from the factory and younger girls would be brought in later to replace them.

He reached the plateau and was shocked to see Shima's slender back just fifty meters ahead of him. Her cornrow braids whipped her shoulders as she sprinted the fence's perimeter. She was headed straight toward the lights, the open gate, the black solar van waiting for the slaves to exit the factory, and the half dozen people inside the fence who weren't expecting her.

What's she doin'? Blaze stopped several meters short of the fence, paralyzed by indecision as he watched his crewmate running straight toward certain death. *What should I do?*

That question was answered for him as something akin to a runaway tram hit him from behind.

Blaze went down hard, face-first into a clump of thorny weeds, the wind knocked out of him by the unseen linebacker who must have been twice his weight.

"Don't move," Cade York hissed in his ear.

He couldn't have moved if he tried. Blaze thought being run over by a tram might have been less painful. When he could breathe again, he opened his eyes and discovered a pair of ancient field binoculars on the ground, about a decimeter from his nose, the same binoculars he thought he left beneath the Banyan tree. He realized Shima must have dropped them before she took off running toward the gate.

"Zuri!"

Even from this distance, he recognized the scream as Shima's. The response was instantaneous—the night was shattered with the *crack crack crack* of gunfire.

York cursed and leapt to his feet. "Stay down, Smith!"

Blaze heard a metallic *click*, followed by the deafening blast of a military-grade pistol. York added his deadly contribution to the raging firefight on and around the factory grounds. Blaze hoped the ISPP captain's split-second pauses between each trigger pull were evidence he was aiming and not just blasting anything that moved.

Empty bullet casings rained down on him from York's handheld cannon. Blaze didn't like feeling helpless and scared. Random screams from the factory grounds made his skin crawl. He prayed none of those screams were Shima's. He extended an arm and picked up the binoculars, wiping dirt from the lenses.

He heard York move off a few steps, pausing only two seconds to reload his pistol with a fresh magazine. "Begin sweep now!" The captain shouted orders to his teams on his earcom. "We're moving up the raids! Repeat—begin sweep now!"

I have to see! Blaze's heart was pounding against his ribs. *I just have to see if Shima* . . . he felt cold, despite the warm night air . . . *if she's been* . . . he couldn't finish the thought. He rose to his elbows and lifted the binoculars to his eyes.

His vision was drawn to the bodies sprawled on the grounds near the gate. He fought back a wave of nausea and looked away, focusing his sights on the two figures still upright in the midst of this gruesome scene. One had a cloth bag over her head, hands bound behind her back, struggling to escape a pair of arms that reached out of the open cargo door of the van to haul her inside.

A long shiny blue pole he recognized as a nerve prod touched the hooded girl. She screamed and stopped struggling, paralyzed by the cruel device.

The other figure still up and covering ground like an Olympic sprinter was Shima. "No!" Her shout of outrage reached Blaze's ears a moment before she reached the van. She threw her arms around the captive, turned so her body was positioned between the girl and the van, and was struck with the nerve prod.

Shima screamed in pain this time. She struggled to hold on to the slave but couldn't get her muscles to cooperate. She lost her grip and both fell onto the gravel road.

Three people leapt out of the van, seized the prisoner and Shima, and hauled them inside. Tires spitting gravel, the van lurched forward, picked up speed, and the taillights vanished into the night.

"Shima!" Blaze dropped the binoculars and scrambled to his feet. "Shima!" The shock of what he just witnessed barely registered in his mind. The gunfire ceased the moment the van drove out of sight. The sudden silence was just as unnerving as the screams a few moments ago.

York was behind him, barking instructions. "Team six, move in! Secure the factory!" Blaze was also given terse orders. "Stay here, Smith! Don't move this time!"

"What about Shima?" He couldn't see York. The ISPP team assigned to raid factory six wore Chameleon suits, which made them invisible to the eye.

"I told you I don't have anyone to spare to follow the van." The ISPP captain's disembodied reply was gruff. "I don't know what Oryang was trying to accomplish— short of suicide—but there's nothing we can do about her right now."

Blaze started to protest again, but York cut him off. "We've got a job to do, so save it!"

He sensed, rather than heard, York leave. He felt frozen in place, unable to organize his thoughts around a single, numbing, terrible fact: *Shima's gone!*

The one thing Shima was desperate to accomplish was to follow the van to discover where the older slave girls were taken during the night. She hoped the van would lead her to her fourteen-year-old niece, Zuri Oketta, who'd been missing for seven years. Blaze had offered to accompany the *Alex*'s first officer into Bangkok for safety, defying the orders of both captains. Now Shima was gone, taken away in the same van she hoped to trail. She disappeared right before his eyes.

Captain Shepherd—what am I gonna say to her? I have to tell her Shima was abducted while I just watched, helpless to do anythin' to stop it! The thought of making that call twisted his stomach into a painful knot, but he knew he couldn't put it off.

Because Blaze was lying close to York's very large and very loud handgun, a buzzing sound filled his ears like audio feedback on a cheap holo-vid. He wondered if he would be able to hear well enough on an earcom to speak to Shepherd. When he reached up to touch his left earlobe and found it bare, he remembered he wasn't wearing the com—it was still in the grass beneath the Banyan tree.

The thought of York confronting him again for disobeying orders was strong incentive not to retrieve the com. The bad news would have to wait.

He walked to the razor-wire fence and stared up at the factory. It was brown stucco, four stories tall, windowless, although he'd seen it from a higher vantage point and knew it was two buildings connected by a four-story wall on each side, leaving a courtyard in the middle. The fence was only ten meters from the factory's exterior wall.

Blaze recalled there was a door on each side of the factory. He began to follow the fence, away from the bodies near the gate, until he turned a corner and found a different entrance. He decided to wait a few minutes to see if anyone would emerge.

What's goin' on inside? How many children are slaves here? How many criminals run this place? Are they all armed like the ones at the gate? The engineer realized he was an easy target, standing in plain view of the door. *Maybe some self-defense would be a good idea.* He reached into the cargo pocket of his jeans for the tiny Excalibur pistol.

As a boy, Blaze often hunted rabbits on the Osage Indian Reservation outside of Tulsa, Oklahoma, using his grandfather's antique 12 gauge. He'd blasted enough armadillos and rattlesnakes to be comfortable with a shotgun, but the pistols ISPP loaned the crew of *Alex's Legacy* were more difficult to maneuver. Despite the fact that he'd logged several hours of target practice with the Excalibur, Blaze didn't think he could hit an elephant if it was standing right in front of him. He worked for a moment to find a comfortable purchase on the too-short grip, which didn't fit his extra-large palm.

Without warning, the door to the factory flew open, and he heard shouts from inside. High-pitched female screams and the sound of running footsteps grew louder. He dropped to one knee and took aim at the dark opening, but something made him pause and leave the safety on.

He was grateful he hesitated.

Children began to pour from the open doorway. Dozens of barefoot girls clad in drab gray tunics, heads shorn in military-style crew cuts, filled the space between the factory and the fence. They ranged in sizes, ages, and nationalities, but each was shouting with excitement in her own language. Some were looking around for an exit in the fence.

"This way!" Blaze yelled to get their attention.

A few of them glanced at him in alarm, but he smiled, made a show of putting his pistol away, and indicated the direction they should go to reach the gate. He began walking, hopeful they would follow his lead.

There was still the problem of the carnage near the gate, but it couldn't be helped. There was no other way for the girls to leave the factory grounds.

"I will show you the way!"

Blaze startled at the booming female voice. He turned back to see an enormous woman emerge from the open doorway behind the last few girls. He'd met Wisdom Moniesa briefly the day before. She was a member of the ISPP surveillance team assigned to cover factory number six with York. It was reassuring to know the weapons officer was one of the good guys because she was the most ferocious-looking person Blaze ever set eyes on.

Moniesa had removed the head covering of her Chameleon suit and turned off the camouflage, giving her the appearance of a body builder in SCUBA gear. She had ink-black skin, a shaved head covered in wild, colorful tattoos, and a muscular physique which would've made any *man* envious. She was also wearing a pair of lethal-looking oversized pistols in holsters strapped to her thighs. He suspected she was packing a lot more weapons than what was on display.

The ISPP officer waded through the crowd of girls. She was at least a meter taller than most of them. The former slaves made room for her to pass and fell into step behind her. Blaze thought the girls were too terrified to disobey her. *I know I'd be runnin' the other way if she showed up at my door in the middle of the night!*

"My name is Moniesa." She turned around and walked backward as she addressed the girls. She had a comforting voice, despite the volume, with an accent Blaze couldn't place. "I am an officer in the Interstellar Peacekeepers Patrol. We came here to liberate you from the factory."

Cheers erupted from the girls, even the ones who didn't speak English and had no idea what she was saying. Moniesa's lilting voice seemed to be the only friendly thing about her persona, yet the girls were smiling up at her, in awe of this grizzly bear of a woman.

"You have been very brave tonight, but I must ask you to be brave once more as we reach the gate," Moniesa said. "Do not be afraid of what you will see. Turn away if the sight of blood makes you sick. Just remember these cruel people can never hurt you again. You are free."

Another ragged cheer went up from the crowd as it made its way to the gate. Blaze walked the fence with growing trepidation as they neared the site of the blood-bath.

A few of the girls gasped, but no one screamed or went into hysterics. They followed Moniesa through the gate, crossed the road, and congregated on the grassy slope a dozen meters from the fence, gathering around the giant woman to await more instructions.

She's got a fan club. Blaze paused at the edge of the group. At two meters, he was as tall as Moniesa. He could see over the girls and take a head count: eighty-three.

"We will take care of you and try our best to locate your families," she said. "But for now we must wait for Captain York to tell us what to do."

The ex-slaves cheered again and began chattering with one another. Blaze couldn't understand what they were saying. He caught some snippets of Chinese and Russian, but no Spanish or Swahili, which were the only other languages he could recognize.

Three more ISPP officers, two men and one woman, emerged from the factory grounds. Each had a large sniper rifle nestled in the crook of his or her elbow.

"All clear," the woman called to Moniesa.

The larger woman nodded in response and turned her attention back to the crowd. She was attempting to answer questions for the girls, if she could understand their language.

One young woman elbowed her way through the group and approached Blaze. She was thin but taller than most of the girls. She was one of the older slaves. She had an auburn crew cut and large, sad brown eyes. Unlike the other girls, who were laughing and hugging each other, this teen was distraught about something.

"*Prieten?*" She studied Blaze's face with a look of desperation. "*Prieten?*" she asked again, a little louder.

He shrugged and shook his head to indicate he wanted to help but didn't know what *prieten* meant.

The girl's eyes filled with tears. "Zuri?"

Blaze's jaw dropped. "Zuri? You know her—you know Zuri?"

Her eyes widened, and she stared at him in shock. "Yes, Zuri! Where Zuri?"

Blaze was at a loss for words. Not knowing what else to do, he got down on one knee and held out his hands to her. Without hesitation, she rushed into his arms, burying her face in his shoulder. He wrapped his arms around the trembling girl. She reminded him a little of his own daughter, five-year-old Niyati.

"Zuri . . . gone." She started to cry. "Where Zuri?"

"Don't worry; we'll find her." He didn't know if she understood what he was staying, but he tried to sound soothing. "What's your name?"

She shook her head; she didn't understand.

He pointed to himself. "Blaze." Then he pointed to her.

"Ekaterina."

"What's going on?" Cade York appeared out of nowhere again, startling Blaze. This time the captain had turned off the camouflage and removed the head covering, like the other ISPP officers. "What's she saying?"

"I'm not sure why she approached me. Maybe I remind her of someone," Blaze said. "She asked me about Zuri—Shima's niece."

"Zuri?" York echoed. "The girl Danae's searching for? Is she here?"

"Let me ask." Blaze spoke to her in a soft tone. "Ekaterina, where is Zuri?"

When Ekaterina glanced at his face with a puzzled frown, he pointed, indicating the crowd of girls around them. "Is Zuri here?"

Blaze wasn't sure if the teen spoke much English, but she got the gist of what he was asking. She shook her head no, and her eyes filled with tears again.

"She *was* here." He was chagrinned to realize how long it took him to put the pieces together. "I heard Shima shout 'Zuri' when she was runnin' to the van. The girl they were takin' away, the one with the bag over her head, must've been Zuri."

York ran a large hand across his brown forehead, wiping away the sweat which threatened to run into his eyes. "If it was the niece getting hauled out to the van, that would explain why Oryang went after her."

Blaze nodded and got to his feet, but Ekaterina wouldn't let go. She wrapped her skinny arms around his waist and looked up at him with sad, pleading eyes. He gave her shoulders a gentle squeeze of reassurance before focusing on York. "Captain Shepherd needs to know what happened to Shima."

"One problem at a time." York got a faraway look in his eyes and listened to his earcom for a few minutes before turning his stern gaze on Blaze again. "We have a lot of children now under ISPP's protection. We'll have to figure out what to do with them. My teams report between eighty and one hundred twenty kids from each factory."

The engineer did the math and grimaced. "*Alex's Legacy* could handle a hundred fifty, max."

"We can't transport nine hundred kids outside of Bangkok," York said. "We can't take them anywhere until we have some answers. We'll have to interview each child and find out where they were abducted so we can reunite them with their families."

Blaze felt a nudge of impatience. "Are you gonna put them all up in a hotel? Didn't you plan on what to do with the kids after you raided the factories?"

"We barely had time to plan a coordinated attack for tonight. And thanks to Oryang's little stunt, we had to move in early."

Blaze opened his mouth to object that it wasn't her fault, but York shouted over him. "I lost two officers tonight! I've never lost a member of my crew, but tonight two of my youngest recruits were shot and killed by slavers!"

Ekaterina clung tighter to Blaze as the captain's volume rose, but the engineer patted her on the back and attempted to keep a leash on his own temper. "I'm sorry for your loss, but you can't blame Shima. She was only tryin' to rescue her niece. Maybe if you'd let the *Alex*'s crew help—"

"Then I'd have half a dozen dead instead of two!" York snapped.

"Captain!" Moniesa's shout interrupted the argument. "CIPs!" She didn't need to announce it because they could already hear the approaching sirens.

York swore and turned away from Blaze. They could see the rotating blue lights coming up the gravel road, illuminating the night sky like a miniature Aurora Borealis. "One more headache I don't need. Stay here while I sort this out, Smith."

"What should I do while you're sortin'?" Blaze was unable to suppress the sarcasm.

"You could figure out what to do with all these kids tonight," York said over his shoulder as he walked toward the road.

Blaze realized he was serious. "Yes, sir."

"Get out of sight and cover me," York called to the three ISPP team members who were standing off to the side, near the gate.

The engineer watched in amazement as the snipers vanished, rifles and all. York walked toward the two CIP solar cars stopped outside the gate, his empty hands in the air. The police silenced the sirens and piled out of the vehicles, weapons leveled at the captain. One of them shouted at York in Thai, but he continued to approach them.

Blaze held his breath. He was sure York was going to get himself killed, but the CIPs held their fire. When the captain was a few meters from the first patrol car, he spoke a short phrase to the CIPs in Thai.

The police holstered their weapons. York removed his earcom and handed it to the CIP who had done all the shouting. Blaze thought it was the police chief. The Thai scowled at the ISPP captain as he clipped the device to his own earlobe. He listened for a minute, nodded, and returned the earcom.

The CIP chief turned to the other officers, spoke to them at length, and that seemed to do the trick. They climbed back into their patrol cars and drove away.

"What did he say to them?" Blaze asked Moniesa, who was close enough that he didn't have to shout.

"All Central Intelligence Police know about ISPP. Our Thai translator on the com told them to cooperate or face arrest for ignoring the slave-run factories."

"Why is it I've never heard of ISPP until now?"

"We like to keep a low profile." Moniesa flashed a mischievous grin.

York walked back to Blaze. "Any ideas?" he asked, as if nothing had interrupted their earlier debate.

The engineer gave Ekaterina's bony shoulders another gentle squeeze. "Actually, I do have one idea."

TWO
DARK ALLEY

"NO! NOOOOO!" DANAE Shepherd could feel the blood draining from her face. She sat down at the com control board before she keeled over. "How can she be missing? What happened?"

A hundred thoughts raced through her mind as she tried to listen to Blaze's report without interrupting him again. *I shouldn't have let her go—I should've gone with her—I should've gone after her—I should've . . .* She wedged her trembling hands beneath her thighs and tried to slow her breathing so she wouldn't hyperventilate. *I can't lose Shima! She's all the family I have left!*

"Captain?" Danae realized Blaze finished telling her what happened at factory number six. Not much of what he said after "Shima's missing" registered in her mind.

"I need to talk to Captain York." Her request came out like a croak, but she swallowed hard and tried to get her emotions under control.

"Yes, ma'am."

Unfortunately, setting her fear aside left an opening for another emotion to take center stage. In the few moments it took for Blaze to switch the com to Cade York, Danae was ready to draw blood.

"This is York."

"Why didn't you follow her? How could you just let them take——?"

"Oryang had no business being here tonight!" Cade shouted over her. "You gave me your word your crew would stay out of the way!"

"You could've shot out the tires! You could've done *something* to stop them!"

"Wrong! Because of her, we had to move in early! She put the entire mission in jeopardy!"

"I don't care about——!"

Cade shouted her down again. "I lost two people tonight because of Oryang!"

"What?" Danae felt a fresh jolt of fear. It took the edge off her anger.

"You heard me! I lost two members of my crew tonight because we had to move in before we were ready!"

Danae slumped back in her chair, a cold, sick feeling in the pit of her stomach. *He's right.* Her indignation drained away like water in a sieve. *I have no right to take this out on him.* She took some deep breaths and reined in her emotions.

"Shima left here against my orders and without my knowledge. I'm sure she convinced Blaze to go with her."

"Smith tried to stop her." Cade's tone was cold, but calmer, his volume coming down to match hers. "He thinks she saw her niece being loaded into the van."

"Shima saw Zuri?" Danae gasped.

"She must've seen *someone* because she almost got her head blown off trying to reach that van."

Danae flinched, unwilling to imagine that scene. She wasn't aware her ship's medic, Erik Sorensen, had walked up behind her until he asked, "What's all the shouting?"

She held up an index finger, indicating she needed a minute to finish the call. "We need to talk about this, in person. I need to know exactly what happened."

"Negative. I've got more urgent problems to deal with right now." Cade sounded weary, but still steamed. "I'll have someone escort Smith back to your ship."

Danae bristled. "You don't think Shima's abduction is urgent? Every minute we delay takes her farther away! She could be anywhere by now!"

"This conversation will have to wait. York out." He severed the connection.

Danae wanted to scream, but she didn't want to have a meltdown in front of Erik. She slammed a fist down on the control board instead.

"Whoa! Don't hurt yourself!" Erik gripped her shoulders, but when she didn't try to take another swing at the hapless console, he massaged them instead. "Did you say Shima was *abducted?* What happened?"

Danae knew the shoulder rub was meant to be re-assuring, but she wasn't in the mood for sympathy. She was too angry at Cade to attempt a rational conversation with Erik. She shrugged off his hands as she stood and stalked across the bridge to the helm control board. Since the bridge was only three-by-four meters, it was a short stalk.

She folded her arms and stared out the window at the night sky. "I don't want to talk about it."

Erik hesitated before offering a cautious reply. "Do you want me to leave you alone?"

Though it was an innocuous question, Danae inter-preted a much deeper meaning in the words. *Alone? Yes,*

I've been left alone. Everyone I love is gone—either dead or missing! Her knees began to shake, and she gripped the back of the helmsman's chair to steady herself.

"Danae?" Erik reached her in two strides. He started to put an arm around her but stopped short of making contact, his expression uncertain. He dropped his arm to his side. "Please let me help—talk to me. What happened to Shima?"

There was also a stark contrast in the men's personalities. Erik was proving himself to be an indispensable member of Danae's crew. He'd been honest about his interest in her as more than a friend, yet he was taking extra care not to pressure her.

Cade had also shown an interest in Danae, although the only thing he managed to do was make her so angry she wanted to punch him.

At the moment, Danae didn't want to think about either of them. Shima was all she could focus on. "I can't . . . I can't talk about it . . . It's too horrible . . ."

"What happened?" he persisted.

She couldn't hold it in any longer. She sank into the chair and buried her face in her hands. "Shima's missing!"

Danae struggled to keep the tears at bay as she explained to Erik what she knew about Shima's abduction. She hated feeling so vulnerable and weak, and she especially hated feeling helpless. She rubbed at her uncooperative eyes. "How will I ever find her? She could be anywhere by now!"

The doctor got down on one knee beside her chair so he could look her in the eye. "You've been up at least forty-eight hours. There's no way we can search for Shima while you're dead on your feet."

"I don't need sleep. I need to find Shima."

"We will." He sounded so sincere she almost believed him.

"How?" Danae shook her head and discovered the movement made her temples throb. The pain worked itself into a migraine.

"I don't need a scanner to see you're hurting."

"I'm fine." She was impressed Erik managed to maintain a poker face at this announcement. "Really." She tried to muster a smile, but was unsuccessful. "I can manage."

"No, you can't. You need a painkiller and some sleep, in that order." He flashed a sheepish grin. "I've been on this ship for two weeks, but I still have no idea where your cabin is."

"I don't think I can walk that far." Danae had to shut her eyes. The overhead lights of the bridge made her stomach feel like the ship was in free fall.

"The infirmary's closer." When she objected, he said, "Doctor's orders."

Danae felt herself being scooped out of the chair by a pair of strong arms. Erik carried her the short distance to the infirmary post-op, set her down on one of the beds, pulled off her boots, and tucked her in like an overgrown baby.

"I'll be fine." She knew it wasn't a convincing argument because her skull felt as if it were going to split in two.

Without saying a word, Erik slipped a hand beneath her neck and pressed a med patch to the skin just below her hairline. Her nausea and pain subsided.

"Thanks . . . doctor."

Danae wondered if Erik included a sedative with the patch. *Jake would've knocked me out without giving it a second thought.*

But, she realized, just before falling asleep, *Jake wouldn't have kissed me on the forehead.*

***

"I have some good news and some bad news, Captain."

Danae opened her eyes and blinked sleepily at her thin, graying Indian navigator, Vipul Ganguli, who was standing at the side of her bed. If anyone else on the crew was standing at her bedside, it would've been awkward, but since she and Vipul spent several days together in post-op recovering from gunshot wounds, his appearance now seemed normal.

"Where's Erik?"

"That's the bad news; he's not here. Dr. Sorensen, Lorina, and Phailin have been recruited by Captain York to help his crew organize a temporary camp for the former slaves in Lumphini Park. I've been requested to relieve the doctor in an hour so he can come back and check on Ting."

"Where's Blaze?"

"I saw him in the galley with Niyati. He just got back from helping ISPP set up the camp. He and Lorina plan to trade off parental duties every shift."

Danae sat up and rubbed the grit from the corners of her eyes. "What's the good news?"

"Captain York requests you contact him as soon as possible."

She didn't think that qualified as good news. "Why?"

"He said he has a way to locate Shima."

"What?" Danae was out of bed in an instant and searching the floor for her boots. "Next time, give me the good news first!"

"Yes, Captain," Vipul said. "Captain York wants you to accompany him to search for her."

Danae abandoned the hunt for her boots and left Vipul, sprinting next door to the bridge. She dropped into the seat at the control board and activated the ship-to-ship com.

A quick glance at the time made her grimace. It was 1027. She was disgusted with herself for sleeping late while her best friend was held captive for over nine hours. She tried not to imagine the worst-case scenarios of what could've happened to Shima during that time.

"You've reached the Interstellar Peacekeepers Patrol warship, the *Title of Liberty*." The ISPP com officer answered the call like a fussy administrative assistant. "Roland Diaz speaking."

Danae skipped the formalities. "This is Shepherd; put York on."

"Yes, Captain. One moment, please."

Before Cade could issue a greeting, she was peppering him with questions. "How can you locate Shima? Where is she? Why didn't you mention this last night when I was worried sick about her?" She didn't attempt to filter the accusation from the last question.

Cade's reply was gruff. "One: Oryang's wearing a personal transmitter, and it's still in range. Two: I don't know. We'll have to use the PT tracker to locate her. And three: I had nine hundred kids and forty ISPP crewmembers ahead of her on my list of priorities last night. And two of those crewmembers required coffins." He didn't attempt to filter the contempt from his last comment.

Danae flinched but didn't apologize. "How soon can we leave to search for her?"

"I'm dirtside at Lumphini Park. We can leave as soon as you get here."

She brought up a map of Bangkok on the console's right-hand monitor and frowned at the immense size of Lumphini. "How will I find you?"

"There's a large Buddha statue near the Rama Road entrance. I'll have Moniesa meet you there. York out." He didn't wait for her reply before cutting the connection.

Danae spoke to the shipboard com. "Vipul, I'm going dirtside. You should accompany me since you have to relieve Erik. It'll be safer if we travel together."

"Yes, Captain. I always feel safer when I'm with you. I'll meet you at the airlock in five."

She didn't give herself permission to blush at Vipul's sincere compliment. "Blaze, take care of the ship and Ting while I'm dirtside."

"Yes, Captain." The engineer's reply was hesitant. "And, Captain, I want to apologize for disobeyin' orders—"

"Save it," she cut him off. "I'm on my way to find Shima. Nothing else matters right now."

"Yes, Captain. Good luck, ma'am. I'll be prayin' for you."

Danae raised her eyebrows at Blaze's last comment but didn't take time to analyze it. *How did I manage to hire such an interesting crew?* They never stopped surprising her.

She descended the ship's ladder one level and raced to her tiny office to retrieve her pistol with a spare magazine, a datapad, and her extra pair of boots. She hopped on one foot, then the other, pulling the boots on as she made her way back to the ladder.

Vipul was waiting for her in the entryway. He was wearing an earcom and loading a fresh magazine into his pistol.

Danae felt her bare earlobes and scowled. "I'm not going to waste five minutes going back for an earcom."

"I understand, Captain. Ready to go?" At her nod, Vipul touched the keypad to cycle open the round, half-meter-thick airlock door. They crossed the antechamber, and she cycled open the airlock outer door to the space-port.

After being inside a climate-controlled starship, the sticky tropical heat of Bangkok felt like a sauna. Danae was already starting to perspire as she and Vipul descended the collapsible staircase to the landing platform.

Once they were across the platform and on the space-port lift, she ran her fingers through her short messy curls, trying to flatten them into some semblance of order. She tucked her tropical-print *Alex's Legacy* shirt into the waist-band of her blue jeans and ignored the incessant growling of her stomach.

"Be honest, how do I look?" she asked.

The navigator shrugged. "Why? Are you trying to impress someone?"

Danae would have laughed if she wasn't so worried about Shima. She shot Vipul a halfhearted glare and tried to smooth the wrinkles out of her shirt until the elevator doors opened to the ground level.

It was half a kilometer across an ancient cracked and pockmarked parking lot to the tramstop. Too anxious to walk, Danae ran. She was pleased Vipul was able to keep up.

"Which line takes us to the park?" she asked when they reached the tramstop, where a few other spacers were waiting to catch a ride into the city. She wiped her sweaty forehead on the shoulder of her shirt. *So much for trying to impress anyone.*

"I'm not sure." Vipul studied the monitor, which displayed a map of Bangkok in Thai and English.

"Ask." She said it more brusquely than she intended, berating herself for not coming prepared with something as crucial as an earcom.

"Yes, Captain." Vipul touched his right earlobe and put in a call to the *Alex*'s cook, Phailin Kim. "What's the fastest route to the park?" He listened for a moment. "Thank you. Ganguli out. Yellow, Captain."

Danae paced up and down the sidewalk in front of the tramstop shelter as they waited five long minutes for a yellow line trolley. The one that pulled up to the stop was lemon yellow, inside and out, with the profile of a silver elephant painted beneath each window. She and Vipul boarded the tram, swiped their left thumbnails through the credit flash slot beside the android driver, and claimed the empty seat right behind it. The captain tried not to fidget, but she silently urged the android to drive faster.

They were in the city proper within a matter of minutes, but Danae knew it was still a long ride to Lumphini Park. She resigned herself to the snail's pace of the tram and watched the city pass by from her window.

Bangkok was a dirty, crowded city, halfway between ruined and rebuilt. Empty shells of crumbling brick apartment buildings sagged next to towering new structures with bright pink stucco siding and gleaming tinted windows. The shops and businesses which lined the streets were either brightly painted, neat and inviting, or they were looted hovels with smashed windows, dark and neglected.

There was little street traffic, but the pedestrian-filled sidewalks more than made up for the empty roads. The locals preferred the economical trams to cover long distances so there were no taxicabs, but there were a few solar cycles and delivery trucks on the streets. Danae counted one CIP patrol car, but little else in the way of vehicles, telling her a lot about the city's economic condition: Bangkok was experiencing the post-war pinch of poverty, just like everywhere else.

The one exception to the poverty was the street vendors, who appeared to be doing a thriving business. Push carts and kiosks selling every type of food imaginable lined both sides of the sidewalks, bordering the curbs and nestled up against the buildings, leaving just enough room for people to walk between them.

The tram made a stop at the entrance to a Buddhist temple, called a wat, with a golden, cone-shaped roof. The wat was surrounded by crowds of Thais, despite the fact that the building was nearly demolished.

Danae watched a young woman leave a necklace of tiny white flowers on the broken tile steps of the wat and turn to a decapitated Buddha statue to the left of the doorway. She placed the palms of her hands together and brought them up into a prayer position, bowing her head until her thumbs touched her chin.

"Do you know what that gesture means?" Danae asked.

"The Thai culture is influenced by both India and China," Vipul said, "so, yes, I know what it means. It's called a *wai'*—it's a sign of respect. The lower the bow, the more prominent the person or idol one is bowing to. It's also used as a greeting, farewell, or apology."

"The Japanese do something like that."

"Most Asian cultures have similar traditions, symbols, and mannerisms, although a Japanese person would be aghast to hear you suggest their bows were the same as a Thai's *wai*'s."

Danae nodded. "I'll try to remember that the next time I'm in mixed Asian company."

As the tram began to move again, Vipul said, "Do you think we'll have to ride through any flooded parts of the city?"

She pulled out her datapad and checked the map of Bangkok. "Looks like it's not close to the river, so I think we're safe."

"I hope so," Vipul said. "My boots still haven't dried out."

"And I still have blisters on my feet." Two days ago the *Alex*'s crew was forced to wade in the putrid, knee-deep floodwaters of the submerged streets near the river, searching for slave-run factories. It was an experience Danae didn't care to repeat.

She turned back to the window and tried to look for interesting details in the city's hodgepodge of scenery to keep her mind off Shima, but she wasn't successful.

Half an hour later, Danae managed to gnaw her right thumbnail down to the quick, but her fingernails were spared the same treatment because the tram arrived at Lumphini Park. She and Vipul disembarked and were met by Wisdom Moniesa on the sidewalk.

"Captain Shepherd." The big woman nodded to her. Moniesa was dressed in olive green military fatigues made of a lightweight synthcotton fabric.

Danae was conscious of her own sweaty and rumpled clothes she'd slept in. *But I'm not here for a beauty pageant. I'm here to search for Shima.*

"Officer Moniesa, this is my navigator, Vipul Ganguli."

Moniesa nodded to him. "This way, please. Captain York is expecting you."

Two of the local CIPs were guarding the Buddha-statue entrance to the park. They moved aside for Moniesa, but one of them stepped forward to stop Danae and Vipul.

"They are with me." The weapons officer added a short phrase in Thai which made the CIP's eyes widen. He stepped back and let them pass.

"They are keeping the public out so we can ensure the children's safety," Moniesa explained before Danae could voice a question. "Plus we told them if they did not cooperate in assisting us, the entire Bangkok police department would be facing criminal charges for allowing child-slave factories to operate here."

Vipul whistled. "Well, that's one way to recruit volunteers."

Moniesa laughed. "Follow me."

Danae had a difficult time keeping up with the giant woman's extra-long strides as she guided them through a maze of wild, overgrown, flowering bushes. The crazy shrubbery gave way to open fields, dotted with just enough palm trees to provide some decent shade for the makeshift refugee camp.

Normally refugee camps were miserable places to live, but the occupants of this camp were anything but miserable. There were laughing children everywhere Danae looked, kids of every size, age, and nationality. They were barefoot and clad in drab gray tunics that reached their bony knees, and most of them had crew cuts, but it wasn't hard to tell the boys from the girls.

The smaller kids were running everywhere, swarming over the swings and slides like youngsters who never had an opportunity to play outdoors. *Which is probably true for the ones who've been slaves for years, maybe for their entire childhoods,* Danae thought.

The bigger kids congregated in small groups, talking or sitting cross-legged on the grass, playing card games. The captain wondered how ISPP was able to procure so many decks of cards.

Some of the children were playing on the banks of the small lake, skipping stones or making mud pies. The overall atmosphere was festive. It was like walking into the middle of an enormous birthday party.

ISPP officers in olive uniforms were scattered throughout the park, supervising the chaos.

"How is this arrangement working out?" Danae jogged a few paces so she could fall into step beside the weapons officer.

"There are enough public restrooms to accommodate everyone." Moniesa pointed out one of the small, tiled-roof buildings in the vicinity. "The children slept on the ground last night, but they did not seem to mind. We emptied the factory dormitories of toiletries, bedding, and fresh food."

Without breaking stride, Moniesa gestured to what appeared to be a white circus tent on the other side of the lake. "That is the mess hall. We do not have the equipment to set up a full kitchen, but the children did not mind fruit and bread for breakfast. Your crewmembers Murphy and Kim are working with the *Liberty*'s kitchen staff to organize something for lunch."

"Phailin said they chopped up most of the confiscated fresh vegetables to make salads," Vipul reported, listening on his earcom as he trailed behind them. "She thinks they've located some commercial-sized grills and rice steamers to prepare a hot dinner."

Danae was impressed, but she wasn't interested in the full tour. "Where's Captain York?"

Moniesa pointed out another white tent they were approaching. "He is at the clinic, assisting with the interviews. Dr. Sorensen and the *Liberty*'s medics are giving each child a brief examination there."

"Checkups for nine hundred kids? That could take weeks," Danae said.

"We have another ISPP ship arriving this afternoon," Moniesa said. "The *Mahatma Gandhi* has a crew of sixty-five, including three medical technicians."

The captain just nodded as they reached the clinic tent. About twenty children were standing in line outside the main entrance, but they didn't appear to mind the wait. They smiled at Danae and Vipul, and one of the girls rushed over to hug Moniesa's leg, the same way Niyati Smith greeted her parents.

The big woman laughed and patted the child's nearly bald head. "Get back in line, Imani. I think you are going in with the next group."

Imani smiled up at Moniesa and returned to her spot.

The weapons officer held back the mosquito-netting door so Danae and Vipul could step inside the air-conditioned tent ahead of her.

They walked into a noisy command central. A dozen ISPP officers were interviewing former slaves, seated in folding metal chairs throughout the tent. As Danae scouted the crowd, she overheard part of a nearby interview and realized it would be a time-consuming task to question the kids who didn't speak English.

The officer spoke into a datapad, "How old are you?" He then let the girl hear the audio translation from the datapad in a guttural language Danae couldn't place. The child gave her reply, and the officer had to wait a moment for the English translation. "I think I am ten. I was taken when I was five, and it has been five rainy seasons since then."

Whew, what would it be like to spend half your life as a slave? Danae thought.

Three folding tables took up the space in the center of the tent. Erik, in blue scrubs, and two Asian men, in white lab coats, were each scanning a child seated on the makeshift exam tables.

Erik's table was the closest. He glanced up briefly from his patient and smiled at Danae. Vipul walked over to speak with him.

She returned the smile but was too busy searching the crowd with her eyes to give the doctor her full attention. "I don't see Captain York."

"He was here a few minutes ago," Moniesa said. "He might have gone out the back." She led Danae past the exam tables, through a second mosquito-netting door at the far end of the tent. "Here he is. Now if you will excuse me, Captain Shepherd, I have another task I must complete."

Danae didn't get a chance to thank Moniesa because the weapons officer already disappeared back inside the tent. She walked over to Cade.

The ISPP captain didn't seem pleased to see Danae. He was standing a few meters from the tent, making an adjustment to the saddle of a cobalt blue solar cycle which appeared to be custom made for him, due to its extra height. One of Cade's officers, a graying, wiry-looking man, was nearby, astride the saddle of another blue cycle which was standard size. A third custom cycle, this one bright purple, was parked a few meters away. Due to its height and wider saddle, Danae assumed it belonged to Moniesa.

"Captain." Cade nodded to her but didn't make eye contact. "This is my acting first officer, Heath Bergen, who will accompany us." He handed her a helmet and put on his own with the visor down so she couldn't see his face. Bergen did the same.

Danae pulled on the helmet. It was too big, but she adjusted the chin strap without complaint.

Another ISPP officer emerged from the tent with a helmet under her right arm and a large pistol tucked into a holster beneath her left. "This is my senior security officer, Tatiana Ghukasyan." Cade's deep voice in Danae's right ear was softened through the helmet's com, but not enough to take the edge off his tone. She didn't need to wonder if he was still annoyed at her, but she considered his sour attitude a minor inconvenience. Finding Shima was all that mattered.

After working with Marco Ting for ten years, grumpy Captain York should be no problem. She nodded to the dark-haired, athletic-looking Ghukasyan, who acknowledged Danae's presence with a suspicious frown before putting on her own helmet and climbing onto the tiny passenger seat of Bergen's cycle.

"Moniesa and our Thai translator will follow about five minutes behind us in case we run into trouble. Climb on." Without waiting for a response, Cade threw his leg over the seat and kicked the engine to life. Bergen started up his own cycle. The roar of two solar engines was barely muffled by her helmet.

Danae hesitated, eyeing the tiny passenger seat behind Cade. She thought it could accommodate someone Niyati's size, or smaller. She noticed Bergen peering at an unusual device mounted to his cycle over the gauges and assumed it was the PT tracker.

Erik emerged from the tent and grabbed her hand before she could climb onto Cade's cycle. He leaned close to her visor and shouted so she could hear him over the engines. "I need to tell you something!"

She opened her mouth to protest, but he added, "It's important!"

"One minute," she told Cade and pulled off the helmet before he could voice an objection in her com. She allowed Erik to lead her a few meters away from the cycles so they could talk to each other without shouting.

"Early this morning I noticed Ting's condition is starting to destabilize. I don't think we should keep him in the infirmary ICU much longer."

Danae bit her lip, ashamed she hadn't given much thought to her helmsman, who'd been in a coma for two weeks. Marco Ting was shot in the head on Mars Station after he and Phailin delivered important evidence to attorney Rosamar Delacruz—evidence that would convict CIP chief Acheron of abducting homeless children and selling them as slaves. "What should we do?"

"The King Bhumibol Memorial Hospital owns a Wang-Ortiz Neuromelder. It's a machine that can re-connect severed neural pathways in the brain."

Danae made an instant decision. "Take him there, today. Transport him by ambulance." Worry clouded Erik's features, but she didn't have time to give him a pep talk. "You revive Ting; I'll find Shima."

The doctor nodded, but she noted the uneasy glance over her shoulder at Cade. "Be careful, Danae."

"I will." For a moment she thought he was going to give her a hug, but the deafening rumble of twin solar engines revved in unison distracted them, and the moment passed.

Danae turned away from Erik and put her helmet back on. She hurried over to the waiting solar cycles. She found a short peg protruding from the axis of the rear tire, and used it to climb up to the seat behind Cade. There were footrests, but she didn't see anything for her hands, so she tentatively placed one on either side of his waist.

"You might want to hold on." Cade leaned forward.

She was forced to lean forward to keep her hands at his sides. A sarcastic remark was right on the tip of her tongue when Cade hit the throttle.

Spacer's reflexes were the only thing that kept Danae on the bike. She seized the fabric of Cade's uniform, flexed her leg muscles to anchor herself to the seat, and leaned forward until she was pressed snugly against his back to cut the wind shear. She reached around his waist until she could lock her hands together just above his navel. Only then did she feel secure enough to start breathing again.

Danae was fuming. *Did he do that on purpose just to scare me? To punish me for inconveniencing him?*

She blew out a breath of frustration and decided to be objective—and a bit more mature. *Or is this normal for him because he always drives this fast?* "Try not to run over anybody."

Cade snorted. "We went the long way around to avoid the kids. People are safe as long as they stay on the sidewalks." He took a corner without slowing down.

Turning her head, Danae saw a different entrance to Lumphini Park fly past her shoulder. She caught a glimpse of two CIPs on guard duty at the gate, their mouths hanging open in shock, but the cycles quickly left them behind. She risked a glance forward and saw Bergen's cycle ahead of them and to the right. The older man seemed to know how to drive just as fast as Cade.

She settled in for the ride, her muscles as taut as bow strings. She knew she would be sore later, but she didn't want to risk loosening her grip on Cade, not at this breakneck speed. He slowed a few times to weave around trams and other cycles, and even a few terrified pedestrians, but never came to a complete stop.

Cade York. Just my luck the one person I need to rely on for help is so infuriating. Danae was uncomfortable being this close to him. She was aware of every firm muscle in his back and waist, every vertebra in his spine, every inhale and exhale.

She shut her eyes and tried not to think about how much Cade's back felt like Alex's. The ISPP captain was physically so similar to her late husband, the two men could've passed as brothers, although their personalities couldn't have been more different.

Memories of Alex crept into Danae's thoughts. *I just wish I could see his face one more time . . . to hear him laugh . . . to feel his arms around me . . .*

Stop! She had to swallow the lump in her throat. *Focus on Shima. We have to find Shima.*

But the ache was impossible to dismiss. The wound was still fresh, no matter how hard she tried to convince herself she was strong enough to ignore the pain. Yet here she was, stuck like glue to a living, breathing replica of Alex Shepherd.

"Are you . . . crying?" The voice in her ear was quiet, but it brought her back to reality with a jolt.

"No," Danae lied, trying hard not to sniffle. She blinked to clear her vision. A few tears trickled down her face, but she had no way to wipe them away. *Ugh, I'm a mess. Focus, Danae, focus.* "Are we getting close to the transmitter?"

"Just a few more blocks, I think. Bergen?"

Danae didn't hear the first officer's response to Cade's query. They turned a corner, and then another. The cycles slowed until they were cruising at a modest speed of ten kilometers an hour.

She was able to unlock her hands, sit upright, and scoot back a few centimeters to put some space between herself and Cade, although she maintained a firm grip on the fabric at his waist in case he decided to hit the throttle again. She ignored the pains radiating up and down her legs as she was able to stop clutching the seat. She stretched her cramped muscles and took a good look around.

They passed through a dark and debris-strewn alleyway between two dilapidated brick buildings. Danae wrinkled her nose at the stench of rotting garbage. There was no one else around. "Nice place."

"This is a red-light district," Cade said.

"What?"

"Do you really need me to explain?" He was back to his old self in a heartbeat, impatient and brusque.

"No." Danae bit her lip and glanced up at the sliver of smoggy sky overhead. Clotheslines crisscrossed the alleyway between the buildings. Most of the laundry hung out to dry was women's lingerie.

There was a painful knot in Danae's stomach. The thought of Shima being held here made her nauseated. She was grateful she hadn't eaten because she wouldn't have been able to keep it down. *We've got to find her, and fast.*

Cade followed the other cycle into an alley just wide enough for a garbage truck to drive through. Her heart skipped a beat when Bergen announced, "The signal's coming from that van!"

Danae leaned to the right so she could see around Cade. Parked in the middle of the street about fifteen meters ahead of Bergen's cycle was the black solar van she recognized from the prisoner exchange at factory number six.

She was halfway off the back of the cycle before it rolled to a stop.

"Wait!" Cade had the unfair advantage of extra-long arms. He collared her the moment her feet touched the pavement. In one swift movement, he cut the power to the cycle, dismounted, and planted himself between her and the van like a human barricade.

"Are you trying to get yourself killed?" The captain let go of her and took off his helmet, but Danae wasn't intimidated by the threatening scowl on his face. "You *never* go into a potentially dangerous situation without scouting the area first. We'll handle this."

She'd reached the limit of her patience. She whipped off her own helmet and threw it on the ground, just missing his feet. "Anyone watching the street already knows we're here! And since nobody's shooting at us, why don't you stop lecturing me and check out the van!"

To his credit, Cade maintained his composure. How-ever, his scowl settled into something darker, which told Danae she'd reached the limit of *his* patience. "*Stay. Here.*" He didn't wait for a response. He withdrew a huge handgun the length of her forearm from somewhere inside his uniform and turned his back to her.

"Bergen? Ghukasyan?"

The other ISPP officers were already armed and ready to move in. They fanned out and cautiously approached the van from three different angles. Bergen reached the driver's-side door first. He glanced at the other two for nods of approval before peering through the window. Then he tried the door handle.

"It's locked. It looks empty, but the signal's definitely coming from inside."

Danae had to bite her tongue so she wouldn't scream at them to hurry up.

Cade joined Bergen at the door. He peered inside before raising his gun and bringing the butt down against the window, shattering the glass.

The sound of breaking glass echoed off the buildings. Danae held her breath and glanced around, but no one came to investigate the noise. No curious faces appeared at any of the windows overlooking the street. She exhaled and focused again on the van.

Captain York opened the driver's-side door and released the locks. Then he moved down the narrow gap between the van and the building to reach the cargo-side door. He yanked it open.

"It's empty," he announced.

Ignoring the warning glance from Ghukasyan, Danae raced to the side door. She stopped short of climbing inside after Cade, who was searching the bare interior.

Her heart plummeted as he crouched down and picked up something from the metal floor.

Cade looked over at her with a grim expression. He was holding something tiny between his left thumb and index finger. She knew what it was, but she felt frozen, unable to move or make a sound until he confirmed it.

"This is Oryang's transmitter."

THREE
NEUROMELD

DR. ERIK SORENSEN felt cold, despite the blistering heat of the midday sun outside the clinic tent. He watched, appalled, as Danae had to grab on to Cade York. The ISPP captain hit the accelerator before she was in her seat.

He did that on purpose! Erik had taken an instant disliking to York from their first conversation over the com, and this reckless move lowered his opinion of York another notch. *Danae could've been seriously hurt!*

He watched until the solar cycles were out of sight before going back inside the tent.

The doctor felt stretched thin, emotionally. The worries were piling up. Ting's coma, Shima's disappearance, and Danae's safety. Of the three worries, Marco Ting was the only one Erik could do anything about, but what needed to be done was risky. Moving the helmsman to a hospital by ambulance could prove fatal, now that his vital signs were declining.

Assuming Ting made the journey without complications and Erik was able to secure an appointment for him to be treated with the neuromelder, there were still no guarantees he would come out of the coma.

The treatment itself could prove fatal in Ting's deteriorating condition. The entire plan was one giant gamble, and Dr. Sorensen would bear full responsibility for its outcome.

He felt the beginning of a tension headache as he walked back to his makeshift exam table. A new patient was already waiting for him, sitting cross-legged in the center of the table and munching on an apple. The boy smiled at Erik. "*Hola.*"

"*No ingles?*" Erik searched his pockets for the translation datapad.

Vipul appeared at his elbow. "Are you looking for this?" He offered Erik one of the ISPP-issued, wafer-thin tablets.

"Thanks, but I really can't take the time to do another physical." He turned to the navigator. "Danae wants me to move Ting to a hospital today, so I need to get back to the ship."

"What do you need me to do?" Vipul asked.

"The ISPP doctors can handle the medical exams. What we need is someone to make sure we get a DNA trace from each child."

Vipul reached into his pocket and produced a different datapad with an ID lock built into the screen. "DNA traces are no problem, but why? All these kids were born after the war, so their DNA won't be in the Earth's database."

"The ISPP engineers are writing an advanced heir-lock program to match these kids to people in the database," Erik said. "We're hoping it'll speed up the process of reuniting them with their families."

"What about the ones who don't match anyone on Earth?"

"ISPP is requisitioning the CIP databases from each of the stations."

"That'll take time," Vipul said.

Erik nodded. "We know, but the other four ISPP ships have liberated a dozen more factories, and it's just the tip of the iceberg. Thanatos's log contains the locations of at least one hundred more factories that need to be investigated. We might be trying to reunite thousands of kids with their families by the end of the week, maybe tens of thousands by mid-December."

Vipul whistled. "It's a ripple effect."

"Yes, Danae Shepherd was just a small stone tossed into a big pond."

"Don't let her hear you say that. She's determined to avoid the hero pedestal."

"I know." Erik turned back to the Latino boy who finished gnawing his apple down to the core. He pointed to the next table where one of the ISPP doctors was finishing up with a little Asian girl. "Um, *vaminos*."

The boy laughed at Erik's pathetic attempt at Spanish, but he hopped down and went over to the other exam table.

The doctor turned back to Vipul. "I need to run. Good luck."

"You too. I think you're going to need it."

Erik grimaced more from the pain in his temples than Vipul's comment. "Thanks."

***

Marco Ting had been in a coma for two weeks. The gunshot wound had healed, leaving behind a thin pink line of synthflesh, fifteen centimeters long, across his pale forehead. Erik didn't like the readings displayed on the monitors. Ting's blood pressure was falling, his brain-wave patterns were becoming irregular, his breathing was labored to the point where he would soon need mechanical assistance, and he was no longer responding to external stimuli.

Blaze's announcement over the com roused the doctor from his worried thoughts. "The ambulance is here."

"Send them up."

"Yes, sir."

Erik left the door open to the surgery/ICU and walked over to the doorway of the infirmary. Two Thai paramedics, one male and one female, rolled their high-tech gurney off the starboard lift and approached him.

"*Sawadeekrup.*" This was the extent of the doctor's Thai vocabulary. "English?"

"A little," the woman said.

Breathing a mental sigh of relief, Erik stood back so they could wheel the gurney into the small surgical room.

The three were able to communicate well enough to work together and prep Ting for the transition. It took them only a few minutes to unhook the helmsman from the equipment, transfer him to the gurney, and hook him up to the portable monitors.

"We're on our way down, Blaze."

"I'm waitin' by the basement airlock."

Erik followed the Thai paramedics as they wheeled Ting to the starboard lift. He kept his medical scanner in hand, keeping an eye on it for any change in the helmsman's condition. The elevator brought them to the lowest level of the ship. Erik had no idea where the smaller airlock was located, but Blaze poked his dark crew cut out of one of the doorways in the basement corridor. "Over here, doctors."

The basement airlock was built into the floor of a small room, and the space seemed barely large enough to accommodate the gurney. "Can we all fit?" Erik was careful to stand back from the outline of the three-by-two-meter rectangle etched into the floor.

"Let's find out." Blaze typed a code into a keypad mounted to the wall, and the airlock floor slid to one side, tucked out of the way like a pocket door.

The paramedics climbed down into the antechamber, which was only the height of their shoulders, and the English speaker worked an anti-grav remote control. Ting's gurney rolled itself over the open space before floating down into the antechamber. The paramedics took hold of the gurney when it settled to the floor and waited for Erik to climb down and join them.

"Hold on," Blaze called down to them.

The exterior door they were standing on worked like a lift, quietly and smoothly descending the four meters to the spaceport landing platform. The paramedics pushed the gurney clear. Erik stepped off too, and watched as the half-meter-thick door ascended to the belly of the ship and snapped into place like a puzzle piece. From the outside, the airlock blended in with the hull so well that only the rectangular outline broke the smooth silvery surface of the ship.

He turned his attention back to his scanner and followed the paramedics as they rolled Ting's gurney to the platform elevator.

When the lift doors opened dirtside, Erik was relieved to see an ambulance parked only a few meters away. The female paramedic worked the anti-grav remote again, transferring the gurney with care into the vehicle.

"Can I ride in back?" He gestured to be certain there was no misunderstanding.

The Thais nodded, waited for him to climb inside, and shut the doors behind him.

"Well, I didn't mean just me," Erik grumbled, but he got to work as he heard the Thais climb into the cab and start the engine. He set the brakes on the gurney and unplugged the portable monitors, reconnecting them to the proper outlets in the walls. He squeezed into the too-small jump seat near Ting's head and gripped the sides of the gurney with both hands to give it extra stability as the ambulance began to move.

It felt as if they drove over every pothole in the ancient parking lot. Erik kept his eyes on the monitors as they lurched back and forth with each bump. Ting's heart rate and breathing seemed to speed up or slow down in time with the potholes.

A particularly jarring bump set off one of the monitors. The doctor rose from his seat just enough to reach Ting's chest with one hand, checking to be sure the helmsman's heart was still beating.

He sighed and sat down again after slapping the heart monitor machine a few times to silence the alarm. "You're not allowed to die on me," he muttered to Ting as the ambulance moved onto the main road and the ride became much smoother.

It took an hour to reach Bhumibol Memorial. Erik fretted the entire time and made the difficult decision to put Ting on the respirator when his irregular breathing became irregular wheezing.

Erik rubbed his aching forehead and breathed a sigh of relief when the ambulance came to a final stop and the rear doors opened. He unplugged the monitors and respirator from the ambulance and reconnected them to the portables. He then climbed out and stood to the side as the female paramedic transferred the gurney to the ER loading dock.

He followed closely as Ting was wheeled inside the pristine hospital, which was so newly constructed it still had that fresh-paint smell. Two attractive nurses, dressed in tailored orange scrubs which appeared to be made of silk, took over for the paramedics, who *wai*'ed to Erik and departed.

The doctor realized he was once again at a disadvantage with no one to translate for him. He shrugged in response to one of the nurse's unintelligible queries and handed her his scanner, hoping she could decipher enough from it to figure out what Ting needed.

The two women put their heads together as they studied the tiny screen. They looked up at Erik, nodded, and began to push the gurney down the hallway.

He followed them down several long corridors—a standard feature of hospitals anywhere on Earth. Ting's respirator sounded an alarm, but one of the nurses made the proper adjustment, silencing it. She glanced at Erik with a reassuring smile, but the women began to push the gurney faster.

They reached a bank of elevators and elbowed a few people out of the way to board the first one that opened up. The lift stopped on the eighth floor, and he recognized the equipment in the room behind the glass doors across the hall from the lift: *neurology department*.

The nurses opened the security doors to neurology and shouted at the medics who were just sitting around the main lab, reading datapads and drinking tea. There was a flurry of activity as several people took hold of the gurney and rushed Ting through another set of doors into a dimly lit, cavernous room which reeked of antiseptic air.

Erik had to jog to keep up. He was grateful no one kept him out of the treatment room, especially since he didn't look as if he belonged with a group of short, brown, skinny Thai medics. Apparently, the others just accepted he was Ting's personal physician and paid him no mind.

Because he had only seen holograms of the Wang-Ortiz Neuromelder, Erik was eager to see one in person. They were so expensive to build that there were only a dozen WONs in existence. He took a good look and couldn't help but wonder how any hospital could afford to maintain a WON, let alone purchase one.

Looks like there's no waiting list. Maybe most people can't afford the treatment. He wondered how much Ting's stay at this fancy hospital was going to dip into Danae's funds from her mother's inheritance.

Four medics removed all the helmsman's restraints, catheters, and IVs, leaving in place only the heart monitor and respirator. They moved him onto a large table covered with shiny pink foam, a substance Erik recognized as suspension gel. The gel was a practical invention but too costly for most surgeons to use except in cases where complete immobilization was an absolute necessity. Brain and open-heart surgeries required the gel, while most other procedures did not.

He watched as the gel began to move, undulating and shifting to accommodate Ting's body, cradling and encasing every part of him below his Adam's apple until he looked like someone buried in sand at the beach, only he was up to his neck in pink goo. Once in place, the gel hardened to a rigid shell.

In the few minutes it took for the suspension gel to encase Ting, a nurse shaved his head bald with an electric razor.

One of the medics took a seat behind a control station and began pushing buttons. The other medics and Erik took a few steps back as Ting's table glided on anti-gravs to the far end of the room until it was just in front of the WON.

The giant doughnut-shaped neuromelder was like something out of a history book—a CAT scan—but with one major difference: the opening in the center where the patient's head would be placed was filled with a clear mass of a self-contained liquid, filled with thousands of tiny probe androids.

The probes swam and swirled in random directions like fiber-optic water snakes. The movements appeared chaotic but patterns could be discerned if someone wanted to watch for several minutes and deal with the headache afterward.

Erik was skilled at using single probe androids for surgical procedures, but he always controlled them with a remote. The WON probes were designed to operate with no human interference, and each one functioned independent of the others. He couldn't wrap his medical mind around the high tech used to create the WON, so he just watched as Ting was moved into position.

One medic checked to see that the patient's respirator mask was sealed around his mouth and nose before extending the tubing so the helmsman would have a clear airway no matter how long the procedure took. The medic at the control board took charge again. The table slowly slid into the WON's round opening until Ting's entire head was submerged in the weird liquid.

Someone handed Erik a folding chair, and he got the message: this might take a long time. He sat and watched the probes swirl faster, obscuring Ting's head from view.

***

"Dr. Sorensen?" Phailin's voice was in Erik's earcom.

He glanced at the time and was amazed to see forty-five minutes had passed since Ting started the WON treatment. *Time flies when you're half asleep.* He tapped his earlobe. "Yes?"

"I'm downstairs in the lobby. I was hoping I could come up and see Marco."

"If you brought me a sandwich, I'd be glad to escort you through security." Erik stood and stretched.

"I did better than that; I brought you some panang curry on jasmine rice and a Thai iced tea."

"I appreciate the first-class service. Please tell me it's not too spicy."

"Hey, this is Bangkok. They make chili pepper baby food here. You'll just have to pick them out, sorry."

"That's fine. I'll be down in five."

Erik tried to explain to the medic monitoring Ting's respirator that he needed to leave briefly and return. The Thai just shook his head until Erik pointed to the security pass clipped to the shirt pocket of the man's lab coat.

A guest doctor's pass was produced. Erik held up two fingers, pantomimed some more, and the medic figured out what he wanted. A visitor's pass was produced.

"*Korb khun krup.*" He butchered the pronunciation for thank you, but the medic gave him a good-natured thumbs-up and opened the security doors for him.

Erik took the lift down to the crowded lobby/ waiting room to meet Phailin, who was standing near the information kiosk.

Any man with a pulse would agree the Thai-Korean-Hawaiian cook was easy on the eyes. Phailin had a creamy taupe complexion, large brown eyes, straight black hair which skimmed her shoulders, attractive dimples, and an incredible figure which strained the seams of her skin-tight blue jeans and a-size-too-small, tropical-print *Alex's Legacy* shirt. The fact that she was a dozen years younger than Erik made it easier for him not to be distracted by her natural beauty, although he was amused to see some jaws drop in the waiting room as Phailin walked over to greet him.

He traded the takeout bag for her visitor's pass. "Thanks. Any word from Captain Shepherd?"

"No." Phailin fell into step beside Erik as they walked to the lift. "I told Lorina to call me when they find Shima. *If* they find Shima." She shot him a guilty look. "Sorry. I know I should be more optimistic."

"Hunting for Shima in this city does seem like a long shot," Erik said. "I'm not sure what Danae will do if they can't find her."

"I can't imagine how she'd react. She once told me Shima is the only family she has left."

I don't want to think about how she'd react. What would I do if something happened to Kirsten? His younger sister on Mars Station was the only family he had left. Erik forced himself to shelve the depressing thought and pushed the button for the eighth floor. He and Phailin rode the elevator up to neurology.

"What's happening?" Phailin asked the moment the lift doors opened.

Behind the glass doors across from the lift they could see several medics running around the neurology lab in a panic, grabbing medical equipment and shouting instructions to each other.

"Something's wrong." Erik whipped out his security pass and pushed his way past the slow-moving doors with Phailin right on his heels.

One of the medics was on her way into the WON treatment room, shouting something over her shoulder at one of the nurses. Phailin gasped and sprinted after her, this time with Erik on her heels.

"What did she say?" he asked, although he had a pretty good idea what was happening.

"She said Marco's heart stopped!"

Inside the neuromeld room, Erik grabbed Phailin's arm to hold her back. "We need to stay out of the way."

"You're a doctor!" She shrilled, "Do something!"

"They are doing something—they're trying to revive him." Erik found himself having to physically restrain the cook. She was becoming hysterical, trying to reach Ting. He stood behind her and kept a firm grip on her shoulders so she could watch but not get close enough to be in the way.

Marco Ting had been removed from the WON, but it must have been just moments ago because his face was dripping wet. Most of the suspension gel was stripped away from his torso. Four medics were using a crash cart on him, trying to shock his heart into beating again.

Phailin stopped trying to squirm free and turned to Erik with tear-filled eyes. "He can't be gone. He can't. I didn't even get to say goodbye."

Erik didn't know what to say. He always hated breaking the bad news to family members when things went wrong, but it was the reality of working in the medical field—sometimes patients died.

"Don't look," was the only advice he could offer.

She scowled at him and turned back to watch.

Another few minutes of CPR was followed by another burst from the defibrillator paddles and a triumphant shout from one of the medics. This time Erik needed no translation.

"They've got a heartbeat."

Phailin responded to this announcement by bursting into tears. She was trembling so much, he found a chair and made her sit down.

All the medical personnel took a step back from Ting's table and issued a collective sigh of relief. One of them waved Erik over.

"I'm coming too." Phailin wouldn't take no for an answer. She was out of the chair and right by Erik's side when he reached Ting.

The helmsman was a mess. He looked as if he'd been dragged behind a horse for a few kilometers. His chest was already starting to display some major bruising from the CPR. His breath was coming in ragged gasps.

But his eyes were open.

Phailin emitted a squeal of shock. "He's awake!"

Ting blinked a few times, his dark almond-shaped eyes clouded with confusion.

"Tell them to take him off the respirator." Erik dug his scanner out of his pocket to check the helmsman's brain-wave activity.

Phailin spoke to one of the medics. The woman nodded and removed the tube from Ting's throat.

Marco coughed, groaned, and glanced around at everything and everyone, his eyes coming to rest on

Phailin. *"Tian shi?"* His voice was raspy and hoarse from the ventilator and lack of use.

The cook shook her head. "English?"

"Am I dead? Are you an angel?"

"No to both questions." Phailin grinned. "You've just come out of a coma."

Erik would have laughed, but the look on Ting's face was sincere. He read the scanner results and was impressed the helmsman's brain function was near normal.

One of the medics spoke to Phailin, who translated for Erik. "They want you to examine him and explain to him what's going on. They said the awakening will be less stressful if he's surrounded by familiar faces, so they're just going to stand back and observe."

"I'm probably not a familiar face, but if his memory's intact, he'll recall seeing me at least once." The doctor put his scanner away and used his hands and a stethoscope to check Ting's vital signs. Even with a daily regimen of movement and massage, the helmsman's muscles had atrophied.

Phailin shifted from one foot to the other with a helpless look on her face. Erik thought of something she could do to assist him. "Maybe you could get him cleaned up?"

She started to blush but nodded and turned to one of the nurses with a request. The nurse left the treatment room for a minute and returned with a basin of warm soapy water and a washcloth.

In hindsight, Erik realized this simple task could be potentially awkward. "You don't have to wash him, um, you know—below the waist."

Phailin shot him an incredulous look but turned to Ting without a word and began to wash his bald head.

Erik tested Ting's memory while he worked, peeling away strips of the dried suspension gel. "Do you re-member your name?"

"Of course I do. I'm Marco Polo Ting."

Sarcasm already, that's a good sign. "Where were you born?"

"Beijing."

"Parents' names?"

A shadow crossed Ting's features. "This is pointless. I know who I am."

"Well, do you know who I am?"

"Sorensen. You're the doctor Shepherd wanted to break out of jail on Mars Station."

"And she obviously succeeded." Erik ignored Ting's scathing tone. "What's your occupation?"

"Starship helm. I'm one of the best."

"And modest too." Erik's comment made Phailin giggle.

Ting gave her a cold look, and her smile faded. She averted her eyes and focused on washing his left arm.

Erik felt a nudge of concern. He picked up his scanner and held it over Ting's forehead. "Do you know who she is?"

"No. I still think she looks like an angel though." His lecherous grin was anything but angelic.

Phailin shot Erik a worried look but remained silent.

"What's the last thing you remember?"

Ting shut his eyes, a crease forming between his thick eyebrows. "I remember waking up in my cabin on the *Ishmael*—I know Shepherd renamed it *Alex's Legacy*—I remember waking up hung over. It was the day we were going to lift for Mars Station to go get you." His tone turned accusatory. "I remember thinking it would be a suicide mission.

53

"I remember Shepherd had me spray-painted as a disguise." Ting tried to look down at himself, but he couldn't lift his head. "Do I still look Indian?"

"No," Erik said. "Your skin tone is back to normal."

"Do you remember anything about the trip to Mars Station or the time we spent there?" Phailin bit her lip.

Ting thought for a minute. "No, but I'm sure it'll all come back to me. Right, doc?"

Erik studied his scanner before answering. The lie was more for Phailin's benefit than Ting's. "Yes, I'm sure your memory will return in time."

FOUR
CHAINS

WHERE IS MY gun? was Shima Oryang's first thought when she was cognizant enough to think. The aftereffects of the nerve prod continued to wrack her body. She couldn't stop trembling, and the paralysis made it impossible for her to move, let alone shout for help. *Danae was right that I would need a weapon. Why did I leave it on the ship?*

She was aware of her niece's shivering body beside her on the van's hard metal floor. She wished she could do something to comfort Zuri Oketta, but they were helpless until the effects of the nerve prod wore off.

The male voices around them were loud and angry, and Shima had no idea what was being shouted back and forth in the confined space. One of the men near her was having a heated argument with the driver.

Something to do with me. They did not expect an extra prisoner tonight. She didn't want to think about what awaited her and Zuri when they reached their destination.

Shima was familiar with the horrors of human trafficking. It was an everyday occurrence in her childhood, war-torn city of Kampala, Uganda. Teenage girls were lured away with lies of glamorous work and good pay. Those who didn't come willingly were often abducted.

I must protect Zuri!

The van took a sharp turn, causing Shima to roll onto her right side. She felt something like a splinter poking her upper arm, and she remembered: *The transmitter!* The tiny device might go unnoticed by her captors in the darkness. *Captain York may be able to locate us!*

She clung to that morsel of hope as the ride came to an end. The cargo door of the van was opened and rough hands gripped her ankles and seized her under the arms, hauling her out of the vehicle like a sack of rice.

"No talk or you die!" The gap-toothed Thai thug who held her ankles whispered the threat. He waited until she made eye contact before tilting his head to indicate the pistol tucked into the holster beneath his left arm.

Shima was able to exert some control over her neck muscles, nodding to indicate she understood. She still couldn't move her arms or legs, although the trembling had stopped. She tried to keep a rein on her fears so she could think straight.

The "no talk" threat was repeated to Zuri as two more men extracted the girl from the van. The thugs carried them a short distance in the darkness. The overpowering stench of decaying garbage made Shima gag. *Smells like an alley. Are we still in Bangkok?*

Yet another scruffy-looking Thai man opened an emergency-exit door from the inside of a building. Shima and Zuri were carried into a dimly lit space that didn't smell much better than the alley.

The *Alex*'s first officer noted every detail of their surroundings as she and Zuri were hauled up three flights of stairs. There were no windows, no signs on the walls to indicate their location. A well-lit hallway led to a door which was unlocked with an old-fashioned key. The door opened to a small room illuminated only by the lights from the hall.

Shima muffled a cry of pain as she was dropped onto a hard tile floor near the room's only window. One of her captors shoved her back against the wall, forcing her to sit upright.

Zuri landed on the floor beside her. One man removed the hood covering Zuri's head and untied her hands. Before either of them had a moment to recover, Shima heard the unmistakable rattle of metal chains.

She could only watch with mounting fear as her wrists were secured in front of her in thick metal bracelets. A titanium chain about two decimeters in length connected the shackles to each other, and another short chain extended outward from each of her restraints. Zuri was handcuffed the same way, and Shima was chained to Zuri on her right and another teenage girl on her left.

A loud whisper warned, "Quiet!" and their captors left the room, pulling the door shut behind them, and plunging the room into darkness. The only light came from the crack at the bottom of the door. Shima heard a key in a lock, and then it was quiet.

"Auntie, auntie," Zuri said in Swahili, "you found me."

"I have been searching for you since the night you disappeared from Mars Station."

"Don't let them hear you or they'll punish all of us!" A scared female voice whispered in English from the other side of the room.

Shima's eyes adjusted to the gloom of the unfurnished three-by-three meter space. It smelled like a locker room which hadn't been aired out in years. She could dimly make out the scared and tearful faces of the dozen multinational teenage girls who shared the stifling space with her and Zuri. They all sat with their backs to the filthy walls, each wrist connected to the ones on either side by a short length of chain. A squeaky ceiling fan set on low moved the air just enough to keep them from suffocating.

She responded to the prisoner across the room. "How long have you been here?"

"Two days."

"She is from my factory," Zuri murmured. "I recognize her voice."

"Did you all come from factories?"

A few "yes"s from those who understood English.

"I haven't had any food since I was brought here three days ago," another girl said. "We're only allowed to use the toilet three times a day, so I hope you have a strong bladder."

"They give us just enough water to keep us alive," complained a young woman with a Spanish accent.

"They weaken us so we'll be more . . . cooperative," the Asian girl on Shima's left spoke up, her tone a mixture of bitterness and fear.

Shima realized she was the only prisoner who wasn't dressed in a skimpy, form-fitting shift. *Dressed for work,* she thought with a shudder of revulsion. *These girls are just children!*

"Auntie, you are bleeding," Zuri whispered.

The first officer was able to turn her head enough to see a trickle of blood oozing from a tiny wound near her right shoulder. She had to bite her lip to hold back a cry of dismay. "No—it is gone."

"What is gone?" Zuri turned her head to look at her aunt with her big brown eyes.

Shima felt a lump in her throat as she got a good look at her niece for the first time. Even with the poor lighting, she could see Zuri looked exactly the way she remembered Ngoma. Shima's second oldest sister was Zuri's mother. Ngoma died many years ago in Kampala, along with all the other members of the Oryang family.

It was hard to believe Zuri was fourteen. She was so small and thin. Shima couldn't imagine the hardships the teen must have endured as a slave for half her life.

She forced herself to focus. *I cannot become emotional.* She explained to Zuri, "I was wearing a tracking device when we were taken away in the van. My friends might be able to trace it and rescue us."

"But where is it now?"

"It must have come off when they dragged me from the van. But it may be close enough that we can still be found."

Zuri looked hopeful, but she turned her face away and leaned her head against the wall. Shima could sense her niece was trying hard not to cry.

She tried to distract Zuri from the overwhelming feeling of despair which permeated the room. "Why did you risk punishment by taking the bag off your head?"

"I do not know how to explain it." Zuri sniffled. "I just wanted to see outside the factory. I knew it might be my last chance to see anything beautiful."

"It was good you took the risk," Shima said. "I would not have known it was you if I had not seen your face."

"How did you find me?"

"That is a long story, and I promise I will tell you everything once we are free."

"What if we are not found by your friends?" Zuri asked with a tremor in her voice.

"We will be. I will think of a plan if they do not come soon," Shima said.

The room grew quiet again as the whispers between the other prisoners faded and stopped. No more advice was offered to the newcomers.

Shima was physically and emotionally exhausted. She leaned her head back against the wall and managed to doze off.

***

The sound of the door being unlocked awoke Shima. She blinked at the sudden illumination from the hallway when the door was thrown open. The two girls sitting closest to it were forced to move toward the center of the room to get out of the way. Everyone sitting near them had to shift their positions to minimize the strain on their wrists from the shackles.

None of the captives made a sound as two people stepped inside the room—a man clad in military fatigues and armed with a heavy rifle and a woman in a sleeveless, Chinese-style, red silk dress and stiletto heels. The armed guard spoke something to the well-dressed woman and pointed at Shima.

Shima felt cold, despite the sweltering heat of the prison room. The woman crossed the small room and crouched in front of her, their faces only a decimeter apart.

The first officer didn't know what to expect so she remained silent as the woman scrutinized her face. Shima guessed her scowling captor was Asian, but not Thai. Her eyes were more like Marco Ting's. She assumed the woman was a *madam*—the only word she could think of to describe a female slaver.

The madam wore heavy makeup and a floral perfume so overpowering, the scent made Shima queasy. Her black hair was pulled up into an elaborate chignon, and she wore a lot of expensive-looking jewelry. She finished staring at Shima and got to her feet, turning to speak to the armed man in a tone of authority. His response was deferential and brief.

That does not sound like Thai. I think it is Chinese.

The woman barked something at the man, and snapped her fingers in the universal signal for *hurry up.* He stepped out of the room and returned in a minute with another Asian man who was built like a Sumo wrestler.

Shima had a brief flashback to the terrifying night aboard the *Ishmael* when a brute named Wade Jackson tried to overpower her. She realized this time there would be no Blaze or Danae to come to her rescue.

The madam stepped aside so the huge man could reach down to unlock Shima's shackles. He seized her wrists, yanked her to her feet, and then immobilized her by turning her back to his chest and looping one massive arm around her waist, pinning her arms to her side. She was lifted off the floor and carried from the room. He paused in the hallway, waiting for the others.

"Auntie! Do not leave me!" Zuri's voice rose to a hysterical scream. "Auntie!"

Shima heard the unmistakable sound of a slap, and Zuri was silent. "Leave her alone!" She struggled, trying without success to kick her Sumo guard.

"Quiet!" The madam pulled the door to the prison room shut and spun the key in the lock. She then marched over to Shima and slapped her hard across the face.

Shima's cheek burned. She stopped struggling and closed her mouth but gave her captor a defiant look.

With the improved lighting in the hallway, Shima noticed for the first time a small tattoo on the woman's neck, just below her left ear. It appeared to be a symbol or trademark: a red letter B was surrounded by a circle of black barbed-wire. The rustic initial seemed out of place on the flashy courtesan.

"You spek Engrish?" Her English was so bad, Shima could barely understand her. "Thet goot! Get bic money fo you!" She snapped her fingers at the men and gave them some orders.

The madam remained at the door, watching with a satisfied sneer as Shima was carried down the hallway by her guard with the armed man close behind. She was hauled up a staircase and down another well-lit hallway. Her captor stopped at one door and pounded on it with his big fist.

The *Alex*'s first officer couldn't see who opened the door. She listened in helpless frustration at the rapid-fire conversation between her handler and the female door opener. She did hear one phrase, "*bai hu*," several times, but she had no idea what it meant since her knowledge of Mandarin was limited to *ni hao*—hello—and *xie xie*—thank you.

The man standing behind her with the rifle listened to the exchange with an ugly smile on his face, nodding with vapid approval. Shima wished she could kick him in the nose, but the muzzle of the rifle pointed at her face was a strong deterrent.

The conversation ended, and she was taken inside the brightly lit room.

No! Shima panicked and tried again to break free. She didn't want to be alone in a room with these disgusting criminals who treated women like property, like cattle.

No, cattle are treated better than trafficked humans. She managed to swing her heel back and strike her handler's kneecap, but this only made him angry.

The fist that connected with the side of Shima's head made the lights flicker and the room spin. She squeezed her eyes shut against the pain and swallowed against the bile rising in her throat.

Her handler dropped her, facedown, onto a cold horizontal surface.

A table? What is happening?

Two powerful hands seized Shima's wrists and held them down. Two more hands did the same with her ankles. The Sumo leaned on her back, pinning her down with his weight. She heard the snip of scissors and fabric tearing. Her jeans were cut to expose the back of her right leg.

Just her right leg.

She heard a high-pitched buzzing sound and something sharp punctured the tender skin behind her knee.

Shima screamed and squirmed, but the weight on her back increased, forcing the air from her lungs. She fell silent to preserve what little breath she had left. She had no choice but to remain still and endure the torture, drawing in shallow breaths to keep from passing out.

And it was torture. It felt as if a razor was slowly being drawn across her skin. Whenever one cut stopped, her skin was punctured in another spot, and the cutting continued, over and over. The skin behind her knee began to sting like it was attacked by hornets. She could feel blood oozing from the cuts, but no one bothered to wipe it away.

Tears streamed down Shima's face as the puncture and cut pattern went on for several minutes. *I think I am being tattooed.* The buzzing noise came from a tattoo needle.

At last the cutting stopped, and she felt a blast of moist, ice-cold air on the tattoo site. The weight on her back eased, enough for her to fill her aching lungs.

Is it over?

The hand on her left wrist moved to her elbow and held her arm against the table so firmly, she started to lose the circulation to her hand. She gasped as a small but deeper cut was made on the back of her arm. Something tiny was inserted into the incision, the blast of cold air was repeated, and this area was bandaged.

Her captors released her and stepped back from the table. "Up," the Sumo guard said.

Shima raised her chin and glanced at each of them, trying to decide if this was a trick. When none of them moved, she shifted her legs over to the side of the table opposite them and lowered her feet to the floor. The skin behind her knee throbbed and burned, making it difficult to put weight on her leg. She held on to the edge of the table to steady herself. Her head ached where she was struck, and she fought the urge to vomit.

She eyed her captors with fear, trying not to imagine what they might do to her next.

An old, gray-haired woman dressed in shapeless pink pajamas was still holding the tattoo needle. She set it down on the top shelf of a bookcase filled with other types of strange tools and nerve prods. The tattoo artist then found a pair of blunt-nose scissors on a different shelf and came around the table toward Shima.

The first officer quickly backed away until she was pressed against the door. She put one hand behind her back and tried to turn the handle, but it was locked.

The tattoo artist laughed at Shima's feeble escape attempt. She seized her wrist and said, "Doon move."

Shima watched in astonishment as the woman reached down and finished cutting off the torn leg of her jeans. The left leg of the jeans received the same treatment and the fabric fell away, leaving her with a ragged pair of cut-off shorts.

The woman barked orders at the Sumo-guard and the man with the rifle. The big man seized Shima again, but this time she was in too much pain to put up a fight. The tattoo artist unlocked the door for the men, and Shima found herself transported back to the third floor and the original room where a tearful Zuri trembled with relief to see her.

She was dropped onto the floor in the same spot and chained between Zuri and the Asian girl.

"Quiet!" The room was warned, and the men left, locking the door behind them.

Darkness and silence settled over the prison room.

Wincing at the raw wound on the back of her leg, Shima tried to find a position that was tolerable. She couldn't rest her legs on the filthy floor, but she couldn't bend them either because the tattoo would touch the back of her thigh. In desperation, she propped up her right leg on her left in an awkward position which would've impressed a yoga instructor.

"Auntie, did they give you a tattoo?" Zuri whispered.

"Yes. How did you know?"

"I have one too. They also put something under the skin of my arm."

"They did that to me, as well. Who has a tattoo on the back of your leg?" Shima asked the room.

Only one responded with "I do"—the girl with the Spanish accent.

Why have they tattooed only a few of us? Shima wondered. It was possible some of the non-English speakers had tattoos, but she had no way to investigate further.

It is like we have been branded, like sheep for the slaughter. With that grim thought, she leaned her aching head against the wall and fell asleep.

***

Shima was startled awake by the sound of breaking glass.

"What was that?" Zuri whimpered.

"It is nothing, it came from outside. Maybe someone dropped a bottle." She tried to sound reassuring, but she knew she wasn't fooling her niece.

Zuri pressed closer, trembling. Shima tried to shift to a more comfortable position, but she hurt everywhere. *How long have we been here?*

The room had grown brighter since the last rude awakening, but when Shima craned her neck to see the window just above her head, she discovered a dark film over the glass. She wouldn't be able to see out, even if she had a way to reach the window.

Reach the window? She had an idea. "Help me to stand," she whispered as loud as she dared.

"Why should we?" the girl on her left said.

"If we all stand at the same time, I can bang on the window and maybe attract the attention of someone outside."

"We will all be punished," another young woman warned.

"You would rather be a slave?" Shima knew she was being hard on them, but she could see no way to escape if they were going to cower like infants. "We must try to summon help."

The English speakers had no response. There was fearful muttering from some of the others as they whispered to each other in their native languages. Shima prayed they understood enough to cooperate in the attempt.

"The chains are too short for any of us to stand by ourselves. I cannot do this without everyone working together."

"Follow my lead," Shima said to Zuri in Swahili.

Her legs were stiff from sitting for so long, but she was able to spread her knees apart and use her thigh muscles to raise her bottom off the floor. She leaned forward as much as the short chains would allow until she was positioned in a low squat. Shima's leg muscles quivered from the exertion, and the sharp burning pain from the pressure on her tattoo site made her dizzy, but she was determined to keep her balance.

Zuri shifted her position until she was also squatting. The other prisoners moved to follow suit, straining at their manacles without complaint.

"Now, on the count of three." Shima didn't know how to count to three in any other language except Swahili. The group would have to stand up together or risk injuring each other.

"One . . . two . . . three." On "three," she slowly straightened up. A few of the girls struggled to control their wobbly legs, but the strain on their wrists forced them keep trying.

In moments, the group was on its feet.

"Quick, help me beat on the window," Shima instructed Zuri, tugging on their connected wrists for emphasis.

They bent their elbows and swung them backward in unison, striking the window loud enough to make a noise.

The immediate reaction wasn't the one Shima hoped for.

The door to the room flew open, throwing the entire group off balance. The two girls closest to the doorway were knocked forward into the center of the room, pulling the rest of the group down with them like dominoes.

Shima fell to her knees amid the screams of her fellow prisoners as several men stormed into the room, shouting at them in Thai and swinging nerve prods.

A piercing scream close to her left ear was evidence her Asian neighbor was touched with a prod. Shima ducked her head, gritted her teeth, and expected to be hit next.

The unmistakable sound of gunfire cut through the din of girls' screams.

Shima glanced up to see their captors go tearing out of the room, pulling the door shut behind them.

The *crack crack* of gunfire continued for several minutes, and the noise was getting closer. Her ears rang from the unrelenting screams of the other terrified prisoners.

"We're going to die!" wailed the girl with the Spanish accent. *"Por favor, Dios nos libre!"*

Shima heard more glass breaking, each gunshot moving closer to their position.

The firefight was taking place right outside the door.

FIVE
CLOSE RANGE

"WE HAVE TO search the buildings." Danae knew what Cade would say, but she used her no-nonsense tone anyway.

He was already shaking his head as he climbed out of the abandoned van. "We'll need backup to organize a search. I won't risk the lives of my officers until we're sure the area is secure."

"How long is that going to take?" Danae snapped.

She didn't wait for an answer as she slipped down the narrow gap between the van and the building, passing Bergen and Ghukasyan, who were covering the alley. She walked to an open space halfway between the cycles and the van and looked around, locating the entrances to the buildings on either side. "Every minute we delay could mean the difference between finding her alive and finding her dead!"

Cade marched right up to her, ready to argue. "Safety first. We'll do this the right way—*my way*. Be patient."

Danae was struck by the irony of his words. *Mr. Impatient is telling me to be patient!* She was spared from further debate by the timely arrival of Moniesa and another ISPP officer on the oversized purple solar cycle.

The weapons officer pulled up beside the captains and cut the engine. She dismounted and waited for her much smaller passenger to climb off. The officers took off their helmets.

"This is Dusit Jiang, junior medical officer and our Thai translator," Moniesa introduced the scowling Asian man to Danae. She recognized him from the clinic tent where he was giving a child a physical. Jiang was wearing a large gray backpack with *ISPP* and a Red Cross symbol embroidered on it.

Moniesa turned to Cade. "What is the status of the search, Captain?"

"Shima's here somewhere," Danae said before Cade could respond. "We have to search the buildings in this area."

"Not until we have an armored backup team." Cade glared at Danae. "And *you* won't be taking part in the search."

She returned the glare. "What're you going to do— throw me in the brig?"

"Don't think I haven't considered it!"

Moniesa stepped between them, a calm yet formidable barrier. "The buildings are only four stories, so we can search them as soon as backup arrives," she assured Danae. "Jiang has already summoned a team."

The weapons officer turned to Cade. "I will look after Captain Shepherd and keep her safe during the search."

"I don't need your babysitter services, thank you!" Danae stalked a few paces away from her watchdogs and turned to stare up at one of the buildings. "The windows on this side are all blacked out," she said over her shoulder. "We should check out this one first."

"We're going to wait—" Cade was on the verge of another tirade but was interrupted by Moniesa's announcement of, "CIPs, sir."

Captain York had a few blistering words for this new development.

Danae turned to see two patrol cars approaching them in single file down the alley, blue lights flashing but no sirens.

The ISPP's assortment of weaponry disappeared in an instant, hidden inside uniforms. Danae was grateful she left her Excalibur in her pocket. It was against the law to possess firearms in Bangkok, and she knew ISPP didn't want to provoke the local CIPs if they could avoid it.

Four CIPs in dark green, short-sleeved uniforms climbed out of their vehicles, but only three drew their weapons. The one not waving a gun approached the group of ISPPs and started hurling questions at them in Thai.

Jiang got right in the officer's face and fired off some questions of his own.

Cade let this go on for about thirty seconds before he joined the huddle and barked at Jiang, "What's he saying?"

"He says this is a restricted area, Captain, and for-eigners aren't allowed to be here."

"Tell him that's the most pathetic lie I've ever heard, and he's interfering in an ISPP investigation."

Jiang spoke to the CIP at length.

Danae watched the policeman's expression waver between fear and anger. She suspected these CIPs were paid to ignore what went on in the red-light district. Unlike the obedient CIPs who were helping guard Lumphini Park, this group could pose a real problem.

She glanced at Cade to gauge his reaction. He looked steamed, as usual. Jiang switched back and forth between Thai and English, trying to mediate what was turning into a shouting match between the ISPP captain and the CIP.

Danae turned back to study the building with the blacked-out windows. There was no handle on the door facing the alley. *How do we get inside?* She walked toward it, putting some space between herself and the verbal brawl.

"Captain Shepherd," Moniesa cautioned, falling into step behind her.

"I just want to get a closer look," Danae said without breaking stride.

When she reached the door, both women heard it: a faint *thump thump*. Someone was pounding on one of the upstairs windows.

Danae snapped her chin upward and tried to hone in on where the sound was coming from. It stopped as abruptly as it began. "Third floor!" was her best guess.

"I do not think—" Moniesa's warning was cut off by a chorus of women's screams coming from inside the building.

"It *is* the third floor! We need to get inside!" Danae glanced at Moniesa in frustration, assuming the weapons office would tell her to wait for backup, as Cade ordered.

But Moniesa surprised her. She shouted, "No more slaves; not on my watch!" and shoved Danae to one side. The huge woman then threw her shoulder against the door, knocking it off its hinges. It fell inward, and she stormed inside with a pistol already in her hand.

The captain swallowed her astonishment, whipped out her own gun, and was right behind the giantess.

They faced a flight of stairs, leading up. A woman with a high-powered rifle was taking aim at them from the first landing, but Moniesa was faster on the trigger.

"Stay behind me!" the ISPP officer ordered as she charged up the stairs three at a time.

Danae stepped over the carnage on the landing, trying to stay close to Moniesa and watch their backs at the same time. She heard Cade shout, "Wait!" from downstairs when they reached the next landing with a large *2* painted on the blacked-out glass door to the building's interior.

A hailstorm of bullets ricocheted off the concrete wall, which separated each section of stairs from the next flight up. The door shattered, sending shards in every direction.

Danae turned her face just in time to avoid a dagger of glass that flew at her. It struck her left temple instead of her eye. She didn't feel any pain, thanks to the adrenaline coursing through her veins.

Moniesa reached around the corner with her right arm. She squeezed off several blind shots and was rewarded with a gasp and then silence.

The ISPP officer paused to load a fresh magazine, but Danae leaned around her to see if it was safe to head up to the next landing. The big woman yanked her back behind the wall.

Another volley destroyed the spot where Danae would have been standing, had she taken one more step.

"Semi-automatic," Moniesa said, "a refurbished AR-15 with slidestock firing." She glanced at the bullets littering the landing. "Full Metal Jacket rounds, and they are wasting ammunition like amateurs. We do not need armored backup."

"We don't?" Danae could only gape at her in astonishment.

Moniesa motioned for the captain to get behind her and then reached around the corner again, just enough to get off a few shots with her handheld cannon.

Another shower left pockmarks in the floor, chipped away at the edges of the wall, and filled the dead assailant with more holes.

Moniesa gasped, dropped her gun, and snatched her arm back. Blood was pouring from the bottom edge of her hand.

"I don't have anything to stop the bleeding." Danae searched her pockets for something to use as a bandage.

Moniesa sat on the top step and pressed her left hand over the wound. "It is not bad," she muttered between clenched teeth. "The bullet only nicked me. Just take them out."

Danae thought the injury was worse than Moniesa was willing to admit, but she knew there wasn't time to play nursemaid. "Yes, ma'am."

She glanced back over her shoulder at Cade, who was rounding the landing below and would reach them in seconds, but she wasn't in the mood for any more of his orders. She didn't wait for him.

She maneuvered around Moniesa and reached around the corner with her tiny pistol. She touched the trigger once, and the magazine emptied itself in less than a second.

Whew! Danae was impressed with the lethal force of the G30. She hadn't used the rapid-fire setting before. She fumbled for the fresh magazine in her left cargo pocket, but thought her marksmanship had the desired effect: silence from the upper landing.

"Get back!" Captain York slipped by Moniesa, shoved Danae aside, and peered around the corner.

Danae had to seize the banister to stop herself from falling. She turned back just in time to see Cade reach around the corner with his right arm, just as Moniesa had done.

Another volley of FMJ rounds peppered the landing, gouging a few more chunks from the wall. Danae heard metal strike metal, the force of the shot wrenching the pistol from Cade's grip. His weapon hit the concrete and skidded half a meter out of reach, into no-man's land.

The suggestion to "use my gun" didn't get a chance to escape Danae's lips because Cade was already in motion. Taking care to keep his head and the rest of his body behind the wall, he dropped to his knees and risked only his arm, reaching across the floor to snatch his gun back.

The first shot missed Cade's arm by a decimeter. The second shot was more precise, clipping him before his arm was safely behind the wall.

He dropped his gun again and uttered a string of curses.

"Captain!" Moniesa was on her feet. She put her left arm around Cade's waist and helped him sit on the step beside her. He was bleeding heavily from a gunshot wound near his right wrist. Like Moniesa, he covered the wound with his left hand and grimaced against the pain.

"Cade?" Danae was torn between getting him and Moniesa immediate medical attention and finishing the fight. The reality of their vulnerable position won the debate—there was still a sniper up on the next landing.

"Wait for backup, Shepherd, before you get us all killed!" Cade scowled at her, breathing hard.

"We're *going* to get killed if they come down here!" She slammed the new magazine into her pistol, set it to single fire, and leaned around the corner.

The thug with the AR-15 probably wasn't expecting to see anyone after shooting Cade. Before he could reach the trigger, Danae took him out with a shot between the eyes.

Bergen, Ghukasyan, and Jiang arrived a moment later, breathing hard from their rapid ascent and mouths gaping as they assessed the grim scene on the landing.

Jiang whipped out a can of Hemorrhage Freeze from his backpack and sprayed Cade's arm.

"You should sit, Captain Shepherd. Let Jiang take a look at you." Bergen appraised her with a concerned frown.

"Why?" Danae didn't wait for an answer. She raced up the next flight of stairs, stepped over her gruesome handiwork, reached around the corner, and touched the trigger several times.

She heard glass shatter, a gasp of pain, and then something metallic clattered down a few of the steps. She assumed she shot out the door to the third floor because the hysterical screams were now much louder.

"Get back!" Bergen edged past Danae, poked his head around the corner, and glanced up to the next landing. He drew back and spoke sternly to her. "The gunman's down, but we'll check the hallway first. There may be more of them."

Danae was tempted to respond with something sarcastic, but she realized the man had years of experience in combat situations. She nodded and lowered her gun.

Ghukasyan joined Bergen on the landing, and the two ISPPs ascended the stairs with caution, their oversized pistols ready to take out anyone careless enough to make a sudden appearance. They reached the third floor, glanced around the corner to make sure no one was waiting up on the next landing, and approached the shattered door from either side, staying clear of the hallway beyond.

Bergen took a moment to look before jerking his head back as the gunfire started up again. Someone was shooting at them from the hallway.

"Take cover, Captain!" Moniesa advised from below.

Danae edged back behind the wall so most of her body was out of range, but she peered around the corner so she could see what was going on up at the landing. She moved her pistol to her left hand and flexed the tired fingers of her right.

It took her a few seconds to realize her left hand was wet. She was reluctant to take her eyes off the firefight so she brought her hand close to her face for a quick examination.

She gasped. Her hand was covered in blood. She moved the weapon back to her right hand and examined her left arm to see where the blood was coming from.

A steady stream of crimson was flowing down past her shoulder. Her neck was wet. She raised her damp arm to touch the side of her head and recoiled from the sudden shockwave of pain. Her hair on that side was soaked with blood. *The shard of glass, and I didn't even feel it.*

Danae was feeling it now. *So that's why Bergen wanted me to sit down. I guess I could use some Hemorrhage Freeze.* She glanced downstairs at York and Moniesa, who were being treated by Jiang, but she didn't get a chance to shout for assistance.

A break in the gunfire from upstairs claimed her attention. She turned her head in time to see Ghukasyan and Bergen vanish down the hallway. She held her breath, expecting more gunshots, but all she heard was a single scream which faded into a cry of, "Help! Help us!"

It was Shima's voice.

Danae raced up the stairs. She was light-headed when she reached the landing and peered through the shattered doorway to see if it was safe to head down the hall.

The ISPP officers were the only people still standing. There were several bodies sprawled on the floor, and they all appeared to be Thai men.

Very dead Thai men.

Halfway down the long hallway, Bergen pushed open one of the doors, and he and Ghukasyan moved inside the room.

Danae ducked through the remains of the doorframe and hurried down the hall. Glass crunched beneath her boots, and she navigated the gore without looking too closely at it. She reached the open doorway to the room and looked in.

The ISPPs were trying to calm the chaos. They unlocked shackled wrists and moved chains out of the way, freeing the young women who filled the small room to capacity.

Shima catapulted from the room and threw her arms around Danae, almost knocking her down. She was laughing and crying at the same time. "You found us! Thank God you found us!"

Blinking back a few tears of her own, Danae Shepherd hugged her best friend. She was at a loss for words. Part of her inability to say something coherent was emotional, but most of it was physical—she was dizzy.

"You are bleeding." Shima released her, held her at arm's length, got a serious look on her face, and helped Danae sit on the floor.

"I'll be fine. Just need to catch my breath." Danae closed her eyes and leaned back against the wall. She could hear talking and commotion going on around her, but she had trouble focusing and lost track of time.

"Auntie?" A youthful, timid voice.

Shima answered in words Danae didn't understand, except for one: "Zuri."

"Get Jiang up here with the Hemorrhage Freeze!" Bergen's voice.

Danae barely noticed the blast of ice-cold air on the side of her head.

A woman—Ghukasyan?—said, "I'll escort Oryang and her niece to *Alex's Legacy*. What should we do with the others? Some are suffering from the effects of nerve prods, and all of them need medical attention."

"Lumphini Park," said a voice Danae didn't recognize. "They're tiny. I can carry one of them downstairs. DiAngelo, see if you can lift that girl curled up in the corner. Be gentle, she looks pretty traumatized. Speaking of trauma—inform the *Gandhi* we'll need any crewmembers trained in trauma counseling as soon as they land."

There was an explosive sound of wood splintering, and Moniesa bellowed, "More prisoners in this room, sir!"

"Release them. Here's the keys," Bergen said. "Open every door on this level."

In a short time, the hallway was buzzing with women's voices, running the gamut of emotions from joyous laughter to hysterical sobbing.

"The ambulances are here," Jiang reported. "They'll take the captains and Moniesa to Bhumibol Memorial. Want me to ride along?"

"No, I need you here," Bergen said. "Tell Freiberg's team I want every room in this building searched, plus all the buildings within a five-block radius. They should transport all the victims to Lumphini, for now. We're shutting down the slave trade in this city—all of it."

"What happened to the CIPs that confronted us in the alley?" Moniesa asked.

"They vanished as soon as the shooting started," Jiang said. "You should have seen the guilty looks on their faces."

"Inform the CIP chief there'll be a full investigation into the illegal activities of the Bangkok police department," Bergen said.

"Yes, sir." Jiang sounded cheerful at this request.

"I have your gun. I will see you back aboard the *Alex* once they repair the gash on your head." Shima leaned closer, kissed the top of Danae's head, and whispered, "Thank you, *rafiki*."

"Captain Shepherd," Jiang said, "the paramedics are going to put you on a gurney and take you to the hospital."

"I'll be fine," Danae whispered, right before she passed out.

SIX
CARETAKER

"NO, DON'T PLAY with that." Blaze took a laser drill out of his adopted Indian daughter's tiny hands. He placed the tool on top of the Velocity drive control panel, out of her reach. "Where's your doll?"

Niyati stuck out her lower lip in exasperation. "Priya sleeping, *baba.*" She put a finger to her lips, but her "shhhh!" was loud enough to wake the dead. She pointed to the alcove off the engine room which served as the engineer's quarters while the ship was in Velocity flight. "She take nap."

That's what you should be doin', he thought with a mental sigh. "You didn't bring any other toys?"

The answer was obvious, and Blaze felt a twinge of guilt. He hadn't been keeping a close eye on her. He'd brought Niyati with him to the engine room, thinking he could get some work done while she entertained herself. She spent fifteen minutes jumping on his cot in the alcove but got bored and looked for something else to do. The dangerous tools Blaze used were much more interesting than her toys.

So much for gettin' any work done today. The engineer hoped staying busy would keep his mind off Shima's disappearance. He couldn't concentrate on anything except the painful knot which took possession of his stomach the moment he saw the van drive away from factory six.

"Hungry." Niyati put her little hands on her hips in a perfect imitation of Lorina when she was annoyed about something.

"You just had lunch." Blaze knew there wasn't much hope of changing her mind. Niyati had a voracious appetite. Dr. Sorensen explained to him and Lorina that their daughter's little body was trying to compensate for the time she was malnourished as an abandoned child on the streets of Mars Station. She gained two kilos and grew four centimeters over the past six weeks. She was currently the size of a healthy three-year-old—still well behind other five-year-olds, but catching up.

Niyati seized Blaze's hand and tugged, trying to get him to move in the direction of the door. "Hungry!"

"I'm comin'." He closed the access panel to the solar engine he'd been working on and followed her through the maze of control boards and machinery to the door. It was a short walk down the basement hallway to the ladder.

Blaze followed Niyati up the ladder for four levels to the top deck of the ship. It was an easy climb for her, but he had to catch his breath when he stepped off the ladder into the short hallway which accessed the bridge, infirmary, and galley. She scampered ahead of him to the galley.

"Are you sure you can't wait an hour?" He reached the doorway and saw Niyati at the crew's mess, pulling a loaf of bread out of a drawer low enough for her to reach. "I get the idea. One PB and J, comin' right up."

His earcom chimed. "I need to go next door. I'm gettin' a call."

"*Amma?*" The child dropped the loaf and raced after him to the bridge.

He took a seat at the com control board, lifted Niyati onto his lap, and pressed a button, opening the ship-to-shore connection. "This is Smith."

"This is Murphy."

"Hey, gorgeous. How're things dirtside?"

"They found Shima!"

Blaze was speechless for a moment as he felt the weight of the world being lifted off his shoulders. "How . . . how is she?"

"She's fine! She was roughed up, but nothing serious. And Zuri was with her. An ISPP officer is escorting them to the *Alex*. They should be there in half an hour."

Blaze was exhausted. He'd been running on adrenaline for the past twelve hours as he waited for word on Shima. "Tell me everythin'."

"I wish I could, but I'm up to my elbows in a trough of salad. There'll be nine hundred kids coming through the mess hall in about twenty minutes. You'll have to get the details from Shima. I'll see you at 1430 for shift change. Love you." She cut the connection before Blaze could formulate a reply.

"Love you too," he said to empty air, provoking a giggle from Niyati. The child was unaware her auntie Shima had been abducted.

He set Niyati on her feet and walked with her back to the galley. He sent up a silent prayer of gratitude as he sat down with her and shared the most delicious peanut butter and jelly sandwich he ever tasted.

***

Blaze cycled open the outer door of the airlock and stepped into the antechamber. A female ISPP officer he didn't recognize nodded to him and turned to descend the collapsible staircase, leaving Shima and Zuri in his care.

He was glad Niyati fell asleep in their suite because she didn't need to see Shima in this condition. He changed his mind about giving the first officer a hug when he got a good look at her.

She was dirty and disheveled. Her jeans had been made into a ragged pair of shorts and her T-shirt was stained with blood. Since he couldn't see where she was injured, he suspected the blood wasn't hers. She also had a golf-ball-sized lump on the left side of her head.

He gave Shima a cautious pat on the shoulder in greeting, but she threw her arms around him and squeezed hard. "If you had not gone with me, I would not have been tagged with the transmitter. I would *never* have been found without it. You saved my life, *rafiki*, and Zuri's too."

Blaze felt undeserving of her praise. "York was the one who tagged us—thank him. All I did was stand there and watch the van drive away!"

"There was nothing you could have done." Shima smiled up at him, but he could tell the gesture took a lot of effort. She looked exhausted.

"Please don't *ever* do somethin' like that again. I'm too young to die of heart failure."

"I promise." She put her arm around Zuri's shoulders. "This is the reason I did such a crazy thing."

"Well, then, it was definitely worth it. Welcome aboard, Zuri."

"She does not speak much English," Shima said.

Blaze smiled and allowed the nervous teen a few moments to look him over. She was wearing a green ISPP uniform shirt over some type of short dress which left most of her thin brown legs on display. Zuri didn't return the smile. She also looked ready to collapse.

"Starboard lift." He ushered them into the entryway but noticed they were both limping, favoring their right legs. A quick glance at the backs of their legs brought up new questions, but he knew it would have to wait. "We can talk after you've had some rest."

"I think we should have something to eat and get cleaned up before we rest. Zuri has not had any food since early yesterday."

"Well, you're in luck 'cause I happen to make the fastest omelets in the Western Hemisphere."

Shima mustered an appreciative smile. "That sounds good."

In the galley, Blaze had them sit at a table. Shima grimaced as she settled into the seat, keeping her right leg extended so the back of her knee didn't touch the chair. Zuri was also careful with her right leg, but she didn't seem to be in as much pain as Shima.

On the small grill in the kitchen, he whipped up two omelets filled with anything he could find in the enormous double refrigerator: cheese, green peppers, tomatoes, scallions. He refilled their water glasses several times and kept their plates loaded with fresh strawberries and buttered toast. Since aunt and niece were quiet, he didn't ask them any questions.

They ate until Shima said, "I am full. Thank you."

Zuri burped and giggled. Blaze took it as a good sign.

"*Baba?*" A sleepy voice came over the shipboard com.

"I'll be right there, Niyati. Stay in our suite." He offered Shima a hand up from the table. "And that's my cue to escort you ladies to your cabin for some shut-eye."

"I will move my things to a cabin with two beds."

"Sounds like a good plan for *tomorrow*." He offered Zuri his hand, but she shook her head no and pushed herself out of the chair.

Shima nodded in mute agreement, and Blaze led the way back to the lift.

A few doors down from the first officer's cabin, he poked his head into a housekeeping closet and found a rollaway bed. "Just what the doctor ordered."

Once Shima and Zuri were inside Shima's cabin, Blaze jogged to his own suite on the opposite wing of the third level.

"I've got just enough time to clean up the galley before *amma* gets back," he told Niyati.

"Hungry, *baba*!"

***

"I need to warn you," was the first thing out of Lorina's mouth when she stepped into the *Alex*'s entryway where Blaze and Niyati were waiting for her.

"That sounds ominous." He noted how sweaty his Irish bride was after being out in the tropical humidity. Her long, strawberry-blonde hair was pulled back into a ponytail, but the loose tendrils that weren't contained were plastered to her glistening neck and flushed pink face. Her jeans and tropical-print shirt were soaked through. He leaned down for a quick kiss instead of a full-body-contact hug.

Niyati didn't care if *amma* got her wet. She hugged Lorina's left leg.

Lorina tousled Niyati's bobbed, ink-black hair but kept her eyes fixed on Blaze's. "I need to warn you about the number of kids at Lumphini."

"There were about nine hundred this mornin'. You're sayin' there's more?"

"I'm saying that number could double or triple by the end of the day. The *Gandhi* is expected to land in a few hours. They've come to assist, but they've brought one hundred and ninety-seven more kids with them from Mandalay, Burma. The *Aung San Suu Kyi* will be here in the morning, but they're also bringing three hundred kids from Dhaka, Bangladesh.

"But most of the children will be coming in this afternoon from the red-light district. None of the ISPPs could give me an estimate on how many that could be. Maybe thousands."

"ISPP is gonna be over their heads." Blaze blew out a breath of frustration. "York needs to call in the Earth Marines or somethin'."

He had a sudden thought and gave Lorina a shrewd look. "Or somethin'."

"Oh no, you don't." Lorina took a step back and wagged a warning index finger in his face. "You're *not* going to suggest I recruit volunteers in Bangkok."

Blaze grinned and nodded. "That's exactly what I was gonna suggest."

"But it's a dangerous city."

"Mars Station is a dangerous city—at least it was before they locked up Acheron—but you had no trouble persuadin' people to volunteer at the juvenile shelter."

"Yes, but most people on Mars speak English."

"Phailin speaks Thai," Blaze reminded her. "She could help."

"Phailin went to the hospital to see Ting, and she told me she plans to stay right by his side. I can't imagine what she sees in that vile little worm." Lorina shrugged, looking disgusted and baffled. "So we can't count on her to translate."

Blaze nodded, trying to think of another option. He glanced with dismay at the time. "Vipul's called me five times this shift, so I need to go relieve him. We can talk about this later." He got down on one knee and gave Niyati a hug.

When he straightened again, he told his wife, "Maybe you could do some research. There's gotta be some local organizations that work with kids."

"I just finished an eight-hour shift," Lorina complained, without much conviction.

Blaze grinned. He could already envision the wheels turning in her brilliant mind. He knew recruiting volunteers would be a better use of Lorina's skills than working in the mess hall. "I'll see you tonight, sugar."

***

Blaze showed up for his shift at the Lumphini refugee camp at 1530. When he stepped off the tram at the Rama Road entrance to the park, he was met by Vipul and the *Title of Liberty*'s senior engineer, a thin, serious-looking Chinese woman with a round face and a long black braid which reached the small of her back. He had seen her before, briefly, along with York, Moniesa, and another officer whose name he couldn't recall, at factory number six.

"Hey, Vipul, ready for me to take over?"

"Yes, please." Vipul attempted to cover a yawn. "I'll show you where I've left off before I head back to the ship. Blaze, this is Annalise Tse."

"Nice to officially meet you, Engineer Smith." She offered her hand for him to shake. "Call me Axe, everyone does."

"Please call me Blaze."

"You sound like a Texan."

"Close—Oklahoma. You sound like you're from *Miz-or-uh*."

Axe laughed. "Yes, Branson, although my parents insisted I speak only Chinese at home, so I'm not sure how I picked up a Missourian accent." She headed into the park, Blaze and Vipul falling into step behind her. They passed a pair of CIPs guarding the main entrance.

"Do they call you Axe because you're sharp or because it's your weapon of choice?" Blaze guessed.

"It's actually short for *battle-axe* because some people think I'm difficult to work with." She shot him a mischievous grin over her shoulder.

Difficult to work with. Great.

"Why do they call you Blaze?"

"Mostly 'cause I can fix things fast."

"That's good to hear because I'm putting together an advanced heir-lock program that needed to be up and running yesterday. Where did you go to school?"

"I was in the next to the last graduatin' class at MIT. How 'bout you?"

"Last class at Purdue."

"That makes you about three years older than me, but I swear you don't look a day over fifteen."

"Thanks, I think."

"Were you one of the snipers at factory six last night? I don't recall seein' you."

"No, I was assigned to lead the raid on number three. It was filled with boys, most of them half-starved."

Axe slowed her pace and turned back to speak quietly to Blaze and Vipul. "The junior officer assigned to my team was one of the fatalities last night. He was ambushed in a hallway." She shot Blaze a haunted look. "It was my fault. I should've given him better cover."

"Please don't blame yourself," Blaze said. "The factories are big, and the teams were spread thin. It was a lot of area to cover. I almost saw my crewmate get shot last night. The only reason she's still alive is because three ISPP snipers were coverin' her."

Axe looked unconvinced, but she nodded, acknowledging his sympathy, and turned her attention to the path ahead.

The two men followed Axe through the maze of wild, overgrown, flowering bushes. The hedgerows gave way to open fields, and Blaze's jaw dropped as he got his first good look at the crowded park in the daylight. "Lorina wasn't kiddin' about the numbers."

"And a lot more kids are on the way. You heard about Captain Shepherd's role in the red-light district liberation?" Vipul asked.

"Just a little bit. I'm waitin' to hear the full details from—"

A child's whoop of laughter interrupted him. Blaze, Axe, and Vipul stopped short as a pair of boys cut across their path, several rolls of toilet paper unrolling behind them as they ran. A harassed-looking ISPP officer ran across the path a few paces behind the boys, shouting, "Stop!"

"Things have been getting out of hand," Axe said.

"I can see that." Blaze took a good look around as they resumed their walk.

The din of children's voices was occasionally punctuated by a scream of laughter or pain—it was hard to tell which. There was a lot of laughing, shouting, and commotion. The freed slaves were running everywhere, despite the heat, and the engineer couldn't blame them for celebrating. ISPP officers were busy breaking up scuffles, bandaging scraped knees and bloody noses, coaxing a few adventurous boys down from the palm trees, dodging mud-pie missiles, and attempting to guard the bathrooms from more toilet-paper thieves.

"We can't keep bringin' kids into the park," Blaze said. "There aren't enough adults to supervise them." He remembered the chaos aboard the ship when Lorina, Shima, and the former cook, Idalis, attempted to supervise the one hundred and forty-eight children Captain Shepherd rescued from the slaver Thanatos.

"The *Gandhi* just landed," Axe said, "so we'll have more help shortly. The sooner we get this heir-lock program running, the sooner we can start returning kids to their families."

Blaze thought what she was describing would require twenty times the number of ISPP officers they currently had on staff. *I hope Lorina comes up with a solution soon.* He had a thought that security was less than adequate with just a few CIPs guarding each of the park's main entrances.

"Think we could set up a protective barricade around the park?" he asked Vipul, half teasing, half serious.

"This isn't a prison camp," Axe said.

"I'm not worried about keepin' the kids in. I'm concerned about keepin' other people out. After seein' the

CIPs' reaction at the factory last night, I just wonder if it's wise to trust them to guard the camp."

"I think ISPP's security officers have things under control," Axe said.

Blaze had his doubts but dropped the subject.

He spotted a familiar face. She was sitting by herself, looking distraught. "Just a second, I need to talk to someone." He left the path and walked over to the freed slave girl.

She saw him coming, recognized him, and broke into a big grin. She leapt to her feet and ran to him, throwing her thin arms around his waist. "Blaze! *Prieten!*"

Blaze now knew the meaning of the word: friend. "Yes, I'm your *prieten*, Ekaterina." He got down on one knee so he could speak to her face-to-face. "And I've got good news for you—we found Zuri."

"Found . . . Zuri?" It took her a moment, but he knew she figured it out when her face lit up. "Zuri! Where Zuri?"

"She's fine. She's safe aboard my ship."

"See Zuri?" There was a pleading look in her big brown eyes.

Blaze stood up, but Ekaterina held on, burying her face in his shirt. "I'm not sure when you could see her. Not today, at least."

"Plez?" She pronounced the word the same way Niyati did.

"Who do we have here?" Axe asked as she and Vipul walked over to join him.

"Just one of the girls from factory six."

"She seems to like you," Axe observed.

"Thinking of adopting another one?" Vipul flashed a sly grin.

"No way. I can barely manage the one I've got." Blaze tried, unsuccessfully, to pry Ekaterina off him. "I wonder if she's had an interview."

"Doubtful," Axe said. "And with so many of them, I'm not sure how we're going to keep track of which ones still need DNA scans."

"Have you considered drawin' stars on their foreheads with a permanent marker after they've been interviewed?"

Vipul agreed. "That worked well for Jake when he had to examine all the kids aboard the *Ishmael*."

Axe nodded. "Sometimes the simplest solutions are the most effective."

To Ekaterina, Blaze said, "Sure, you can come with me." He took her hand and pointed the way they needed to walk. "Let's go."

The teen kept a tight grip on his hand as she skipped to keep up with his long strides. He glanced down at her a few times before they reached the tent. She looked happy. *I hope we can find her family.* He could imagine the expression on Lorina's face if he brought home a child half their age to raise. This thought triggered some new concerns.

He turned to Axe. "What happens to the kids who don't have any family members still livin'? Or what if their families can't be located?"

He hated to give voice to one more thought. "What if a child's parents are the ones who sold him or her to the traffickers? I've heard that happens sometimes when people are desperate."

Axe nodded. "We're aware of the potential barriers to reunification. Captain York thinks we'll need to find orphanages for the children who can't go home."

"Adoption would be a better solution, in my opinion." Blaze exchanged a knowing glance with Vipul. "There're millions of people who're infertile, thanks to the war. Captain Shepherd's had an easy time findin' homes for the abandoned kids from Mars Station."

A crease formed between Axe's eyebrows. "I'll run the idea by Captain York."

They reached the large clinic tent, and Axe held the mosquito-netting door aside for them.

"Can Ekaterina go inside?" Blaze asked.

"Sure, why not?" Axe said, "They can figure out if she's been interviewed."

There was a lot going on inside the crowded, air-conditioned tent. Ekaterina held on tight to his hand. He decided to be patient with the frightened girl.

Vipul directed Blaze to the *Liberty*'s medical officers, who were finishing up with two small boys at the make-shift examination tables. The boys climbed down from the tables and went to be interviewed, and the medics handed Blaze their datapads with ID locks built into the screens.

"We've gotten traces from three hundred and seventeen kids so far," said a weary-looking Asian officer named Jiang. "We should keep working until the *Gandhi*'s medics arrive."

"When's the last time you slept?" Blaze asked.

Jiang looked at the ceiling. "Hmmm, not sure. It's been a while."

"Forty-eight hours," the other medic, Yamato, supplied with a scowl.

"Why don't you let Axe and me collect DNA traces until the *Gandhi*'s medics show up?" Blaze said.

"Not me." The ISPP engineer shook her head. "If I don't get the heir-lock program working soon, the kids'

DNA won't do us any good. I thought you were here to help me," she added, an edge to her tone.

Blaze wasn't pleased to note the emergence of Officer Tse's battle-axe side. He glanced around at the dozen ISPP officers scattered throughout the tent, hoping to find someone free to assist him, but they were all interviewing former slaves. He resigned himself to a long afternoon. "I'll help you as soon as reinforcements arrive."

"Captain York left instructions for the red-light district children to be examined as soon as they arrive. They'll go to the front of the queue," Jiang said. "Most of them have more urgent medical needs than the factory slaves."

"It makes my blood boil to think of children being forced into prostitution. It's too bad you didn't shoot all their handlers," Axe said to Jiang.

Jiang didn't bat an eye at the engineer's macabre complaint. "It helps to have a few witnesses so we can get some names of the CIPs that were involved." He turned to Blaze, shook his hand, and added a heartfelt, "Good luck."

"Sorry, mate." Vipul patted him on the back. "I'd stay and help if I could keep my eyes open."

"Wait a minute—" Blaze felt a flutter of panic as the medics and Vipul exited the tent. He turned to Axe before she could slip away. "How am I supposed to do this by myself? What if one of them needs to see a doctor—?"

"Then have them sit down and wait for the *Gandhi*'s medics," Axe spoke over him. "Ask your little friend to help you." She glanced at Ekaterina and turned away, heading to another part of the tent where several computers had been set up at a makeshift work station.

Great. Blaze smiled down at the teen, who had no idea what the adults were discussing, and extracted his hand from hers. "I have to work now."

Ekaterina gave him a mystified look. "Blaze, *prieten?*"

He glanced around for something to keep her occupied and out of the way. His dilemma was solved a moment later when an ISPP junior officer he recognized came in the back entrance to the tent, guiding several cases of bottled water stacked on an anti-grav unit. He directed the load over to Blaze and lowered it to the floor beside him.

The officer was a short Latino with a solid build. "Roland Diaz," he said before Blaze could ask. "I was at factory six yesterday morning."

"Sure, I remember you. Blaze Smith. I'm the *Alex*'s engineer, but I guess I've been promoted to medtech."

Diaz shrugged. "I'm a com officer, but I've been demoted to delivery boy."

Blaze chuckled. "I assume the water is for the kids."

The ISPP officer nodded. "Most of the red-light district slaves are suffering from dehydration."

"Could you hand out water to the girls comin' in?" Blaze turned to Ekaterina and tried to pantomime the message by taking a bottle out of the first case and handing it to Diaz.

She just looked up at him with a quizzical smile.

"Here, try this." Diaz pulled a datapad out of one of his cargo pockets and handed it to Blaze. "This will translate for you."

"Thanks."

"I don't have anything urgent to do right now so I'll give you a hand. I'll stand outside and direct the kids to you, one at a time. Let's link our coms."

Blaze nodded and tapped his earcom twice to create the new link.

By the time the translation datapad finished explaining Ekaterina's task to her, the first group arrived. Diaz hurried to the entrance and gestured for the first teen to approach Blaze's table.

Oh, dear Lord. The engineer reflexively shut his eyes when he realized the former slave was wearing next to nothing, just underwear which had seen better days. *I'm the wrong person for this job!*

When she was standing in front of him, he cautiously opened his eyes, but kept them fixed on her careworn face, determined not to glance any lower than her chin.

The slender black young woman reminded him of Zuri, especially with her close-cropped hair. Blaze tried to appear friendly and harmless, but he couldn't stop his face from turning red with embarrassment.

Ekaterina handed her a bottle of water. The teen regarded Blaze with a worried frown as she gulped down the drink in less than a minute. Ekaterina handed her another bottle.

"Good job," Blaze told his assistant. He touched his ear and hissed to Diaz, "We need some clothes for these girls, ASAP."

"We had a donation of several hundred T-shirts, but they won't fit because they're all extra large."

"Extra large is exactly what they need. See if someone can deliver them here." He cut the connection before Diaz could reply and shifted his attention back to the nervous teen in front of him.

Blaze held the datapad out to her at arm's length in his left hand. He held up his right thumb and held it over the ID lock on the screen, hoping she would get the idea.

She pressed her thumb to the right spot.

He turned the datapad around to make sure it captured the trace. Since she was born after the war, her information didn't appear on the screen. He realized he would need some identification with her DNA.

He took a hologram of her face and asked, "What's your name?"

She just stared at him.

Blaze picked up the translation datapad and repeated the question.

"Katya."

He recorded it with her file and tapped his com again. "What should I do now?"

"Send her to the first open interviewer," Diaz said. "I can have those T-shirts here in about fifteen minutes."

"Thank you." Blaze repeated the instruction to Katya on the datapad. He waited until she was sitting across from a female ISPP officer before turning to greet the next newcomer.

After getting the DNA traces, holograms, and names of the first five young women, he was confident enough to move the rest of the group through the process at a faster pace. He was able to finish with the last one before Diaz announced in his ear, "The next tramload is here."

"Great." Blaze sighed.

"I've got a case of the T-shirts outside. I'll hand them out to the girls before they come in."

"Please give some to the first group that's just leavin'."

"Will do. They'll have something to wear, and I'll direct them to the mess hall for something to eat. It'll feel like paradise after what these poor kids have been through."

Blaze agreed, and in a minute he was able to greet the first teen from the new group. She was wearing a new, red, baggy T-shirt that came to her knees, making his task much less awkward.

The young women in this group looked as if they were used as punching bags on a regular basis. Each one had some type of facial contusion, such as a black eye, scabbed or puffy lip, or a fist-sized bruise. Many displayed fresh injuries, purplish-blue and swollen, while all of them bore older injuries, yellow or faded green. A few of them were limping.

The teens appeared defeated in body and spirit. Some of them glanced around with wide eyes, shying away from any adult who came near them. Those who weren't scared were numb to all the excitement as evidenced in their slumped shoulders and vacant stares.

Blaze took a trace from the smallest girl in the group. The thumb she pressed to the ID lock was crooked, as if it had been broken but not properly set. She had so many cuts and bruises on her petite face, he decided not to take a hologram, since no one would recognize her in this condition.

"What's your name?" He whispered the question. She was obviously terrified of men and couldn't look him in the eye.

"Oluremi," the datapad translated, "but I have been called Worthless Dog for many years."

Blaze had to swallow his rage. He'd never wished harm on anyone, but he found himself feeling morbidly grateful ISPP hadn't bothered to arrest most of the human traffickers they encountered in the factories and brothels. "No one will ever call you that again, Oluremi."

"I'm going to need medics, ASAP," he told Diaz after he sent Oluremi to sit on one of the examination tables.

"Well, you're in luck because they're here," the com tech said. "Bonus: they're all women."

Three ISPP officers in pink scrubs walked into the tent and went to work treating the former slaves. Blaze made sure each medic had translation and DNA datapads, and breathed a mental sigh of relief as he turned his back on the most emotionally draining task he'd ever performed.

He had one more thing he needed to take care of before he could help Axe with the heir-lock program. He got down on one knee and had a quick chat with Ekaterina with the aid of a datapad.

"I'm gonna be right over there." He pointed across the tent to Axe's workstation. "Can you be a good helper and make sure everyone who comes in gets a bottle of water?"

After hearing the instructions in her native Romanian, she nodded.

"Please do not leave without me," the datapad told him. Ekaterina batted her big brown eyes at him.

Great. There was no way for him to escape. Blaze nodded at his little shadow and walked over to join Axe Tse at the computers.

SEVEN
PATIENT

THE HEADACHE WAS bad, but Danae had to cope with it until she figured out what was going on. She glanced at the purple curtains which formed the walls of her cubicle. She was lying in a white-blanketed bed with a Quickheal IV bag suspended above her shoulder, the IV tube connected at the back of her right wrist. She noted the familiar cloying scent of antiseptic air and came to the obvious conclusion: hospital. The voices outside her curtained walls were speaking Thai.

"Hello? Um, *sawadeeka*?" It came out like a whispered croak, so she tried again. "*Sawadeeka*?"

The curtain to her left flew open, and a stout female nurse in orange silk scrubs appeared at her bedside, asking her something in Thai.

Danae shook her head, which increased the pain, to indicate she didn't understand.

The nurse repeated the same phrase louder and slower, as if the captain was just a bit dim.

"English?"

The nurse made an impatient noise and stepped out, pulling the purple curtain shut.

Why did I leave the ship without an earcom? Danae had been a hospital patient enough to know she could be stuck here for hours unless someone showed up to sign her out. *Unacceptable,* she thought. *I'm not staying here all day.*

She found the bed controls and raised the head until she was more upright. Her skull throbbed in protest at the movement.

Where's Jake with a painkiller when I need him?

She glanced down and saw she was wearing only a standard hospital gown, which didn't conceal much. She still had dried blood on her left arm. She felt the left side of her face and discovered a large bandage covering her temple. Her hair was stiff with dried blood.

I'm glad there's no mirrors in here.

As she pondered how she could escape the ER with a crushing migraine, she heard a familiar voice just outside the curtain, arguing with the not-too-friendly nurse.

"Phailin!" Danae hissed. "In here!"

The cook threw open the curtain. She yanked her arm free of the nurse's grip, snarled "*kon bah!*" and pulled the curtain closed on the protesting woman.

"What did you say—?" Danae heard the nurse stomp off.

"I called her an idiot. She said only family members are allowed back here," Phailin said. "She's probably calling security. Let's get you out of here, Captain."

"Best idea I've heard all day. Where are my clothes?"

Phailin glanced around the cubicle and found a tote bag underneath the bed. She examined the contents with a grimace. "I don't think you'll want to put these back on."

"Then I'll leave in this lovely ensemble." Danae swung her legs over to Phailin's side of the bed. "Help me up."

Phailin took hold of her left arm and gently pulled her to a standing position. Danae swayed on the spot, unable to find her balance.

"Captain!" Phailin grabbed Danae's shoulders and helped her sit again. "You can't leave in this condition. I'll tell the nurse you need some pain meds."

"No, I'll be fine. Whatever's in my IV is making me groggy. I don't want any meds, I just want to get back to the ship. I need to see Shima."

"Shima's fine. She and Zuri are sleeping, they're exhausted," Phailin said. "And I guess you haven't heard about Marco."

"What about him?"

"He's conscious! He came out of the coma!"

"That's great news." Danae wanted to cheer but didn't because she knew it would make her headache worse. "How is he?"

"His memory is a bit . . . spotty, but Dr. Sorensen thinks he'll make a full recovery."

"Erik?" Danae tried to connect her scattered thoughts. "That's right, he brought Ting here. Could you ask him to come to the ER? Maybe he could give me a painkiller and get me signed out of here."

"Yes, ma'am." Phailin slipped her hands under Danae's knees and lifted them, helping her shift her legs back up to the bed. Once she was tucked in again, the cook said, "I'll send Dr. Sorensen down as soon as possible, Captain."

"Thank you." Danae closed her eyes, and the sounds around her faded away.

***

"So here's where they hid you!"

Danae struggled to navigate her way out of the persistent fog of drug-induced drowsiness. She pried her eyes open and appraised Cade York, who was standing at her bedside in a spotless ISPP uniform. A thick cast and a sling on his right arm didn't seem to bother him. He appeared well-rested and cheerful for someone who had just been shot.

"Hi," was all she could manage, unable to put a complete sentence together.

"Head wounds tend to bleed profusely. We think you lost a liter before Jiang got to you with the Hemorrhage Freeze. He removed a sliver of glass about eight centimeters long. It was embedded in your temple."

"That long? Didn't feel it." Danae closed her eyes again to shut out the glare from the overhead lights.

"So why haven't they patched you up yet? Wisdom and I were cleared to leave an hour ago."

"Wisdom?"

"Moniesa. Wisdom's her first name."

"Right, I forgot."

"Must be the ISPP uniforms," Cade said. "Military priority."

"Must be."

It was quiet for a few minutes, until she heard Cade ask someone about an English-speaking nurse. *Why didn't I think of that?*

Danae dozed off for what felt like five minutes. When she awoke again, her headache was gone. She opened her eyes.

She was in a private hospital room. Cade was reclining in the chair at her bedside. His eyes were closed. She couldn't tell if he was asleep or just waiting around for her to wake up so he could yell at her for racing into the building like a lunatic with a death wish.

Danae glanced down at herself again. She was still in a hospital gown, but her left arm was clean. She felt her neck: clean. The bandage on her temple was gone, and only a tiny scar remained, thanks to synthflesh and fusion laser technology. And her hair felt clean, although she had no idea how someone managed to wash it without waking her.

She decided to see if her visitor was awake. "Don't you have an army to command?"

Cade's eyes snapped open, and he sat up. "How are you feeling?"

"I'm feeling confused. Isn't there a lot going on that needs your attention? Why are you hanging around here?"

He didn't smile, but there was no scowl this time, no trace of anger or animosity in his features. There was warmth in his dark eyes she hadn't seen since the first time they met aboard his ship on Mars Station. That cordial interview, when he offered to loan her crew the Excalibur handguns, seemed like such a long time ago, although she knew it had only been two weeks. Since the debriefing aboard his ship, their relationship had become so adversarial, she was amazed neither of them had thrown any punches.

It looks like Cade wants to be friends again. Danae wasn't sure what to make of this development.

"Someone needed to stay and make sure you got the proper treatment." He answered her question with a one-shouldered shrug.

"I'm not the one who was shot. How's Moniesa?"

"She'll be fine. The bullet only grazed her hand. We've both been shot several times over the years. You get used to it."

Danae gave him a dubious look. "She's not up for court-martial or something for storming inside without your authorization?"

Cade looked thoughtful and fidgeted with his sling. "No, I've decided to let her off with a warning. I trust her instincts. She did . . . well, to be honest, she did exactly what I would've done if I'd gotten there first. Plus she kept you safe, like she promised."

"Yes, up until the moment she was shot."

The ISPP captain reached over with his left hand and rubbed the cast on his right wrist. "This was an easy repair. FMJ rounds leave clean entrance and exit holes. Just some synthbone and a few muscles to regrow. Nothing like what you went through when Thanatos tried to kill you."

"Vipul," Danae said. "He tried to kill my navigator, and I was in the way."

Cade seemed eager to change the subject. He got to his feet and turned his head to show her the com attached to his left earlobe. "I'm not taking time off. ISPP's workload just doubled with the children we've liberated from the red-light district."

"It does seem like we've opened a Pandora's box."

Captain York needed to get something off his chest, and since Danae felt responsible for adding to his burdens, she closed her mouth and donned an attentive expression.

He paced the floor beside her bed. "I have a small crew and limited resources. It'll take an army of volunteers to sort this out. We have thousands of children who need to be returned to their families.

"I have to make sure we find and liberate all the slave-run factories and brothels in Bangkok, and this is just one city! Thanatos's log lists thirty-one other cities that purchased the kids he trafficked, and ISPP will need to investigate every one of them. I have five ships, only two hundred fifty officers, to accomplish all of this.

"How am I going to shelter and feed all these people while we sort this out? How am I going to return children to their families? Who can I depend on for assistance if the local CIPs are corrupt? I need volunteers I can trust. These kids have been used, abused, and treated worse than animals. They're scared, they're scarred, and most of them need medical attention and probably a lifetime of therapy. I'm responsible for what happens to them from this point on, and I can't risk recruiting anyone who's going to take advantage of them or even traffic them again.

"I need volunteers—generous people, like your crew—to make sure these kids get the care they deserve. And I need to return them to their families."

Cade stopped pacing and turned to stare at her, a pained look on his face. "And my personal mission, my highest priority, has been swept aside in all the confusion."

"You need to find your son."

He hesitated, his voice dropping to a whisper. "If he's still alive."

Danae was stunned at this admission. "Why wouldn't he be? Did you learn where he was taken from Thanatos's log?"

"Yes, the log listed the port where Linc was delivered. It's in Malaysia." Cade bit his lip and stared past her, at the window. "We flew over it right before coming to Bangkok. The city's been bombed—completely wiped out."

Danae drew in a sharp breath. "I had no idea what you've been going through." Her thoughts leaped ahead, and she offered him some theories. "The log could be wrong. He could've been delivered somewhere else. Or the slaves might have been moved to another site before the city was bombed. I'm sure we can find out when it was bombed. If it happened during the war, or at least before Linc was taken, then we'll know he wasn't there."

She waited for Cade to make eye contact. "You *can't* give up hope. It took us seven years to find Zuri. Shima refused to give up."

"She risked her life to get to her niece. And then you risked your life to get to Shima." He moved close to her bedside and put his left hand over hers.

Danae felt a flutter of concern and was tempted to pull her hand away, but the intense expression on his face made her hesitate.

"Today when you ran inside the building after Moniesa, I couldn't believe my eyes. I couldn't believe one woman could be so reckless—"

Danae flinched and tried to move her hand, but Cade closed his fingers around hers and wouldn't let go.

"—so headstrong, so . . . brave," he stammered. "Even when I was so angry at you I couldn't see straight, I thought, 'York, you've met your match. This woman has more courage and determination in her little finger than you have in your entire body.'"

His face was only a few decimeters from hers. "We're so much alike, you and I. We've experienced the same tragic losses, we have the same ambitious goals, we know how to lead, and we're not afraid to make the tough decisions. You're resourceful and smart and . . . fearless. I need you, Danae."

Uh oh. She could tell by the way he was gazing at her that he wasn't referring to a need for her tactical assistance. She felt the flutter of concern ratchet up to heart-pounding fear. So many thoughts raced through her mind, she was unable to vocalize a single one. She could tell how Cade intended to finish this speech by the way he was leaning closer . . . and closer. She felt frozen, trapped physically by the IV and hospital bed and trapped emotionally by indecision.

And then it was too late to decide.

She hoped it would be a quick thank-you type of smooch, but Cade was persistent, determined to coax some participation from her. Danae stopped trying to resist and lost herself for a few moments. It was easy to imagine, with her eyes closed, that she was kissing Alex.

A little voice inside her head warned her to check back in with reality. *He's not Alex.*

Cade released her from the compulsory kiss. He straightened up with a roguish grin and gave her hand a squeeze.

Then she heard a noise so soft it was almost imperceptible. It was the sound of a door closing.

EIGHT
PAIN

ERIK DIDN'T HAVE much experience with physical therapy, so he sat and observed Ting's first session in the anti-grav suspension unit.

Sirikit, a cheerful therapist with a frizzy perm and the patience of Job, took an hour to attach tiny electrode androids to each of Ting's major muscles on his back, arms, legs, neck, hands, feet, and hips.

The helmsman complained each time she adjusted the unit. "I feel like a puppet!"

And he looked like a puppet—a bald, skinny, Chinese marionette in purple boxer shorts. The anti-grav kept his body upright with a simple harness across his back tethered behind each elbow, and a second harness across the backs of his thighs, tethered behind each knee.

Sirikit rotated Ting so his back was to her, his toes a few centimeters off the floor. She then picked up a different remote unit used to control the androids.

Ting's left arm jerked as she directed a tiny jolt of energy into his forearm, contracting the muscles. In response, he started to curse, calling Sirikit every vulgar name in English he could remember.

Too bad his tongue is the only muscle he can control. Erik was glad Sirikit didn't speak English, but he noticed Phailin looking uncomfortable. He caught her eye and mouthed "Sorry."

The cook nodded, looking helpless, but then touched her earlobe. "I'm getting a call. It's Lorina." She moved to a quieter part of the room, listened for a few seconds, and then screamed, "Yes!" and pumped a fist in the air. "They found Shima! Dr. Sorensen, they found Shima!"

Yes, thank God! "Patch me in." Erik tapped his earcom.

"Zuri was with her," Lorina was saying. "They're shaken up but no serious injuries. Captains York and Shepherd found them in a building where about one hundred other girls were being held captive before being forced to work as—" She stopped there and didn't go into details.

"It's been a very successful day," Erik chimed in. "Marco came out of his coma a few hours ago."

"That's wonderful news! I don't suppose he woke up with a new personality?" Lorina asked, half kidding, half serious.

"No, he's as charming as ever. How's Danae—I mean, Captain Shepherd?"

"I was getting to that. The captain helped raid the building with some of the ISPP officers. Actually, she led the charge. There were a few injuries."

"Who?" Erik felt a twinge of dread. *Please not Danae.*

"Captain York was shot in the arm and Officer Moniesa in the hand. A piece of glass hit Captain Shepherd on the side of her head. She lost a lot of blood, but she should be fine."

"Where were they treated?" Erik tried not to sound anxious.

"They were taken to Bhumibol Memorial. As far as I know, they're still there."

"Good, I can go see her right now."

"Thank you for the update, Lorina," Phailin said. "We'll keep you posted on Marco's progress."

The doctor said goodbye and turned off his earcom. "Phailin, please tell Sirikit I need to leave for a few minutes."

She nodded and approached the smiling therapist, who was blissfully unaware Ting was cursing her ancestors back to Adam and Eve. She spoke to Sirikit, frowned at the response she got, and turned to Erik.

"She said you can't leave now. She needs a doctor here for the entire session. She said newly awakened coma patients can sometimes have breathing problems, vomit, lose control of their bladders, or become hysterical. Their bodies need time to . . . *reboot* is I think the word she used."

Erik suppressed a sigh of frustration. "How long is this going to take?"

Phailin asked and reported back. "She said two hours is optimal if he can handle the strain on his joints."

Two hours! Erik found a chair by the wall, sat down, and took out his scanner. "Tell Sirikit I'll stay for the full session."

Phailin relayed the information. "I could check on Captain Shepherd and let you know how she's doing."

"I'd really appreciate that," Erik said.

The cook left the room, and the puppet show continued. Ting's right arm jerked, and he cursed some more.

Erik wished for temporary hearing loss. *Two hours of this? Someone, please sedate me.*

***

Dr. Sorensen was beginning to utter a few curses himself when Phailin returned.

"I brought your lunch. You left it in neurology. It's cold but I think there's a staff lounge on this hall. I could warm it up for you."

"A smart woman knows food is the fastest way to a man's heart," Erik said.

"That's why I'm a cook. Plus, I figured you were half-starved."

"How's Danae? Is she still here in the hospital?"

"I found her in the ER." Phailin hesitated. "She looks like she's in pain. I don't think they've treated her yet. She wants to leave, but she was too woozy to stand, even with my help."

"What?" Erik was on his feet. "I need to see her. Please ask Sirikit if another doctor could sub for me for a few minutes."

Phailin opened her mouth to ask, but Ting picked that moment to start screaming. "I can't do this! This hurts! Let me down! Let me down!"

The therapist shouted something at Phailin, who was getting upset too. "Sirikit says do something!"

"What am I supposed to do, sedate him? I don't have any meds on me. Tell her I need access to a micro-pharmacy."

"Let me down!" Ting sounded close to tears. "It hurts!"

Erik's frustration had reached its limit. He marched over to the helmsman, getting right up in his face. "Stop it! *Shut up!*"

The silence was refreshing as Ting stared at Erik, incredulous, his lips still flapping but no words coming out.

"That's better! Now you're going to cooperate with the therapist so *all* of us can leave this hospital in a few days. Am I making myself clear?"

"It hurts," Ting complained, although much quieter.

"No, it feels strange, and it might be a little uncomfortable, but it's the only way we can get your muscles fully functional again, so you need to do as you're told."

Ting's expression was insolent, but he had no response.

"The goal is for you to walk out of here on your own two feet and reclaim your life. You want that, don't you?" Erik felt as if he were talking to a petulant teenager—which was probably an accurate description of Ting—but his firm approach was working.

"Yes," Ting whispered.

"Good! So keep it together, and do what Sirikit tells you." Erik returned to his seat. He caught Phailin's eye and winked. "Substitute doctor?" he reminded her.

She nodded. "I'll see if I can find someone. Thank you, Dr. Sorensen."

He rubbed his aching forehead. "You're welcome."

***

It was close to 5:00 p.m., local time, when Marco was stable enough to be left without a doctor's supervision for a few minutes. Erik had to sit through the entire physical therapy session because all the doctors Phailin spoke to were too busy to take his place for fifteen minutes. It was a long and frustrating afternoon.

Erik left Phailin at Ting's bedside with an admonition to call him, if needed. He rode the lift down to the lobby and went straight to the information kiosk.

"Danae Shepherd," he told the screen.

Fortunately, the answer on the screen came up in both Thai and English: *observation room 6, emergency department, first floor.*

She's still in the ER? He headed over.

Language once again became a stumbling block as Erik attempted to get some information from the ER triage nurse. She kept shaking her head no. He wasn't sure if it meant, "No, I don't understand you" or "No, you can't go inside."

He showed her his doctor's security pass. She pondered this, suspicion written all over her face, before reluctantly opening the doors for him.

Erik walked around the crowded emergency department, trying to act as though he was supposed to be there. He was able to glance into each of the curtained cubicles before being confronted by an orderly who threatened him with a wet mop.

The doctor held up his hands in the universal sign of surrender. "I was just leaving." And he was, because Danae wasn't in any of the observation rooms. Room 6 was empty.

He returned to the information kiosk and tried again. *Maybe she was just discharged.* "Danae Shepherd."

Room 472.

She was admitted? Maybe she did lose a lot of blood.

Erik rode the lift to the fourth floor and discovered more corridors which seemed to go on for kilometers. He walked up and down for fifteen minutes until he found the 400 wing of patients' rooms. Room 472 was way down at the end of yet another corridor, but he found it at last.

He raised a fist to knock on the door but hesitated when he heard Cade York's voice inside.

The doctor didn't intend to eavesdrop, but he knew how abrasive the ISPP captain could be. He didn't want to walk in on an argument. If York was giving Danae any grief, Erik would be tempted to punch first and ask questions later.

So he listened for a minute to see if it was safe to barge in.

"Even when I was so angry at you I couldn't see straight, I thought, 'York, you've met your match. This woman has more courage and determination in her little finger than you have in your entire body.' We're so much alike, you and I. We've experienced the same tragic losses, we have the same ambitious goals, we know how to lead, and we're not afraid to make the tough decisions. You're resourceful and smart and . . . fearless. I need you, Danae."

Erik felt as though a bucket of ice water had been dumped on his head. *What did he say?* His mind was churning with so many questions that he couldn't hear any more of York's syrupy-sweet speech.

Only one question demanded an answer: *How is Danae responding to this?*

He had to know.

The room had become suspiciously quiet so Erik took extra care not to make a sound. He turned the handle and pushed the door open a few centimeters, grateful the hinges didn't squeak. He paused when the gap was just wide enough for him to get a glimpse of Cade York and Danae Shepherd . . . kissing.

Serious kissing, like mouth-to-mouth resuscitation without the drowning.

Erik felt as if he were drowning; he couldn't breathe. He silently pulled the door shut and walked away.

***

"Dr. Sorensen, they're discharging Captain Shepherd at 2000," Phailin reported in his earcom. "She's going to stop by and see Marco before Officer Moniesa escorts her back to the *Alex.*"

Thanks for the warning. Erik got up from the uncomfortable and undersized visitor's chair in Ting's private room. The helmsman had fallen asleep when Phailin left to get something to eat, so Erik had used the quiet solitude to sit and think.

"I picked up some cucumber salad and chicken satay for you," Phailin continued, "and I'm on my way upstairs. I can stay with Marco tonight if you want to go back to the ship and get some sleep."

"Thank you, but I'm not hungry. You can have the satay; I'm sure it's delicious." He invented a plausible excuse. "I need to check in with the head of neurology to see what they have Ting scheduled for tomorrow. Sirikit also needed some time to train me to take over for her when he's discharged."

"Do whatever you need to do, but I'm still camping out in Marco's room."

What does she see in the obnoxious loudmouth that the rest of us can't?

Erik didn't wait for Phailin to reach the room. He knew she would want to discuss Ting's condition, but he wanted to disappear before Danae and York showed up. He headed to the neurology department.

There was no one in the neurology lab. The lights were off in the room behind the glass doors. The doctor leaned his back against the wall and tried to think.

I could bunk here at the hospital until Ting's released in three days, but none of the scrubs these tiny Thais wear will fit me. Plus it'll look odd if I ask Phailin to bring me clean clothes every day. I could go back to the ship and hide out in my cabin, but it'll be hard to avoid running into Danae, even if I come and go at odd hours.

Erik sighed. He knew he couldn't avoid Danae indefinitely, but he had no idea what he would say to her or how he would react when he saw her. *Especially if York is hanging around.* He knew he was behaving like a love-sick teenager who'd been stood up for a big date, but he needed time to process the whirlwind of emotions he was experiencing. The shock, disappointment, and jealousy had to be dealt with before he could dredge up any mature emotions, like acceptance. He knew this, subconsciously, but it hurt too much to see the long-range view.

"Erik?" Lorina's voice was in his com.

"Yes?"

"I was wondering if you were coming back to the ship this evening. Zuri should have a medical exam. Shima too."

"Of course. I'm leaving the hospital now." He couldn't loiter around feeling sorry for himself. He still had a responsibility to the entire crew of *Alex's Legacy*, not just Ting. *I'm still on the payroll, for now.*

He caught a tram back to the spaceport. It was getting easier to ignore the stares of the other passengers. They gawked at him as if he were a circus sideshow exhibit. The doctor was used to standing out in a crowd. He kept his nose pressed to the window and watched the nightlife of Bangkok roll by.

Back aboard the *Alex*, Erik paged Shima and Zuri and went straight to the infirmary to meet them.

"Dr. Sorensen!" Shima was in high spirits. She gave him an unexpected hug and introduced him to her niece. "This is Zuri. She does not speak much English."

The attractive teen looked a lot like Shima, although she was much smaller than her aunt. Zuri's coarse black hair was buzzed short, and she had big brown eyes which grew larger as she studied Erik. She appeared to be wearing one of Shima's long T-shirts, belted around her tiny waist as a makeshift dress.

"Nice to meet you, Zuri." Erik offered his hand, but she just glanced down at her bare feet.

Shima spoke soothingly to Zuri in a language he never heard before.

Zuri's answer was a whisper.

"She is afraid of men, and you are the biggest man she has ever seen," Shima said.

"Please assure her that I won't touch her." Erik ushered them into the exam room.

"Perhaps you should check me first," Shima said, "so she will feel more at ease with you."

"Good thinking. Have a seat on the table."

"I would prefer not to." Shima looked embarrassed. "It hurts to sit down."

Erik took out his scanner. "You can stand, but you need to turn around so I can scan everything."

Shima nodded, understanding, and did a full turn for him. He could tell she'd been physically mistreated, but suspected most of the damage from her abduction was psychological.

"Just some bruises. Nothing broken, if you were wondering about your tailbone. The lump on the side of your head could use an ice pack." He paused, frowned at the readings. "Let me see your left arm."

Shima raised her arm above her head so Erik could see the bandaged site.

"It's a Sterilite Guard implant, used to stop menstruation, prevent pregnancy, and block STDs."

Shima nodded, grim. "And the tattoo?"

He got down on one knee so he could take a closer look at the bright yellow ink on the back of her leg. "It looks like some kind of writing."

"I think Zuri's tattoo is identical to mine."

"Let's find out." Erik turned to Zuri, who observed his every move with a worried frown. "Ask her to sit on the table, if she can."

Shima spoke to Zuri, and the nervous teen did as instructed.

He passed the scanner in front of Zuri. He gave her a smile of encouragement and held up the device so she could see the information flow across the tiny screen.

"She's also wearing an implant, Shima. She's got a few bruises and some tendonitis in her knees, but I can treat it when she feels more comfortable around me. I can remove the implants whenever you're ready, but I can't remove the tattoos, not without a specialized laser."

"Of course, I understand."

"Please ask her to roll onto her front side."

Shima took Zuri by the hand and encouraged her to change positions. She and Erik studied the tattoo behind the girl's right knee.

"It does look identical to yours. It's Chinese, I think." He took a datapad from the side counter and took a hologram of Zuri's tattoo. He got down on one knee again and took a hologram of Shima's tattoo.

Erik put the images side-by-side on the screen and did some quick research. "They're so similar it looks like they used a template. They're Mandarin characters, but just random words, not any kind of message."

"Can I see?" He handed Shima the datapad, and she read, "Large . . . bird . . . white . . . water . . . oyster or clam . . . seed . . . fast or swift . . . water, again. What does it mean?"

"I have no idea, but it must be important. Did you notice tattoos on any of the other girls locked up with you?"

"No." The first officer appeared uncomfortable relating this detail. "We were all sitting down so I could not see the backs of their legs. Only one girl said she was tattooed, but some of them did not speak English and did not know what I was asking."

"I'll ask the ISPP medics to watch for the tattoo on girls from the red-light district."

Erik glanced at the time and remembered he wanted to be in his cabin before Danae returned to the ship. He took a tube of arnica gel out of an overhead cabinet and handed it to Shima. "You should both use this on your bruises."

"Thank you, Dr. Sorensen."

He waited until Shima helped Zuri down from the table before ushering them to the door of the infirmary. "If you'll excuse me, ladies, I desperately need some sleep. I'll check on you again tomorrow."

"Thank you. Goodnight."

Danae's cheerful voice came over the shipboard com before Shima and Zuri reached the ladder. "First Officer Oryang! Meet me in the galley in five minutes!"

"I am already there!" Shima crowed back.

Erik felt trapped as he watched aunt and niece walk down the short hallway, past the bridge, to the galley. He was on the wrong level if he wanted to avoid Danae. There were only two ways to reach the top deck: ladder or starboard lift. *Which one will she use?*

He would have to make an educated guess. *Just got out of the hospital—she'll use the lift.*

Moving to the ladder, Erik descended to the third level. He hurried to his cabin on the port wing, grateful he didn't encounter Lorina or Vipul on the way. Any crewmembers would wonder why he was skulking around the ship like a stowaway.

You're a big, pathetic coward, he told himself as he showered and got ready for bed. *I should've volunteered to stay on as The Lost Sheep orphanage director. Maybe I should have stayed on Mars Station and reopened the Outreach Clinic.*

I don't belong here, on a starship . . . with Danae Shepherd.

***

Danae was standing at his bedside, looking down at him. She smiled and suddenly began to shrink, growing smaller and smaller until she was the size of a child's doll. The doll-sized Danae laughed in a high-pitched little girl's voice and started to shrink again until she disappeared.

Erik awoke with a start, his heart pounding. "Lights, dim." He sat up and looked around his empty cabin. He had the eerie sensation someone was standing at his bedside while he slept.

Relax, Sorensen, it was just a dream. But it felt familiar, as if he'd had this dream before.

"Lights, off." He had a hard time getting back to sleep.

NINE
REUNION

"YOU CAN TRUST the people here on the ship," Shima told Zuri as they left the infirmary after their brief examinations with the doctor, and headed to the galley to meet Danae. "Dr. Sorensen cared for homeless children on Mars Station."

"What about this Ting person? I have heard his name many times today."

Shima shrugged. "He has a big mouth, but he is harmless—like a little dog that barks a lot but is too scared to bite. Just ignore him, like I do."

"Are you sure I can live here too?" Zuri toured the ship earlier with an expression reminiscent of a child set loose in a candy store. Shima remembered feeling the same way when Danae informally adopted her after Zuri was abducted from Mars Station seven years ago.

"This is our home." She put an arm around her niece's thin shoulders. "Your only work here will be to catch up on the schooling you have missed. I will set up an education program for you as soon as you are ready to begin. You will need to learn English."

"I know a little already but just simple words like *toilet*."

Shima laughed. "That is a useful word, but aboard a ship a bathroom is called a *head*."

"I thought this is a head." Zuri patted her scalp, a confused look on her face.

"Yes, English can be hard to understand. Some words have many different meanings." Shima had just finished setting three cups of chamomile tea on Danae's favorite table near the kitchen when the captain walked in.

Danae gave her a bear hug and startled Zuri with the same greeting. "This has been the longest day of my life!" She dropped into a chair and took a gulp of hot tea.

Shima and Zuri joined her at the table with more decorum, although Shima thought it was great to see Danae looking so happy after watching her taken away unconscious in an ambulance a few hours ago. She was relieved to see that the gash on the side of Danae's head was better. Only a thin line of synthflesh remained.

She did a double take at the captain's attire. "What are you wearing?"

Danae glanced down at her orange silk nurse's scrubs and laughed. "I sort of *borrowed* them from the hospital. It was either that or go home in a gown that didn't quite cover my butt."

"You must tell me everything but pause often so I can translate for Zuri."

"Welcome aboard!" Danae gave Zuri a big smile. "We've been searching for you for a long time, young lady."

The teen shyly returned the smile, sipped her tea, and listened with rapt attention as the women spent an hour comparing stories.

The captain stopped Shima's narrative at one point to clarify, "They used a nerve prod on both of you? Those are illegal, and they're the most horrible torture devices ever invented."

Shima shrugged. "Human trafficking is also illegal, but so is carrying a gun in Bangkok."

Danae returned the shrug. "You should've seen the look on Cade's face when I picked off the thug who was shooting up the place with a semi-automatic."

"You were crazy to go charging up those stairs while people were shooting at you."

"I'm crazy? I didn't go sprinting across an open space, unarmed, with bullets flying all around me. It was a miracle you weren't hit."

"We are just a pair of miracles, then. You know, you did not keep your promise to me about staying out of another shootout."

"I had a compelling reason to break that promise."

"I know. And I am grateful you did. More tea?"

"Yes, please." Danae handed over her empty cup. It was just a few meters from their table to the crew's mess, but she let out a gasp before Shima reached it. "What happened to your leg?"

Shima paused mid-step and explained over her shoulder. "It is a tattoo. Zuri also has one. Dr. Sorensen researched the characters and believes it is Chinese writing—"

"Erik's on board?" Danae cut in. "Where is he?"

Shima turned around and studied her friend's furrowed brow. "He examined us a few minutes ago, just before he went to his cabin. He said he was very tired."

Danae nodded, looking thoughtful. "I thought he would want to see me since we missed each other at the hospital." She gave Shima her full attention. "I'm sorry, what were you saying about the tattoos?"

Shima filled the cup with hot water, dropped in a tea bag, and returned to the table. "Zuri was tattooed before being taken from the factory yesterday. I was . . . held down and given the tattoo last night after a woman— someone in charge—looked closely at my face. I do not know how many of the other girls in our prison room were tattooed since many of them did not speak English. It might have been one or two. It might have been all of them. Dr. Sorensen wants the ISPP medics to watch for the tattoo on other girls."

"To see if there's a pattern of who gets a tattoo and who doesn't. It might be a clue to help ISPP find other slaves." Danae nodded.

Shima had a sobering thought. "I wonder if they caught that horrible woman who told them to give me the tattoo. She might have information ISPP needs to find other traffickers."

"I heard most of them were gunned down when ISPP searched the red-light district this afternoon."

Shima bit her lip. "I am glad those monsters can never hurt any more children like Zuri."

"I'm just grateful you weren't one of the casualties." Danae's face grew pale. "The gunfight could've ended badly for either of us."

"I know." A knot formed in Shima's stomach. "Can we talk about something else?"

***

Shima didn't realize how late it was until she noticed Zuri had put her head down on the table and dozed off. "I should take her back to the cabin. I moved my things into 310 because it has two beds."

Danae nodded and reached across the table to grasp Shima's free hand. "Before you go, I need some advice."

Shima expected this. "Something to do with a certain doctor who cannot take his eyes off you?"

"No, it's not about Erik. It's about Cade—he kissed me."

"*What?* I thought Captain York did not like you."

"So did I! But now he insists that he needs me and we're perfect for each other. I was stuck in a hospital bed so I couldn't fend him off . . . but I wasn't sure I *wanted* to fend him off."

Shima could guess why. "Did it feel like you were kissing Alex?"

"Yes." Danae looked ashamed. "Now I feel torn. I know Erik's interested in me. He doesn't exactly hide his feelings. He's calm and considerate and dependable—I could really get used to all the attention.

"Cade, on the other hand"—she furrowed her brow—"has so much raw energy, and passion. But he's like a loaded gun with no safety switch. I never know when he's going to go off. Maybe that's more excitement than I need.

"I shouldn't even be thinking about other men, not now . . . not so soon after losing Alex."

"Blaze once told me that love does not follow any predictable timetable."

Danae pursed her lips. "Yes, he's right about that. But I'm not looking for love. I'm not even looking for a dinner date. I shouldn't be sending out signals to Erik or Cade that I'm interested. It wouldn't be fair to them or me."

"I am not sure I am the right person to ask. I have never had two men interested in me at the same time."

"Neither have I!"

"If you want me to be honest . . . I must first ask if you plan to keep wearing that mask around Dr. Sorensen and Captain York."

Danae froze, a crease forming between her eyebrows. "What do you mean by that? What mask?"

Shima studied Danae's face to make sure she under-stood the implication. "Your mask . . . it is like a wall you use to protect yourself, to keep other people out. You do not let people get close to you. You push them away and hide your true feelings."

Danae regarded her with a suspicious frown. "Have you been talking to Jake?"

"No, not since we left Maui."

"Jake's the only person who's ever confronted me about the walls I put up." Danae thought about it. "No, that's not true. Blaze and Erik both mentioned it, in a roundabout sort of way, but Jake's the only one who's ever advised me to let down the wall."

She set her empty mug down hard enough to rattle the other cups on the table. "I like my wall—or mask, as you put it—because it keeps me safe. I don't let people get close to me because the people I care about tend to die—or disappear!"

Shima didn't mean to strike a nerve. "I did not plan to be abducted last night." She frowned. "Do you not think I know how you feel about people dying or disappearing?"

Danae sobered. "Of course you know how I feel." She glanced over at Zuri, who was sound asleep. "I'm sorry. I didn't mean to snap at you. It's been a long day, and I'm feeling stretched, emotionally."

"Emotions can cloud our vision when we need to make important decisions."

"That's deep." Danae grinned. "Are you turning philosophical on me?"

"No." Shima returned the grin with a shrug. "I mean, not really. I just think you need to examine the situation objectively."

"If you have some words of wisdom, I'm listening."

"Captain York reminds you of Alex." She paused to let Danae think about it. "If you can see past that, you would still need to consider if a relationship with him is even possible."

Danae frowned and nodded, urging her to continue.

"If you want to be with Captain York, one of you would have to sacrifice your career for the other. I do not think he intends to leave ISPP. He does not seem"—she had to search for a tactful word—"flexible to me, which is why you argue with him so much."

"That's true. He'd want me to be an officer on his ship. He practically begged me to help him organize a volunteer effort to return the kids to their families."

"He did?" Shima eyebrows went up. "So you also need to consider how you would feel about taking orders from him."

Danae chewed her lip for a moment. "Alex and I . . . were a team. He wouldn't take orders from me, and I never expected him to." Her eyes met Shima's again. "But this is all just speculation, right? You don't think Cade would treat me like a co-captain—his equal?"

"Are there co-captains in the military?" Shima added, "Are you suggesting you would give up everything to be with Captain York?"

Danae shook her head and reached across the table to grasp Shima's hands in her own. "No! *You* are my family, you and Zuri, and the ship is my home!" She released Shima's hands and sat back in her chair with a heavy sigh.

"To be honest, up until the moment I found you and Zuri, I hadn't given a single thought about what to do next. I mean, what are we doing tomorrow or next month or even next year? I'm responsible for The Lost Sheep, but we need to get back to the business of passenger transport before my inheritance money runs out. Doing both at the same time isn't realistic.

"On the other hand, maybe the *Alex* could be put to better use if we formally joined ISPP. We could shuttle kids back to their homes. There are so many of them, it could take years."

"Yes, there are many paths you could take, *rafiki*," Shima said, "but you must do what is right for *you*, not what you think Dr. Sorensen or Captain York would want you to do."

Danae cracked a smile. "How did you get to be so smart?"

"I had a very good teacher," Shima said with complete sincerity.

The captain blinked hard a few times and cleared her throat. "Do you think it's safe for me to take off the mask? I get tired of saying goodbye to the people I care about."

"I do not know enough about Captain York to offer an opinion, but I believe Dr. Sorensen would never betray your trust, even if you decided you did not want him in your life."

Danae nodded. "Erik would probably wait years for me to make up my mind."

"Captain York would wait maybe five minutes."

"That sounds like an opinion to me!" Danae burst out laughing.

Shima chuckled too, and patted Zuri on the back to wake her. She helped her sleepy niece to her feet. "Goodnight, Danae."

"It's good to have you home, Shima."

"It's good to have a home." She noted Danae's thoughtful half smile and turned and left the galley with Zuri in tow.

TEN
BRAINSTORM

BLAZE'S EIGHT-HOUR SHIFT turned into a twelve-hour ordeal as he worked into the night, struggling to debug a hastily cobbled-together computer program with a Type A who lived up to her battle-axe nickname.

The command central was down to a skeleton staff, but ISPP continued to do medical exams and interviews. Instead of three exams and a dozen interviews going on simultaneously, there was one medic and four interviewing officers trying to keep up with the steady flow of freed slaves.

At one point during the evening shift, the ISPP medics received orders to keep an eye out for a certain tattoo behind the right knees of girls from the red-light district. Blaze left his terminal for a few minutes to report to one of the medics that he saw the tattoo on Shima and Zuri.

"Please add their information to the file," the officer said. "We're trying to find a pattern. It may help lead us to others who are still slaves."

"Why some are tattooed and others aren't?"

"Exactly." The ISPP officer thanked him and went back to work on a young girl's broken nose, and Blaze reluctantly returned to Axe's workstation.

That short break was several hours ago.

Quittin' time! Blaze knew he had to stop when he could no longer focus his eyes on the screen. "I'll be back in the mornin'." He glanced over at Ekaterina, who was sound asleep, curled up on a pile of the donated T-shirts. "Please tell her I'll be back."

The ISPP engineer looked as if she was about to say something sarcastic, but her eyelids were also drooping. She nodded, and he left before she could change her mind—she did that with annoying frequency.

Officer Diaz escorted Blaze down Lumphini's dark paths with only a small handlight to guide their way. The light revealed sleeping children everywhere they looked, stretched out on any spare patch of grass. Some had pillows or blankets to lie on, but most of them just used each other as pillows. They were huddled together like litters of kittens. Not everyone was asleep; they overheard a few giggles and muted conversations, but the park was peaceful compared to the earlier chaos.

"I'm still concerned about security," Blaze said when they passed the guards at the Rama Road entrance to Lumphini. He glanced back over his shoulder at the CIPs. "Aren't those the same two guys from this afternoon?"

Diaz turned around and squinted at them. "I think so. It's hard to tell in the dark."

"Does the CIP chief expect them to stay awake all night?"

"I don't know." The com officer emphasized his answer with a yawn. He walked Blaze to the tramstop and waited with him for a trolley back to the spaceport.

"Please make sure Ekaterina knows I'll be back in the mornin'."

"You're such a lady's man," Diaz joked.

Blaze thought of his wife, daughter, boss, and crewmates. "You have no idea. Goodnight, Roland," he said as he boarded a tram.

Although it wasn't safe for anyone to wander around Bangkok alone, particularly at night, the engineer wasn't nervous about returning to the spaceport without an escort. He felt safe with his Excalibur pistol tucked into the cargo pocket of his jeans. He made the trek without incident.

He was so tired, he almost forgot where his cabin was located. He hesitated halfway up the ladder to recall if he needed to climb to the second level or the third.

Blaze wandered slowly down the corridor, forcing his feet to keep moving forward. He found the ID lock on the control panel beside the door and pressed his thumb against it. The door slid open, and he quietly stepped inside the two-room suite he shared with Lorina and Niyati.

A nightlight in the head provided just enough illumination for him to move around without finding the furniture with his toes.

He stepped into the head, stripped off his sweat-soaked clothing, and stuffed it into the laundry chute. Blaze squeezed into the tiny shower stall and hooked up the breathing tube. The ultrasonic pulses of warm water cut off after the standard sixty seconds. He debated hitting the repeat button, but was too tired to stay upright any longer. He hit the dry button instead and was out of the head a minute later, cinching the waistband drawstring of his pajama pants as he shuffled over to the bed.

He stopped short when he saw there was no room for him on the bed. Lorina was lying right in the middle with her arms draped across both pillows. Niyati was curled up next to Lorina, hogging his side of the bed.

Blaze sighed. His normal impulse would be to pick up Niyati, who weighed maybe sixteen kilos soaking wet, and carry her to the twin bed in the adjoining room. But since she was still having nightmares due to post-traumatic stress disorder, she would be back in her parents' bed within minutes of being moved. Privacy was a lost cause.

It was a short honeymoon. But Blaze reminded himself he was willing to sign on for this instant family. Lorina and Niyati had formed a mother-daughter bond long before he came along, so he was the one who needed to adapt to his new roles as husband and father.

He still couldn't believe a woman as vivacious, clever, and beautiful as Lorina Murphy would want to spend her life with him. Blaze didn't consider himself much of a prize, so he vowed never to take his new family for granted.

Lorina was still grieving from her mother's recent death. She often had trouble falling asleep, so disturbing her while she looked so peaceful was out of the question.

He found his way to Niyati's room, made an attempt to offer a prayer, but managed only a mumbled "thank you" and fell asleep the moment he was horizontal, his big feet hanging off the end of her bed.

***

"What are you doing?" The voice in his ear was so soft it tickled.

"Sleepin'." Blaze didn't open his eyes. It took too much effort. "Is it time for your shift? Do I need to start daddy duty?"

"I'm not working today and neither are you."

Lorina had his attention. He pried his eyes open. "What?"

"The crew of the *Alex* has the day off. Captain York thinks ISPP can get a lot more done without us getting in the way."

Blaze sat up, a thought taking shape in his sleepy brain. "I need to tell Ekaterina. I'm sure she's upset I left her in the clinic tent last night."

"Who's Ekaterina?" Lorina sat on the bed beside him. She raised an eyebrow, but her smirk gave away the feigned-jealousy act.

"One of the slave girls from Zuri's factory. She and Zuri were friends, I think. Let's just say Ekaterina's taken an interest in me."

"It sounds like she might be getting attached to you."

"I hope not. I think she'll stop clingin' when she sees Zuri's fine. Maybe we could bring her back to the ship today so the two of them can say goodbye."

"It might be easier to take Zuri to see her at Lumphini."

Blaze frowned. "I'd like to avoid Lumphini until ISPP gets things under control."

"That may happen sooner than you think." Lorina flashed a mischievous grin and leaned over for a kiss. "You should thank me."

"Yes, ma'am. Thank you." He leaned to meet her halfway. Their lips hadn't quite met when Niyati barged into the room and bellowed, "Ewww!"

"I need to install a lock on that door." Blaze sighed.

"Well, this is *her* room." Lorina stood and took Niyati's hand, leading her over to the dresser to choose some clothes.

"The lock would be for the other side, so she can't come in *our* room."

His wife shrugged. "Maybe when she's not scared to sleep by herself."

"She takes naps by herself just fine," Blaze grumbled. "I just hope she breaks the nighttime habit before she starts high school." He pretended not to notice the scathing glance from Lorina. He stood, stretched, and wisely changed the subject. "You were sayin' somethin' about volunteers?"

Lorina put a bundle of clothes in Niyati's hands and sent her to the head to get dressed. "I spoke to two organizations yesterday and vetted both of them—their employees and volunteers submit to thorough background checks before they're allowed to be around children.

"One is a US-based adoption agency called Asian Child. Their office here in Bangkok has sixty volunteers who help out in the local orphanages. All the volunteers are headed to Lumphini this morning. The other group is a charity called Stop Traffic."

"That sounds self-explanatory." Blaze nodded with approval.

"They plan to send two shifts of volunteers, one morning and one evening. They're all Thai, so communication will be one less hurdle to deal with."

"How many people are we talkin' about with Stop Traffic?"

Lorina smiled. "Almost one hundred."

He did the math. "Three hundred adults should be able to manage thirty-five hundred kids. But I don't think the park's facilities can handle that many people twenty-four/seven."

"ISPP can sort it out. Officer Moniesa is the liaison for the new volunteers. She was grateful we found them some help so fast."

"Not *we—you*." He put his arms around her and leaned down for another attempt at a kiss, but Niyati emerged from the bathroom and announced, "Hungry!"

Lorina winked at Blaze. "Save that thought." She ducked beneath his arms and went over to Niyati to comb her hair. "How's the heir-lock program coming along?"

"There's still a few bugs, but Axe—I mean, Officer Tse—intends to start usin' it today. We're still waitin' on the CIP databases from the stations, but there's no reason why some of the kids can't go home if their parents live on Earth."

"That's going to be a massive undertaking," Lorina predicted. "Tracking down families one at a time?"

"I know." Blaze wanted to steer the conversation to a less stressful topic. "A day off, huh? Niyati hasn't been dirtside yet. Maybe we could be tourists today."

"You mean *falangs*?" Lorina grinned. "That's the only Thai word I know besides *sawadeeka*. I'd like to see the inside of a wat, if there's one still standing."

"Let's get goin' before it's an oven outside." He walked into his and Lorina's bedroom and pulled on shorts and a T-shirt.

The family climbed the ladder to the galley for break-fast. Blaze was just about to sit down when his earcom chimed. "Be right back," he told Lorina before heading next door to the bridge.

It was a ship-to-shore call. He opened the connection on the com. "This is Smith."

"It's Axe."

I thought we had the day off. "How's the heir-lock program workin'?"

"It's up and running, and we've matched about one hundred kids in the database to their parents. Now we just need to find the current addresses of the parents, but that's not why I'm calling."

"Is somethin' wrong?" He knew she hadn't called just to give him an update.

"Do you remember yesterday when you and Vipul mentioned putting a barricade around the park?"

Blaze scowled. "Security problems?"

"Yes. You were right about the CIPs. None of them were at the entrances this morning. Anyone could've walked in during the night. We're not sure if any of the kids are missing."

His empty stomach gave a nervous twinge, derailing his appetite. "Didn't York put some ISPPs on security detail?"

"We don't have enough people," Axe said. "Captain York is furious, but we can't do anything to confront the police department until we have the camp better organized and secure."

"What do you need me to do? You know Vipul and I were just jokin' about a barricade."

"We've got to find a larger space to put these kids. I guess we could split them into smaller groups, but then we'd need even more security for multiple areas."

"What do you need me to do?" Blaze repeated, frustrated this enormous responsibility was being dumped on him.

"Captain York says you're resourceful. He wants to know if you have any ideas."

"Lorina managed to find you some volunteers on short notice."

"Yes, and we appreciate it—"

Blaze didn't think she sounded sincere.

"—but ISPP has never handled a large-scale rescue mission, and we've never managed a refugee camp. We need a long-range plan."

"We can't let any children fall prey to traffickers again. I'll get back to you with some suggestions ASAP." *As soon as Lorina thinks of some, that is.* He was fresh out of ideas.

Axe sounded relieved. "Thanks for your assistance. Tse out."

Blaze returned to the galley and sank into the chair across the table from Lorina and Niyati. He pushed aside the bowl of oatmeal his wife set out for him.

"What's wrong?" Lorina raised her eyebrows at him.

He repeated the conversation with Axe. "They've got half a dozen engineers and security officers on staff, but suddenly this is *my* problem?"

Lorina pursed her lips. "York can be a real task-master—"

"That's one way of puttin' it," Blaze grumbled.

"—but we should assume ISPP is over their heads—"

"They're *way* over their heads."

"—and brainstorm a possible solution," Lorina continued without missing a beat. "All ideas are fair game, no matter how farfetched." She noted his pout and added, "I'll start. So, we know the park isn't safe because it's in the middle of the city and covers a large area."

"We need a place bigger than Lumphini," Blaze said.

"What about a high-rise hotel? It would only need the lobby secured, but—"

"I can't imagine a hotel that'll allow thousands of kids to have the run of the place."

"I also think traffickers will continue to be a problem in the city. They'll find a way to lure the kids outside, past security."

"They need an area with security already in place, like a military base."

Lorina shook her head. "Not in Asia. Most were leveled during the war."

"That's true." Blaze frowned. "The only intact bases are in the US and Europe. How 'bout an area more isolated, like an island?"

She narrowed her hazel eyes at him. "An island? Well, I guess we could hop over to the Philippines and find an island for sale, although we'd need one with a tourist resort already in place to house and feed thousands of kids."

"I think resorts are scarcer than military bases. And even if we could find an island, just shuttlin' the kids to and from the mainland would be a real chore, so scratch that idea."

He noted Lorina's sudden grin. "Do you wanna tell me what's goin' on inside your brilliant mind?"

"I'm thinking what ISPP needs is a large hotel, but on a *mobile* island."

"You're talking about . . . a ship?"

"Yes, but not a starship—an ocean liner," Lorina said. "It would be easy to secure because no one could sneak on board when it's not in port, but it would be easy to move kids and supplies on and off when it's docked."

Blaze tried to shelve his doubts and go along with this crazy idea. "Where do we find a ship?"

She pulled out her datapad and did some quick research. "The Khlong Toei Port is just up the river, north of the city, but its marina can only handle yacht-sized vessels—nothing bigger." She widened the map area to include the ocean. "It looks like there's a cruise terminal two hours northwest of Bangkok called Laem Chabang. That's where we need to go."

"Two hours?" Blaze noted the determined look on his wife's face and knew any attempt to talk her out of this idea would be wasted breath. "How far north do the trams run?"

Lorina flashed him an appreciative smile and consulted her datapad again. "We can transfer to a bullet train at the end of the orange line."

He glanced over at Niyati, who finished scraping her bowl clean. "Hungry, *baba*."

Blaze pushed his untouched oatmeal across the table. "I guess we'd better pack some snacks for the bottomless pit."

***

Laem Chabang cruise terminal turned out to be a mammoth port where several luxury ocean liners were docked. An air of neglect surrounded the vast concrete pier. The area was deserted; the salt air tinged with the unmistakable scent of dead fish.

Some of the ships were old, their white paint marred by barnacles at the waterline, and some of their round passenger-cabin windows were either boarded up or broken. The giant chains which secured the ships to the concrete cleats along the pier were rusty and draped in green slime.

"I can't imagine taking a cruise when most people can barely afford to put food on the table." Lorina said, "I think it's safe to say these have been abandoned."

Niyati skipped ahead as they walked down the pier. Lorina wanted to take a closer look at each of the anchored ships. It took them several minutes to walk the length of an unnamed cruise ship with faded Mickey Mouse ears painted on the bow.

The second ship had the silhouette of a mermaid with *Princess Kate* painted beneath it on the stern.

"What does that say?" Blaze moved closer to a moss-covered wooden sign hanging from the gangway. The enclosed wooden ramp was barricaded with a door made of rusty iron bars. Beneath the Thai writing on the sign was *For Sale* in lettering so small they had to squint to read it.

"It's for sale?" Lorina put her hands on her hips and looked up at the massive ship.

Blaze counted twelve decks from the waterline, and it was at least four hundred meters from bow to stern. It appeared to be in fair condition from the exterior.

"What do cruise ships go for these days?" Lorina asked.

"No idea. More than I've got."

She laughed. "I'll bet ISPP can afford it."

"Go on boat?" Niyati had raced back to join them in front of the gangway.

"Not unless we can break in, sugar," Blaze said.

"That'll be our backup plan."

Blaze looked askance at his wife but realized she wasn't kidding. "I forget sometimes I married a felon."

Lorina rolled her eyes at him. She cupped her hands to her mouth and shouted up the gangway, "*Sawadeeka*! Is anyone on board the *Princess Kate*?"

They were shocked to hear a faint reply—and in English. "Yes! Be right down!"

Blaze and Lorina exchanged a curious glance as they waited for the speaker to descend the gangway.

A Thai man in his thirties, clad in pressed khakis and a short-sleeved, button-down fuchsia shirt, reached the bottom of the ramp. He grinned at them through the bars and took out a ring of old-fashioned keys to unlock the door. It swung open with a mighty *screech* of rusty hinges.

"Welcome!" The man stepped forward and shook Blaze's hand. He had a sizable gap between his two front teeth. "War Supatcha, Tropical Paradise Real Estate."

"You're a realtor?" Lorina asked as Supatcha turned to shake her hand. "You're selling this ship?"

"Yes, ma'am." Supatcha's smile widened. "And it's a real bargain."

The realtor reminded Blaze of a used solar car salesman. He had the personality to go along with the oily smile, although he spoke good English without a noticeable accent. "Could we get a tour?"

Supatcha looked over the Smith family with a skeptical eye. "I can only show the ship to prospective buyers."

"We represent a buyer," Lorina said. "Ever hear of an organization called the Interstellar Peacekeepers Patrol?"

"No." Supatcha scratched his head, thinking. "But I suppose I could give you a tour. I haven't had a showing in fifteen months."

"Do you spend much time on the ship?" Blaze asked as the realtor led them up the ramp to the ship's lowest deck.

"All the time. I live here."

"You live here by yourself?" Lorina's mouth fell open. "Why?"

"I'm also the security guard," Supatcha said. "My wife lives here with me, so I'm not alone. She works days at the real estate office in the city, or she would also be here to greet you."

"Big boat," Niyati said.

Supatcha gave her a smile. "Yes, it is, although the guest rooms are very small."

Lorina took out her datapad. "Would you mind if I take some holograms while you show us around, Mr. Supatcha?"

"Of course, but please call me War." The realtor beamed. "So, where would you like to start?"

ELEVEN
DANAE'S CHOICE

DANAE SET her alarm, but she had a difficult time convincing herself to get out of bed. She ached all over from the solar-cycle ride, the shootout, and the long hours spent at the hospital. The spot where the glass sliced her temple was still tender to the touch. She sighed, found an analgesic patch in the bedside table, and applied it to the skin behind her left ear. She waited a few minutes for the aches and pains to fade, then threw off the covers.

Moving slowly, she dressed in athletic shorts and an old scoop-neck T-shirt which was stretched out of shape and really needed to go in the recycler. But Alex had bought her the T-shirt at a cheesy amusement park on Titan Station on their first date. She would never part with it, even if it disintegrated to rags. She ran her fingers through her curls and opted not to wear shoes to breakfast.

The captain left her cabin and climbed the ladder to the top deck. She wasn't expecting to see anyone else up this early, but she discovered Erik in the galley, at the crew's mess. His back was to her.

Clear the air, like Shima said. Danae felt a nervous flutter in her chest as she tried to decide what to say to him, and how to say it. "Erik?"

He froze, and she thought his mind had been elsewhere and she startled him, but there was so much tension in his posture, she could tell something else was wrong.

He took his time securing a lid on his cup of coffee before turning to face her. "Good morning." The smile didn't reach his eyes. "I heard you had quite an adventure yesterday."

Danae's eyebrows went up, and the smile left her face. She could tell Erik was nervous, and he was doing a lousy job of disguising it.

"Yes, it was pretty exciting. I want to hear all about Ting's WON treatment. Phailin said it was scary."

"Yes, it was." Erik sounded as if he was reading from a script. "And I want to hear how you were able to find Shima and Zuri without getting yourself killed, but this conversation will have to wait. I have to get back to the hospital as soon as possible. There's a full day of therapies and tests scheduled for Ting."

Danae folded her arms and gazed up at him with the intimidating glare she reserved for whiny passengers. "I should go with you to see Marco."

Erik's hesitation spoke volumes. Danae assumed the next words out of his mouth would be an excuse—and she was right.

"You're welcome to come with me, but doesn't ISPP need all the assistance they can get at Lumphini Park?"

"I informed Captain York we'd be willing to help wherever he needs us, but we'd wait to be called in for specific assignments. There's already enough confusion at Lumphini without the *Alex*'s crew getting in the way. We have the day off unless I hear otherwise."

An awkward pause followed. Danae waited for Erik to say something.

He made a point of glancing at the time. "Ting's first physical therapy is in an hour. I really do need to run. Come by the hospital when you have time." He walked by her, heading to the door.

"Is something wrong?" Danae called after him.

The "no" over his shoulder didn't sound convincing. "I just have a lot of work to do if you want Ting back on the job anytime soon. We can talk later—"

Without even a backward glance, he was gone.

Danae knew she'd just been the recipient of a cold shoulder. The question was: why? She had an uneasy thought she knew the answer.

She filled a cup with hot coffee, rummaged in the bread drawer for a cinnamon bagel, and took a seat in the dining area. She stirred the coffee and stared at the shiny surface of the stainless-steel table reflecting the recessed lights overhead.

She was still lost in thought, stirring her cold coffee, when Shima and Zuri came into the galley.

"What is wrong?" was the first thing out of Shima's mouth as she sat down across from Danae.

Although it was tempting to say nothing, the captain knew Shima would never fall for that lame excuse. "I think he knows."

"Who knows? And what does he know?" Shima gave Danae a minute to mull it over as she gave some instructions in Swahili to Zuri, who was investigating the drawers in the crew's mess, opening and closing each one.

"I think Erik knows about Cade. I'm not positive, but I *thought* I heard the door to my room close yesterday, right after Cade finished giving me a tonsillectomy." She almost laughed at Shima's puzzled frown. "I mean, when he finished kissing me."

"You think Dr. Sorensen saw you kiss Captain York?"

"I didn't kiss him; he kissed me."

Shima rolled her eyes. "You said you kissed him back—same thing."

"Maybe Phailin saw us and told Erik."

"I do not think Phailin is a snatch." Shima accepted a cup of coffee from Zuri, who sat at the table with the women and began to eat a bowl of yogurt covered with granola and blueberries.

"The word is snitch," Danae said, "not snatch."

"If you say so. Tell me why you think Dr. Sorensen saw the kiss."

The captain frowned. "Erik did a complete one-eighty just a few minutes ago."

Shima's furrowed brow did evoke a laugh this time. "I mean, he wasn't happy to see me like he usually is. He seemed tense and invented an excuse to leave."

"Are you sure he was not distracted by your shirt?"

It was Danae's turn to look puzzled. "What?" She glanced down at her clothes and noticed for the first time that her stretched-out T-shirt left a lot of cleavage on display. "Oops." She reached behind her back and tugged the shirt hem down to raise the neckline a few centimeters. "Well, since he barely glanced at me, I don't think the view distracted him."

Shima appeared thoughtful as she picked up Danae's cup and rose from the table. She stepped over to the crew's mess and returned in a minute with a fresh cup of coffee and a glass of orange juice for Zuri.

"So," she said, resuming her seat, "you must make a decision and tell them what you decide."

Danae opened her mouth to object, but Shima kept talking. "Since you work with both of them, it is important to clear the air."

"What I was going to say is I haven't made a decision. I'm not even ready to consider making a decision."

"Then they need to know that."

"You make it sound so simple."

"It is simple. Tell them you need a few years to decide if you are ready to start dating again."

"A few years!" Danae laughed.

Zuri glanced curiously back and forth at the women and said something to Shima.

The first officer nodded to her niece and told Danae, "Zuri and I are going to the open-air market, before it gets too hot, to buy her some clothes."

"You're going out alone?" She was impressed by Shima's courage to venture into the city.

The younger woman stood and patted the lump at the small of her back, tucked into the waistband of her shorts. "We will not be alone. We are bringing . . . a friend."

"Good idea. I'll be sure to do the same when I head over to the hospital."

"I am sorry to be out of uniform but"—Shima glanced at the back of her leg—"it still hurts to have anything touch the tattoo."

"No need to apologize. We're off duty today so wear whatever you like."

Zuri got up from the table, but before they departed, Shima asked, "What are your plans for today?"

Danae feigned a dramatic sigh. "I guess I'm scheduled to do some soul-searching."

***

Captain Shepherd arrived at Bhumibol Memorial around 0830, dressed more modestly in a clean *Alex's Legacy* uniform. A quick call to Phailin told her where to find Ting: physical therapy department, room 23. She got a visitor's pass at the lobby information kiosk and headed for the lift.

Danae was startled to find only Phailin and a therapist in the room with Ting when she arrived. *Maybe Erik heard I was on my way up and found another excuse to avoid me.*

Come on, Danae, when did you become such a cynic?

"Didn't you tell me a doctor was supposed to be here for the session?" she asked Phailin.

"Erik just stepped out for a minute."

I'm sure he did. Danae glanced at the time to see how long this minute would actually take.

The Thai therapist Phailin introduced as Sirikit had Ting harnessed to an anti-grav suspension unit. With a remote control, Sirikit directed the electrode androids to stimulate muscle movement. The helmsman wasn't shy about letting her know how much he hated the experience.

"I think I need earplugs," Danae said.

"He's quiet when Erik's in the room, just wait." Phailin was quick to change the subject. "Marco had something to eat this morning. It was just gelatin and a cup of broth, but hopefully it will get his digestive system working again."

Danae nodded, acknowledging the information, and studied the cook's haggard features. "You should go back to the ship and get some sleep."

"I'm fine, Captain." Her yawn wasn't convincing. "Really, I want to stay."

"He still doesn't remember you." It wasn't a question.

"No." Phailin's shoulders slumped. "How long will it take him to get his memory back?"

"I have no idea, but don't beat yourself up about it. He's fortunate to have a supportive friend like you, and I'm sure he'll realize it sooner or later."

Phailin nodded, looking unconvinced. "I knew he was unpopular with the crew, but I didn't realize how rude he could be. He's so disrespectful to everyone, not just me. He wasn't like this before getting shot."

"Give him time." Danae tried to sound sympathetic, but she doubted Ting would turn into a gentleman if Phailin waited long enough. She couldn't imagine how he managed to charm the cook in the first place. *I should've given him more credit for his acting skills.*

The man's been a porcupine for as long as I've known him, even to his friends—no, make that friend—singular. Giovanni Medici, Danae's former engineer who'd died from the Zenithian Flu which also claimed the lives of Alex and two other crewmembers, had been Ting's only friend.

Maybe he was nice to her because he needed a friend after losing Vanni. Danae shook her head. She assumed the helmsman had an ulterior motive for being nice to Phailin. *Since she's so attractive and he's . . . Ting.*

Maybe I was wrong about his intentions. Danae glanced at the younger woman's unhappy face. *Too bad he's sabotaging his earlier efforts.*

"Don't neglect your own health. Go back to the ship for some shut-eye. Captain's orders," she added when Phailin opened her mouth to protest.

The cook nodded, cast a dejected look Ting's way, and left the room.

Danae found a chair and watched the show for a few minutes. Sirikit directed the electrode androids to rotate Ting's hands and flex his fingers, one at a time.

All this Pinocchio needs is a nose that gets longer when he tells a lie. "If you cooperate with the therapist, you could get out of here sooner," she advised Ting when he paused mid-harangue to catch his breath. "All that swearing uses up energy you need to get stronger."

The helmsman glowered at her before settling into a moody silence. As his ankles rotated and his toes flexed, one at a time, Danae worked hard to stifle a giggle. *He does look like a puppet.*

Behind Ting's back, Sirikit gave her a thumbs-up to thank her for getting the helmsman to be quiet. The therapist glanced past Danae to the doorway of the room. She assumed Erik was standing there. His short break—or rather, his escape attempt—was over.

The doctor brought a chair over and set it down a meter away from Danae. He sat, took out his medical scanner, and appeared to be concentrating on its screen. The cold shoulder had morphed into the silent treatment.

Ugh. Why does this have to be so difficult? Danae spent some time soul-searching, as Shima advised, but still had no idea what to do. In order to have a cordial working relationship with Erik, however, she would need to discuss what she already suspected he knew.

She decided to see if he would bring it up himself. "Something you need to talk about?"

"No." Erik kept his eyes fixed on his scanner.

Well, that was abrupt. "Since you're acting so distant, I just assumed you're mad at me. Would that be an accurate assumption?"

No response.

Feeling irritated, she tried again, this time with sarcasm. "Since I failed Mind Reading 101, maybe you could try verbal communication."

After another uncomfortable silence, Erik spoke in a quiet monotone. "There's nothing to talk about, really. I think I made a big mistake. I should've stayed on the station."

Danae was waging a losing battle with her patience. "No one's keeping you here. Find passage back to Mars if that's what you want to do."

"I'm under contract."

"I'll expunge it from the ship's legal files. You're free to go." The thought of Erik leaving made her sick to her stomach. *But he should know by now I don't play games.*

There was another long silence as she waited for a response.

Erik turned his head to look at her. "I mentioned once, not too long ago, that I never wanted to do anything that would add to your pain. I feel like I might be . . . standing in the way of an opportunity for you . . . to be happy."

Don't say it. Danae hated being on the defensive, even if it was her fault they were having this awkward conversation. She could feel her anger building and knew she would say or do something she would regret if Erik didn't stop being his usual calm, levelheaded self. He was clearly trying to give her an easy exit, and she couldn't explain why this made her furious.

The doctor wasn't making eye contact or he might have noticed she was about to go nuclear. He kept talking. "If you've found someone else—"

"Where did you get such a *stupid* idea?" Danae ignored the shocked looks on Sirikit's and Ting's faces. She was on her feet, facing down Erik with her hands on her hips.

"What you saw yesterday—don't deny it!" she snapped when he started to shake his head. "What you saw was a *mistake!* Cade had me cornered and I—!"

"*You weren't cornered!*" He sprang from his chair, glaring down at her from his towering two meters, his pale complexion taking on a bright pink hue. "You think I would've just stood there and *watched* if I thought he was trying to take advantage of you?"

Erik took a deep breath and made a visible effort to rein in his own temper. "I would've given York a brain biopsy without anesthesia if I hadn't seen with my own eyes how much you were *enjoying* that kiss!" His bass voice cracked on the last word, but he wasn't finished hurling accusations at her.

"Just be honest with me, Danae! That's all I'm asking! Just admit you're interested in York and—!"

"I'm *not* interested in him! What happened yesterday was a *mistake!*" Even as she said it, she realized it was how she really felt. "It was a stupid, impulsive mistake! I should've said no and pushed him away." She hesitated, lowering her gaze to the breast pocket of Erik's scrubs shirt so she wouldn't have to see the hurt in his eyes. "I don't know why I didn't. I shouldn't have given him the wrong impression."

Mingled with her fresh pang of guilt was an overwhelming feeling of loneliness. *Why do I keep pushing people away, like Shima said?*

"I wanted to tell you in the galley this morning, but you took off like I had some kind of incurable disease." This thought rekindled her temper, and she glanced up at his face again. "I guess expecting you to be understanding was my second mistake."

Erik flinched at her words, but she didn't give him a chance to respond. "I don't need people in my life who are quick to judge me and bail out at the first sign of trouble. You may have noticed I seem to attract trouble."

Her emotions were jockeying for position, but Danae couldn't decide which one should win. Was she angry or was she afraid? Was she right to send Erik packing, or was her stubborn pride pushing her to make a huge mistake? Her hands started to shake, but she slipped them into her hip pockets, hoping he wouldn't notice.

The doctor glanced down, following her hand movement, but then he brought his eyes back up to her face. His disgruntled look seemed frozen in place, but she thought she saw a flicker of remorse in his eyes. He looked as though he wanted to say something but was making a concerted effort to keep his mouth shut.

Danae's energy was fading. She was tired of arguing with oversized men who questioned her decisions and felt an irrational need to protect her as if she were dainty and helpless. *Cade wants to guard my body, and Erik wants to shelter my emotions, even after they've both seen me handle situations under pressure—under gunfire!—without their help.*

She was tired of the emotional roller coaster. She wanted to get off the ride, permanently. But before she walked away, she had a few more things to say. "I can't believe I risked *everything*—my ship, my crew, my freedom, and possibly my life—to return to Mars

Station for you! I must have been out of my mind! It was a stupid, dangerous—!"

Danae wasn't sure how it happened. Even with her spacer's reflexes, she was taken by surprise. She experienced a split second of fear when Erik lunged at her, his hands out as if he intended to throttle her, but he grabbed her by the waist instead and picked her up, cutting off her rant mid-sentence with a kiss that was nothing like the one Cade pressured her to accept.

Erik's warm lips briefly touched hers, and then he drew back a few centimeters, not saying a word. He looked into her eyes as he held her in this awkward hug, with his arms around her waist and her feet half a meter off the floor.

Danae was confused, and her conflicting emotions only added to her perplexity. It took her a full minute to figure out he was waiting for her to respond. She could demand that he put her down, or she could accept his unspoken invitation. It was her choice.

My choice. The indecision was gone, replaced by a fleeting moment of clarity.

Her hands were still trembling as she placed them on either side of Erik's face. There was a hint of white-blond stubble on his cleft chin, but she thought it suited him. She studied the unusual white eyelashes which brought out the startling turquoise color of his irises. She saw only warmth and concern in those eyes, and a trace of apprehension.

Erik mustered a hopeful smile and that's what broke down the last of her defenses.

She closed her eyes, brought her chin forward until she found his lips again, and responded to his invitation with an RSVP he could appreciate. He was more than willing to let her take the lead, and it turned into a long, passionate kiss.

Danae didn't need to use her imagination, not with Erik. All of her worries melted away and she lost track of time. She forgot she was angry, forgot she was lonely, forgot about the empty place in her soul Alex left behind.

"Get a room!" Ting's shout jolted them back to reality.

They broke off the marathon kiss, but Danae was reluctant to let go. She pressed her cheek to Erik's so she could whisper in his ear. "I'm scared . . . and I'm not ready."

What she wasn't ready for, she couldn't articulate. *Not ready to let my guard down, not ready for a relationship, not ready to get serious . . . not ready to take a chance on love again?* Somehow she knew he would understand what she meant, and she was right.

"I'm scared too," he whispered back. "You take all the time you need."

"Shima told me you'd say that." Danae couldn't help it; she giggled.

"Shima's a wise soul." Erik was unsuccessful at keeping a straight face. His laughter bubbled up until his entire body shook. He set Danae on her feet.

They laughed until Ting got impatient and told them to chill. This struck Danae as so hilarious she couldn't stop laughing until Erik handed her a tissue to blot her streaming eyes.

She couldn't remember the last time she laughed so hard. *I could get used to this.*

***

Danae awoke with a start when she felt a gentle touch on her left temple.

"Sorry." Erik snatched his hand away from her face. "I didn't mean to wake you. I was just checking your scar."

"No, it's fine. It didn't hurt." She blinked and looked around. She had fallen asleep in the recliner in Ting's private room. She sat up and worked the stiffness out of her neck. "What time is it?"

"It's 1230." The doctor leaned against the wall.

Danae got to her feet. "How could you let me sleep for two hours?"

"You didn't miss anything." Erik smirked. "Ting spent the past half hour in the bathroom, trying to—"

"I wish someone would *leave me alone* for two hours!" Marco interrupted from his hospital bed. "Why don't you two get your own room?"

"Believe me," Erik said, "we would love to leave you alone, permanently."

Danae was grateful the doctor didn't respond to the *get a room* suggestion, but felt herself blushing anyway. "We can leave as soon as Phailin gets here."

"That girl doesn't give up, does she?" Ting grumbled. "She's like a human leech. What's her problem?"

The captain's temper flared. "Her problem is she cares about you—don't ask me why! You're lucky to have Phailin around, and you're a fool to treat your only friend like garbage!"

Ting sniffed, unimpressed. He turned his attention to the remote control on his lap, extending an unsteady hand until he could reach the button to turn on the holo-vid screen mounted to the wall.

"You're scheduled for another physical therapy session at 1530," Erik informed Ting over the blare of a commercial for over-the-counter Banspace patches.

"What?" Ting protested. "Why?"

"So you can get out of here tomorrow," Danae fired back. "You're not on vacation, you know."

"After tasting the swill they call food, I'd have to agree." The helmsman sneered.

"You ungrateful little—" Danae was on the brink of a full-scale tirade when she felt a large arm around her shoulders, corralling her a few steps away from Ting's bedside. The contact helped to diffuse the tension building up in her like a volcano ready to erupt.

She cut her rant short with, "Do us all a favor, Marco, and shut your mouth."

Danae leaned against Erik, grateful to have his physical and emotional support. *I could really get used to this!*

"Speaking of food, I'm hungry." The doctor commandeered the exchange of barbs before Ting could get in another word. "Let's get something to eat before his next session."

"Bring me back something that doesn't look or taste like baby food," Ting demanded.

Danae gave her helmsman a cold look and turned her back to him so she could give Erik a warm look. "Shouldn't we wait for Phailin?"

"You're asking my advice?" He arched one white eyebrow at her.

"Yes, I guess I am. Do you have a problem with that?" Her earcom chimed. "But hold that thought a moment." She tapped her earlobe. "This is Shepherd."

Shima sounded like she was out of breath. "Zuri and I are in trouble."

"*What?*" Danae shrieked. "What happened? Where are you?"

Shima didn't answer. Instead she shouted, "Stop! Do not come any closer!"

Danae could hear the hysteria in her own voice. "Shima, where are you?" She noted Erik's wide-eyed concern. He was silently mouthing, "What's wrong?" and pointing to his earcom to remind her to link him with the call, but it was all happening so fast. She felt paralyzed with fear, unable to move a muscle.

"How you got 'way?" said a male voice in the background of Shima's com.

"We are not slaves!"

The blast of a gunshot echoed over Danae's earcom. "*Shima!*"

TWELVE
THE TATTOO'S SECRET

SHIMA HAD NOTICED an open-air clothing market on the tram ride to and from factory number six. Since it was close to a major tramstop, she felt confident she wouldn't get lost, even if the market sprawled for blocks in several directions.

She and Zuri disembarked and walked down the first street, which was filled with open stalls offering both traditional, handmade, Thai silk clothing and basic synthcotton, factory-made, American-style clothing.

"Shoes." Zuri pointed to the first stall selling synth-leather sandals.

"What, you do not want to keep mine? Just because they are three sizes too big for you?" They walked over to a table in front of the stall where several styles of shoes were on display.

An elderly Thai woman stood behind the table, hanging up neon-colored T-shirts on a portable display rack. Realizing she had potential customers, she turned to greet them with a *wai'* and "*sawadeeka.*"

"How can we communicate with her?" Zuri asked.

"We will manage." Shima pointed to the teen and then to a basic pair of women's shower sandals or *flip-flops*.

The gray-haired shopkeeper gave a quick nod and handed them a universal foot-measuring ruler.

Zuri measured the length of her left foot. "Seven." She returned the ruler and pointed to a pair of pink sandals. "These in size seven, please."

The shopkeeper gave her a puzzled look.

Shima held up seven fingers.

The old merchant smiled and nodded, reached into a large box under the table, and produced a pair of the sandals in the right size.

Zuri tried them on. "They fit. Ask her how much."

Anticipating the question, the shopkeeper pulled out a datapad and wrote *600* on the screen.

Shima was shocked at the price. "That is too much. We will try a different booth."

Zuri took off the sandals and reluctantly returned them. She put her aunt's flip-flops back on and they turned to walk away.

"*Ka ka ka.*" The old woman sounded like a crow, trying to get their attention.

They turned back to see her waving the datapad at them with *500* written on it. Shima caught on. "We must bargain with her, just like we did in the markets in Kampala."

They returned to the table and negotiated a price for the shoes by writing numbers back and forth on the datapad. It took only a minute to agree on two hundred and fifty.

Shima showed the shopkeeper her left thumb. "Can I pay with this?"

A different datapad with a credit flash slot was produced. The first officer swiped her thumbnail and made sure only two hundred and fifty was deducted.

Beaming, Zuri slipped on her new sandals. "I have forgotten how good it feels to have something of my very own."

Shima felt a pang of sympathy for the suffering her niece must have endured as a slave. "How about underwear next?"

"Auntie!" Zuri rolled her eyes but allowed Shima to lead her to another stall with stacks of brightly colored panties on the table out front.

Several hours of shopping later, with only a short break to sit and enjoy some fresh mango, Shima turned down a new street and led Zuri over to a stall filled with colorful Thai silk skirts and blouses. "We should each have a nice outfit to wear to church or on special occasions."

"How do you have enough money for all of this?" The teen paused to admire a glittery purple dress on a mannequin.

"I do not have much but at these prices I can afford to buy what we need."

Shima set her shopping bags by her feet and examined a rack of short-sleeved blouses. There was a variety of gorgeous styles and colors with delicate gold-threaded embroidery accents on the sleeves and collars. She knew she would have a hard time choosing just one item. She looked over each blouse, trying to decide which one she liked best.

After several minutes, Shima wondered why no shopkeeper had interrupted her browsing to steer her toward the more expensive merchandise, which was their normal routine. She turned away from the rack to look for Zuri.

Her niece was standing a few meters away, examining a red skirt with a chevron detail woven into the hem. Standing near Zuri was a male shopkeeper. He was leaning against a table covered with men's neckties, his dark eyes riveted on the teen.

He is not smiling. This struck Shima as odd since all the other merchants they encountered were delighted to have customers. *Does he think she is planning to shoplift?*

She moved over to a nearby rack so she could see the Thai's face in her peripheral vision. She realized he was staring at Zuri's tattoo. The cold, hard look in his eyes made her nervous.

Something is wrong. Trying to appear nonchalant, Shima moved to Zuri's side. "We should try a different shop."

"But I want to buy this one, auntie."

I must not frighten her. She pretended to admire the skirt. "Yes, it is beautiful but too expensive here."

Shima turned around in time to see the shopkeeper avert his gaze, but not before she caught him staring at the back of her leg. Their tattoos were attracting some unwanted attention.

She nudged her niece in the direction of the exit. "We can try next door."

"Could I please have this one?" Zuri wheedled.

"Sorry, no." Shima didn't take her eyes off the shop-keeper, who was muttering quietly into his earcom. "I do not have enough credits to buy it."

"But we do not know the price yet," the girl argued reasonably, still unaware something was wrong.

Shima gave up discretion and grasped Zuri's arm. "We need to leave *now*."

The teen's eyes widened as she noticed the grim-faced shopkeeper standing nearby. "Why is that man staring at us?"

"I do not know, but we should not stay here. Just walk away." She tried to sound confident but her stomach was in knots.

The salesman said something harsh sounding in Thai and took a few threatening steps toward them. Shima moved faster, herding Zuri in the opposite direction.

Two large, rough-looking men materialized from the street, blocking the only exit out of the stall. Their hostile expressions sent Shima's fear into full-scale panic.

The big men stepped inside the stall and approached them, and the shopkeeper moved to flank them. They were trapped.

"Run!" Shima gave Zuri a shove in the direction of the street. "Climb over the table! Get out of here!"

Her niece wouldn't budge. "No! I will not leave you!"

One of the big men seized Zuri from behind, pinning her arms to her side. She screamed in terror.

No! Not again! Shima felt a rush of adrenaline. It replaced her fear with a sense of calm and determination. *Never again.*

The other thug made a grab for Shima but stopped short when she drew her pistol and leveled it at his broad forehead. "Get back!"

She pivoted to the right, dodging the shopkeeper who was rushing her from behind. He also stopped and backed away, his hands in the air, when she pointed the gun at him.

"Let her go!" Shima covered all three men as she moved the small black Excalibur slowly back and forth between them. Even if they didn't understand English, the gun made her point clear.

The thug holding Zuri hesitated but let her go when Shima released the safety with an audible *click*.

The teen was close to tears as she rushed to Shima's side. "What should we do?"

"Get behind me. Watch our backs."

Zuri scrambled to comply, moving behind Shima and turning to face the street.

The three thugs-turned-hostages consulted with each other in rapid-fire Thai. Shima took advantage of the distraction by touching her left earlobe with a trembling finger. She didn't take her eyes off the men.

"Zuri and I are in trouble."

"*What?*" Danae's shriek hurt her ear. "What happened? Where are you?"

She didn't get a chance to explain because one of the men risked another step forward. "Stop! Do not come any closer!"

"Shima, where are you?" There was a trace of hysteria in the captain's voice.

"How you got 'way?" The thug who moved closer spoke in halting English, his expression dangerous.

"We are not slaves!" Shima touched the trigger.

The blast made all three men jump, but she aimed low. The bullet ricocheted off the concrete in front of their feet. Still, it had the desired effect—they backed away.

"Danae?"

There was no answer; the connection was lost. The fact that she was on her own worried Shima more than the three brutes standing in front of her.

"You go back!" said the English speaker, who still appeared determined even though his face was pale.

"You stay away from us! We are not slaves!"

Attracted by Zuri's scream and the gunshot, a crowd of curious bystanders gathered in front of the stall. Shima could hear them behind her, whispering to each other.

She hoped her niece would be alert for any attempt to rush them.

"What should we do?" Zuri asked again, her voice quavering.

Shima didn't know what to say. They were boxed in on all sides.

The distant sound of an approaching siren changed the dynamics of the crisis again. The three men exchanged conspiratorial grins and visibly relaxed.

The CIPs are involved in human trafficking. We are the ones in danger, but I am the one holding the illegal weapon. Shima didn't have to wonder whose story the CIPs would believe.

"Grab our bags, Zuri. We are walking out of here."

"But what if someone tries to stop us?"

"It will be all right. Just go!"

Shima took a step forward, pointing her gun at the merchant's head. She gestured for the men to move away from the exit. They got the message and complied.

Her niece snatched up the shopping bags left near the blouse rack and raced out of the stall. Shima followed by walking backward, her gun still trained on the three thugs as a warning for them to stay back.

When Shima reached the street, she made a break for it, turning on her heel and running after Zuri. She discovered the gun made it easy to part the crowd. People scurried out of her path, horrified. She remembered to thumb the safety back on before shoving the pistol into the pocket of her shorts, but it was all she remembered for several minutes as she concentrated on keeping up with her niece.

"Head for the tram!"

Zuri made the proper course adjustment, but Shima was dismayed to see blue lights approaching from that direction. A CIP patrol car was slowly edging through the crowd of shoppers, coming toward them.

"Never mind—go left!"

The teen pivoted without breaking stride and headed down an unfamiliar street. Shima was only a few paces behind her. They left the market behind but ran for a few more blocks until they reached a busy intersection.

"Stop! We can stop running!"

Zuri slowed to a brisk walk until Shima fell into step beside her on the sidewalk. Her niece handed over some of the shopping bags. "I think I dropped one." She panted and wiped the sweat from her forehead with the back of a trembling hand.

"It does not matter. I am just grateful we got away." Shima took time to catch her breath as she glanced back over her shoulder. She was relieved to see no one following them. "I cannot believe we just ran eight blocks in flip-flops."

Zuri forced a laugh and glanced down at her feet. "I will have some blisters tomorrow."

They walked in silence for a few minutes, dodging other pedestrians and the food-cart vendors who shared the sidewalks with them.

Shima looked around for a street sign, but the one she spotted had only Thai writing on it. She searched for anything written in English to help identify their location.

"Where are we? And why did those men attack us?"

"I think we are lost." Shima didn't answer the second question because she needed more time to think about it.

"Could you ask someone for help?"

Shima nodded and tapped her earcom. "Danae? Are you there?"

A relieved voice said, "I swear you're going to send me to an early grave. Where are you?"

"I do not know. We are not near any tramstops, and the street signs are all in Thai."

"What happened?"

"I will tell you about it when we are back aboard the ship, but right now Zuri and I are lost in the city, and we are scared. Can you help us?"

"Can you see the river?" Dr. Sorensen's deep voice spoke up. "Are you near any wats?"

Shima stopped at an intersection and looked as far as she could down the street to their left. Nothing stuck out as unusual, but when she peered to the right, she spotted a golden roof. "Yes, I see one."

"There's a tramstop near each wat."

"Good thinking, Dr. Sorensen." She took Zuri's elbow and steered her in the direction of the Buddhist temple.

The sign in front of the crumbling front steps of the wat was in Thai and English. "We are at—I cannot pronounce this long word—Wat Ben-jama-bo-fit?"

After a brief pause, the doctor said, "There should be a green line tram close by."

Aunt and niece walked around the outside of the wat until they found the tramstop sign at the west corner. "Yes, it is here, but where will it take us?"

"The northbound will take you back to the spaceport," he said.

"Yes, but the southbound will bring you within a block of Bhumibol Memorial," Danae said. "That's where we are."

Shima breathed a sigh of relief. "We are on our way. Thank you."

***

The hospital room reached maximum capacity when Shima and Zuri walked in, but only the room's primary resident seemed bothered by it.

"Aren't visiting hours over yet?" Marco growled.

"Nice to see you too," Shima said.

Phailin glanced over at Ting with a disgruntled frown, and turned her attention to Zuri. The teen took a seat in the room's only chair, pulled some items from her shopping bags, and showed them to the cook.

"Oh, that's a gorgeous color." Phailin admired one of Zuri's new shirts. "It will look great with those pants."

Zuri didn't know what Phailin was saying, but she was enjoying the attention. Shima was relieved to see her niece looking so cheerful after their frightening experience at the marketplace.

"Could you keep it down?" Marco said. "Better yet, could you take your little fashion show outside?"

Phailin ignored him.

Meanwhile, Danae enveloped Shima in a bear hug and took her aside to the room's only square meter of free space, in front of the window. Dr. Sorensen squeezed past Phailin to join them.

"What happened?" The captain had abandoned her usual calm demeanor. Her face was flushed, and she still looked shaken.

Shima described the attack in detail. Danae and Dr. Sorensen listened without interrupting. She couldn't help noticing how comfortable they seemed around each other. They were standing close together, his big hand resting on her elbow. The contact seemed to be a show of support, not romantic or even a tiny bit possessive. There was no trace of the tension Danae mentioned over breakfast.

It is amazing how fast relationships can change, Shima thought, stealing a glance at Phailin again.

"Erik, you still have the tattoo images on your datapad?" Danae asked.

"Yes, I do." Dr. Sorensen pulled out his datapad, found the file, and handed the device to her.

Danae flashed him a smile of thanks, and Shima was amused to glimpse the dazed look on the doctor's face.

After studying the holograms, the captain spoke up, bringing everyone in the room into the conversation. "The men who attacked Shima and Zuri at the market recognized the tattoo. We should assume they work for traffickers. They probably thought Shima and Zuri escaped from the red-light district."

"Well, technically, they did," Ting said.

Danae shot the helmsman a frosty glance and went on without missing a beat. "Did the ISPP medics say how many girls have the tattoos?" she asked Dr. Sorensen.

"One in four, at last report. Twenty-five percent."

"What do the tattooed girls have in common? There must be a pattern."

The doctor shook his head. "ISPP hasn't figured that out yet. The girls are all different ages, races, and nationalities."

"What about physical features?" Phailin asked.

"All different shapes, sizes, and skin tones." Dr. Sor-ensen looked over Danae's shoulder at the datapad screen. "There must be a clue in the tattoo itself."

The captain glanced over at her helmsman. "We need someone who knows Chinese. Marco, can you still read Mandarin?"

Ting snorted. "You never forget how to read it when you have to memorize every single character."

"Your memory is perfect," Phailin muttered under her breath. Ting didn't hear her, or he chose to ignore the remark. Shima suspected it was the latter.

"Maybe you can make sense of this." Danae stepped over to his bedside and held the datapad so he could read it. "We think it's a message."

Ting scowled at the screen for a minute and then glanced at the ceiling. "It's not a message; it's an address."

"What?" Danae said. "You figured it out just like that?"

Ting's grin was smug.

"What address?" Dr. Sorensen was getting impatient. "Just tell us what the tattoo says."

"If it was easy to read, anyone could decipher it, so I think it's deliberately vague for that reason. Plus you have to know something about China's history." Ting scowled. "History was another subject I had to memorize."

"Tell us what it says!" Danae was losing her patience too.

"Don't rush me. Look at the first four characters: large, bird, white, water. What's a large white water bird?"

"A crane," Shima said.

"Think bigger." Ting announced the answer before she could guess again. "It's a swan. The next two characters are oyster and seed. What kind of seeds do you find in oysters?"

"Pearls," Phailin said.

"Exactly. The last two: fast or swift and water. This one should be easy."

"A river." Danae began putting the pieces together. "Is there a Pearl River?"

"Yes there is, and it runs through Guangzhou, China."

"What does a swan and the Pearl River have to do with history?" Dr. Sorensen asked.

"Not just any swan—the White Swan. It was a famous fancy hotel on the Pearl River a century ago, but it's long gone."

"How can it be an address if it's not there anymore?" Danae asked.

"The hotel was on Shamian Island. It's a very small area of the city." Ting appeared pleased with himself. "My guess is White Swan is a code name for a trafficking organization headquartered on Shamian Island."

"Or the White Swan could be a person," the doctor said, "the leader of a trafficking organization."

Shima's mouth fell open. "I just thought of something. It might be important. How do you say white swan in Chinese?" she asked Ting.

"*Bai hu'*."

"That was the phrase I heard many times, just before they gave me the tattoo."

Danae turned to Erik with a worried frown. "I need to tell Cade we've figured out what the tattoo means."

"I know." Dr. Sorensen tried to appear unconcerned, but Shima could tell by Danae's raised eyebrows that he wasn't putting on a convincing performance.

"In person would be best," she added.

The doctor nodded. "I'll come with you."

"Zuri and I are coming too." Shima explained to her niece they were leaving.

"I want to come too," Phailin said. "There's no reason for me to stay here."

Marco looked askance at her. "What about me? Isn't someone going to keep me company? Don't I have another stupid therapy this afternoon?"

Dr. Sorensen grimaced. "Yes, you do. I guess it means I'm stuck here for the duration."

"No offense, ghost giant, but you're not much for company." Ting glanced at Phailin with a hopeful leer.

"It's not our job to entertain you, Ting," the cook said.

Shima exchanged a startled glance with Danae. *Did it just get cold in here? She is calling him Ting now?*

"I guess we'll see you later, Erik." Phailin helped Zuri gather up the shopping bags and led the way out of the room.

Shima was right behind them, but glanced back over her shoulder in time to see Danae go up on her tiptoes to give Erik Sorensen a goodbye kiss.

"Is there something you need to tell me?" she whispered as Danae fell into step beside her in the corridor.

"Later. I'm still trying to figure it out myself."

Shima laughed.

***

An ISPP officer and a Thai volunteer wearing a red Stop Traffic T-shirt were guarding the Rama Road entrance to the park. They wouldn't let the *Alex*'s crew past the gate until the officer called Captain York to confirm their identities.

"The meeting is being held in the mess hall," the ISPP officer informed Danae.

"Meeting?" Shima asked when they were past the gate.

"I think there's lots of details to discuss," Danae said, "although I didn't expect Cade to call a big meeting, at least not one that requires our participation."

The three women and Zuri walked into the park and found themselves having to navigate their way through rambunctious crowds of children. Shima glanced around in awe at the throngs of former slaves. The ISPPs and adult volunteers were having a difficult time keeping the chaos to a minimum. It was like being back in the homeless village at McConnell Park, where she and Zuri lived for four months, although the young residents of Lumphini were enjoying a raucous party, compared to the people on Mars Station who would just lie around in a depressed stupor all day.

Shima asked Zuri, "Do you see your friend Ekaterina?"

The teen craned her neck, trying to look around, but it was impossible to scan all the faces. "No, but I am sure she is here somewhere."

They reached the large mess tent and went inside. Eight ISPP officers and six androids were busy in the food-preparation area, tending what appeared to be a dozen black witches' cauldrons. Each was being stirred with a spoon the size of a canoe paddle. Shima watched as giant bags of frozen peas and corn were added to each steaming kettle. She recognized the tantalizing aroma of fried rice.

"Yum," Zuri murmured.

"Sorry, but dinner will not be ready for another hour." Officer Moniesa intercepted them a few steps from the entrance and directed them to a section of the dining area where two long tables were placed end-to-end to create a makeshift conference table. The twenty folding chairs surrounding it were occupied by ISPP officers, although five chairs at the far end were vacant.

Captain York sat at the head of the long table. He got to his feet and smiled at the newcomers, although Shima could tell the greeting was directed specifically at Danae. She had never seen the ISPP captain smile before and thought the affect was frightening.

"Please have a seat, Captain." York indicated a chair to his left where Diaz was sitting. The junior officer took the hint and scrambled to vacate the seat.

"I'd like to sit with my crew, if you don't mind." Danae shot York a grin as she walked past him to the far end of the table, where Vipul was sitting by himself. Danae sat at the end, directly opposite York, with Shima and Phailin on either side.

The *Alex*'s first officer stole a quick glance at the ISPP captain to gauge his reaction, but there was nothing in his countenance to suggest he felt slighted by Danae's refusal to sit beside him.

Looking around for Zuri, Shima discovered that her niece made a detour toward another table a dozen meters away. The teen broke into a run to reach the thin, redheaded girl who had gone unnoticed by the adults in the tent.

"Ekaterina!"

The two girls embraced, squealed, jumped up and down, and hugged again.

Everyone else in the tent watched the reunion for a minute, and then York cleared his throat. "Back to business?"

Making eye contact with Zuri, Shima put a finger to her lips so the girls would get the message to lower their voices. The former slaves sat across from each other at a small table and launched into a whispered, giggly conversation.

Shima was grateful her niece found a loyal friend while she was a slave, someone who brought a ray of light into an otherwise dark, lonely, and cruel existence. *Bless you, Ekaterina. I pray ISPP can reunite you with your family.*

"So what have we missed?" Danae directed her question at the ISPP end of the conference table.

"Not much," York said. "We've been tossing around ideas for fifteen minutes."

"Blaze and Lorina are on their way," Vipul informed Danae. "They've uncovered a potential solution to the security problem."

"They have?" Danae chuckled. "*Of course* they have. But we have some new information to share, as well." She raised her voice so everyone at the table could hear. "My helmsman figured out the message in the tattoo."

Captain Shepherd had everyone's attention, but before she could begin, Blaze, Lorina, and Niyati walked into the tent. "Just a minute."

Shima stood and beckoned her crewmates to join them. "There are two chairs here." She indicated the empty seats between Phailin and Vipul.

Blaze and Lorina sat down, and the engineer set their daughter on his lap.

"Hungry," Niyati announced, loud enough for the entire table to hear.

"Shhhhh," Lorina cautioned.

A plate of carrot sticks and cucumber slices was passed down the table until it was in front of Niyati. She emitted a squawk of disapproval but started to eat anyway.

"So what did we miss?" Blaze asked.

"Not much," Danae said. "I was just about to explain what Ting figured out about the tattoo."

"Which is—?" Lorina prodded.

The captain addressed the entire group. "The tattoo is a code for an address. There was a hotel called the White Swan, which used to be a famous landmark on the Pearl River in Guangzhou, China. Since the hotel no longer exists, we think White Swan refers to either a trafficking organization or its leader."

"Tse, can you verify this?" York asked.

The Chinese engineer studied her datapad for a minute and looked up with a nod of approval. "I agree with the interpretation of the characters—White Swan, Pearl River. I thought I'd figured out the part about the Pearl River, but very few would remember the White Swan unless he or she happened to be a historian."

"Ting's father is a historian," Phailin said. "His mother was an archeologist."

"Tell Mr. Ting well done," Tse said.

Phailin lowered her gaze to the table and didn't reply.

After a brief, uncomfortable silence, Captain York spoke up. "It sounds like Guangzhou needs to be our next stop, just as soon as we sort out the huge mess here in Bangkok."

"We need to investigate the entire police force," Moniesa said, "just like we did on Mars Station."

"But we didn't have to take care of thirty-eight hundred refugees on Mars," Tse said. "We don't have the manpower to do both tasks, even with the extra volunteers."

Danae drummed her fingernails on the table. "So . . . what's the next step?"

"Is there even a next step for us?" Blaze spoke up before York could formulate a response. "No offense,

Captains, but I think our little crew has done all we can do here."

Seeing he had the attention of everyone at the table, Blaze glanced over at Zuri for emphasis. "We've accomplished what we came here to do. I think it's time we returned the Excaliburs and went home." He turned to Danae. "Sorry to spring this on you, ma'am, but I had to speak my mind."

"I can understand why you'd feel that way," Captain Shepherd said. "I've given it some thought myself."

Shima noticed Danae didn't make eye contact with York when she said this. The ISPP captain scowled, more so than usual.

The table was quiet again until York cleared his throat. "You mentioned on the com you had an idea for securing the park, Smith?"

"It's Lorina's idea." Blaze turned to his wife with a proud smile.

"It's more than an idea," Lorina spoke with confidence. "This is a solution that will keep all the kids safe until they can be returned to their families." She pulled a datapad out of her shorts' pocket and brought up a file. "There's just one little problem . . . pass this down to Captain York."

"One problem?" The datapad reached the ISPP captain, and he glanced at the screen in confusion.

"Does ISPP have enough funding to purchase a cruise ship?" Lorina asked.

"*A what?*" Tse asked.

"A cruise ship—an ocean liner," Blaze said. "We found one for sale."

Moniesa, Tse, and several other officers rose from their seats and crowded around York, looking over his shoulders at the datapad. He waved his eager audience away with some impatience. "Sit down, calm down. I'll send you copies of the file."

The ISPPs returned to their chairs and pored over their individual datapads. The initial mutterings of "this is crazy" turned into thoughtful queries.

"How many passengers can it accommodate?" Tse asked.

"Over five thousand," Blaze said. This elicited some whistles of approval.

"What kind of shape is it in?" Diaz asked.

"It just needs a good cleaning," Lorina said. "No structural problems."

"Where can we find a captain and crew?" Tse asked.

"The realtor has three hundred former crewmember applications on file," Blaze said. "Since jobs are scarce, most of them are available to begin work immediately."

"How soon can we start transferring children to the ship?" Moniesa glanced over at the Smiths with a grin of approval.

York turned to Diaz. "Contact the realtor and the bank. Let's see if Murphy's idea will work."

The com officer nodded and left the tent.

"Well done, you two." Danae said. "It's brilliant."

"I help," Niyati piped up with a mouthful of cucumber.

Captain Shepherd grinned at the girl. "Thanks for your assistance, Niyati."

The ISPP officers split off into smaller groups to discuss logistics, and the *Alex*'s crew put their heads together to consider ideas, as well. Blaze repeated his recommendation to allow ISPP to take over all the headaches.

"Let me think about it," Danae said.

Captain York approached the *Alex*'s end of the table, walking past Shima's chair before stopping at Danae's. "Could I have a word, in private?"

Captain Shepherd was the picture of calm as she said, "Of course," and got to her feet.

"Let's step over here."

The moment York turned away from the table, Danae shot her first officer a nervous look and touched her earcom.

Shima looked away before anyone noticed the exchange and pretended to scratch her earlobe to link their coms. She didn't understand why Danae was worried about having a private chat with York, but she trusted the captain's instincts in allowing her to eavesdrop.

Danae walked around the table and followed the ISPP captain to an unoccupied area of the mess hall. Shima noted the tension in Danae's posture. After twenty meters, York stopped and turned to face her, still in plain sight but far from listening ears—as far as he knew.

Lorina's voice drew Shima's attention back to the table. "Do we have any theories as to why some girls are tattooed and others aren't? What do they have in common? That seems to be an important piece of the puzzle that's still missing."

Shima faced the impossible task of listening to two conversations at the same time. She didn't want anyone at the table to suspect she was eavesdropping on the captains, so she focused on answering Lorina. "I guess you have not heard about the attempt to abduct Zuri and me at the marketplace today."

"*What?*" Lorina's eyes widened. "What happened?"

She described the attack to them. She was careful to omit the more frightening details for Niyati's ears.

"Lucky you had your gun this time," Blaze said.

Shima nodded, her expression grim.

Phailin spoke up. "If the tattoo is easy to recognize, many of the girls who were just freed may still be in danger from traffickers."

Shima realized Danae and Captain York had dispensed with the small talk and were venturing onto a more serious topic.

York was saying, "This thought just came to me after you explained the meaning of the tattoo, so I don't have all the details worked out yet." He paused. "I need to ask a favor."

Danae was right to be concerned. Shima tried her best to look as if she was following the conversation at the table. Fortunately, no questions were directed at her for a few minutes so she could concentrate on York's request:

"There's a lot of work to be done here before ISPP can head to China, but your ship can leave anytime. I could use an advanced scout to check out Shamian Island."

Danae hesitated. "What would it involve?"

"You and your crew would go in as tourists, check out the area, locate the White Swan if it's the location of their headquarters, and send me word." York pressed on with some reassurances. "I don't expect your crew to put themselves in any danger. Don't confront any traffickers and don't attempt to rescue any slaves. I just need basic information to plan a coordinated attack. We'd like to round up all these maggots as soon as possible."

"It seems risky. Your people are trained to do this type of undercover work—we aren't."

"We're military. We stand out like sore thumbs even when we're not in uniform. Your crew would be less likely to attract attention and thus be able to gather information more easily."

"You heard what Blaze said. My crew won't agree to further involvement at this level. They love aiding children, but—"

"Then we'll motivate them to continue the aid." Shima thought York's impatience was beginning to tarnish the sales pitch. "We've already matched some of the kids with families who live in or around Guangzhou. The *Alex*'s official mission could be returning them home. You could say the investigative work is just a side job."

"I'm not going to deceive my crew," Danae snapped.

"I don't expect you to," York fired back. "Just appeal to their sympathies by putting the most emphasis on returning the slaves to their families. I went out of my way to help you locate and rescue Oryang, despite the fact that it was her own fault she was abducted."

Shima was appalled. *Do not listen to him, Danae! He is trying to make you feel guilty to get you to agree!*

"Please do this, for me. One small mission, and we'll call it even."

"Give me a minute to think it over." Danae sounded upset.

"Are there any slavers in custody who could tell us about the tattoo?" Lorina's question to Moniesa drew Shima's attention back to the conversation at the table.

The big woman broke off her discussion with Tse and turned her attention to the *Alex*'s crew. "We are holding five people in the brig aboard the *Title of Liberty*. The only reason they were arrested is because they were unarmed."

Shima shuddered at the image this casual remark stirred up. *Only five, out of how many slavers?* But she consoled herself with the grim thought that the monsters who enslaved children like Zuri didn't deserve comfortable prison cells and three hot meals a day. ISPP's brand of justice might seem brutal to some, but it was quick and efficient.

She had a new thought. "Is there a Chinese woman in the brig? She would have worn a nice dress with a lot of jewelry and makeup, and she had a small tattoo of the letter B on her neck."

Moniesa studied Shima's face for a moment before responding. "Yes, we did apprehend a woman who appears to be Chinese and matches that description." The weapons officer glanced down at her datapad, scrolled briefly, and slid it across the table. "Is this her?"

Shima felt a chill as she recognized the mug shot. "Yes, this is the same woman who ordered me to be tattooed. I think she will have the answers we need." She glanced over at the weapons officer. "I would like to question her."

"No. It is not your responsibility. But I will allow you and your captain to listen on surveillance while Ghukasyan and I interrogate her. So far all the prisoners have refused to answer any questions, but we have not asked them about the White Swan tattoo."

"How soon can you question her?" Shima asked.

"I will return to the ship after dinner," Moniesa said. "You can listen on the com aboard your own ship. Shall we say 1900?"

Shima nodded. "Thank you."

She then realized her earcom had gone silent and chided herself for missing Danae's response to York's request. She glanced over at the captains. They were returning to the conference table.

The crews waited in silence as York and Shepherd resumed their seats.

Danae's expression was calm, but Shima could sense her tension level was high. *Did she agree to the dangerous mission?*

"Blaze is right—we've done what we came here to do," Danae announced without preamble, "but breaking ties with ISPP doesn't seem to be as simple as we assumed."

"What do you mean, Captain?" Vipul asked.

Shima glanced at York's confident grin and had a sudden urge to slap him.

"I can't discuss it here. I'll share it with the entire crew when we're back aboard the *Alex*."

Danae caught Shima's eye, confirming what she already guessed. *We are not going back to Maui.*

THIRTEEN
INTERROGATION

ERIK WAS SUPPOSED to be monitoring Ting during his latest physical therapy session, but his mind wandered the entire time.

Was I too assertive? He didn't doubt himself too much on this point. Although he expected to be pummeled for picking up Danae while she was shouting at him, she finally let down her guard and responded in a way he could only describe as *incredible,* which led to more questions.

What should I do now? If Danae was still mourning the death of her husband, Erik had just set the stage for a rebound relationship. He was worried she'd dump him the minute she finished grieving and no longer needed Erik as a source of comfort. He'd taken extra care not to pressure her for this reason, but thanks to some unexpected and poorly timed competition from Cade York, things were already set in motion, whether she was ready for a relationship or not.

Erik couldn't backtrack, but he wasn't sure how to move forward either. *Try to stay on her good side* was the only practical advice he could give himself. He'd been fortunate to break through her emotional wall, but he knew how fast she could put it up again if he wasn't careful.

What's she going to tell York? A part of Erik wanted to be present for that conversation, but a more rational part of his brain wondered, *would that be giving York an invitation to rearrange my face?* He was grateful dueling was outlawed centuries ago.

His thoughts also turned to more practical concerns. *Where can I purchase a tattoo-removal laser? How can I help treat the former slaves if they're terrified of men?*

Erik noticed Sirikit had finished Ting's session and was removing the electrode androids from his body. He walked over to assist her.

"Ouch!" Ting yelped every time the doctor or physical therapist peeled off a probe.

"You do realize you're moving without assistance?" Erik said.

"Huh?" Ting lifted his left forearm, bringing his hand up to his face. His movements were slow and jerky, but the effort was his own. "How 'bout that?"

"Shall we try walking back to your room?"

The helmsman appeared worried at the prospect. "Let's see if I can stand first."

"I think you'll be surprised."

With the androids removed, Sirikit lowered the anti-grav unit until Ting's feet were flat on the floor. She fetched a walker and positioned his hands on it before removing the suspension harness.

Erik stood behind Ting, prepared to catch him, if necessary, but the patient was able to bear his full weight. He swayed a bit, but Sirikit cheered and gave him an enthusiastic thumbs-up before fetching a wheelchair.

Marco Ting had a genuine smile on his face for the first time since awakening from the coma. Erik told him,

"Good job today," but wasn't surprised the helmsman failed to thank him in return.

The doctor pushed Ting's wheelchair back to his room, assisted him in the bathroom, and helped him into bed. He sat by and watched Ting feed himself a bowl of soup without spilling too much. Erik wished Phailin would take over for him, but he suspected the helmsman burned that bridge. She wouldn't be back.

He turned the chair so he could look out the window at the half-blue, half-gray smog sky. He had just begun to doze off when his earcom chimed. "This is Sorensen."

"This is Shepherd." Danae's contralto brought him fully awake.

"How was your meeting with York?" Erik tried not to sound anxious.

"We met with most of the *Liberty*'s senior officers."

Good, he thought, relieved it hadn't been a private meeting.

Danae told him about the plan to move the refugee camp to the cruise ship. "I don't know who funds ISPP, but they must be loaded. It's already a done deal."

"Does that mean they don't need us anymore?" Erik tried to keep his tone neutral, but he suspected she could detect the underlying eagerness in his voice.

She hesitated. "Not exactly."

"What does 'not exactly' mean?"

"I'll explain it to you in person."

Erik resisted the urge to pressure her for an answer. *Stay on her good side,* he reminded himself.

"Can you come back to the ship? I'd like you to be here to listen when Moniesa interrogates the Chinese woman who ordered Shima's tattoo."

"She's alive?" Erik was amazed to hear this.

"Yes, it seems ISPP was able to keep a few bad guys out of the morgue. If Moniesa can get her to explain how they choose their victims and why, we might be able to shut down one of the galaxy's biggest trafficking organizations."

"I'm sure ISPP can handle it without our help."

"You sound like Blaze." Danae paused. "He hasn't complained, but I think he'd prefer to have his family in a safer location, doing safer work."

"I agree with him. You've risked life and limb for this cause." Erik took a deep breath and confessed something on his mind. "The next time someone decides to shoot at you may be the last time your luck holds out."

"I know. So do you think Marco could manage on his own tonight? I'd really like you to be here . . . with me."

Although she hesitated on the last two words, Erik felt their impact. "I'm leaving now. Sorensen out."

"What about me?" Ting was eavesdropping.

The doctor turned off his earcom and got to his feet. "I'll be back in the morning, if you're lucky."

***

An hour later, Erik was back aboard *Alex's Legacy*. He went straight to the bridge to meet Danae. She was sitting alone at the helm, staring out the window.

He had a flashback to the last time he came up behind her on the bridge and put his hands on her shoulders, but he was hopeful she wouldn't shrug him off this time.

She was tense, her shoulder muscles rigid. Without saying a word, he massaged them.

Without saying a word, she let him.

Although her shoulders relaxed, he could sense she was holding on to some anxiety. "Anything you need to talk about?"

Danae reached up to grasp his hands. "I still need to tell the crew there's one more thing we have to do before we go back to Maui."

"What would that be?" he asked cautiously.

"We need to take a few children home to their families."

"That sounds like a safe assignment, but why is it our responsibility?"

"Because I owe Cade a favor."

Erik bristled before he could stop himself. "You don't owe him anything."

He was grateful the helmsman's chair stood between them, for his own safety. Danae sprang to her feet and spun around to face him. He expected an argument, but was astonished at her lack of emotion, the uncertainty in her words.

"Cade saved Shima's life. He's the reason she's still alive, the reason she's not a slave. I don't care about him, if that's what's bothering you, but he asked me to help ISPP one more time, and I felt it was my duty to say yes."

Her cheeks flushed pink with guilt. "I usually meet with the crew to weigh their concerns before making a plan, but I made an executive decision this time. I'm not sure how they're going to react." She searched his face, her large blue eyes clouded with worry. "Do you think I should've refused?"

Erik was grateful again for the chair between them because it gave him something to lean on so he wouldn't keel over from the shock. *The strong, confident Captain Shepherd wants me to reassure her she made the right decision?* He honestly didn't understand what motivated her to continue aiding York. He thought the ISPP captain already put her in too many dangerous situations. *Yes, you should have refused!*

At the same time, Erik felt pressured to give her the answer she needed to hear. One disparaging word from him and her wall might go up, shutting him out, perhaps permanently. He knew she wasn't testing him, at least not consciously, but it sure felt as if he was taking the final exam for a course he hadn't studied for.

"I think the crew will understand. We'll support your decision." He included himself in that statement, despite his misgivings, but the brilliant smile which broke through her dark expression drove all his doubts away.

Danae climbed up onto the seat of the chair so she was eye-to-eye with him. She threw her arms around his neck, and it was their first kiss all over again only this time it felt more incredible than he remembered from this morning.

The doctor reluctantly came up for air. "Where will we be returning these kids?"

She hesitated before answering. "Guangzhou."

Erik felt all the pressure and doubts come crashing back down on him like an avalanche. "York's sending us into the lion's den? You can't be serious!"

Danae was calm as she hopped down from the chair. "Please keep your voice down."

The doctor stomped over to the com controls and punched the *mute* button for the shipboard speakers. "What else have you neglected to mention about this mission? Tell me—" he stopped and tried again with more tact. "Your crew *deserves* to know exactly what you're getting us into."

Danae nodded, her face an odd mixture of defiance and contrition. She shoved her hands into her hip pockets before explaining. "ISPP has to stay in Bangkok until they move the kids to the cruise ship and investigate the police department, so we'll be the vanguard in Guangzhou. Cade wants us to check out Shamian Island so ISPP can plan the best way to attack White Swan."

Erik thought York had no right to give them such a dangerous assignment. *We're just ordinary people, not soldiers.*

She pressed on before he could formulate a counter-argument. "We're not expected to confront any slavers. If we see any slaves, we shouldn't attempt to rescue them. Cade wants us to keep a safe distance. Our mission is just to observe and report—"

"In other words, he wants us to *spy* on some of the most ruthless criminals in the galaxy?" Erik wanted to say more, but he realized he was too close to turning this into a personal attack. *I can't believe you agreed to this! This isn't our fight! This feels wrong—it's too dangerous!*

"Cade's loaning us an officer for extra protection," Danae added.

"I hope it's Moniesa." *Someone who can keep you safe!*

"Actually, it's Tse, because she speaks Chinese."

What's Chinese for 'we're all going to die?' Erik forced himself to set aside his fears, but he needed to express some valid concerns. *How can I do that without setting off more fireworks?*

He had an idea. It was sneaky, but communicating with the temperamental captain sometimes required creative maneuvering. Jake had warned him what Danae was like, and Erik experienced it for himself, but this time he needed her to listen.

He took a deep breath, squared his shoulders, and held out his arms to her. She moved closer with some hesitation, eyes narrowed in suspicion, but he managed to maintain a sympathetic face long enough to get his arms around her. He drew her into a tight embrace.

Erik nuzzled the top of her head, breathing in the citrusy fragrance of her wavy brown hair. He waited until he felt her body relax. He waited some more until she pressed closer, rested her cheek against his sternum, and encircled his waist with her arms. Only then did he feel safe to speak his mind. He kept his tone gentle and soothing.

"You've got a big heart, Danae. It was the first thing that attracted me to you—your compassion." He took a deep breath. "I appreciate the fact that we were able to team up with a common goal to help homeless kids and orphans"—he blew out the breath and pressed on before he lost his nerve—"but to confront the criminals who exploit these kids takes the risk to another level, a level we're not trained or equipped to handle."

She apparently didn't like what she was hearing because she tried to squirm free, but he held her firmly. "Let me finish, please—and no biting."

Danae didn't crack a smile at his feeble attempt at humor, but she stopped struggling and just stood there, stiff once again and radiating tension.

"I'm willing to support your decision because I trust you. But I need to hear you say we're going to take every precaution. We're not going to put ourselves in any situation that feels unsafe. You've experienced firsthand what these people are like. They won't hesitate to kill anyone who gets in their way." He added, "So I want your word: no unnecessary risks."

Slowly, Danae nodded.

"Let me hear you say it."

"I thought you trusted me."

"I do trust you, completely." He let it sink in. "Repeating a phrase aloud makes it easier to remember. I need you to remember because in Guangzhou, it won't be a matter of *if* we find ourselves in a dangerous situation, but *when*."

"I could say you're being paranoid and overprotective." Danae tilted her head back and looked up into his eyes. "But I won't . . . because you're probably right."

"I'm waiting." Erik gave her a stern look.

"No unnecessary risks." She sounded like a robot. "We'll take every precaution. Now let me go."

She didn't have to ask twice. He took a hasty step back the instant he released her.

Danae put her hands on her hips. "If you want *me* to trust *you*, don't ever do that again."

Erik nodded, trying to appear contrite. "I'm sorry."

Her expression softened, and she dropped her hands to her side. "Am I so stubborn that you have to force me to listen?"

"Do you want me to answer that honestly?" He cracked a smile.

***

Dr. Sorensen was able to take a short nap in his cabin before returning to the bridge for the interrogation. Shima sat at the com control board, and Erik and Danae stood behind her chair so all three could listen to Moniesa question the Chinese prisoner in the *Liberty*'s brig. Although the doctor thought it would be more helpful to observe the interrogation, he suspected it wouldn't be a friendly chat. The weapons officer would be joined by the security officer Ghukasyan with engineer Tse translating.

"Good evening." Moniesa came on speaker promptly at 1900. "I will leave my comlink open during the interrogation, as promised."

"Thank you," Shima said.

"I will first ask the prisoner her name."

Tse's lilting voice could be heard in the background, speaking fluent Mandarin with a trace of a South-western accent, similar to Blaze's. Erik found the com-bination amusing but kept that opinion to himself.

There was silence. Tse repeated the question, but the silence continued. Then they heard the unmistakable sound of a slap.

"How does it feel to be on the receiving end?" Shima muttered under her breath. "Slap her again, for Zuri."

Erik exchanged a startled glance with Danae.

"Yes, she has a temper," the captain confided in a whisper. "I rarely get to see it, but when it does emerge—look out."

Shima, overhearing, huffed and shook her head.

The prisoner answered the question in a high-pitched voice, and Tse translated. "Her name is Cai."

"Who do you work for?" Moniesa asked.

It took three slaps to get the prisoner to answer this question. "*Bai hu'*—White Swan," Tse reported.

"Is *bai hu'* a person or an organization?"

More slaps. The prisoner groaned and let loose a torrent of short, clipped words.

"It's a crime syndicate," Tse said, "a mafia."

Erik felt a real jolt of fear at this response. *This has to convince York the mission is too dangerous for civilians.*

"How does White Swan choose its victims?"

The doctor wasn't sure what Moniesa used to loosen the prisoner's tongue, but whatever it was made Cai gasp and speak without further persuasion.

Tse kept a running commentary. "White Swan selects only exceptionally beautiful young women for its high-paying customers."

"Beauty is what the tattooed girls have in common." Danae gave Shima's shoulders a squeeze. "Of course, it makes sense now."

"The organization is well known among other traffickers because they post rewards for the return of any girls who run away," Tse said. "The tattoo is how they're identified."

"The slaves are branded like cattle so they can never escape." The look of disgust on Danae's face and in her tone of voice reflected what Erik was thinking.

Shima spoke up. "Moniesa, ask Cai about the tattoo on her neck. What does it mean?"

"What tattoo?" Erik was confused. "I thought we solved the mystery of the tattoo."

Without turning around, the first officer pointed to a place on her own neck, just below her left ear. "Cai has a different tattoo here. It is a letter B, surrounded by a circle of barbed wire."

Danae drew in a sharp breath and gripped the back of Shima's chair.

Alarmed, Erik glanced over at Danae's profile. Her mouth was pinched into a thin, tight line. "You've seen the B tattoo before?" he whispered. "You know what it means?"

She gave a barely perceptible nod and stared straight ahead at the helm window.

Tse spoke to the prisoner and relayed her response. "She says the tattoo is a symbol of her loyalty to Baronowski."

Shima gasped.

"The Baronowski Brothers murdered my father," Danae whispered to Erik. Her knuckles on the chair turned white.

"*What?*" Before he could ask her to elaborate, she fired off another question at Moniesa.

"What was her role in the Baronowski organization?"

After some back-and-forth, Tse reported, "Before the brothers were imprisoned, she arranged hits for their hired assassins."

Danae and Shima gasped in unison.

Erik had only a vague idea of what the answers meant to Danae. He recalled her mentioning that her father was poisoned—*but by the space mafia? Why would the infamous Baronowskis want him dead?*

"Ask her what she knows about the murder of Ishmael Thompson," Danae said.

"Please fill me in," Erik whispered while they waited for Tse to translate Cai's response.

Danae kept her voice low. "Liam Baronowski threatened to murder Rosamar Delacruz's family—she was the prosecutor for his trial. I told you my dad was in a serious relationship with her, but I pressured him to break up."

Erik nodded. "I remember that part, but why did they go after your father if he wasn't family?"

"He was *almost* family. They did it to scare Rosamar, of course. She assumed Dad was safe because they'd split up before the trial began." Danae took a deep breath. "A few months after she left, I found him dead in his cabin. He'd been—"

"Poisoned." Erik reached over and turned Danae's face toward his, but she continued to stare straight a-head, refusing to make eye contact. There was a dangerous look in her eyes, a smoldering rage he had seen only twice before—once when she shot Acheron while he was attempting to arrest Jake, and the second time when she was being held captive by a pair of street thugs in Bangkok.

"For eight years I'd wondered what really happened to him and who was responsible for his death. Rosamar told me a few weeks ago, when we were in jail on Mars Station. She didn't know he was dead, and I didn't know she was responsible. He would still be alive today if she'd warned him."

"She did not know they were after your father." Shima sounded distressed. Erik wasn't the only one concerned about the venom in Danae's tone. "You told me you forgave her."

"I did forgive *her*. But *they* got away with murder."

"But—" Erik wanted to reason with her that the Baronowskis were serving life sentences for their crimes, but he thought she was too angry to hear what he had to say.

Tse announced, "She does not remember the names of any of the victims. She just passed along their information to the assassins."

Danae scoffed. "She doesn't *remember*? Ask her if she arranged to have a starship captain poisoned eight years ago."

The atmosphere on the bridge was heavy with tension as they waited for Cai's answer. Erik put his arm around Danae's shoulders. She didn't resist, but she didn't lean against him as she usually did. As a doctor, he couldn't help noticing her racing pulse and shallow breathing, but he had no idea what was going on inside her mind.

"Cai says she doesn't know. She wasn't told what weapons or strategies they used. She was just the messenger."

That should be enough information to help Danae find some closure, Erik hoped. He had never seen her so angry, compared to the other times he watched her lose her temper—too many to count.

However, the captain wasn't satisfied with Cai's answer. If anything, she looked ready to hurt someone. "Moniesa, White Swan must be part of the Baronowski empire. They had ties to every type of organized crime, including human trafficking."

"I thought Delacruz put those scum out of business." Cade York's voice was filled with contempt.

"Captain York has just joined us," Moniesa informed the *Alex*'s crew.

"Tse, tell that filth she's going to lead us to White Swan's headquarters," York said.

"And if she refuses?" Moniesa asked.

York snorted. "I don't know. Use your imagination. Captain Shepherd, if you're listening, you'll have one extra passenger in addition to Tse. I recommend you keep Cai in your brig."

"No!" Erik couldn't believe his ears. "No! No! Absolutely not! There's no way you're putting her on this ship!"

"It's not your decision to make, Sorensen!" York roared back. "You're not the captain!"

"You can't expect us to take responsibility for a dangerous criminal!"

"Hit the mute button," Danae told Shima.

York's next retort was silenced.

Danae shrugged off Erik's arm and turned to face him, poking an index finger at his chest. "You: calm down!" She pivoted back to the com. "Shima: inform Captain York I'll call him after I meet with the crew."

Her first officer nodded and focused on the control board with a worried frown.

Erik hooked Danae's elbow and turned her to face him again. "This isn't a simple scouting expedition anymore, not if we bring that viper on board. This should be a military operation, and you know it."

"I already gave my word."

"Then break it. What's he going to do, sue us? You don't have to risk your life for ISPP. It's time we went back to Maui."

"I'm not doing this as a favor to Cade, not anymore." Danae's expression was dangerous.

That's what I'm afraid of, Erik thought. *Just when I thought she might be convinced to renege, York decides to up the ante.*

"Maybe you should calm down and think this over." He was more concerned for Cai's safety than Danae's. It would be too tempting for the captain to confront the slaver if she were on the ship.

"You heard what Cade said—we need her to help us find White Swan. It makes sense."

"It makes *no* sense! It's an open invitation to trouble—it's way more than we can handle!"

"It'll be fine. Tse will be in charge of the prisoner, and we'll never let her leave the brig."

"So are you allowing her on the ship because York demands it or because you want *revenge?*" He didn't wait for an answer. He turned on his heel and walked out of the room.

"Erik!" Danae called after him, but he didn't look back. He needed to calm down or he might do something he would regret, like force her to put up a wall which would shut him out of her life forever.

FOURTEEN
RELUCTANT VOLUNTEERS

DANAE REVIEWED THE *private* conversation with Cade in the mess hall. Though her normal instinct was to rebel against any requests made under coercion, Captain York presented a compelling case.

Do we owe ISPP anything? She thought of Shima and Zuri. *Yes, we do.*

Does he really need my help? ISPP could send in some scouts after they finish up here. What's the rush? She chewed her lower lip, considering this angle. *They don't have enough officers. They could be here for months, and if word gets out to White Swan that ISPP is coming after them, the traffickers will be long gone.* She knew how much Cade wanted to shut down the galaxy's child slave trade and find his son, so she dismissed the it-can-wait theory.

Does he think my crew can be an effective vanguard after our disastrous attempt on Mars Station to rescue Erik? She tried to imagine what types of dangers they might encounter in Guangzhou. *No one knows us there. I'm not wanted by the CIPs for murder. Posing as tourists shouldn't arouse too much suspicion, should it?*

She shook her head in frustration. *Couldn't we just return some of the children to their families and skip the rest? Can we ensure their safety with Cai on board?*

Danae reflected on the fact that she made a decision contrary to her gut feeling—something she'd never done before. *Yes, we faced down powerful criminals on Mars Station, but we knew what we were getting into. We knew who our enemies were: Acheron and Thanatos. There are so many unknowns about scouting Shamian Island. We have no idea who or what we're up against.*

Fast-forward a few hours to the prisoner interrogation and everything changed. Danae didn't doubt her decision anymore. Her path was clear, and she wasn't afraid of what they might find on the island. The news reports after the trial had insisted the Baronowskis's businesses had all been uncovered and forced to close. *But evidently they missed one—White Swan.*

Danae tried to rein in her emotions so she could look at the situation objectively. She knew vengeance fueled the type of blind ambition which could lead to disaster, and she had other people's safety to consider. *I can't expect everyone to feel the way I do—Erik made that point clear. I'll let each crewmember decide. Risking one's life should be voluntary, not compulsory.*

***

Captain Shepherd leaned back against the long counter and studied the concerned faces of her six employees. Blaze, Lorina, Shima, Phailin, and Vipul sat near her at various tables, each waiting to hear what she had to say. Erik sat in the back of the room. His mood was anything but calm. Zuri was assigned to supervise Niyati in the third level port lounge just in case the meeting didn't go well, and Danae had a nagging feeling it wouldn't.

Although she toyed with the idea of composing a speech to garner sympathy and support, Danae knew she'd lose everyone's respect if she wasn't completely honest. She made that mistake with Erik and his response was sobering. She couldn't expect him, or any of them, to support her decision. *This isn't a 'thank you for helping us, Cade' mission anymore. This is personal— this is for Dad.*

The mantle of leadership weighed heavy on her shoulders. Danae hadn't been this nervous in front of a crew since the day after her father was murdered, leaving her in charge of a passenger starship and a struggling interstellar business.

"I made a"—she glanced at Erik with an apologetic frown—"controversial decision without consulting the crew beforehand. What I agreed to do is potentially dangerous and involves all of us, so I overstepped my authority, and I'm sorry. I need you to please hear me out. I promise to answer any questions when I'm through."

Danae explained Cade's request: the two-fold mission of returning the former slaves to their families and then posing as tourists to gather information on White Swan. She talked about their potential asset: Tse—although she noticed Blaze grimaced when she mentioned the ISPP engineer's name—and their potential liability: Cai. Without going into a lot of detail, she mentioned the connection between the slaver and the Baronowski mafia that murdered her father. She would let them draw their own conclusions.

"Captain York believes Cai could lead us straight to White Swan's headquarters, but for everyone's safety, especially the children's, I don't plan to let her out of the brig."

"She shouldn't be brought on board." Erik's tone was flat.

The others exchanged uncomfortable glances, but no one else offered any comments. Danae waited for questions, but none were forthcoming. She gave them a minute to think about it before proposing a vote. "This assignment should be voluntary, so each of you should decide for yourself."

She was amazed the first one to speak up was Vipul. "Captain, I worked for Thanatos for nearly a year. I *helped* that monster traffic children. Even after I realized what was taking place on the *Elmina*, I was a coward and did nothing to stop him. I ran away and kept this terrible secret until you were wise enough to confront me. You've helped me realize how much one courageous person can accomplish. I don't think you made a mistake in agreeing to this mission. I would welcome another opportunity to make amends."

"Thank you, Vipul." Danae was touched by his sincerity.

Shima dropped the second bombshell. "I would also welcome another opportunity to help rescue children like Zuri. If we could save just one more child from a life of slavery, it would be worth the risk."

"I agree with Shima," Lorina said. "I signed on with this crew to rescue homeless children. I think you were right to speak for all of us."

Danae met Erik's slack-jawed gaze and was tempted to say, "I told you so," but she flashed him an understanding smile instead.

"This is the most rewarding work I've ever done," Phailin said. "I can be timid sometimes, but I want to do whatever I can to help."

Blaze looked troubled but said, "If I can ensure my family's safety in China, if we're careful to not go lookin' for trouble, I think I'm up for one more adventure."

"I can assure you we'll take every possible precaution," Danae said. "Hopefully we won't run into any trouble—"

Erik gave a loud snort of disapproval.

"—and can report anything suspicious we see to ISPP. This is *only* a scouting expedition. We won't be confronting any slavers." She shifted her gaze to Shima. "No more shootouts, I promise."

Her first officer shrugged. "We trust your judgment, Captain."

Danae was careful not to reveal the guilt she felt at Shima's statement. She tried to lighten the mood by asking, "What would Marco's vote be?"

There were a few weak laughs from everyone except Erik and Phailin.

"I can't repeat what Ting would say because there are ladies present," Vipul said.

"Just keep him on board for his own safety," Lorina said.

The galley was quiet again as everyone turned to look at Erik Sorensen. Danae caught his eye, noted his disapproving scowl, and wondered if this would be a deal breaker for their fledgling relationship. She'd become so accustomed to having his support that she felt abandoned.

The thought of Dr. Sorensen quitting the crew, leaving the ship, and walking out of her life made Danae's stomach turn to ice. She was surprised at the depth of her feelings, but she couldn't deny they were real.

The words were out of her mouth before she could stop them. "Erik, you don't have to do this for me. You don't owe me anything. I'm the reason you were in jail, and I didn't even get you out—Rosamar did that. You didn't sign on with this crew to risk your life"—she glanced around at the others—"none of you signed on to be spies for ISPP to hunt down dangerous criminals, and I'll understand if you change your minds and want no part of it."

Erik got to his feet, his mulish scowl still fixed in place. "I need more time to think about it." He left the galley without another word.

Danae's heart sank. "You're dismissed," she told the others. "Marco will be discharged from the hospital late tomorrow. Hopefully the doctor will have an answer for us by then."

Shima shot her an understanding glance. "We can talk later. I sense you would like to be alone. I will inform Captain York that most of the crew has agreed to accept the mission."

Danae nodded, grateful for the reprieve. "Thank you. I think I'll turn in early."

***

Annalise Tse presented herself at the *Alex*'s airlock at 0700. She was dressed in jeans and a T-shirt, her long black braid coiled into a bun on the back of her head. "Captain Shepherd." She offered her hand for Danae to shake.

"Officer Tse." She ushered the engineer into the antechamber and tapped the visitor's code into the keypad so she could pass the security barricade.

"Please call me Axe."

"Let me show you to your cabin . . . Axe." Danae glanced at her heavy rucksack, suspecting it contained more weaponry than personal items. "Shall we take the lift?"

"No, ma'am." Axe eyed the ladder. "I can manage." She shouldered her bag and grasped the rungs. "Which level?"

"Third." Danae climbed after the ISPP officer, who nimbly ascended the two levels. "This way."

The captain escorted her to 312 on the starboard wing. Axe pressed her thumb to the ID lock beside the door, creating the pass-key to her cabin.

"My first officer, Shima Oryang, is in 310 next door if you need anything."

Axe dropped her heavy bag on the floor and turned to face Danae. "Captain, I know you have reservations about bringing me on board, but—"

"On the contrary," Danae cut her off. "I'm grateful to have your assistance. I don't anticipate any problems working with you, so long as you remember I'm the captain on this ship and my orders take precedence over ISPP's if there is ever a conflict of interest."

Axe looked taken aback but managed to say, "Yes, Captain. I understand."

"It's the prisoner that concerns me. We'll have children on board who must be kept safe. My brig has never been used as a prison before." *Only as a morgue,* she thought with a pang of sadness. "I'm not sure how secure it is."

The brig needs to keep me out as effectively as it keeps Cai in. Danae had been up half the night, trying to pick the knots out of her tangled emotions, but to no avail. *Why did Cade have to throw a wrench in the machinery? Now that I know who orchestrated Dad's death, what am I supposed to do with Cai? It would've been much easier to hate her from afar.*

Axe's voice cut through Danae's worried thoughts. "My presence here will ensure your passengers' safety, Captain."

"You seem confident, but you're just one person— not a garrison. No doubt you're capable of handling any problems that arise, but I need to make one rule crystal clear: I know soldiers are expected to protect their leaders, but if there's ever a situation where you must choose between covering me and covering a member of my crew, you will protect my crew first. Do you have a problem with that?"

Axe opened her mouth, but Danae spoke over her before she could respond. "My crew is doing this as a favor to me, not ISPP. Given the option, a few of them would've chosen not to be involved."

Who can blame them? Searching for traffickers with ties to the space mafia is the most dangerous thing we've ever done. Danae had many reasons to doubt her own sanity for agreeing to this mission, but she was determined to uncover the last remnant of the Baronowski empire. *For Dad—and for all the kids who've had their childhoods stolen, their lives ruined, by White Swan.*

"My crew's safety comes first because I'm responsible for their lives, and I take that responsibility very seriously. Do you understand?"

"Yes, Captain." Axe was disgruntled but added with respect, "Your crew's safety takes precedence over all other orders."

Danae nodded and hoped Officer Tse meant every word. "Please make yourself comfortable and acquaint yourself with the layout of the ship. The crew's mess is available twenty-four/seven. I'd give you a tour, but my presence is needed at the hospital today so my helms-man can be discharged on time."

"Yes, Captain." Axe pressed her thumb to the lock again, and the door to her room slid open. "Thank you."

***

Danae met Erik in the entryway at 0800 so they could commute to the hospital together. He still appeared sullen, so she just said, "Good morning," and cycled the airlock doors open.

His "good morning" sounded forced.

They descended the staircase and walked side-by-side to the lift, mostly avoiding each other's eyes. She assumed the ball was in his court and he would talk when he was ready. The ride down to the ground was silent, as was the half-kilometer walk to the tramstop.

Danae didn't relish a mute hour-long tram ride to Bhumibol Memorial, so when they sat down together on the tram—she was surprised he sat beside her when there were empty seats available—she pulled out her datapad and handed it to him so they would have something neutral to discuss.

"This is the file of the twenty-eight kids we'll be bringing aboard this evening."

Erik scrolled through the holograms and information without comment.

"As you can see, we have very few addresses to work with, so we'll depend on Axe to translate the city directory and do some sleuthing to locate their families.

A dozen of them are from Foshan, which is only a few kilometers from Guangzhou, so we'll head there first. Half of them remember the name of the street they lived on. The rest only remember the name of the city. I suspect this will be a time-consuming task."

"Their families won't recognize them." Erik kept his eyes fixed on the screen. "I'll bet some of them won't be welcomed back because of what they've been through."

"I can't imagine what kind of parents would reject their daughter for being forced into prostitution. Arranged marriages, dowries, and sanctimonious family honor attitudes went the way of foot-binding, centuries ago."

"I think we need to consider the possibility that a few of them might be rejected, or their families may have moved away or might even be dead. How do we want to handle that?"

Danae was relieved to hear him say *we*. "I'm not going to abandon them with nothing but the clothes on their backs, just so they can be picked up by traffickers again. I guess we could take them to The Lost Sheep and find places for them to live if they're too old to be adopted."

Erik's large hand found hers and held it for a minute before he turned his head to look at her. "I've been thinking . . ."

She was tempted to say something sarcastic, but she donned her calm face instead. "About what?"

"I sat up most of the night, trying to decide what to do about us."

Danae felt a twinge of fear at his use of *us*. "Did you make a decision?"

Erik sidestepped the question. "It occurred to me if anyone else asked us to go to Guangzhou—anyone except York—I would've been the first to volunteer."

She nodded, pretending to understand why he was still jealous, but she kept quiet, hoping he would share more.

He took a deep breath. "When you said we were going to spy for ISPP, the first thing that came to mind was you getting shot by Thanatos. I couldn't stop seeing you with the thug holding a knife to your throat, or you in that shootout on the stairwell. I know you can handle yourself in dangerous situations, but the thought of losing you makes my blood run cold.

"I've been beaten, threatened, tortured, arrested, and thrown in jail several times, but I've never had to worry about someone else being murdered right before my eyes."

Danae hesitated, trying to think of something to say to reassure him. "Would it help you feel better if I promised that after this is over, I'm packing up my gun for good? No more adventures. We'll let ISPP take care of the criminals. We'll go back to the quiet business of placing kids for adoption and maybe transporting passengers between stations, if you'd care to tag along for that."

"Except for the takeoffs and landings, I'd like that." Erik leaned over to kiss her on the forehead. He didn't give her a chance to relax, however, because he had one more point to make. "I don't want Cai on the ship. I think her presence would be inviting trouble, and I'm not just saying that because I'm worried you've got revenge on your mind."

"Now wait a minute—" Danae tried to get a word in, but he spoke over her.

"The real reason I'm objecting is because she's a dangerous criminal, and I think we can find White Swan without the added risk of her presence."

"But—" Danae tried again, to no avail.

"She was just the messenger, like she said—just an employee. I doubt we can force any more information out of her. Confronting her won't help you avenge your father's death."

Danae's temper flared. "Who said I was going to confront her?"

"I did." Erik leaned closer so she couldn't escape seeing his flushed face or hearing every word he had to say. "I can see it in your eyes, Danae. You've got an agenda that goes way beyond scouting for White Swan."

"An *agenda*? What happened to that nice little speech about trusting me? Don't you think if I had an ulterior motive, I'd discuss it with you first?"

It was obvious Erik wasn't expecting her offer to 'discuss it with you first,' and floundered for a reply. "It's just that . . . you tend to bottle things up when you're angry."

"No, I don't." *Yes, I do.* "Stop questioning my motives and maybe I'll share more."

"I don't question—" He stopped himself, sighed, and rolled his eyes in frustration. "I know you want justice for your dad—I get that. I understand. But you have to admit this mission is way over our heads. It's too dangerous—"

"And I understand your concerns but—"

"Do you?" Erik spoke over her, exasperated. "I just told you how I feel about losing you, and you still—"

Danae didn't know how it happened. It was as if her brain flipped a switch, shutting off all the anger and defensiveness and turning on a light which filled her mind with all the positive emotions she'd been suppressing. She moved fast, cutting off his diatribe with a kiss that drew a few wolf whistles from some of the other passengers on the tram.

Erik decided he'd done enough arguing and pulled her closer. "We haven't finished this discussion."

"Yes, we have. You've made your point." She had no trouble persuading him to be quiet.

They almost missed their stop.

As they walked into the hospital holding hands, Danae said, "I don't think Thais approve of kissing in public. Do you think we offended anyone?"

"Maybe. I heard some muttering, but I don't know the Thai phrase for 'get a room'."

Danae could feel her face turning red, but she couldn't help laughing.

FIFTEEN
PASSENGERS

DESPITE THE HEAT, Shima and Zuri felt safer leaving the ship dressed in long pants. Shima's concealed pistol also contributed to their sense of security. They took the tram to Lumphini Park. Moniesa had requested Shima's assistance in locating the twenty-eight children who would be lifting with the *Alex's Legacy*, and Zuri wanted to spend time with Ekaterina, knowing it would be the last time she would see her Romanian friend.

"I wish Ekaterina could go with us," Zuri said to Shima for the umpteenth time while all three of them helped the ISPP cooks and Stop Traffic volunteers serve lunch to the thirty-eight hundred ex-slaves.

"I understand how you feel, but Ekaterina needs her family. They must miss her terribly."

"She does not even remember them," Zuri said. "She was only four years old when she was taken."

"All the more reason to return her to them," Shima said with firmness. "Eight years is a long time to wonder what happened to your child. I am sure they are still heartbroken."

"Were you heartbroken when I was gone, auntie?"

She put down her serving tongs and hugged her niece. "I think you know the answer to that question."

Ekaterina glanced over at them with a puzzled grin. Shima beckoned the younger girl over so she could be included in the hug.

"Back to work." Shima released them, picked up her tongs, and worked faster to compensate for the slowdown in the line she'd created. She was able to blink back a few tears before either girl noticed.

They continued to serve whole baked sweet potatoes and steamed corn on the cob for over an hour until all the children were through the lines. Next they got their own plates and claimed a table the moment one became available.

"I will be at the clinic this afternoon, helping Officer Moniesa locate the girls who will be leaving with us for China," Shima said.

"Yes, auntie," Zuri said around a mouthful of corn.

"You and Ekaterina must not leave the park. Come to the tent at 1700, five o'clock, so we can return to the ship."

"Yes, auntie."

Shima rose from the table before the girls finished eating. "Do not forget, five o'clock." She gave them each a smile before leaving, threading the maze of crowded tables to reach the exit.

There were hundreds of children sitting on the grass outside the tent, eating their lunches in small groups since there weren't enough tables inside to accommodate everyone. Shima maneuvered between them, sometimes having to step over legs, and made her way to the clinic. The noisy crowds, though cheerful, made her tense. She knew she needed some time alone to meditate, but it would have to wait.

Outside the clinic/command tent, Shima saw a dozen children lined up for physicals, DNA traces, and counseling with ISPP officers. She went inside and had an easy time locating Wisdom Moniesa, who was decimeters taller and wider than everyone else working there. The weapons officer had created a small waiting area for the Chinese girls who were returning home aboard the *Alex*. Currently, there were only eleven in the group.

"If you are still collecting DNA traces, how will we know if you have located all the children who need to go to Guangzhou?" Shima asked.

The big woman shrugged. "We cannot wait to interview every child. We must begin the process of returning them home. We are already overwhelmed by their numbers."

The *Alex*'s first officer looked over the Chinese girls, who were sitting cross-legged on the ground, talking or playing cards with each other. Five of them wore drab gray factory tunics and the other six wore purple or red oversized T-shirts. "Where are the other seventeen?"

"Somewhere in the park," Moniesa said. "It is like—what is the expression?—looking for needles in a haystack." She handed Shima a datapad. "Here are their holo-grams. The facial recognition program may be helpful."

Shima did some quick thinking. "It will be impossible for me to locate all these children by myself. Here is a better idea: send a message to the officers and volunteers stationed around the park, asking them to send any Chinese children they see to the command tent."

The big woman smiled. "Process of elimination instead of needles in a haystack? Good thinking."

Shima glanced over at the group of eleven. "Could one of these girls assist me?"

"More good thinking." Moniesa handed her one of the translation datapads. "I will put a table and two chairs out front. There is some shade beneath the tent awning so it will not be unbearably hot. I will check to see how you are doing later this afternoon."

"Thank you." As Moniesa left the tent to set up, Shima considered which girl would make a good assistant. She noticed one appeared older than the rest, maybe fifteen or sixteen, and was talking a lot with her neighbor. She approached the young woman with a friendly smile.

"*Ni hao.*"

Curious, the teen glanced up at her. She was beautiful with long-lashed eyes, wavy black hair, and lots of dimples.

She gestured for the young woman to join her in a less-crowded area of the tent. When the teen got to her feet, Shima wasn't surprised to see the White Swan tattoo on the back of her leg.

Shima said, "Mandarin," to the datapad, introduced herself, and explained the assignment. The device translated it back to the young woman who thought about it before offering a response.

The datapad said, "My name is Hua. Yes, I will help. I think some of the children will be afraid to go anywhere with strangers, but I can convince them you are taking them home."

"*Xie xie!*" Shima used up the rest of her Chinese vo-cabulary.

Hua said something and giggled. The translation was, "You should probably just use the datapad."

The two sat down behind the tiny table outside the tent.

An hour later Shima thought, *Maybe this was not such a good idea.* Forty-three children had come to her table so far, but only two of the forty-three were part of the Guangzhou group. Some weren't even Chinese, but other Asian nationalities. Many of those she turned away were devastated to learn they weren't going home yet.

"Maybe we should not tell them we are taking them home," she said to Hua as she watched a small Korean boy walk away with tears in his eyes.

The teen pursed her lips. "I have to tell them something or they will not agree to go. They do not trust adults."

Shima sighed and tapped her earcom. "Moniesa?"

"Yes?"

"Please remind the volunteers to send only Chinese children and to please do it quickly."

The ISPP officer chuckled. "You are bossy when you sit out in the sun too long."

By 1630, Shima located twenty-seven members of the Guangzhou group—twenty-six girls and one boy. She fretted over the one who hadn't turned up at the table. She told Hua, "Thank you for your help," and sent her back inside the clinic to rejoin the others.

She put in another call to Moniesa. "We need to escort the children to the *Alex* so the ship can lift at 2000. The time has already been confirmed on the port master's schedule. I do not know what to do about the missing boy." She pulled up his hologram. "Yao—he is only nine years old."

"I will call the volunteers once more to ask them to look for a small Chinese boy." Moniesa added with sympathy, "If he is not found, you must go back to the ship without him."

Shima reluctantly agreed. She signed off the com and drowned her sorrows in a bottle of cold water.

"Auntie?" Zuri and Ekaterina arrived five minutes later. Both girls looked as if they'd been crying. The pleading look in her niece's eyes needed no explanation.

Shima felt a fresh wave of guilt wash over her. *It could be many months before ISPP returns children to Romania. There are so many of them, and they are from every country on Earth. It is an impossible task.*

"One moment, I need to make a call." Shima was grateful Zuri didn't speak much English. She didn't want to get her niece's hopes up when she explained the situation to Danae.

"Hello, Shima." The captain gave her a brief update. "We're just on our way back to the ship with Marco. Blaze, Vipul, Phailin, and Lorina took care of the food, supplies, fuel, water, and septic. Are we ready to lift on schedule?"

"We are hoping one more child turns up, but I am planning to leave here at 1700, regardless. I am bringing twenty-seven Chinese children"—she took a deep breath—"and Ekaterina."

"That doesn't sound like a Chinese name. That's Zuri's friend, right?"

"Yes, I wondered if she could accompany us . . . for a while."

"How do you propose we return her to her family?"

Shima had no response.

Danae sighed. "I guess I should be used to taking in strays by now. Sure, bring her along."

"Thank you. See you back at the ship."

Shima turned off her com and smiled at the girls. She told Zuri in Swahili, "I guess you can share 310 with Ekaterina and I will move back to my old cabin."

Zuri shrieked with joy and threw her arms around Shima. There was more shrieking and hugging after Zuri explained to Ekaterina in the collection of words from different languages they used to communicate.

"Calm down. We need to leave soon." Shima led the girls inside the tent.

Moniesa was already speaking to the group of Guangzhou children with the help of a datapad. They were on their feet, chattering excitedly to each other, ready to go. They were also wearing new flip-flops.

"Recent donation," Moniesa said when she noticed Shima staring at their feet.

"Good." The first officer wondered how they'd be able to walk over scorching hot sidewalks in bare feet. "Any sign of the missing boy?"

The weapons officer shook her head. "Maybe I can look for him in the dinner line at the mess hall."

"If you find him, maybe someone could escort him to the ship before we lift." Shima doubted ISPP could spare an officer for this errand, but she didn't want to give up hope. She handed the translation datapad back to Moniesa. "Thank you, for everything."

"Goodbye, *rafiki*."

Shima turned to the group of freed slaves and gestured for them to follow her. She took Zuri's right hand and Ekaterina's left, and led the way.

***

It was after 1800 when Shima herded her charges through the airlock. "Show them to the galley," she told her niece. "I am sure they would like some dinner."

Zuri headed up the ladder, and the ex-slaves followed her, single file.

"Phailin, are you ready for our guests?"

"Soup's on," the cook said. "Axe is here to brief them on ship's rules and cabin assignments."

"Shima, stay put," Danae spoke up. "Erik and I are coming down to the entryway. Cade will be here in five minutes with the prisoner."

"Yes, Captain." Shima dreaded seeing the cruel madam again. She knew Danae hadn't accepted this mission as a favor to York. She might have been coerced to agree at first, but her motivation changed the moment Cai revealed her former career included arranging assassinations for the Baronowskis.

Danae is determined to avenge her father's death by uncovering White Swan—the mafia's last stronghold. It is not about the children anymore—it is personal. Shima made a silent vow to support Danae, no matter what happened, but the whole situation made her nervous.

Shima was also worried about having Cade York and Erik Sorensen in the same room. *This is going to be awkward, or worse.*

The captain and the doctor descended the ladder and waited in the entryway with her.

"How is Marco?" Shima asked.

"He's walking without help and eating solid food, but he still needs another week of intensive physical therapy." Dr. Sorensen frowned. "Which should be loads of fun for me, of course."

"He's not ready for the helm yet," Danae added. "He needs to build up his arm strength."

"He may also need a refresher course on piloting the ship," Sorensen said. "We'll see if his memory is intact for that task."

"Why does he not remember Phailin?" Shima asked.

"There's permanent damage to a small portion of his short-term memory. I'm no neurologist, but that's my best educated guess. He can't recall a specific block of time because a tiny portion of his brain where the bullet hit is missing." The doctor drew a finger across his forehead for emphasis.

"Permission to come aboard?" Captain York appeared at the open outer airlock doorway with Cai beside him. One of his big brown hands gripped her shoulder, and she was gritting her teeth as if angry or in pain, or both.

Shima recalled York's paralyzing grip on her own shoulder when he had caught her and Blaze at factory number six the night of the raids. She also remembered the painful, stinging slap Cai gave her and Zuri. She secretly hoped Cai would have an uncomfortable stay in the *Alex*'s brig.

Officer Ghukasyan was standing behind York on the stairs, covering Cai with a large rifle. The slaver's wrists were handcuffed behind her back and she was wearing an orange prison jumpsuit. Shima didn't realize ISPP was so well-equipped to handle prisoners.

Danae shot the slaver a hard look before stepping forward into the antechamber and entering the visitor's code into the security keypad.

Captain York and Dr. Sorensen exchanged scowls. Shima was reminded of a pair of bull elephants because they were both such large, muscular men. *This will not go well, no matter how diplomatic Danae tries to be.*

The ISPP group walked into the ship, but York had eyes only for Danae. "We'll see her to the brig. After that, Tse will take charge of her."

"This way." Danae led the group to the starboard lift and they rode down to the lowest level in silence. At the end of the basement corridor, the captain pressed her thumb to the ID lock beside an unlabeled door.

The door was new, having been replaced after the rough landing on Maui which almost cost Blaze his life. The new door was designed for a brig. It was made of indestructible glass on the top half and solid titanium on the lower half. It slid open with a soft hiss, revealing a two-by-three-meter compartment equipped with a single cot, a toilet, and a wall-mounted holo-vid screen controlled from the remote on the outside of the cell, beside the ID lock.

Ghukasyan gave Cai a push, forcing her to step inside the cell. The security officer removed the handcuffs and backed out of the tiny room. The prisoner turned around to glare at her captors.

Danae touched the keypad, and the door slid shut, but the captain remained where she was, staring at the prisoner's neck tattoo.

Cai stared back at Danae through the glass and made an obscene gesture. Shima turned away so she wouldn't have to see the hatred in the slaver's eyes.

"She shouldn't be here." Dr. Sorensen spoke through clenched teeth. "We shouldn't have to take responsibility for a dangerous criminal. This is a private ship, and there are children on board. Their safety is our top priority."

"We've been over this too many times." York's reply was sharp. "You need her to locate the White Swan. With Tse in charge of her, the risk to the crew and passengers is minimal." He turned his back on a furious

Dr. Sorensen and headed for the ladder at the other end of the corridor with Ghukasyan on his heels.

Back in the entryway, Shima could sense the tension radiating off York, Sorensen, and Danae as they faced each other in an awkward triangle.

"Thank you for your help." Captain York nodded to Danae with a small smile.

"I'll thank *you* not to expect her to do your dirty work." Dr. Sorensen's pale face turned pink, his fists clenched at his side.

"Erik, calm down." Danae moved closer to him, placing a cautionary hand on his arm.

York's black eyebrows shot up. He glanced back and forth between Danae and the doctor. "All this bluster isn't just about the prisoner, is it?"

Sorensen sidestepped the question. "The only reason that woman was allowed on board is because I trust Danae's judgment. If it were up to me—"

"But it's not up to you, is it?" York said, "You're not the captain."

"You seem to have forgotten *you* have no authority here, either. Don't tell Captain Shepherd how to run her ship."

"Erik!" Danae placed herself between the men as they took a few menacing steps toward each other. She shoved them apart and turned to face York with a stern look. "You should leave now."

The ISPP captain glared at the doctor over the top of Danae's head. Shima hoped York would get his temper under control. She knew Danae wouldn't hesitate to throw the first punch if things turned ugly.

"It never would've worked out between us, Cade." Danae's tone was kind but firm. "I've agreed to this one last mission to return the favor of rescuing Shima and

Zuri, but I have my own ship and my own life, and I'm not willing to give them up for anyone."

"Not even for Sorensen?" York's tone was bitter.

"I think the captain told you to leave!" the doctor shouted.

"Would you people please behave like adults?" Shima blurted before she could stop herself.

Everyone turned to stare at the first officer as if she'd sprouted antlers. Even Ghukasyan looked embar-rassed.

The hostilities faded into a tension-filled silence. Cade York gave Danae a cold look before turning and walking out of the airlock without another word. Ghukasyan nodded politely to them before hurrying after her captain.

Danae exchanged an eye roll with Shima before turning around to face a still-angry Dr. Sorensen. "I think we could've handled that with a little more tact."

"So . . . I think I will go have some dinner." Without waiting for a response, Shima moved to the ladder and climbed to the second level, not pausing to eavesdrop this time.

***

At 1900, Shima was forced to admit the last Guangzhou passenger wouldn't be located in time to leave with the *Alex*. She left Zuri, Ekaterina, and Niyati in the third level starboard lounge where they were watching Disney's 'Snow White' on the widescreen holo-vid with a few of the Chinese passengers. The ex-slaves were all munching popcorn and howling with laughter at every scene, even though they couldn't understand the English dialogue or song lyrics. Shima wondered how long it had been since these girls laughed.

"Do not forget to strap down when the captain makes the announcement," was her parting instruction to Zuri.

"Yes, auntie."

Niyati and Ekaterina echoed "yes, auntie" before lapsing into hysterical giggles.

I guess I have three nieces now. Shima walked to the ladder and climbed to the top level. She found Danae and Vipul on the bridge, running pre-flight.

"Any word from Moniesa?" Shima asked.

"None, sorry." The captain glanced over her shoulder with a sympathetic smile before turning back to the helm.

Shima felt a pang of sadness but made an effort to keep a straight face. "What is the plan for this evening?"

"It'll take an hour and fifteen minutes to reach Foshan," Danae said. "They're an hour ahead of Bangkok, so we'll get a good night's sleep before venturing out."

"Sounds good." Feeling restless, Shima walked next door to the infirmary where she observed Dr. Sorensen for a minute as he supervised Ting's physical therapy.

The helmsman was complaining, as usual, as he struggled with a set of hand weights. "This is too hard!"

"Bring your arms all the way down." The doctor shot Shima a quick smile but kept his focus on Ting's jerky arm movements. "Now slowly raise them straight out to the side."

"I'm tired! I don't want to do this anymore!"

"Shut up, and don't bend your elbows."

Shima retreated and walked past the bridge to reach the galley, where she found Lorina and Phailin securing the drawers in the crew's mess for liftoff.

"I've never boiled eggs in tea." Lorina shot Shima a mischievous grin. "And Axe assumes I know how to make steamed buns with bean-paste filling? Yuck."

"Let's just make oatmeal." Phailin covered a yawn. "Too much work for too early in the morning."

"Do you need any help here?" Shima asked.

Lorina shook her head. "No, we're finished." She glanced at Shima's face. "What's wrong?"

"There is one little boy who should be on board, but we were not able to find him in time."

"We can't save them all." Lorina's tone was gentle. "When I volunteered at the juvenile shelter, I realized I had to focus on the few I could help or I'd go crazy."

"It can be overwhelming," Phailin said.

Shima nodded, although their words didn't buoy her spirits. "Where is Axe?"

Lorina frowned. "Well, she *was* in the engine room, trying to tell Blaze how to do his job until he kicked her out. I think she's in the second port lounge, annoying some of the passengers."

"How is she annoying them?" Shima asked.

"She's been asking them dozens of questions, trying to get an idea of where their homes are, but most of them can't remember. A few of them don't even remember the names of their parents, it's been so long." Lorina shot Phailin a bemused look. "Like I said, Axe is annoying them."

"Did the DNA traces help her locate their families?" Shima asked.

"The DNA helped ISPP match them to family members in specific cities," the cook said, "but the universal database doesn't store complete addresses, since that information often changes. For instance, my DNA would show I'm from Kapaa, Kauai, but that's it.

If I didn't know my mother's name or my street address, it would be tough figuring out where I lived."

Shima felt sorry for Axe. "It is too bad Marco cannot help with the search. Another translator would make things much easier."

"I don't think he'd be willing to help even if he was fully recovered." Phailin's tone was bitter.

Lorina exchanged a helpless glance with Shima. No one knew how to respond to Phailin when she griped about Ting—just like the rest of the crew.

"I guess we should go through the ship and make sure our passengers have strapped down," Shima said.

The other two nodded. "I'll take the third level, portside," Phailin said.

"Third level, starboard." Lorina was already on her way out of the galley.

"I guess I will take the second level." Shima followed her crewmates to the ladder.

In the second level starboard lounge, the first officer found five of the younger children rummaging in the storage bins beneath the window seats. They had gathered a collection of toy cars and baby dolls into the center of the room but were scrounging for more.

She clapped her hands to get their attention and walked over to one of the armchairs facing the holo-vid screen. She pulled out the padded seat belts from the recesses of the chair and showed them how the straps went around her waist and over each shoulder.

"Now you try." Shima gestured to the other chairs, and the youngsters got the idea. They each took a seat and struggled with the straps, laughing at each other's efforts.

Shima glanced at the time. It was 1945, so the strap-down announcement would come at any moment. She got up and made sure each child was properly secured. "Stay." She wagged a warning finger at them, hoping they got the message.

She was on her way down the corridor to the lounge on the port wing when an announcement came over the ship's speakers, but it wasn't the one she'd been expecting.

Danae shouted, "Blaze to the airlock! We have another passenger!"

Shima raced to the ladder and beat the engineer to the entryway by a few seconds. The ship had to lift on schedule or risk a hefty fine, so she pounced on the airlock controls. Blaze slipped by her the moment the inner door cycled open and deactivated the antechamber security barricade.

"Strap down for liftoff." Danae's general announcement made Shima's heart race faster. Axe repeated the announcement in Mandarin for the passengers.

"Lower the staircase!" Shima dashed to the open outer door and looked down at the landing platform.

Officer Diaz was standing below, flanked on each side by a small Chinese boy. He grinned sheepishly and called up to her, "Sorry we're late."

Shima's heart leapt. She recognized Yao, and the other boy looked so much like him, they must have been brothers. "Stand back a few meters."

The collapsible staircase which extended from the *Alex* seemed to move slower than usual, but the instant it touched the platform, Diaz rushed the boys up the steps.

"Thank you!" Shima called to the ISPP's retreating back. She herded the boys into the entryway so Blaze could retract the stairs and seal the airlock again.

"We need to lift in five." Danae's warning alerted Shima to the fact that she needed to get these boys strapped down somewhere.

"Almost there," Blaze coaxed the inner airlock door to cycle faster.

Shima shooed the wide-eyed brothers up the ladder to the second level. She grabbed their hands and made a dash for the port lounge, half dragging them along behind her. "Sit, sit!" She rushed them into two open chairs and strapped them in.

"Thirty seconds to lift," Danae announced.

Shima threw herself into an open seat and strapped in. She couldn't stop smiling at the boys who just stared at her, mouths gaping in shock. "*Ni hao*. Welcome aboard."

PART II
GUANGZHOU

SIXTEEN
FOSHAN REUNION

BLAZE WAS SECRETLY relieved Annalise Tse had work to do which didn't require his assistance. The overbearing ISPP engineer was busy keeping an eye on the prisoner, plus she spent hours poring over maps and a city directory in the captain's office, trying to determine the home addresses for the twelve girls they were returning to their families in Foshan, Guangdong, China.

Once the ship docked at Foshan and the engines were shut down, Blaze wandered around the corridors, assisting his crewmates wherever he saw a need. There was a lot going on aboard *Alex's Legacy*. The young passengers ate like, well, teenagers. They were in and out of the galley all evening.

The kids watched holo-vids, ran up and down the corridors, played on the ladder, and took apart all four lounges. A few times Axe and Ting asked them to settle down—actually, Ting didn't ask, he shouted threats—but the quiet lasted only a few minutes before the volume returned, louder than before. Blaze didn't know how thirty-one kids—Zuri and Ekaterina were enjoying the festivities as well—could make more ruckus than the original one hundred and forty-eight orphans from Mars Station.

Shima attempted to supervise the passengers, but she went easy on them. She was so relaxed, he assumed she'd done some meditating to rejuvenate her calm demeanor. She spent the evening moving her personal belongings back to her cabin on the third level of the port wing.

"Need some help?" he asked when Shima passed him near the ladder. She was carrying some clothes on hangers.

"No, thank you. I do not own much, and these are the last few items." She flashed him a smile and kept walking, humming a cheerful tune he didn't recognize.

Lorina kept a close eye on Niyati, removing her from the festivities promptly at 2100 and putting her to bed with earplugs.

Blaze attempted to be discreet as he observed his other crewmates over the course of the evening. Phailin sequestered herself in the kitchen and went out of her way to avoid Ting whenever he ventured into the galley. Ting spent most of his time in the infirmary so he could work on his physical therapy. Vipul found some earplugs and retreated to his cabin, and Captain Shepherd and Dr. Sorensen spent a lot of time on the bridge, arguing. The arguments were interspersed with periods of mysterious silence.

The first time Blaze's curiosity led him to investigate the silent bridge, he discovered Shepherd and Sorensen communicating in a way that didn't require words. He ducked back into the corridor before they noticed him. However, after walking in on one of their smooching sessions a second time, he thought, *I'll ask Shima when I see her.*

He headed back to his cabin at 2400.

***

The ship was quiet when Blaze awoke, but he was bleary-eyed from trying to sleep through the racket in the lounge closest to his suite. His family enjoyed breakfast together in the empty and messy galley.

After they ate, he took the android from its storage niche beneath the huge kitchen sink and put it to work washing the mountain of dishes left behind by the passengers. He spent several minutes putting food away and wiping the counters while Lorina made a large pot of oatmeal for everyone on the ship.

"How can a few kids make so much noise?" His wife yawned as she set brown sugar and butter out on the counter beside the stacks of bowls.

"Imagine your first real day of freedom after bein' in a prison half your life."

"And knowing you'll be reunited with your family again soon." Lorina nodded.

"Hopefully," Shima added to the discussion as she walked into the galley. "Hopefully we can find their families. There are no guarantees."

"Where Zuri?" Niyati asked.

Shima flashed a sleepy smile. "I do not expect to see her or Ekaterina until noon. I do not know when they went to bed, to be honest." She poured herself a cup of coffee from the crew's mess and sat down beside Niyati, who was working on her second bowl of granola. "Has anyone heard from Axe this morning?"

Blaze tossed the sponge into the sink and wiped his hands dry on the legs of his jeans. "No, and I know we're dependin' on her to organize our excursions. I'm not keen on wanderin' around a strange city without knowin' where we're goin'."

"I wonder if the prisoner wants breakfast now," Lorina said.

Shima scowled. "If she does, I am not taking it to her."

Blaze agreed. "The only person who should be allowed to open the cell door is Axe."

"And only if she is armed," Shima said.

With perfect timing, Officer Tse walked into the galley. A large handgun was secured in a holster beneath her left arm, over her tank top. "I think our guest would like some breakfast." She looked offended when Blaze, Lorina, and Shima burst into laughter.

"We are not laughing at you," Shima was quick to explain. She prepared a cup of green tea at the crew's mess and secured it with a spill-proof lid.

Lorina scooped some steaming oatmeal into a bowl. "Does her majesty want juice?"

"Only if it's lychee," Axe said.

"Sorry, it is not on the menu." Shima pulled a tray out of a lower cabinet and placed the tea, oatmeal, and a spoon on it.

"Is that it?" Axe picked up the tray.

"That is a better meal than most slaves get." There was an edge to Shima's tone.

Axe shrugged, unconcerned. She went to the crew's mess and found a tangerine in the fruit drawer. "For dessert."

"It is more than she deserves."

Blaze was startled at Shima's caustic remarks, but when she paused to scratch the back of her right leg, he remembered Cai was the slaver who ordered her to be tattooed. *Captain Shepherd's not the only one carryin' a grudge.*

"Planning meeting at 0900?" Axe turned to leave the galley with the tray.

"Sounds fine, just let the captain know," Lorina said.

The moment Axe was out of earshot, Blaze said, "Speakin' of the captain . . ."

Shima raised her eyebrows at him as she returned to her seat and sipped her coffee. "What about her?"

"She and Dr. Sorensen . . . ? Blaze prodded.

"They are just friends." Shima hid a smirk behind her cup.

"Friends with benefits?" Lorina asked. "Do I need to cover Niyati's ears for this conversation?"

Shima chuckled. "Their relationship is none of our business."

"It's kinda hard to mind our own business when they're—"

"*Robert,*" Lorina warned, rolling her eyes in the direction of their daughter.

"—not bein' too discreet with their PDA," Blaze concluded with a mischievous grin.

"What PDA?" Niyati asked, intrigued.

"Kissin' where everyone can see you." Blaze demonstrated by blowing a kiss to Lorina, who was glaring at him.

"Oh, ewww," Niyati said. "PDA yucky."

Blaze and Shima laughed until Captain Shepherd and Dr. Sorensen walked in together and Niyati announced, at the top of her lungs, "*Baba* say he see you kissin'— PDA yucky!"

Lorina attempted to cover Niyati's mouth and apologize, but Shepherd's and Sorensen's only reaction was to exchange a bemused grin.

"Don't worry about it, Lorina." The doctor cleared his throat. "Although I'd have to disagree about the yucky part, Niyati."

Captain Shepherd jabbed him in the ribs with her elbow before marching over to the crew's mess. She took her time pouring a cup of coffee and poking around in the bread and fruit drawers. "So . . . is Axe awake?" she asked Shima without turning around.

"Yes, Captain." Her first officer covered her mouth with one hand but was unable to muffle a giggle. "She would like to meet with everyone at 0900."

"I'm sure Marco will be thrilled to have fifteen minutes' notice." Shepherd announced over the com, "All crew members will meet in the galley at 0900."

When she turned away from the crew's mess, her cheeks were still pink. Blaze also noticed that her calm expression morphed into a genuine smile whenever she caught Dr. Sorensen's eye.

They're definitely more than friends.

Marco, Vipul, Phailin, and Axe walked into the galley when it was time for the meeting. Ting complained about the early hour and his lack of sleep, but Shepherd told him, "Shut your mouth, and keep it that way."

"What's the plan for today, Axe?" the captain asked when everyone was seated.

The ISPP officer pulled out a datapad. "Since the Guangdong province was never bombed during the war, Foshan's population is huge. It also covers a large area. The girls are from all five of the city's districts. Even though the spaceport is centrally located, it'll take hours by tram to reach the areas we need to search. I think we should go out in two groups, maybe three crew members to escort two or three girls at a time." She glanced at Ting. "It would help to speed things up if we had two translators."

The helmsman said something in Mandarin that sent Axe into a rage. She was on her feet and shouting back at him in the same language, but Shepherd took control of the situation.

"Enough!" The captain glared at Axe until she was silent and seated before focusing her piercing gaze on Ting. "You will go out with my group, and you will do exactly what I say while we're in Foshan. Do you have a problem with that?"

"Translation services aren't in my job description." Ting sneered.

"Spending a small fortune on medical services for a foul-mouthed, ungrateful helmsman aren't in *mine*," Shepherd countered.

Ting seemed to realize he was treading on thin ice. He gave his boss a defiant look but had nothing more to say.

"Erik and Marco are with me. Blaze, Axe, and Vipul, you'll make up the other team."

Lucky me. Blaze suppressed a sigh with effort.

Captain Shepherd handed Axe her datapad. "We'll need a detailed map."

The ISPP engineer loaded a file, handed the datapad back, and explained as Shepherd studied the screen. "This is the Gaoming district. Jing Ping, Fang, and Ma Pei live within ten kilometers of each other. My group can take Hua and Xiao, who live on opposite sides of the Shunde district. I was able to determine building numbers from the city directory, but not specific apartment numbers."

"How many apartments are in an average buildin'?" Blaze had a feeling he didn't want to hear the answer.

"Between two hundred and five hundred," Axe said.

Even Vipul groaned at her response.

"Well, let's get started," Captain Shepherd said. "Meet in the entryway at 0930 with your passports and pistols. Lorina, Shima, please round up the girls for this first outing."

"Yes, Captain." Lorina took Niyati's hand and left the galley with Shima right behind them.

"How's the weather?" Vipul asked. "What should we wear?"

"Hot," Axe said. "As hot as Bangkok. The Chinese don't care what they wear, so shorts would be practical."

Blaze had just enough time to change into shorts and track shoes, and put together a backpack of essentials. He stepped out of his suite, gave Lorina a goodbye kiss when he passed her and Niyati in the corridor, patted their daughter on the head, and climbed down to the entryway.

Hua and Xiao were already waiting by the airlock, looking sleepy but excited. The young women were still dressed in oversized purple T-shirts. Hua had a White Swan tattoo on the back of her leg. Blaze recalled the attack on Shima and Zuri in Bangkok, and wondered if it would be safer for all of them if they covered Hua's tattoo with a bandage or even a pair of pants.

Vipul and Axe stepped off the ladder, and Blaze asked their opinion on hiding the tattoo.

"Yes, absolutely." Axe took off her backpack, rummaged in it, and pulled out a roll of gauze. She spoke to Hua, who consented to hiding the tattoo. The engineer wrapped Hua's knee, concealing it. "Let's go. Captain Shepherd's team left ten minutes ago, so we're behind schedule."

Blaze kept his mouth shut. *It's gonna to be a long mornin'.*

***

Axe's team caught a tram dirtside at the bottom of the spaceport lift and spent a long hour gazing out the grimy windows of the packed trolley as the city of Foshan crawled by. They changed trams near an outdoor marketplace and spent another hour gazing at scenery.

Hua and Xiao giggled and pointed out landmarks to each other, excited to be back in familiar surroundings. Vipul dozed, and Axe kept her nose in a datapad. Blaze had never been to China before, so he took in all the sights with great interest.

He saw kilometer after kilometer of high-rise apartment buildings with laundry hung out to dry on every balcony. Parks were numerous, and every green space he saw was filled with groups of people practicing *tai chi* or fan dancing. Pedestrians crowded the wide sidewalks, and bicycles clogged the dusty roads. It was common to see an entire family on a solar scooter—a mom or dad driving, a child on his or her lap, and someone sitting behind the driver, sometimes with a dog or, on rare occasions, a *baby* tucked beneath one arm. It was fascinating and horrifying at the same time.

"Next stop, we get off and walk six blocks north," Axe announced.

Hua jabbered excitedly as they disembarked. She pointed to the building in front of the tramstop.

"What's she sayin'?" Blaze asked.

"This was her primary school. She recognizes it." The ISPP officer allowed herself a rare smile. "Hopefully she'll remember the way home from school so we won't have to knock on hundreds of doors."

Blaze hoped so too.

They walked six blocks with Hua confidently leading the way. The ex-slave turned down a trash-strewn alleyway. When they emerged onto the next street, she led them around the corner to the gated entrance of a red-brick building.

"This is it," Axe confirmed, checking the address on her datapad.

Hua spoke to the uniformed doorman stationed behind the caged-in lobby. He frowned and made a call. He then spoke to Hua at length.

Axe translated for Blaze and Vipul. "He said to wait, and that her mother will be right down!"

Five minutes passed before a small woman with short salt-and-pepper hair appeared in the lobby. She rushed to the bars and stared out at the team, her tear-filled eyes coming to rest on Hua. Fortunately, the guard buzzed the doors open, or Blaze thought Hua's mother might have torn them off the hinges with her bare hands.

"*Hua Hua!*"

It was an emotional reunion, and Blaze found himself swallowing a lump in his throat as mother and daughter hugged and sobbed for several minutes. Axe spoke to the mother and was swept into a hug of thanks.

They were drawing a crowd with all the excitement, and Blaze noticed Xiao looking worried and impatient. "I think we should go, Axe. Be sure to tell the mom Hua should keep the tattoo hidden when she's out in public—for her own safety."

Axe pried herself free of the mother's embrace and spoke to her for several minutes. The woman nodded in agreement and kept repeating, "*Xie xie, xie xie*," to each of them.

"Let's go." Axe consulted her datapad. "Four blocks east; then we catch a southbound tram."

Blaze, Vipul, Axe, and Xiao said goodbye to Hua and were able to slip away without too much fuss.

The team changed trams twice, riding for another hour before reaching Xiao's rundown apartment building. It didn't have a gated lobby or a doorman, so Axe and Xiao pored over the directory in the dilapidated mail room.

"They rarely update the names on the boxes," the ISPP officer complained, "but I think it's this one." She pointed to the Chinese characters beside 2416.

They rode a rickety elevator up to the twenty-fourth floor and found apartment 16. Xiao gave a happy nod of recognition and knocked on the door. There was no answer.

"Everyone's probably at work," Blaze said. "I guess we'll have to wait until someone gets home."

"In China, most people go home to eat lunch and take a nap, then go back to work until late in the evening." Axe spoke to Xiao and got a nod and a short response. "She says her parents always went home for lunch, so they should be here any minute."

If this is the right apartment. Blaze wasn't enthused about this needle-in-a-haystack search technique, but he knew their efforts were crucial to getting these children returned to their families.

They waited for half an hour, leaning against the walls or sitting on the white-tiled floor. Several people passed the team in the hallway, walking to or from their apartments. Blaze hoped one of the gawking neighbors would recognize Xiao, but no one said a word.

"I'm sure she's changed a lot in seven years," Vipul said, guessing his thoughts.

"I just pray they still live here after seven years."

"Housing is scarce in China," Axe said. "Most people are forced to stay put once they find a place to live. Sometimes the same family keeps an apartment for generations, so the odds are good Xiao's parents still live here."

He was about to suggest they go downstairs and watch the lobby for Xiao's parents in case the team was in the wrong place when the elevator doors opened. A middle-aged couple walked toward the team, their guarded expressions turning to incredulous joy as they recognized Xiao.

Xiao sprang to her feet. *"Mama! Baba!"* She ran to meet them.

It was another emotional reunion with two adults sobbing over their long-missing daughter.

Xiao's parents invited the team into the tiny, cluttered apartment for tea, but Blaze hovered just inside the doorway, reluctant to sit down. The family was shedding so many tears, he felt like an intruder at a private ceremony. "They'd probably like to be alone, Axe."

The ISPP engineer spoke to the parents at length, explaining the team needed to go back to the spaceport. Xiao's parents kept offering them food, but Blaze shook his head as he and Vipul slipped out the door. Axe extricated herself from the grateful parents' clutches, and the team headed to the lift.

"Here." Axe had three exquisitely detailed, royal blue cloisonné teacups in her hands. She gave one each to Blaze and Vipul. "They insisted. They wanted to give us something as thanks, so I thought it would be rude to refuse."

The *Alex*'s engineer shrugged, seeing no practical use for the ornate cup. "Niyati might like it."

"These are probably the most valuable items the family owned," Vipul said.

Blaze shook his head. "We just gave them back their greatest treasure."

***

It was close to 1600 when Blaze, Vipul, and Axe returned to *Alex's Legacy*.

"How did it go?" Lorina asked when Blaze located her in the galley. She was taking homemade cookies out of the oven for Niyati and the guest passengers.

"It was . . . very movin'." He helped himself to a warm chocolate chip cookie. "I'm glad I got to experience it, even if my butt is worn out from ridin' trams all day."

Niyati giggled. "*Baba* butt hurt."

Lorina rolled her eyes at Blaze as a reminder not to teach Niyati words they didn't want her to use in public.

"And I guess we'll have to head out again tomorrow to return the other girls. Is the captain back yet?"

"No, they had some delays—some issues with Ting."

Blaze raised an eyebrow at her. "What kind of issues?"

"He was being an uncooperative little tyrant. He claimed he was too tired to walk to the tramstop after they returned Ma Pei to her grandmother. Captain Shepherd was so mad she threatened to leave him on the side of the road, but Erik found a shop that sells wheelchairs. The girls took turns pushing him, and the doctor taught them how to say *old man* in English. They called Ting *old man* until they were returned to their families."

Blaze laughed. "Somethin' tells me Ting'll refuse to leave the ship tomorrow."

"I think the captain will tie him to the wheelchair if he does."

"Were they able to find the girls' families?"

Lorina nodded.

"Good. Five down, seven to go." Blaze wondered if they'd have an easy time returning the other seven, but he was more concerned about what they would face in Guangzhou once the children were all reunited with their families.

***

The passengers were too tired to party that evening, so Blaze was able to get a good night's sleep. He left the ship with Vipul, Axe, and five of the girls at 0700 the next morning. Axe was hopeful they could cover two of the districts so *Alex's Legacy* wouldn't have to remain in Foshan another day.

Blaze came prepared with something to read on his datapad this time, although he looked out the window often, just in case the scenery changed—it never did.

By noon they had returned three of the ex-slaves to their families in the Sanshui district. They stopped to eat a spicy noodle soup at a little hole-in-the-wall restaurant. Blaze was grateful to be with someone who could read the menu. He was also grateful to have a ceramic spoon to eat with since his chopstick skills were pathetic.

Three hours and four tram transfers later, they reached the Nanhai district. The last two girls lived only four blocks from each other, and both were reunited with their parents.

Four hours later, the team was back aboard the *Alex*. "It'd be great if someone else could search for families in Guangzhou," Blaze told Vipul as they climbed the ladder to the galley for some dinner.

"That would be my vote. Too bad no one else speaks Mandarin."

"We lift at 2000," Phailin informed them as she handed out plates of lemon beef salad at the long counter.

Blaze inhaled his dinner and headed down to the engine room for the short flight. Basically, the ship would lift, fly five minutes, and dock again at the Guangzhou spaceport.

Next stop, Maui. But he couldn't shake the nagging feeling that things wouldn't go as smoothly in the huge province capital as they had in Foshan.

SEVENTEEN
VULNERABILITY

ERIK CAUGHT UP with Officer Tse as she stepped into the starboard lift. She was heading down to the basement with a breakfast tray for the prisoner. "Mind if I tag along?"

Axe shrugged. "She hasn't told me where to search on Shamian Island, if that's what you're wondering. Actually, she hasn't said anything that should be repeated in civilized company."

"York insisted she could lead us to the White Swan." Erik felt a spark of anger as he recalled the last unsatisfactory confrontation with the ISPP captain when he'd delivered Cai to their custody. "Since we're not going to let her out of the brig, she has to tell us where to search."

"Ghukasyan and Moniesa can get prisoners to talk. I'm just an engineer. I have some influence over machines, not people."

"How did Moniesa get her to talk?"

Axe hesitated. "That's confidential. Let's just say Cai thought confessing would be easier than losing some fingers."

Erik grimaced. Inflicting pain wasn't an option for someone who took an oath to *first, do no harm*. "Maybe you could find something in your toolbox to persuade her?"

They stepped into the basement corridor and walked down to the brig.

"Does your girlfriend, Captain Shepherd, know you want me to torture the prisoner for information?"

"She's not my girlfriend." Actually, Erik wasn't sure what term he would use to refer to Danae if he had to introduce her to someone. Their relationship had evolved so fast that *girlfriend/boyfriend* didn't describe it.

The engineer smirked. "If you say so, but you didn't answer my question." She glanced through the glass to make certain Cai wasn't near the door before pressing her thumb to the ID lock.

The slaver was lying on her bunk, staring at the ceiling. She barely glanced at Axe as the ISPP officer set the breakfast tray on the floor and thumbed the lock again to close the door.

"Captain Shepherd doesn't know I'm here," Erik admitted." Could I talk to Cai?"

"What do you want me to ask her?" Axe turned to the door controls and pressed the intercom button.

"Ask her if she's ever been to White Swan's headquarters."

Axe asked.

Cai stared at them through the glass as she sipped her tea with an arrogant smirk on her round face. It was obvious she wasn't going to answer the question.

"Ask her how long she's been involved with the mafia."

The ISPP officer rolled her eyes at his persistence, but she asked.

The edges of Cai's mouth slowly moved upward, forming an evil little smile. She said something that made Axe wince.

"I can't repeat that in English."

Erik wasn't ready to give up. "Ask her if she'd be willing to show us White Swan's headquarters on the map in exchange for some privileges."

"Privileges?" Axe glanced at him with suspicion. "You can't promise her any favors."

"Just. Ask."

Cai did have something to say in response to this question. She spoke animatedly for a minute, banging her fist on the glass for emphasis.

Axe turned to Erik. "She says she can only take us to their headquarters in person. It's not on any map. She'd be willing to do that in exchange for her freedom."

"She's lying. Look at that face. The woman has no soul. She used to arrange assassinations, and who knows how many children's lives she's destroyed? She knows we're not going to release her."

"Are we through here?" Axe turned off the intercom. "I told you she wouldn't talk. This is a waste of time."

Erik was beginning to understand why Blaze didn't like working with Officer Tse. "The point is there's no reason for her to be here if she refuses to give us any information. You've got to keep asking questions—wear her down."

Axe headed down the hallway toward the ladder. "And how many prisoners have *you* interrogated?" she said over her shoulder.

"None," he called after her, "but I've been a prisoner before. I've been tortured. I know what it's like to spend a month in solitary confinement."

Axe turned around to gape at him. "You've been tortured?"

"We have to figure out what makes her feel vulnerable." Erik tried to reason with the skeptical ISPP. "Everyone's got a weakness. Once we know hers, we can use it as leverage to make her talk."

"Did they find your weakness? Did they break you?" Axe asked with morbid interest.

Erik was reticent to unlock that memory. "Yes . . . Acheron figured out my weakness. But he didn't break me. He came close though. Very close." He shut his eyes. "Another day, maybe just another hour in solitary would've done it."

"I'll keep working on her." There was newfound respect in Axe's tone. "Every chance I get, I'll try to make her talk."

"Thank you." Erik waited until the engineer was ascending the ladder before opening his eyes. He was cold but had to wipe his sweaty palms dry on the legs of his scrubs. When he felt in control of his emotions, he turned around to face the prisoner again.

Cai was still watching him through the glass, gloating at his obvious frustration. Erik wished he knew a few words of Mandarin so he could tell her off.

He settled for giving her a cold look before turning his back to her and heading to the ladder—only to meet Danae on her way down.

She stepped off the rungs and turned to him with a suspicious frown. "Going somewhere?"

"I could ask you the same thing. You're not here to see the prisoner, are you?"

Danae's hands settled on her hips. "Do you want to tell me why I passed Axe in the entryway?"

"I convinced her to ask Cai a few questions." Erik wrestled with his guilty conscience. "All right, let me save myself some grief and admit I was trying to run interference for you."

"After everything you said about not confronting her, you took it upon yourself to question her anyway?" Danae was furious, as he knew she would be.

"I was worried about your emotional state. I thought if I could get her to talk, it would save you a lot of anxiety."

"Yes, I know what *interference* means. Haven't you learned by now I can take care of myself?" Danae switched gears, from furious to curious. "So? Did she say anything helpful?"

"It was a waste of time. We need Moniesa here to loosen her tongue." Erik went on the offensive. "She refused to answer any questions, and you haven't answered my question: what are you doing here?"

He expected more defensiveness, but Danae appeared to have run out of steam. Her shoulders sagged, and she lowered her gaze to somewhere around his Adam's apple. "I'm not sure why I'm here. Having her on board has been eating away at me. It's so frustrating to be this close to the answers I need about Dad's murder and to know she'll never disclose them. You were right about allowing her on the ship—it was a mistake."

Erik bit his tongue to hold back an "I told you so." He tried to appear empathetic and nodded, urging her to continue.

"There's no way I can exact justice on the Baronowskis vicariously through Cai. Taking my frustrations out on her isn't going to help me feel vindicated." Her voice dropped to a whisper. "And it won't bring my father back."

Erik reached over and lifted Danae's chin so she could look him in the eye. "I don't know why I'm here either. I thought asking her a few questions wouldn't be a problem since I'm not as emotionally invested in the answers. But the experience was . . . unsettling. It reminded me too much of my stay in Acheron's prison."

Danae stepped forward and wrapped her arms around his waist. "Maybe Axe can pry some information out of Cai, in time, but it sounds like you and I need to stay away from her."

He nodded and kneaded her stiff shoulders. "I will if you will."

"I will, because I need to." She gave him a squeeze. "Let's keep in mind Cai's a temporary passenger. I figure we'll be out of here in four or five days, and she definitely won't be coming with us to Maui."

Erik wished he could siphon a portion of her confidence. "Four or five days? Did Ting predict that time-frame?"

Danae frowned. "Now that I think of it, Marco hasn't threatened us with any premonitions since he came out of the coma. I'm hoping the trend will continue."

"Hmmm." The doctor didn't want to think about Ting. He'd spent an entire week with the obnoxious helmsman and came to the conclusion he liked Ting better when he was comatose. Erik didn't want to admit he needed a break from the verbal abuse, especially since Danae never took a break from her own responsibilities.

She had the uncanny ability to guess his thoughts, even when she wasn't giving him *the look*. "Stay here today. I'll mix up the teams for some variety. Maybe Vipul and Axe could go with me. Blaze and Shima can deal with Marco. Have you had anything to eat?"

Erik was amazed at how fast she changed the subject. "I was on my way to breakfast when I took . . . this detour."

"The basement's not on the way to the galley." She gave him a mischievous grin before turning around and heading up the ladder.

Erik ascended after her. He tried not to gawk at her long legs above him on the rungs as they climbed, but it was a challenge.

The galley was deserted. Danae walked over to the counter, took a plate, and filled it from the assortment of muffins and fruit Phailin set out. When she turned around to offer Erik a plate, he picked her up by the waist and sat her on the counter. She was now at the perfect height for kissing.

"Wouldn't it be easier to sit at a table?" Danae set the plates down on either side, freeing up her hands so she could drape them over his shoulders.

"Instead of giving me the day off, here's a better idea: Vipul and Lorina could go with Axe, Blaze and Shima could go with Ting, and *you* could stay here with *me*."

"That sounds tempting, if you don't mind babysitting Niyati all day."

He couldn't think of a response so he tried some nonverbal persuasion. It lasted for all of five seconds before Ting walked in.

"Can't you two take the slobber-fest somewhere private?"

Erik winked at Danae and glanced at Ting over his shoulder. "What's the matter? Are you jealous?"

Ting snorted. "Jealous of two thirty-somethings who think they're teenagers at a drive-in movie?"

"At a what?" Erik asked.

"Check a history book." The helmsman smirked and went to the crew's mess for coffee. "Don't we need to go into the city so we can take these brats home?"

Erik had a sharp retort ready, but before he could open his mouth, he found it blocked by a small hand.

"Let me handle this." Danae hopped down from the counter and walked up behind Ting with her hands on her hips. "I'll give you a choice today. You can go into Guangzhou with Vipul and Lorina—"

"No!" Ting spun to face her, spilling half his coffee on the floor. "I'm not going anywhere with Murphy!"

"—or you can go into the city with Blaze and Shima." Danae folded her arms, boring a hole through him with her intimidating glare. "Either way, you're going dirtside and translating for one of the teams."

"That's not much of a choice!"

"Too bad."

Ting scowled in defeat. "When's Smith leaving?"

"In ten minutes."

Ting gulped his remaining coffee and brushed past Danae, exiting the galley.

"You need to clean up this mess!" she shouted after him, but Ting was already gone.

Erik grabbed a handful of napkins and went over to help her sponge up the spill. "So Vipul, Lorina, and Axe are on the other team?"

"No, it'll be Vipul, Axe, and me," Danae straightened up, her hands full of soggy napkins, and looked Erik in the eye. "Lorina told me she doesn't want Niyati left with anyone except her or Blaze for more than a few minutes."

Erik sighed. "I forgot about her PTSD. Why don't I go in Vipul's place?"

Danae tossed him a stern look over her shoulder as she deposited the napkins in the recycler. "Maybe tomorrow. You're off duty today—captain's orders. Do you have a problem with that?"

Erik was tempted to say something mushy about missing her but instead returned the stern look when she turned around to face him. "Promise me you'll be careful."

Danae whipped out her pistol, ejected the magazine, and reloaded it in one fluid motion. "I never go looking for trouble, but it always seems to find me." She slipped the Excalibur back into the cargo pocket of her shorts. "I'll be as careful as circumstances allow."

Erik wasn't satisfied with her answer, but he didn't get a chance to respond before she went up on tiptoes to give him a goodbye kiss.

"I can promise to see you tonight." She flashed him a smile and left the galley.

He watched Danae leave, thinking *déjà vu*. It was the same feeling he had when he watched her ride off on the back of York's solar cycle, hanging on for dear life.

And we know how that little excursion turned out.

"Dr. Sorensen to the bridge." Lorina's voice came over the shipboard com.

Erik closed the door to the surgery's refrigerator, where was checking the expiration dates on the synthblood supplies. "Please call me Erik, like you always have."

"The rest of the crew calls you doctor. I'm just trying to be consistent."

He walked next door to the bridge and responded in person. "If you want consistency, have everyone call me Erik. What's up?"

Lorina was sitting at the com with Niyati on her lap. "Transmission from Jake. Want to view it with me?"

"Yes, please." Erik looked over her shoulder at the screen.

Jake O'Brien's holographic image grinned back at them. "This transmission is intended for the crew of the passenger ship, *Alex's Legacy*, docked at Guangzhou, Guangdong, China, and was recorded on December fifth."

"Jek." Niyati giggled.

Lorina's cousin ran a hand through his dark crew cut, finishing the move with an awkward wave. "Hey, Lorina, Blaze, Niyati. I wanted to give Captain Shepherd a status update. Things are going well here at The Lost Sheep. Grey's placed twenty-five kids with families on Oahu, and we're processing applications for thirty-six more. At this rate, we expect the orphanage to be empty by the end of the year, although I have a feeling we won't have an empty house for long—right, Lorina?"

"What's that supposed to mean? He acts like I go around collecting orphans."

Erik laughed. "Well, we did pick up a few in Bangkok."

Jake continued, "I went to Oahu with Grey last trip, and one of the parents we placed a child with is a surgeon at Waikiki General Hospital. Long story short— she called in some favors and offered me a residency. I could be licensed in as little as three years if I accept."

Erik whistled. "Well done, Jake."

The apprentice medic looked pleased and a little worried. "Obviously I can't hold down two jobs on two different islands. I know you need me here at the orphanage, Captain, but I'd be a fool to pass up this opportunity. Please let me know if I should hire a director, or if the *Alex* plans to return to Maui soon so someone on the crew could take over as director. O'Brien out."

The screen went blank.

"It sounds like we need to head back to Maui as soon as possible," Erik said.

Lorina nodded and set Niyati on her feet. "That sounds good to me. I wish we could skip Shamian Island and leave ASAP."

"So do I. How are the passengers behaving this morning?"

Lorina got to her feet and turned around to face him. "Eight of them left with the teams this morning, so that leaves only nine. Believe it or not, they're confining their mess to one lounge. The girls are playing cards, and the boys are busy with Legos. It's been pretty calm."

"Good. Thanks for asking me to view the transmission."

"You're welcome." Lorina took Niyati's hand and headed to the door. "I was just about to make some sandwiches for lunch. Do you want to join me?"

"If you really mean, 'Do you want to help me?' then the answer is yes."

In the galley kitchen, Lorina took two loaves of bread and a jar of peanut butter from the pantry. "Could you get the jelly from the fridge?"

They formed an impromptu assembly line at the counter. Lorina spread the peanut butter, Erik wrestled with the grape jelly, and Niyati put the halves together and set the finished sandwiches on a platter.

"Do Chinese kids like these?" The doctor tried to keep a glob of jelly on the slice of bread. He scraped it off the counter with his knife and tried again.

"They'll eat anything. I don't know what or how often they ate as slaves, but their eyes sure light up at mealtimes around here."

"I know how they feel. You wouldn't know it by looking at me"—Erik patted his stomach for emphasis—"but I remember what it's like to be hungry all the time and to wonder where the next meal is coming from."

"That's why Jake always fed the homeless kids on Mars. He couldn't bear to see them suffer for something so easy to remedy."

"I fed them for the first year at the Outreach Clinic, but then I couldn't afford to feed myself. I started sending them to Mother Teresa's so Kirsten could feed them—since she actually had a food budget from her sponsors."

Lorina paused to count the sandwiches on the platter. "Fourteen, but we should make some extras. Good job, honey," she told Niyati. "Can you go see how many apples are in the crew's mess?"

"Yes, *amma*."

When her daughter was on the other side of the galley, Lorina cleared her throat and set her knife on the edge of the peanut butter jar. "So what's the deal with you and the captain?"

Erik laughed and set his sticky jelly knife on the counter. "I knew you made up an excuse to get Niyati out of hearing range. What about us?"

"You seem to"—Lorina snorted, trying to hold back a laugh of her own—"really like each other."

He shrugged, embarrassed. "I'll be honest with you—I'm worried things are moving too fast. I was hoping to create some sparks, not start a fire that's going to burn itself out in a hurry."

"Leaving you with just a handful of ashes?" Lorina asked.

"I'm more concerned about leaving Danae with a handful of ashes. She's been through so much, and I think she's still grieving. I wonder if I've inadvertently cast myself into the role of convenient emotional crutch."

"So you're afraid she sees you as just a warm body to snuggle or a shoulder to cry on?"

"Exactly, except Danae doesn't cry—not much, anyway."

Lorina pursed her lips. "She's not shy about expressing other emotions though."

"I don't mind her temper." Far from minding it, Erik found Danae's spicy side rather attractive, but he didn't plan to confess everything to Lorina. "She keeps it under control most of the time."

"If you know her so well, what's the problem? Are you just feeling insecure? Do you need some advice on women?"

Erik sighed. "Yes, because I'm an idiot when it comes to understanding women. My last two relationships are proof of that."

"Did they want a commitment?" Lorina guessed on the first try.

"Yes, and no. They wanted a trial run *before* the commitment, but I think that's a surefire way to ruin a good relationship. Plus there was the major issue of my limited and sometimes nonexistent income, due to my focus on the homeless. Don't get me wrong—they were both nice, intelligent, attractive women, but they couldn't be satisfied with me unless I was willing to change, and I can be awfully stubborn, if you haven't noticed."

"I didn't know that about you." Lorina grinned. "I've definitely noticed your stubborn streak, but I've got to say I admire you for sticking to your convictions. You sound a lot like Blaze."

"Now it's ironic I'm in a . . . I'm not sure what to call this . . . a *relationship* where I'm willing to change anything if it'll make Danae happy."

Lorina looked astonished. "Really?"

"Yes, really." Erik scratched the stubble on his chin, lost in thought for a moment. "I'm afraid I'll look weak if I'm so eager to please, like a dog that'll chase a stick over and over, anything for 'good boy' and a pat on the head."

"Nice analogy, doctor, but you're not weak. I've never seen a hint of physical or emotional weakness in you, so give yourself some credit. You don't have to act tough to impress Captain Shepherd. Couples who are compatible tend to balance each other's strengths and weaknesses. It's fine to want to make her happy if she's willing to do the same for you."

Erik was frustrated the discussion had come full circle. "But I don't know how she feels about me, and I'm afraid to ask."

"So you're feeling vulnerable—it's normal."

He frowned, thinking. "Yes, vulnerable, and scared of doing something stupid that'll make me lose her."

"I think Blaze went through all the emotions you're describing. You should ask him for some advice."

"I will when I get a chance." Erik glanced over at the crew's mess where Niyati was digging apples out of the fruit drawer and sorting them by color. "How did you react when Blaze proposed, after only knowing him for three days?"

"How did I feel about being swept off my feet by the first man I'd ever kissed?"

Erik looked askance at her. "You're kidding."

"It's true." Lorina laughed. "When Blaze dropped the bombshell, I could've done the logical thing by running the other way, but I didn't . . . because it felt right. Once I got past the initial panic, I realized I had to make a decision with my heart, not my head. I knew I'd talk myself out of it if I listened to my logic, and I'd probably regret it for the rest of my life if I was too scared to take a leap of faith.

"I know men are more logical than women. Maybe that's why some men are so afraid of commitment. They have to put faith in their *feelings* instead of their familiar old friend logic."

She paused, a dreamy smile on her face. "I had no problem letting go of logic because I *loved* being swept off my feet. I think most women go weak in the knees at any type of romantic gesture."

Erik raised an eyebrow at her. "Most women?"

"I'm serious. This is one stereotype that's accurate. Flowers, candlelit dinners, slow dancing. Just turn on the charm, and she'll be the one fetching sticks for you."

He laughed. "I don't think Danae quite fits the golden retriever mold, but I'll keep that in mind."

"So here's my advice: continue with the whirlwind romance. You don't have to make any changes, just let her get to know the real you—the whole package. Don't exaggerate your strengths and don't try to hide your weaknesses."

"You make it sound easy."

"It *is* easy if you don't overthink it with endless what-if scenarios. Dump the logic, doctor and listen to your feelings, not your insecurities."

Erik sighed. "Dump the logic? Thank you, I'll give it a try."

"Good. Now let's summon the gang to lunch before the sandwiches get stale."

EIGHTEEN
SHAMIAN ISLAND

DANAE COULDN'T SEE any difference between Foshan and Guangzhou. The trams were equally dirty, crowded, and stuffy. The scenery was the same: kilometer after kilometer of apartment buildings, open-air markets, and parks. The adults—very few children, as was the case in most cities—were doing the same things, going through the motions of their daily routines. Axe even mentioned Foshan and Guangzhou overlapped—they were the same city.

"Do you ever miss China?" she asked Axe, who had been gazing out the window for several minutes.

"I've never lived here, and I've visited enough times to know I'd never want to live here." Axe turned back to her datapad. "Meng's apartment should be coming up in three more stops."

The four young women they were returning to their families had formed a bond aboard the *Alex*. They sat together on the long bench at the back of the tram and held hands, looking excited and apprehensive as they chattered nonstop.

Axe noticed Danae kept glancing over at the ex-slaves. "They're worried they'll lose touch with each other. Meng thinks they'll need each other for moral support as they transition back to normal life."

"I agree. She's a wise girl. I wish I had some paper so they could write down each other's addresses."

Vipul, overhearing the conversation from the seat behind them, searched his backpack and produced a piece of paper and a pencil. He tore the paper into four sections and handed it to Axe.

The engineer wrote down the same information four times and gave the scraps of paper to the young women.

"*Xie xie.*" Meng blinked back a few tears.

"This is our stop." Axe got to her feet and ushered the group off the tram.

Danae was relieved at how easily the girls were returned to their families. Despite Erik's concerns, no one was rejected, none of the families moved away, and none of the girls were orphaned while they were slaves. Her team spent only two hours escorting them home, despite the immense size of Guangzhou.

"At this rate we should have them all returned to their families by tomorrow." Danae sat beside Axe on the crowded tram back to the spaceport with Vipul holding the overhead bar near their seat.

The engineer didn't look up from her datapad. "Canal Street."

"Is that near the spaceport?" Vipul asked.

Axe didn't seem to hear him as she turned her head to look out the window. "There's the Pearl River."

Danae and Vipul gazed out at the wide expanse of silvery-brown water as the tram crossed over a bridge.

"Let's get off at the next stop." The ISPP officer didn't offer any explanation. She herded Danae and Vipul down the aisle to the door.

They disembarked in front of an ornate pedestrian bridge which arched over a narrow canal. Danae felt a tremor of fear as she looked across the bridge at the shady, tree-lined streets and old cream-colored brick buildings that would have appeared more at home on the streets of Paris.

"This is Shamian Island." She turned to glare at Axe. "We shouldn't be here."

"But we shouldn't waste the opportunity. Since the island is only three hundred by nine hundred meters, it would only take us a few minutes to walk the perimeter."

"We shouldn't be here without the rest of the crew."

Axe headed across the bridge. "It's fine; it's the middle of the day. Let's just take a quick look around. There are plenty of other tourists here. No one will notice us." She glanced over her shoulder at Danae. "No one will notice us unless you stand there like a deer in headlights."

"Captain?" Vipul was at her elbow. "Should we go back to the tram?"

Danae blew out a breath she didn't realize she was holding. "We might as well take a look while we're here." She forced her feet to move forward.

On the other side of the bridge, they crossed a narrow street and stepped onto a wide sidewalk. Axe turned right and led the way, walking at a leisurely pace.

Danae wondered if a Chinese-American woman, an Indian-British man, and a Caucasian-Martian woman would raise any eyebrows. They were too few to be a tour group, but they obviously weren't a family unit.

On impulse, she slipped her arm through Vipul's and whispered, "We should act like a couple. Pretend you're my husband."

"I'm flattered you'd choose me for such an honor," Vipul whispered back. "But don't you think your boyfriend will be jealous?"

"Erik's not my boyfriend." The response was automatic, but it forced her to give the question some thought. *Are we "just friends" with benefits, are we testing the waters to see if this will lead to something serious, or is this just a shipboard fling, like the last few guys I dated before Alex joined the crew?*

She chided herself for being so shallow. *I don't have flings anymore. I'm a grown woman. I was married for six years. I'd still be happily married if . . .* she forced herself to shelve that thought.

"My apologies." The navigator chuckled. "Who is he, then, if not your boyfriend?"

"I haven't figured that out yet." Danae forced a loud laugh, as if Vipul said something hilarious.

Axe turned back to give her a questioning look.

"Keep walking like you know where you're going," Danae said. "You're our tour guide."

The engineer nodded and walked on. As they pretended to tour the island, Axe occasionally stopped and pointed out an architectural detail on a building. Vipul and Danae feigned interest.

The navigator gave a superb performance, looking over at Danae often with a smile on his thin brown face. He walked in step with her and let her go first when they traversed narrow areas between trees or other pedestrians. He held her hand when they crossed the street after each block, even though there were few vehicles on the island.

"You're a natural at this," Danae whispered as they stopped to watch two tour boats pass by on the river.

"I was married once, a long time ago."

"I didn't know that," Danae said. "I guess there's a lot I don't know about you."

Vipul didn't respond. He pulled out his datapad and took a few holograms of the river. "Like a real tourist," he said.

"Good idea." Danae kept her eyes peeled for anything unusual as the team continued to stroll around Shamian Island. She didn't know what she expected to find. *A clearly marked brothel? A sign with a picture of a white swan? An armed guard in front of one of the buildings?* So far everything seemed innocuous.

They passed the ruins of an old church, a few hotels and restaurants, some nondescript shops selling souvenirs like silk fans and calligraphy scrolls, and a small park where a few people were playing badminton. Danae found it odd that, compared to the crowded streets of Guangzhou, there were few people on the island. She also observed there were no CIPs in patrol cars or on foot.

"Have you noticed the word *swan* in any of the Chinese characters on the street signs or buildings?" Danae asked Axe as they paused at another scenic spot on the riverfront.

"Just one."

The captain was startled she hadn't mentioned this before. "Where?"

Axe pointed a few meters off to their left, to a small informational sign facing the river. "This is the site where the White Swan Hotel used to stand. That's all it says."

Danae studied the sign's neat calligraphy. "So the only White Swan we've seen here no longer exists?"

"It appears that way," Axe said, "but we didn't look inside any of the buildings."

"And we're not going to," Danae said, frowning.

"We should get back to the ship," Vipul said.

"I agree. Axe, we'll have to come back with the entire crew to do a more thorough search."

The ISPP engineer led the way back to Canal Street. "We need to come back tomorrow with my surveillance scanner. It will help us locate any high-security areas."

"No, what we *need* is for Cai to tell us exactly where to look," Danae said irritably. "So far she's been useless."

Axe stopped and turned back to speak to them in a hushed voice. "I'll bet she'd lead us to the White Swan if we let her go."

"What, are you insane?" Danae said. "We're not letting her go. Even if we did, she's not going to lead us anywhere."

"She would if she didn't know we were following her." Axe flashed a conspiratorial grin. "A personal transmitter could easily be hidden inside her clothing while she's in the shower."

"She's clever. You'd have a hard time convincing her the release was legit," Vipul said.

"Well, what if instead of letting her go, we let her figure out a way to escape—with a little help from us, of course?" The engineer was bouncing up and down on her heels.

Danae didn't want to burst Axe's bubble, but she had strong reservations about both ideas. "We're not trained to deal with criminals in any capacity. Even if Cai was convinced she hadn't been set up to escape, I wouldn't trust her to lead us to her bosses. For all we know, she could be on the next flight back to Bangkok, and then we'd have to explain to Cade why we let a dangerous slaver go free."

"Even if she did lead us straight to her bosses," Vipul added with a note of caution, "we'd be fools to confront them. Erik is right—this should be a military mission. We have no business spying on criminals."

Axe was impatient. "Let's not dismiss the idea until we've had time to think about it."

Danae frowned. "I've thought about it, and I say no."

"But, Captain—"

"Let's go back to the ship," Danae interrupted. "If you want to let Cai escape so you can track her to the White Swan, you'll have to wait until ISPP gets here."

Axe looked as though she wanted to argue some more but turned on her heel instead and began to walk at a brisk pace, leading them back to the tramstop.

Danae took Vipul's arm, and they resumed a leisurely walk, trying to appear less conspicuous than their pretend guide who was stomping down the sidewalk like a petulant teenager. Danae wanted to shout at Axe to stop acting like an idiot, but she didn't want to draw attention to the team.

When they reached the pedestrian bridge where Axe was waiting impatiently for them on the other side, Danae paused and looked around, an uneasy feeling settling over her.

"Is something wrong, Captain?" Vipul murmured in her ear.

"No," she lied. She didn't mention the hairs standing up on the back of her neck. *I think we're being watched.*

***

"I hope your day was better than mine." Danae settled into the chair across the table from Erik and took a sip of her chamomile tea. They were alone in the galley except for the android washing up the dinner dishes, and "Charlie" wasn't programmed to eavesdrop.

"Was there a problem returning one of the kids?" Erik pushed aside his empty soup bowl and reached across the table for her free hand.

Danae didn't know how he would react, so she just went ahead and told him. "Axe, Vipul, and I walked around Shamian Island."

"What?" Erik let go of her hand. "Why would you do that? Did you let anyone know you were going? Did you have any backup arranged?" He kept his tone even but his face reflected strong disapproval.

Danae retrieved his hand with both of hers. "It was Axe's idea. Our tram took us right by the island, and she pressured us to get off and take a look."

At his skeptical frown, she dove into more detail. "There was *nothing* there, Erik. We walked around but didn't see anything out of the ordinary. It's quiet, not much foot traffic—"

"No CIP presence?"

Her mouth fell open. "How did you know?"

"Because a small, innocent-looking spot like Shamian that's right on the river would be perfect for a trafficking organization. Since it's off the beaten path, it would be easy to bribe the CIPs to ignore the area. Remember why the factories in Bangkok were on the river."

"Easy and discreet access." Danae nodded. "That means we won't visit it at night, under any circumstances, right?" She hoped asking for his approval would soften his scowl.

"I can't believe you went there at all, even if it was in broad daylight." Erik leaned halfway across the table so his face was just a few decimeters from hers. "You promised me you wouldn't take any chances. You don't consider your little excursion today a serious breach of trust?"

Whew! He sure knows the direct route to my conscience! "I wish you'd been there with me. I'm sure I'd have felt safer."

Erik shook his head. "I *offered* to go. And that's not going to work with me—stop it with the lost-puppy look. I'm not naïve enough to believe you needed me there for protection"—he gave her a searching look—"unless there's something you're not telling me."

Danae squirmed, but confessed. "I felt like we were being watched."

His disappointed look turned into a full scowl. "The whole time you were on the island?"

"No, just in one little area."

"Then we'll be extra vigilant around that area tomorrow, after we get the rest of the kids returned home. We'll *all* visit the island—the entire crew, in the daytime—so we can provide York with the location he needs for target practice. And then we're out of here, whether we learn anything about the Baronowskis or not. Agreed?"

Danae leaned across the table to meet him halfway. "Yes, agreed."

Judging by the way he kissed her, she felt confident all was forgiven.

NINETEEN
BAIT

"YOU WANT ME to walk around Shamian Island in shorts? You think the traffickers will reveal themselves when they see my tattoo?" Shima glared at Axe across the basement corridor where they were standing outside the brig. Shima had brought down Cai's dinner tray and planned to go straight back to the galley after she handed it over to Axe.

Cai watched them with interest through the glass, even though she couldn't hear what they were saying.

Shima avoided the madam's malevolent gaze. "I think it would be safer to let her escape. Yes, your first idea was a much better plan."

"You'll be wearing a transmitter," Axe persisted. "We'll be covering you from every direction."

"I was wearing a transmitter when I was abducted at the factory! It did not keep me safe!"

"We'll go in the middle of the day. Just one lap around the island, and if anyone approaches you, I'll arrest them before they get within five meters of you."

"It sounds like a good plan for ISPP," Shima retorted. "I am not risking my life for you."

"It's not about me. As soon as White Swan gets word ISPP is coming here, they'll be long gone. Don't you want to see these criminals behind bars?" Axe waved a hand in Cai's direction. "Don't you want to help liberate the millions of children who are still being held in slavery?"

"Of course, I want to—" Shima stammered.

Axe increased the pressure. "I'll walk five paces behind you. I don't care if it blows our cover. The point is I just need to see if anyone notices your tattoo. There are traffickers on that island somewhere, and we need a clue to find them—anything that might give away their location."

"The captain will never agree to this."

"Captain Shepherd will go with us. The entire crew will be there, and we'll all be armed. Once we have a location, your crew comes back to the ship, and you can all leave, safe and sound."

Shima frowned, thinking hard, weighing her options. "What happens to her when we leave?" She shifted her gaze to the prisoner, and then back to Axe.

"You'll just leave her in my custody. I'll find a place to hold her until the *Title of Liberty* arrives."

"But what about—?"

"The sooner we do this, the sooner your crew has fulfilled its obligation and you can leave! I can't do this alone!"

Shima's stomach was in knots. All she could think was, *This is a bad idea, a very bad idea*, but she kept seeing Zuri's face in her mind. She pictured the thousands of children who filled Lumphini Park and knew there were millions more like them, desperate to be freed.

She knew she wouldn't be risking her life to help Axe, or ISPP. She'd be risking it to help save more children like Zuri. Shima blew out a long breath and tried to set aside her fears. "When do you want to attempt this?"

Axe smiled. "Tomorrow after the last of the kids are returned home. We'll plan for 1600."

***

"I still think this is a bad idea," Shima announced halfway through the crew's morning meeting. "Why do I have to be the bait?"

"We can't ask Zuri to do it." Axe only succeeded in making Shima more uneasy every time she opened her mouth.

"I think I should go instead of Lorina," Blaze said for the fourth time, avoiding his wife's icy stare.

"We need you at the com," Danae said for the fifth time.

"Lorina knows how to use the com, or Ting could take care of it."

"Frankly, I don't want to leave Marco and Lorina on board together. He doesn't remember the knuckle sandwich she served him, but I'd prefer to find my ship in one piece when we return."

Ting shot Lorina a suspicious glance but kept his mouth shut.

"Can we move on?" Lorina glared across the table at Blaze until he leaned back in his chair, arms folded across his chest in silent defeat.

Shima had never experienced this level of frayed nerves and short tempers among her crewmates. It was obvious no one liked Axe's plan, but they were all resigned to the fact that it was the only viable plan. With all the ex-slaves returned to their families, the crew had to move forward with the next part of the mission: scouting the island.

Axe tried to assure the crew they wouldn't be doing a blind search. She would bring a handheld scanner which could detect many types of surveillance devices, including holo-cams and audio sensors. However, constantly monitoring the scanner would draw too much attention. "I could keep it in my pocket and have it send a signal to my earcom, but the scans won't be as accurate if it's bumping against my leg."

"No, that's fine. I think it'll be a big help." Danae glanced at Shima and Erik for nods of approval. "Keep it in your pocket, and let's try to do this as discreetly as possible."

"Now let's talk about logistics." The captain glanced at the notes on her datapad. "Erik and Axe will stay behind Shima, Vipul and Lorina will stay ahead of her with the rear-vision holo-cam Axe so generously provided." She probably didn't mean for it to sound sarcastic, but the ISPP officer didn't appear offended. "Phailin and I will stay off to one side or the other, depending on which side of the street Shima's on. Everyone will keep her in their sights, but try not to attract attention. We're supposed to be tourists so we'll act like couples."

Phailin shot her an incredulous look. "Couples?"

"Phailin and I will act like *friends*," Danae said.

Erik and Axe scrutinized each other from across the room, each looking disgusted at the thought of *pretending* to enjoy each other's company. Shima resisted the urge to giggle.

Shima thought Lorina and Vipul would have no trouble with the assignment, and Blaze trusted both of them.

"My wives keep getting younger," Vipul said.

Danae burst out laughing. It served to diffuse the tension as the rest of the room joined in. Shima was sorry the captain brought the levity to an end by announcing, "We'll meet in the entryway at 1500."

***

"I am going dirtside with the crew at 1500," Shima informed Zuri over lunch. She glanced at Ekaterina, who was sitting beside her niece, savoring a peanut butter sandwich as if it was the best thing she ever tasted. "You two can find something to do. We will not be gone long. Blaze will be here to take care of Niyati and the ship." She frowned. "Ting will be here too, but try to avoid him, and do not go down to the basement for any reason. Do you understand?"

She waited until Zuri nodded before explaining further. "The rest of the crew and Officer Tse have one more task to complete before we can leave China."

"What task?" Zuri asked.

"ISPP needs us to look around a part of the city— take some holograms, that sort of thing." Shima knew she wasn't convincing Zuri, but she hoped her niece wouldn't ask for more information. It was one thing to withhold some of the details, but it was another thing to lie about them. If pressured, Shima would be honest and disclose everything, and she didn't want her niece to worry.

Zuri's big brown eyes reflected a trust Shima felt she didn't deserve. "Yes, auntie. Is it safe for you to wear shorts into the city?"

Shima mustered a smile and got up from the table. "I will be with Danae. She will keep me safe. And big Dr. Sorensen will *flatten* anyone who comes near me."

Zuri giggled and seemed convinced. "See you later, auntie."

***

Shima could feel the tension radiating off Axe and her crewmates, minus Blaze and Marco, as they assembled in the entryway. Cargo shorts, T-shirts, athletic shoes, and small backpacks comprised the team uniforms.

Do we look like tourists? Shima didn't think so. *We look like tourists who are planning to feed sharks with our bare hands.* She glanced at each crewmember and saw only worried faces, except for Danae's.

"Are there any questions?" The captain wore her usual calm mask, although Shima noticed a thin sheen of perspiration on her forehead.

Heads moved back and forth in silent *no*'s.

"Everyone knows exactly what to do once we reach Shamian Island?"

This time heads nodded. It bothered Shima that the crew was so quiet.

Danae had everyone check his or her weapon, spare magazine, and earcom, and she watched closely as Axe reached inside the neck of Shima's T-shirt and applied a personal transmitter to the back of her left shoulder.

Shima flinched as the tiny device broke the skin, but she forced herself to present a brave face to the others—an emotion she definitely wasn't feeling.

"Let's get this over with." It was the first time in Shima's memory that Danae didn't have a pep talk prepared. The captain opened the airlock, and Axe led the way to the platform lift.

An hour later, the team got off the tram at Canal Street. The first officer walked across the bridge with the others, though her feet felt like lead weights.

"Just stick to the plan," Axe said quietly to the group. "Good luck."

The team split into their assigned pairs and spread out, trying their best to look like tourists taking in the historic charm of Shamian Island.

Shima turned left and walked by herself toward the river. She felt scared, vulnerable, and exposed with her tattooed leg on display. There were other people scattered around the island, but their numbers were small. Compared to the bustle of Foshan and Guangzhou, Shamian was quiet.

Too quiet. Shima ran her tongue over her parched lips. Her mouth had gone dry. She couldn't hear Axe's and Erik's footsteps on the sidewalk behind her, she could barely make out the backs of Lorina and Vipul walking twenty meters ahead of her, and she couldn't see Danae and Phailin in her peripheral vision. They were all supposed to be shadowing her at a distance, but the distance seemed vast. Shima hoped someone would offer a word of encouragement via the open comlink, but the tiny device on her earlobe remained silent.

Axe thought it best not to use the coms unless absolutely necessary, in case the island was rigged with audio surveillance.

Yes, we should try to act casual while we search for a mafia hideout. Shima tried to breathe normally despite her pounding heart.

She followed the plan to the letter. She walked the entire length of the riverfront, pausing a few times to look at passing boats. She turned right and walked up the first street, which ran perpendicular to the Pearl River, passing a dozen row houses. She went around the corner and walked down the next street.

Shima walked up and down each block, threading her way through the center of the island, pausing briefly to look at the church ruins and the park. When she was one block over from the last street which ran parallel to the little canal, she began to wonder if all their fears were baseless. No one appeared to have noticed her tattoo. None of the real tourists gave her a second look in passing.

Maybe the White Swan is not on Shamian Island. Maybe Ting was wrong about the address.

Shima walked past a modern hotel which appeared out of place alongside the old-style French architecture. She paused to look through the glass doors, into the ornate lobby, but there was no one working at the front desk, not a bellman or a hotel guest in sight. There wasn't even a name on the doors in Chinese characters to indicate the name of the hotel.

She did a quick search with her eyes and spotted a symbol etched into the flat, titanium door handle, so small it was barely noticeable. It was a thumbnail-sized B with a black circle around it.

She felt a chill, despite the afternoon heat, and glanced up in time to see a reflection in the glass—a big man was approaching her from behind.

Danae's terrified voice was suddenly in her ear. "*Run, Shima!*"

TWENTY
PLAN A

THE UNEASY FEELING they were being watched returned the moment Danae stepped off the pedestrian bridge onto Shamian Island. She resisted the urge to glance back over her shoulder at Axe and ask if the surveillance scanner detected anything.

Relax, Danae. She'll warn the team if the scanner goes crazy. She squared her shoulders, determined not to show fear, and started walking.

Phailin stayed in step with Danae, not speaking except to remind her occasionally not to stare at Shima. "We're tourists, remember? Maybe we should browse in a few of the stores."

Danae shook her head. "We'll lose sight of Shima."

"Are you sure you're not feeding your own fears?" Phailin stopped at a souvenir shop and glanced at the window display. "How about a fake jade bracelet, for good luck?"

"I'm not being paranoid, and we're not shopping today." She grabbed the cook's arm and pulled her away from the store.

Phailin issued a disgruntled sigh but dutifully kept pace.

Shima turned the corner. Danae and Phailin crossed over to the opposite side of the street and followed her down the block, staying about a dozen meters behind her.

After several blocks of this routine, the cook began gnawing her right thumbnail.

"Sorry I'm not much company," Danae said. "Would you rather be doing this with Marco?"

"I've given up on him, if you haven't noticed. It's hard to maintain a one-sided friendship. Why punish myself if he's determined to alienate everyone?" Phailin cleared her throat. "How about you? Wouldn't you rather be with Erik right now?"

"Not with all this tension," Danae said. "I'd be a distraction if we were working together, and I need everyone focused on Shima."

"Are you sure you wouldn't be distracted too?" Phailin flashed a sly grin.

Danae couldn't think of a snappy retort before they turned the next corner and got ready to cross to the opposite side of the street again.

Phailin seized Danae's wrist just as they stepped off the curb, pulling her down behind a parked solar car.

"This doesn't look conspicuous at all," Danae whispered as they squatted behind the back bumper. "What is it?" She leaned around the side of the car, keeping Shima in her sights as her first officer kept to the sidewalk.

"Look over there," Phailin whispered, leaning around the opposite side of the car so she could see the street. "That man."

Danae had to get on her hands and knees on the pavement so she could lean around Phailin to see across the street. She spotted a larger-than-normal Chinese man moving slowly along the opposite sidewalk, parallel with Shima. Danae couldn't see his face, but she could tell his head was turned to the side, his eyes fixed on Shima.

"Should we warn her?" Phailin asked.

"Let's wait and see what he does, but we should definitely move in closer." Danae's pulse began to race. "Where's Axe and Erik?"

Before she finished asking the question, the doctor and the ISPP officer crouched down beside them, startling Phailin. She let out a gasp but slapped a hand over her mouth to muffle it.

"This street's being monitored by holo-cams," Axe whispered, "too many to count. This is the first time the scanner's picked up any surveillance," she added before Danae could ask.

"Holo-cams or not, Shima's picked up a stalker." Danae drew her pistol. "Where's Vipul and Lorina?"

"I told them to turn around and walk back toward her. They'll reach her in a minute." Axe reached for the holster inside her blouse and withdrew her G50 semi-automatic.

"He's crossing the street!" Phailin warned.

"We don't have a minute." Danae got to her feet and looked over the roof of the car. She had a clear view of the entire street.

Shima had stopped and turned to look at the doors of a hotel, and the suspect was moving across the street, heading right toward her.

"*Run, Shima!*" Danae was on the move before anyone could stop her, running as fast as her feet could carry her.

"Spread out! Stay out of sight!" Axe's advice was in everyone's ears, but Danae ignored it. She heard running footsteps not far behind her, but she didn't risk a glance back to see who was on her heels.

Shima heeded the warning shout and dodged to one side, avoiding her attacker's outstretched arms, but he was joined by another man who emerged from the hotel's front doors.

Danae's fear turned to panic as the two men trapped Shima between them, disarming and overpowering her. She put on an extra burst of speed but couldn't close the gap fast enough.

"Stop! Stay back!" Erik's shout rang in her ear, drowning out Axe's order, "Everyone take cover! Hold your fire! Captain Shepherd, *do not* confront them!"

Danae heard them, but she was laser-focused on one goal: protecting Shima. She skidded to a stop a few meters from the men, who were holding Shima between them, one on each arm, with their backs to her. "Let her go!"

Shima's captors turned around, manhandling her to rotate with them. All three mouths gaped in shock when they saw Danae. Shima looked as if she wanted to offer some advice, but she was trembling too much to speak.

"Let her go!" Danae moved her pistol back and forth between the men, aiming at their foreheads to let them know she meant business.

The man on the right yanked Shima away from the one on the left, forcing her to stand in front of him. The other man appeared incensed he hadn't thought of this.

Déjà vu. The scene was chillingly familiar with an oversized brute trying to use rail-thin Shima as a human shield. The only difference this time was that there were two men and neither seemed concerned Danae was holding a gun on them. The one who took Shima's pistol had tucked it into the waistband of his slacks, but made no attempt to draw it.

"Look behind you!" Shima found her voice at the same moment Axe hissed, "Captain, behind you!" in her ear.

Danae heard a single footstep, but before she could turn, the barrel of a gun was wedged between her shoulder blades. She let the Excalibur fall to the sidewalk and slowly put her hands in the air.

"Hit the ground!" Axe hissed.

How does she expect me to do that? Danae caught a glimpse of a strawberry blond head leaning out from behind a tree a dozen meters behind the men, followed by the *crack* of a pistol.

The man on the left gasped and crumpled to the sidewalk, a fatal wound in the back of his skull.

A second shot came from behind Danae, and she felt her captor drop like a sack of potatoes. Without hesitation, she lunged straight at Shima, tackling her hard and knocking her and the slaver to the sidewalk. They landed together in a heap with Danae on top.

Shima grunted, the wind knocked out of her, but the man beneath her cushioned their fall. His head smacked the concrete, and he lay still.

Danae didn't get a chance to catch her breath. Six more men burst from the hotel's front doors and moved to stand over her, each of their pistols aimed at her head. One of them shouted at her. She didn't need a translator because the chorus of metallic *click*s made their intentions clear. Shima whimpered in her ear, but Danae didn't budge from her position. She shielded her best friend

289

with her own body, determined to keep her alive as long as possible.

The deafening *crack* of a gunshot made Danae flinch, but she wasn't hit. *I'm not the target?*

The street exploded with gunfire. Bullets zinged back and forth *over* her head—the slavers were shooting at someone across the street. She watched as the men went down in quick succession like a gruesome lineup of dominoes, the last one coming to rest across her right leg.

Seconds after the first shot was fired, it was over. Danae realized she underestimated Axe's military training. The petite engineer was a force to be reckoned with.

The ISPP officer emerged from her hiding place behind a bullet-riddled parked car on the other side of the street. She kept her head down as she dashed over to the tree closest to Danae and Shima, poked her head out from behind it, and glanced up and down the sidewalk to make sure it was safe to move into the open.

As soon as Axe had visual confirmation that the women weren't injured, she drew the surveillance scanner from her shorts' pocket, glanced at the screen, and headed back across the street. "Let me see if I can disable some of the holo-cams. Stay down until I secure the area," she told Danae over her shoulder.

"Yes, ma'am." For once Danae felt humbled enough to let someone else lead. She kicked the dead thug off her leg with her free foot, and then shifted her weight off Shima. She stayed low, hugging the sidewalk.

Shima rolled off the unconscious slaver, coming to rest shoulder to shoulder with Danae. She shakily propped herself up on one elbow and glanced around.

"Lots of holo-cams, so we're not safe yet." Danae had to turn her face away from the carnage a few meters from them.

"I knew this was a bad idea," Shima said.

"So did I." Danae spotted her pistol where she dropped it a few meters away and wondered if it would be safe to marine-crawl over to retrieve it, but Erik chose that moment to poke his blond head out from behind another parked car on the other side of the street.

Danae could see he was unscathed and breathed a sigh of relief. He started to move across the street toward her and Shima. His Excalibur seemed tiny and foreign in his big hand, and she wondered if he'd fired it. She knew how reluctant he was to use it, but she figured he was more afraid of not using it to defend someone's life. She raised herself onto her elbows and nodded to let him know she wasn't hurt.

Erik's lips were moving, but she couldn't hear what he was saying. The shootout had been so loud, a dull, buzzing noise filled her ears. A thought crossed her mind that it would be safer for him to regroup with Phailin, Vipul, and Lorina before approaching her and Shima. *Where are they?*

She was looking into Erik's eyes when he was shot.

Danae screamed, watching in horror as a fountain of blood erupted just below his right shoulder, the exit wound as large as his fist. He went rigid, his face reflecting utter disbelief, the force of the impact sending him forward to his knees. He looked at Danae, tried to say something, crumpled facedown onto the road, and lay still.

"*Erik!*" Danae tried to get up, but Shima seized her arm and held her down.

"Do not move!"

Danae heard more gunshots and knew she didn't have a choice about keeping her head down. *Where's Axe? Why didn't she cover him?*

These questions were answered as five men emerged from the hotel and three more materialized from unseen lairs across the street, converging on their position. They were all armed with military-grade pistols.

One of the men crossing the street had Axe and was forcing her to walk in front of him. He had one arm around her neck, and the other held her left arm behind her back. The ISPP's right arm hung limply by her side, blood dripping from a gunshot wound near her elbow.

The thug holding Officer Tse shouted something at Danae.

"He said don't run, or he'll kill me." Axe spoke between labored breaths.

The man spoke again, his face contorted with rage.

"He said to get up and go inside. We are now prisoners of White Swan."

TWENTY-ONE
PLAN B

"CALL AN AMBULANCE!" Lorina shrieked. "Erik's been shot! I think he's dead, or will be soon if we don't get him to a hospital!"

Blaze had never heard his wife this frantic before, and it took a major catastrophe to rattle her. *I knew I should've gone instead!* He'd waited at the com control board for over an hour, and this was his first call from the dirtside team.

"Ting to the bridge!" Blaze shouted at the shipboard com.

"Why do I—?"

"*Move it!*" Blaze muted the speakers so he wouldn't have to listen to Ting whine. "What happened?" he asked Lorina. "Where are you?"

"We're trying to get to him." Her words tumbled out in a rush. "We're waiting to make sure the coast is clear so we don't get ambushed like he was."

"Who ambushed—?" Blaze began, but Lorina spoke over him.

"I don't have time to explain. Erik has medical supplies in his backpack, and I need to get to the Hemorrhage Freeze—if there's a chance he's still alive. I can't tell if he's breathing!" She took a moment to quell her hysteria before continuing.

"Tell Ting to call the CIPs. We're in front of some kind of hotel on the island, one block over from the canal. Some men abducted the captain." Lorina's voice cracked, but she pressed on. "They took Shima and Axe too. Axe was shot in the arm. They took them inside the hotel, but I can't do anything until we help Erik. *Please hurry!*"

"What's the name of the hotel?" Blaze got up and moved to the doorway of the bridge. "*Ting!*"

"It doesn't have a name," she said, "not even a street number!"

Ting wandered into the corridor from the infirmary with a bored look on his face. "What's your problem?"

"You're my problem." Blaze seized the helmsman's shoulders, hauling him onto the bridge and over to the com controls. He shoved Ting into the chair. "Erik's been shot! The team needs an ambulance and the CIPs, so get on the ship-to-shore and make some calls!"

"You think China has emergency services?" Ting scoffed. "I can probably find a com code for the CIPs, but an ambulance wouldn't be any faster than taking him on the tram."

"*What?*" Blaze and Lorina gasped.

Lorina took control of the conversation. "You listen to me, Ting. You find the address of the nearest hospital, and you get us some kind of transport immediately. A cab, anything, I don't care!"

For once Ting didn't argue. He tapped the keypad to retrieve the Guangzhou directory from Shepherd's office and began to search the listings.

Blaze touched his earlobe, switching to a private link with Lorina. "He's workin' on it. What can I do?"

"There's nothing you can do, and I can't wait any longer. I've got to get to Erik. Vipul, cover me!"

"But—" Blaze closed his mouth. He knew it was useless to give Lorina advice when she was determined to take action. "Be careful!" He could only bite his lip and pray as he listened to the background noises and her running commentary on the open com.

"Phailin, cover the other side of the street." Blaze heard running footsteps, and Lorina swearing under her breath. "There's so much blood. Please don't be dead, Erik."

She gasped. "I've got a pulse! But it's weak." Blaze heard a zipper and plastic rustling. "The bullet shredded his backpack but the Hemorrhage Freeze can is intact." There was a loud hissing sound for half a minute.

"I don't know if I can turn him over to spray the other side."

"Don't move me." Blaze was stunned to hear the doctor's voice. His words slurred, and it sounded as if he was struggling to breathe, but he was coherent. "Artery was severed. My weight's keeping pressure on it. Don't move me, or I'll bleed out."

"I wish Jake was here," Lorina's voice quavered. "What should I do?"

"Paramedics?" Erik wheezed.

"Sorry, but we're going to have to get you to a hospital ourselves. Ting's calling a taxi for us."

Erik groaned. Blaze couldn't tell if he was expressing pain or frustration, or both. "You'll have to hold the bone."

"What?" Lorina squeaked.

"Let me help." It was Phailin's voice. "I've butchered sheep before. Blood doesn't bother me."

Blaze didn't think that was a reassuring image, but he refrained from commenting.

"There's a taxi on the way," Ting reported from the com. "I told the dispatcher we'd pay the driver one thousand credits if he could get there in five minutes. I gave them the address of the hospital."

"Is a thousand credits an impressive bribe?" Blaze asked.

"It is in China," Ting said.

Blaze repeated the news to Lorina.

"How can we get him into the cab? I don't think the three of us can lift him."

The engineer hated feeling so helpless. "Maybe the driver can help."

"Hold what bone?" Phailin was asking in the background.

"Collarbone." Erik's voice sounded weaker. "You'll have to reach underneath me and put your hand inside the wound. Press hard so it slows the bleeding long enough for Lorina to raise my shoulder and hit it with the Hemorrhage Freeze. You'll have to be quick."

Phailin's "ready" sounded terrified.

Lorina said, "On three—one, two—"

On "three" Blaze heard both women grunt with exertion and the hissing of the Hemorrhage Freeze again.

"He blacked out!" Phailin said.

I'm not surprised. Blaze couldn't imagine how much pain Erik was in. The engineer had also torn a major artery, but he was fortunate to be sedated while Jake and Shima handled his splintered femur.

"Where's that taxi?" Phailin asked.

"There! I see it! Wave the cab over here, Vipul!" Lorina shouted, and then added in a much quieter voice, "I'd better hide his gun."

There was more commotion with the arrival of the cab. The driver was upset by the carnage in front of the hotel and was complaining loudly. Blaze knew there was no time to waste.

"Lorina, give the driver your com so Ting can talk to him." Blaze stepped over to the helmsman and put a firm hand on his shoulder, just in case he tried to bolt.

Ting shot him a belligerent scowl, but he didn't have to yell at the driver for more than a minute before Lorina took her com back and reported, "He's nodding. He's going to help us lift Erik."

"Where did all these people come from?" Phailin asked.

"What people?" Blaze felt a stab of fear. *More slavers?*

"I guess the other tourists have been keeping an eye on all the excitement," Lorina said. "Five people just walked over to help us lift Erik."

Blaze offered a silent prayer of gratitude. He heard lots of excited Mandarin chatter in the background, and then several car doors slammed shut.

"Phailin will ride with him to the hospital. Ting needs to stay linked to her com so he can translate." Lorina's tone turned serious again. "Now what can we do to rescue Captain Shepherd?"

"What about the CIPs?" Blaze asked Ting.

The helmsman shook his head. "I was told the police don't patrol Shamian Island."

"Which means they're either scared or complicit." Blaze explained the situation to Lorina, who didn't take the news well.

"We've got to do something! Contact York! It's his fault we're in this mess! If anything happens to them—if Erik dies—I'll personally *wring his neck!*"

An idea took shape in Blaze's mind during Lorina's rant. *But it's crazy—crazy with a capital C.* But he could see no other option. His wife was right—they had to do something, and fast.

"Let me talk to Vipul, privately."

"Why?" Lorina asked.

"Just trust me."

She didn't hesitate. "Once you've worked out the details, please let me know your plan."

"Absolutely. In the meantime, you and Vipul find a safe place to stake out the hotel, and let me know if anythin' changes."

"I love you." Lorina cut the connection before he could respond.

"What's on your mind, mate?" Vipul's voice was in Blaze's ear.

"I've got an idea, but I don't know if it'll work. Stay on the line and listen."

"Listening is easy."

Blaze grabbed Ting's sleeve and yanked him out of the chair. "Come on. We're goin' down to talk to the prisoner." He released the mute button for the shipboard com before leaving the bridge. "Niyati?"

"Yes, *baba?*"

"I'm gonna be busy for a while in the basement. Tell Zuri and Ekaterina to put on another holo-vid for you."

"Yes, *baba*."

Blaze knew Lorina wouldn't approve of leaving Niyati with the teens for more than a few minutes, but it couldn't be helped.

***

"Tell her she's gonna talk to White Swan on the com about a prisoner exchange." Blaze glared at Cai through the brig window. "Her freedom for the captain's, Shima's, and Axe's."

Ting hesitated at the keypad. "She won't agree. White Swan won't agree, either. What's she worth to their organization? Nothing, I'll bet."

"Just tell her." Blaze attempted to keep a leash on his impatience. "We've gotta do somethin', and she's our only leverage."

Ting punched the intercom button and conversed with Cai for several minutes.

"This is your idea?" Vipul's incredulous voice was in Blaze's ear. "What do you need me to do?"

"I need advice. If everyone agrees to the exchange, we'll have to move her to Shamian." Blaze tried to keep his voice low so Ting wouldn't overhear. "Obviously we can't put her on the tram in handcuffs or holdin' a gun to her head. I'm open to suggestions."

"Knock her out."

Blaze wasn't sure if he heard correctly. "What?"

"If she's unconscious, you can move her without attracting too much attention. Ting can tell people she's sick and you're taking her to see a doctor."

Blaze tried to wrap his mind around this outrageous idea. "How do I—?"

"Check the infirmary for something to sedate her. Put a hygiene mask on her so people won't get too close—they'll assume she's contagious. Use a wheelchair to move her."

"I can't do that! I'm not a medic. What if she has an allergic reaction to whatever I give her? It sounds like a good idea, but I'm the wrong man for this job."

There was nothing but sympathy in Vipul's voice. "At the moment, you're the only man available."

Blaze had no response because the navigator was right. His heart was pounding, and he was dripping with sweat. He glanced over at Ting, who concluded his animated discussion with Cai.

The helmsman turned to Blaze with a troubled frown. "She's fine with the swap, but said she can't guarantee White Swan will agree to it. If they do, she can't guarantee they won't kill us and the prisoners once we reach the hotel. You can't make bargains with these people."

No honor among thieves—or human traffickers. Blaze grimaced. "What choice do we have? Let's get her to the com." He took out his pistol and pointed it at Cai. "Time to go."

The prisoner glared at Blaze as Ting pressed his thumb to the ID lock and the door slid open. She eyed the gun with a resentful scowl but turned and followed Ting to the lift without a word.

Once on the bridge, Ting directed her to the com. She sat down, and he spoke to her at length, gesturing to the keypad she needed to use for a ship-to-shore call.

Cai hesitated, her fists clenched in her lap, but Blaze moved around to the front of the control board, facing her, and waved the pistol at her face. She bared her teeth at him, hissing like an angry cat.

Ting shouted something at her, and she relented, lowering her eyes to the keypad and typing in a code.

"Make sure she doesn't try to arrange a way to escape or double-cross us," Blaze said.

"I worked out that part without your help, cowboy."

Blaze clamped his mouth shut on a sharp retort as a gruff voice answered the call. Cai and the male speaker conversed in rapid-fire Mandarin for several minutes.

Ting listened closely and gave him a synopsis. "Well, she is one of the higher-ups in the organization, and they're willing to trade for her, but . . ."

"But—?" Blaze bit his lip.

"But they won't agree to a three-for-one deal. They want you to choose just one of the prisoners."

Blaze felt a cold trickle of sweat run down his back. "That's impossible! I can't leave two of them with those animals!"

"Ask for Axe," Vipul said.

"What?" Blaze said, "Just a second," to Ting, kept his eyes and gun fixed on Cai, and had a quick discussion with Vipul on his earcom. "Why her, aside from the obvious fact she's been shot?"

"Shima's wearing the transmitter, so we'll be able to find her and Captain Shepherd, assuming they're in the same location inside the hotel. They'll handle the crisis better if we keep them together. White Swan will expect us to ask for whoever's wounded. Any other request will seem suspicious."

"It makes sense, but I still don't like it. This whole thing stinks like roadkill in August."

"Charming." Ting smirked, eavesdropping on Blaze's side of the conversation. "Have much experience with roadkill?"

Blaze glared at him. "Tell Cai we agree to a one-for-one exchange, and we want the injured woman, but don't mention she's an ISPP officer."

"You're willing to strike a deal with these criminals?" Ting whistled. "Shepherd will make roadkill out of you when she finds out you're abandoning her and Shima."

"We're not abandonin' them," Blaze said. "Just tell her what to say."

Ting smirked again and spoke to Cai at length.

After more discussion with the representative from White Swan, Ting got a sober look on his face and explained to Blaze. "They expect Cai to walk in the front doors of the hotel promptly at 6:30 tonight before they'll release Axe from the same front doors. They said she needs to come alone." He took a deep breath. "If anything seems out of place—if they suspect a trap—they'll shoot all three of them and dump their bodies in the river."

"*What?*" Vipul hissed.

Ting continued. "They said don't bother with the CIPs because they won't help you. He said, 'They're on our side.'"

"Do they know about ISPP?" Blaze could feel a giant block of ice taking up residence in his stomach.

The helmsman's frown deepened. "They know ISPP isn't here in Guangzhou. I'm sure they're already making plans to skip town as soon as they have Cai, and they'll probably take Shepherd and Shima with them."

"We have to make sure that doesn't happen." Blaze spoke with more courage than he felt. "We don't have much time, and it'll take us at least an hour to get there. Vipul, tell Lorina I'll call her back to explain everythin' in a few minutes—just as soon as we're ready to leave."

He thought of one more detail. *I'd better get some of Lorina's clothes for Cai 'cause she can't wear the prison suit in public.*

"What're you going to do when you reach the hotel?" Vipul's voice was filled with concern.

"I don't know. I feel like I'm walkin' straight to my own execution. Please tell me you have an idea."

Vipul paused a moment. "I do have one idea."

Blaze felt a spark of hope. The navigator's creative mind had saved their necks on more than one occasion. "Tell me what I need to do."

"You'll need to find several items in the spare-parts workshop. Just put them in your backpack, and I'll assemble them when you get here. Bring a set of small hand tools too. And a lighter—that's very important."

Blaze whipped out a datapad and wrote down the items Vipul rattled off. Only one thing on the list stumped him. "What's Propoflurane?"

"It's an anesthesia. I'm sure there's some in the infirmary. If not, it's easy to make in a lab with mostly isopropanol and phenol, although it would take time."

"Then let's pray Erik has some Propoflurane in stock 'cause my chemistry skills are kinda rusty. See you soon. Smith out."

***

Ten minutes later, Blaze, Ting, and the prisoner were in the infirmary. Cai was dressed in Lorina's shorts, T-shirt, and flip-flops, and seated in a wheelchair. She looked quizzically at Blaze, who was still holding his gun on her.

"Now what?" Ting asked. "Are you going to tie her to the chair?"

Blaze put his pistol in the helmsman's palm. "Make sure she doesn't move. I'll be right back." He stepped into the exam room, took a hygiene mask out of a labeled drawer, found a syringe in an overhead cabinet, and checked the wall-mounted monitor for medications.

I wish Jake was here! His hands were starting to shake. He tried to recall how the medics accessed the micro-pharmacy.

Fortunately, the program was user-friendly. Blaze typed in a search for a fast-acting sedative which would wear off in an hour for a woman who was forty kilos—he guessed on her weight. He was astonished to see the anesthesia recommend was Propoflurane.

A vial appeared in a slot beside the screen, and he filled the syringe to the recommended dosage. Then he pried the vial out of the slot and checked the remaining amount of the drug. *Is this gonna be enough for whatever Vipul has in mind?* He shoved the vial into his pocket.

Blaze had a thought and acted on it without hesitation, hurrying next door to the surgical room and checking its micro-pharmacy for Propoflurane. Since anesthesia was typically used for surgery, the vial which appeared in the slot was much larger than the one he just pilfered from the exam room. He pocketed the second vial, feeling more confident it would be enough.

"What's taking so long?" Ting called.

"Comin'." Blaze emerged from the surgical room, walked over to Cai before he lost his nerve, and plunged the syringe into her exposed upper arm.

Her mouth gaped open in shock, and she slumped down in the chair, out cold.

Ting chuckled, impressed. "I didn't know you had a ruthless side, Mr. Sunshine. This is great. Now you won't need me along to translate."

Blaze felt something snap at Ting's blasé attitude and went ballistic. "You worthless coward! I can't do this by myself! People will be suspicious if I try to take her on the tram, and I won't be able to answer their questions! We don't have to worry about her makin' a scene or tryin' to escape while she's like this, but I still need a translator!"

He was tempted to pick up Ting by his collar and shake him, but the helmsman saved him the trouble by reluctantly agreeing.

"I don't get paid enough for this," Ting grumbled.

"Just shut your mouth!" Blaze knew they were short on time, so he forced himself to calm down. "Put this on her face." He traded Ting the hygiene mask for his gun. "Just wait here. There's two more things I need to do."

"You'd better move fast if we have to be there by 1830."

"I know." Blaze slipped the Excalibur into the right cargo pocket of his shorts and hurried to the ladder.

Off the basement corridor was a small storage room of floor-to-ceiling drawers housing a collection of items most people would consider junk. The drawers contained everything from coils of wire to salvaged android circuit boards and even scraps of wood, fabric, and leather. The drawers had been filled to capacity since Vipul joined the crew. The navigator was fond of scavenging dirtside for anything interesting he could find.

Blaze didn't take time to wonder about the items he shoved into his backpack. He was grateful the drawers' contents were well-labeled so he could find everything on the list in less than five minutes, leaving him time to complete the second task.

He climbed the ladder to the bridge and sat at the com. He wasn't sure what he was going to say, but he didn't have time to compose a message to read aloud. He hit the *record* button and faced the right-hand monitor. "This transmission is intended for Captain Cade York of the Interstellar Peacekeepers Patrol warship, the *Title of Liberty*, docked at Bangkok, Thailand, and was recorded on December seventh. This message is *urgent* and requires an immediate response."

I don't have time for this! Blaze dumped all pretense of politeness and gave York a condensed version of the crisis:

"A few minutes ago, Captain Shepherd, Shima, and Axe were taken prisoner in White Swan's headquarters on Shamian Island. Axe was shot, so I'm sure she's in bad shape. Marco Ting and I are attemptin' a prisoner exchange with Cai in less than an hour. This is probably a terrible plan, but we have no other options without some *immediate assistance*. Dr. Sorensen's been shot too—we don't even know if he's still alive—and one crew-member's with him at the hospital, which leaves only four of us against an unknown number of criminals."

He glared at the screen. "In case I didn't make myself clear: *we are desperate* and people are gonna die—includin' your own officer—if you don't move fast! You got us into this mess, York, so *get us out!* Smith out."

Blaze's hands were shaking again as he found the transmission code for the *Title of Liberty* and sent the message. He returned to the infirmary where Ting was sitting on one of the post-op beds, looking bored.

"Let's get movin'." Blaze arranged Cai's head against the backrest and her arms across her lap so she appeared more natural. "Just tell people she's your wife and we're takin' her to a doctor 'cause she's sick."

"My wife?" The helmsman was repulsed by the idea.

"Yes, your wife. And I know you tire easily but try to keep up." He spoke to the shipboard com while he pushed the wheelchair to the lift. "Niyati, I need to go into the city. Be a good girl for Zuri and Ekaterina, and *amma* will be back soon."

Blaze thought it best to wait until they were dirtside before explaining the plan to Lorina. He suspected she'd be upset with him for leaving their daughter without parental supervision and for letting Cai out of the brig. He was counting on his wife's motherly instincts to kick in—she would want to return to the ship instead of sticking around to witness the disaster unfold on Shamian.

His family would be safely out of harm's way. That was the theory, at least. Blaze offered a silent prayer that Vipul's plan would work—whatever it was.

"Bye, *baba*." Niyati didn't sound distressed about being separated from both parents. "Be careful."

Yes, sugar, I'll try not to get us all killed.

TWENTY-TWO
PAPER TRAIL

SHIMA TRIED TO keep Erik in sight for as long as she could. There was so much blood on the street that she thought he was dead, but she couldn't allow herself to lose hope, for Danae's sake.

Her handlers made sure she wasn't going anywhere by overpowering her. One held her arms behind her back, one held her ankles, and one tore off her backpack, yanked out her earcom, and clamped a dirty hand over her mouth. Danae and Axe were immobilized the same way by several other men, although they didn't touch Axe's bleeding right arm.

Their captors were well-dressed Chinese men of various ages, shapes, and sizes, but all of them were armed and angry about the loss of their brothers in crime, although they didn't appear to be in a hurry to clean up the mess.

Shima suspected the slavers had no fear of the CIPs showing up. *Why else would they abduct us in broad daylight?*

Several of the men argued with each other as they carried Shima, Danae, and Axe inside the hotel lobby.

Balconies to the upper floors overlooked the lavish enclosed atrium, filled with flowering plants and full-sized trees. Shima counted five floors from lobby to ceiling.

There was no one else in the lobby or on the balconies, and she guessed the hotel's occupants were nocturnal. It made sense, considering their depraved line of work. *The men Axe shot, and the others who took their places and abducted us—are they part of the day shift?* She wondered how many more of them came out at night.

Their handlers carried them past the registration desk and down a dimly lit hallway. Shima thought they would be taken to one of the rooms and chained up, as she was in the Bangkok red-light district, but she was shocked when they were thrown into a small, windowless office.

Axe cried out in pain as she was dumped on the floor beside Shima and Danae. One man shouted something at them in a threatening tone, and their captors withdrew, slamming the door shut behind them.

"They said there'll be guards outside the door, and if we try to escape, they'll chop off our fingers, one at a time." Axe remained flat on her back on the dingy carpet. Her face was pale, and she was trembling.

Danae knelt beside Axe and said, "Sorry," before tearing the engineer's blouse down the middle. She slipped the shirt over the ISPP's left arm and tore the fabric into long strips, which she used to bind up Axe's bleeding right arm.

"I wish we had some Hemorrhage Freeze but since we don't, I'll have to elevate it and apply pressure." Danae raised Axe's forearm with one hand and clamped the other hand over the gunshot wound.

The engineer groaned and shut her eyes, breathing hard. "I'm sorry I didn't give Dr. Sorensen better cover. I didn't know he was in the open until I heard the shot, and when I turned around to see what was happening, I was hit. I wasn't fast enough."

Danae's lips were pinched into a thin, tight line. "It's not your fault. It's *Cade's* fault. We told him this mission was too dangerous for us to attempt." She chewed her lower lip and shot Shima a guilty look. "It's my fault, too, for letting him talk me into it."

"It is not your fault," Shima said with firmness. "We all agreed to accept the risk."

The captain shook her head. "You agreed to do this because you trust me to make sound decisions. But I was so fixated on the Baronowskis's connection to Cai that I didn't listen to anyone's advice or to my own gut feeling that this was a disaster waiting to happen. No one would've volunteered for this, especially not Erik."

At the mention of his name, Danae lost what little control she had over her emotions and started to sob. "I should've listened to him! He was just trying to keep me safe—trying to protect all of us! And now it might be too late to tell him I'm sorry!"

"Shush. They will hear you." Shima's heart was still racing, but she was determined to put on a brave face for Danae's sake. She had never seen the captain lose her composure like this, except once—at Alex's funeral. "We must hope for the best and right now we must take care of Axe."

Danae nodded, blinking hard, and took a few minutes to pull herself together, wiping her eyes on the shoulder of her T-shirt. "You're right, we need to take care of Axe. See if there's anything in here we can use."

The first officer did a quick search of the three-by-three-meter room. It was furnished with an old steel desk which held a few wooden pencils and some plastic paperclips in the drawers, a filing cabinet with hanging files filled with papers covered in faded Chinese script, a single wooden chair, and an old-fashioned paper shredder with a basketful of shreds.

"We could use shredded paper to pack the wound if it does not stop bleeding," Shima said, "but I do not think anything else is useful." She sat on the floor beside Danae. "I can take over when your arms get tired."

"Why do they still use paper?" Danae asked Axe.

The ISPP officer tried to grin but it turned into a grimace. "The Chinese love paper—they invented it. Plus, datapads are too expensive for the average person to own, even if they're manufactured here. Ironic, huh?"

"Yes, that is ironic." Shima glanced at Danae's eyes. *She is still in shock. I must say something to give her courage.* "Do not forget I am wearing the transmitter, and Vipul has the tracking device. And I am sure Vipul, Lorina, and Phailin were able to help Dr. Sorensen."

Danae shook her head. "We can't assume anything." A tear slipped from the corner of her eye, but she made no attempt to wipe it away. "I don't want to talk about it."

"I understand." Shima scooted closer and put an arm around Danae's shoulders.

"Déjà vu," Danae said.

"What is that?" Shima asked.

"It means I've had this feeling before. Remember our conversation about the people I care about dying or disappearing?

"Erik is not dead." Shima tried to sound confident.

Danae didn't argue the point. "Where's Marco with a premonition when we need one? I'd like to know how we're getting out of this."

Shima shook her head in frustration. She noticed Axe looked drowsy. "I think we should keep her awake."

"I don't . . . want to talk," Axe whispered between labored breaths.

Shima had an idea. "Let me see what is in the filing cabinet." She stood and walked over to examine the faded yellow cards taped to the front of each drawer. "These are dated by year. The top one is the most recent."

She pulled open the top drawer and removed a handful of papers from the first file. She sat down again beside Axe. "What does this one say?"

Axe opened her eyes and squinted at the paper Shima held up in front of her face. "It's some kind of invoice, made out to White Swan."

Danae's eyes widened with interest. "What's the invoice for?"

Axe pondered the writing. "White Swan took receipt of . . . fifteen cows and three bulls, and they were shipped to Zhongshan Cabinet Works."

Danae inhaled sharply. "Thanatos listed the children he trafficked as *animals* in his log. Cows could mean girls and bulls could mean boys. Are these all invoices? Show her another one."

Shima held up a different paper for the engineer to read.

"Eight ewes and six rams. And this one says they were delivered . . . to a chair factory in Foshan."

"It must be children," Shima said. "Sheep do not make chairs."

"What's the date on it?" Danae asked.

Axe squinted. "February of this year."

"Check some of the invoices in the third drawer," Danae said.

"Why?" Shima was startled to see her so animated.

"It's just a hunch. It might not mean anything but if I'm right, it might be *very* important to Cade."

Shima stepped over to the cabinet and opened the third drawer. This time she selected papers at random from several different files. She sat beside Axe again. "Just a few more." She could tell the ISPP officer was struggling to remain conscious.

Axe focused on the next paper. "This one isn't an invoice. It's a shipping notice from . . . Thanatos."

Shima and Danae exchanged shocked looks. "Shipped from where?" Danae asked.

"Venus Station."

"Does it say anything about port of delivery?" the captain persisted.

"No." Axe shut her eyes. "No more, please. It makes my head hurt."

"I'm sorry." Danae glanced at Shima. "Which file did you get this from? Do you remember?"

Shima went back to the drawer and opened it wide. She pulled out the entire folder. "This one."

Danae looked down on Axe with a sympathetic smile. "Could you translate just one more? Please? It's really important."

Axe took a labored breath. "And I thought York was a taskmaster."

Shima took that as a yes. She selected a paper from the thick file and held it over Axe's face.

"Shipping notice . . . from Thanatos. It says eighty-five goats were transferred from Kuala Lumpur to Taipei because the factory . . . was scheduled to be demolished."

Danae got an incredulous look on her face. "Shima, take over for me."

Axe groaned as the women traded places, although they tried not to jostle her arm. Shima could see that the makeshift blouse bandages were soaked through, but the bleeding had tapered off.

The engineer's eyelids fluttered until they remained closed. Shima was worried Axe lost too much blood. "What should we do?"

Danae didn't reply. She took a handful of papers from the shipping notice file, folded each piece into quarters, and filled her shorts' pockets. "If we get out of here, we need to make sure ISPP sees the contents of this filing cabinet."

Shima didn't like the way she said *if*. "What can we do for Axe?"

The captain looked exhausted. "I don't know."

"Would you mind if I offered a prayer?"

"Sure, we could use all the help we can get."

TWENTY-THREE
MORE PAIN

AM I HAVING a nightmare? Erik was lying flat on his face in the middle of the road, listening to gunshots all around him. When the shooting stopped, he thought about getting up but realized he was bleeding from his right shoulder. Not just bleeding—gushing. The pavement was growing wetter on his right side. He assessed his condition, based on what he could feel since he couldn't see anything except concrete.

The good news: he could breathe, so he hadn't punctured a lung.

The bad news: the subclavian artery was damaged or severed, and he had less than ten minutes to live without medical intervention. His shattered clavicle, ribs, and scapula were just a minor inconvenience, in comparison.

His medical training advised him to shift more weight onto his right shoulder to put pressure on the artery. He concentrated, forcing his muscles to cooperate. The shift was incremental, but it took every bit of his strength.

He blacked out for a minute from the intense pain. When Erik came to, he realized he wasn't dreaming. This road was his reality. *Please, God, I don't want to die.*

He heard footsteps. "There's so much blood. Please don't be dead, Erik." It took him a moment to identify Lorina Murphy's voice. He felt a small, warm hand on the left side of his neck.

"I've got a pulse! But it's weak." There was some tugging at his back that sent a fresh shockwave of pain through his shoulder. He struggled to remain conscious.

"The bullet shredded his backpack, but the Hemorrhage Freeze can is intact." Lorina was keeping someone informed. Erik felt the lifesaving blast of cold air on his back. The frigid feeling penetrated his shoulder and trickled down into his chest like an icy waterfall, but he knew it wouldn't be enough to stop the bleeding.

"I don't know if I can turn him over to spray the other side."

"Don't move me." Erik mustered his last bit of strength, forcing his lips to move. "Artery was severed. My weight's keeping pressure on it. Don't move me or I'll bleed out."

"I wish Jake was here." Lorina spoke to him in a quavering voice. "What should I do?"

"Paramedics?" *Doesn't China have emergency services?*

Lorina answered the question for him. "Sorry, but we're going to have to get you to a hospital ourselves. Ting's calling a taxi for us."

A taxi? Erik forced himself to focus on how to stay alive. "You'll have to hold the bone."

"What?" she squeaked.

"Let me help." Another voice joined Lorina's, and he recognized Phailin Kim. "I've butchered sheep before. Blood doesn't bother me."

Do I look like a butchered sheep? Erik's thoughts wandered, and he realized he was close to losing consciousness again.

"How can we get him into the cab?" Lorina asked. "I don't think the three of us can lift him."

"Hold what bone?" Phailin asked.

"Collarbone." Erik struggled to speak; he could barely breathe. "You'll have to reach underneath me and put your hand inside the wound. Press hard so it slows the bleeding long enough for Lorina to raise my shoulder and hit it with the Hemorrhage Freeze. You'll have to be quick."

"Ready." Phailin sounded terrified.

Lorina said, "On three—one, two—"

Erik didn't hear her say "three."

***

When the doctor awoke, he was in a different place, but it took too much effort to open his eyes. There was no pavement beneath him. He was sitting upright in some type of compact vehicle. He could hear loud car horns all around him and wondered if the vehicle was sitting in the middle of a traffic jam—which would be the norm for China. He could feel someone applying pressure to his shoulder, but the pain was so intense, he couldn't stop shaking.

"We're almost there." Phailin's voice was close to his ear. He suspected that she didn't realize he was conscious and was just trying to console herself.

He tried to say something, but his thoughts became foggy, and he slipped into darkness again.

***

When Erik became aware of his surroundings, he could hear raised voices speaking in Chinese. He suspected he was the topic of the highly charged conversation. He was lying on his back on a soft surface, and he couldn't feel his right shoulder anymore. He couldn't muster the strength to raise his eyelids.

Phailin's voice was near him again. "Tell them he needs more than painkillers and bandages, Ting!"

It was quiet for a minute; then the argument seemed to pick up right where it left off. After several minutes, the voices departed, still arguing. The silence was refreshing.

Phailin was still speaking to someone in a low voice, although she sounded quite upset. "I can't believe you're attempting something so dangerous! I don't know what else I can do except stay here with Erik and pray for Shima, Axe, and Captain Shepherd."

Danae! Where is she? Erik pictured her lying on her stomach beside Shima, the sidewalk around them littered with dead Chinese men. He recalled the look of horror on her face when he was shot and wondered if she knew he was still alive.

Erik was devastated to think he failed to protect her, both physically and emotionally. *Despite my efforts, I've added to her burdens.*

He tried to speak to Phailin but it came out as a groan.

He felt a gentle hand on his left arm. "Just go back to sleep. There's nothing you can do." Phailin broke down and started to cry. "There's nothing any of us can do without ISPP's help, but it may be too late by the time they get here."

TWENTY-FOUR
PRISONER EXCHANGE

"PHAILIN'S CALLING," TING announced, nonchalant.

Blaze looked across the tram aisle at the helmsman with his slumbering *bride* sitting beside him. Marco had his arm around Cai's shoulders, but this was only to prevent her from falling out of the narrow seat.

One thing Blaze hadn't anticipated was that trams in China offered no accommodations for the handicapped. To get Cai on the trolley, he had no other option except lifting her out of the wheelchair and carrying her on board. And she was heavy—he was already feeling the strain in the muscles beneath his lumpy backpack. Moving the prisoner when they had to change trams was also a chore. Ting had to fold up the wheelchair and haul it on and off the tram, taxing his already limited strength.

Their excursion attracted plenty of unwanted attention. The suspicious whispers didn't bother him, but the unblinking stares were wearing on his already-stretched-thin nerves.

"What's happenin'?" Blaze focused his scattered thoughts on Ting's report. "Is Erik alive?"

"Yes, he survived. Phailin needs me to tell the doctors how he was shot. They need to file a CIP report."

Blaze felt a nudge of impatience. He'd heard rumors Chinese hospitals were crowded, bureaucratic nightmares of inefficiency. It wasn't hard to imagine the doctors letting Erik bleed to death while they filled out paperwork. "Aren't they treatin' him for the gunshot wound?"

Ting was staring at the ceiling, listening to his com and ignoring Blaze. He began to speak in Mandarin, and it escalated into an argument.

Blaze tried again. "What's his condition? What did Phailin say?"

He noticed Ting's heated discussion was attracting a number of eavesdroppers seated around them. The stares morphed into suspicious frowns. He tried to get the helmsman's attention, motioning for him to bring the volume down.

Ting snorted in disgust and reached up to turn off his earcom. "Sorensen was bandaged, but he'll need major surgery. We'll have to pay in advance before they'll do anything more for him, and Phailin doesn't have enough money on her credit flash."

"What about the doctor's flash?"

"He has to be conscious to use it. Phailin said he's on heavy-duty painkillers, and he's weak from losing so much blood, but at least he's alive."

Blaze agreed. "What were you arguin' about?"

"The idiot on the com didn't believe me when I said Sorensen was shot on Shamian Island by a member of White Swan. He kept insisting I was mistaken, that there were no traffickers on Shamian. Isn't it interesting he knows White Swan is a trafficking organization?" Ting snorted again. "He implied I was withholding information, and I might be the one who shot him. I told him he could go—"

"Stop!" Blaze cut him off. "I get the idea. Did you let Phailin know we can't do anything until we rescue the captain, Shima, and Axe?"

Ting nodded, glancing at Cai, who was beginning to stir. "What do you plan to do when we get there?"

Sweat was pouring down Blaze's back again. "I'm still workin' on that part."

"Well, you might want to work faster! Even if they don't shoot us on sight when we do the exchange, how are we going to free Shima and Captain Shepherd? This is insane, and you know it!"

"Vipul has a plan." Blaze refused to let himself get swept up in Ting's anxiety. *Don't give in to the nerves—too many lives are at stake. Stay focused.* "When's our stop?"

Ting glanced out the window. "Coming up next, and just in time."

Cai's eyelids were fluttering. She raised an unsteady hand to her face and pulled the mask off her nose and mouth.

Ting said something terse to her in Chinese. She scowled but seemed too dazed to vocalize a response.

When the tram reached the stop, Blaze stood and pulled Cai to her feet. He put one arm around her waist and grabbed her wrist with his free hand, hoisting her arm over his shoulder to keep her upright. It was awkward, but he didn't have the strength to pick her up again.

"Tell her to walk!" he told Ting over his shoulder as he half-dragged her down the aisle.

The helmsman followed him with the wheelchair. "The angry mob already thinks we're mistreating her."

Blaze ignored the scowling passengers and concentrated on getting Cai off the tram. She began to struggle, but her efforts were clumsy and weak.

Once they were on the sidewalk, the tram drove off, but not before one of the passengers shouted something at them through an open window.

"Someone said they'd call the CIPs," Ting translated.

"Good, I hope they do." Blaze wrestled Cai into the wheelchair. "Tell her to calm down! Remind her why we're here—we've only got twenty minutes till the exchange!"

He moved around to the back of the chair and grasped Cai's shoulders to keep her seated. She kicked, flailed her arms, and muttered slurred threats, like a bad-tempered drunk. "She's gonna be fully awake in a minute so we need to find Vipul ASAP."

"We should've tied her to the chair. I don't suppose you have some rope in your bag?"

"No, I don't." Blaze struggled to subdue Cai and push the chair at the same time to get across the bridge.

Vipul appeared out of an alley near the bridge and motioned them over. Blaze had the backpack off and in the navigator's hands the moment they joined him in the putrid-smelling, narrow passageway.

"Lorina left about half an hour ago." Vipul sat on an overturned plastic crate and pulled items from the backpack. "And in case you're wondering—yes, she's mad at you for leaving Niyati."

"She'll get over it." Ting snapped something in Mandarin at Cai. She was agitated but stopped trying to get out of the wheelchair.

Blaze ignored Ting's remark. "Is that enough Propoflurane for what you have in mind?"

Vipul eyed the vials with a worried frown. "I think so."

Please don't tell me it's not enough. This plan has to work—it's our only hope. The engineer tried to ignore his shaking hands so he could stay focused. "What can I do to help?"

"Just hand me tools."

"Encourage her to stay in the chair." Blaze handed the helmsman his pistol and got down on one knee beside Vipul.

"I need a tiny Phillips-head."

Blaze found the screwdriver and watched the older man work his magic. Vipul must have studied the instructions earlier because he knew exactly what he was doing.

"Ten minutes," Ting warned.

"Almost there." Vipul poured the vials of Propoflurane into a small chamber inside the metal canister he assembled, added a fuse, and screwed the lid shut. "Lighter?"

Blaze put it in his free hand. "It looks like somethin' the old SWAT teams used for tear gas."

"It's the same basic idea. There's so much alcohol in the Propoflurane that it should create heavy fumes as it burns." Vipul picked up the last spare part he devised for an earlier crisis—a short metal tube which functioned like a harpoon gun—and slipped the canister inside.

"Five minutes. You know she's going to warn them as soon as she steps across the threshold," Ting said.

"I know." Vipul stood. His voice was steady, but his face was etched with worry lines. "The entire street is under surveillance, so we'll need to move fast. They'll be watching for us."

Blaze exchanged a worried glance with Ting. "Remember if anything seems suspicious, they'll shoot Axe, Shima, and the captain."

"They might shoot them anyway," Ting said. "You can't bargain with criminals."

"We know that," Blaze said, "but we're out of options. This *has* to work."

"Let's get into position." Vipul handed Blaze the binoculars. "Marco, get that maggot on her feet. Make her walk ahead of you to the other end of the alley."

"Sounds like fun, but I'd prefer if you two handled the rest of this adventure." Ting handed back the Excalibur.

Blaze had a sharp retort ready but, on closer inspection, decided the helmsman was pale and shaky. "We'll need an extra pair of eyes." He gave Ting the binoculars. "Sit somewhere at a safe distance, and warn us if someone tries to sneak up behind us."

Ting nodded and headed back up the alley to Canal Street. Blaze assumed he would go around the block and watch from a distance. *But who knows, really, what Ting'll do.* They couldn't depend on him to save their necks if things went wrong.

Somethin'll go wrong—somethin' always goes wrong—but I don't have time to be scared. Blaze pulled Cai to her feet and gestured with the pistol for her to walk ahead of him down the alley. She swayed a little, found her balance, and began to move in slow, halting steps. Vipul left the wheelchair and backpack and followed right behind Blaze.

At the end of the alley, they stepped out onto a wide, tree-lined sidewalk. The hotel was diagonally across the street from them, and there were no bodies out front, although several large bloodstains dotted the sidewalk and the middle of the road. The entire street appeared deserted.

I guess the tourists decided they'd had enough excitement for one afternoon.

"Pick a tree to hide behind." Vipul's voice went up an octave. "We've got less than a minute."

Blaze prodded Cai in the back with the gun and pointed at the hotel, just in case she wasn't coherent enough to recognize it. She turned and gave him one last vicious look before heading across the street to the front doors.

"Axe is in the lobby." Ting startled Blaze with this announcement in his earcom. "She's coming out alone."

Blaze squinted out from behind his tree and held his breath as the two women slowly approached each other at the glass doors. He kept Vipul in his peripheral vision. The navigator was crouched behind a tree directly across from the doors.

I hope you know what you're doin', my friend. Blaze prayed Axe wouldn't be shot by a sniper the moment she stepped out onto the sidewalk.

The ISPP's arm looked bad, wrapped with blood-soaked strips of cloth and supported by a temporary sling which appeared to be made from a belt. She used her left shoulder to push open the door on the right at the same time Cai pulled open the door on the left. They exchanged a nervous glance as they passed, giving each other a wide clearance.

Blaze glanced over at Vipul, just in time to see him light the fuse, take aim, and pull the trigger on the harpoon tube.

The homemade missile streaked through the open double doors and exploded in the lobby, filling the space with clouds of white vapor.

Both women screamed and threw themselves on the ground. Cai landed on the floor inside, and Axe on the sidewalk outside. The ISPP officer tried falling onto her left side to protect her arm, but the look on her face told Blaze she was in agony.

Several armed men emerged from the cloud-filled lobby, burst through the doors, and collapsed onto the sidewalk like rag dolls before they could start shooting.

A few more men stumbled through the fog but didn't make it past the doors. They keeled over on top of each other, out cold. Axe and Cai were also overcome by the fumes. Blaze grimaced as one man landed on the ISPP's prone body, but he couldn't do anything to help her at the moment.

He raced to Vipul's side. "That was genius! Now how do we get to the captain and Shima?"

"We'll have to wait until it clears. Everyone in the building should be unconscious by now, but we can't go in without gas masks."

"CIP patrol cars headed your way," Ting announced from wherever he was hiding. "I recommend you ditch the weapons before they see you."

Blaze and Vipul exchanged a concerned glance and deposited their pistols and the harpoon tube into the nearest trashcan.

"That'll only buy us a few minutes," Blaze said. "We're gonna need a translator."

Ting emitted a disgruntled sigh. "I'm coming."

Two CIP patrol cars pulled up in front of the hotel and four astonished-looking officers climbed out to gawk at the pile of slumbering bodies around the hotel's doors.

Blaze and Vipul threw their arms in the air, waving to get the CIPs' attention. "Don't get too close!" Blaze knew it was pointless to shout in English, but he couldn't help it.

The CIPs responded to Blaze's shout by turning around to face him and Vipul and drawing their sidearms. One of them bellowed something which probably meant, "Freeze! Put your hands in the air!"

Ting appeared at Vipul's elbow, raised his arms too, and shouted in Chinese.

"Tell them what's goin' on," Blaze said. "Tell them everythin'."

Ting hesitated. "What if they arrest us?"

"What does it matter?" Vipul said. "We just need to get Shima and the captain out alive. We can sort it out later at CIP headquarters if we have to."

Ting launched into a monologue which kept the officers' attention for a few minutes. When he was finished, one of the officers shouted back.

"He said to get down on the ground and put our hands behind our heads."

"They don't believe you?" Vipul went down to his knees.

"They don't know what to think." The helmsman dropped to his belly on the sidewalk.

"Did you tell them about ISPP?" Blaze hesitated, watching as two of the officers went to the trunk of their patrol car and unearthed a pair of ancient gas masks. The other two approached the crewmembers with their guns still drawn.

One of them barked something at Blaze, and he got the message. He promptly got down on the sidewalk.

"I told them. I also told them two women were being held prisoner inside somewhere."

"Can't say I've ever been arrested." Vipul was calm as he was frisked and handcuffed.

"Me either." Blaze grimaced as metal bracelets secured his wrists behind his back.

"I don't get paid enough for this," was Ting's only comment.

"What now?" Blaze whispered to Vipul. The back of the navigator's gray head was just a few decimeters away.

"Now we wait for ISPP to show up and straighten this out."

Ting groaned. "Reality check, old man. York'll let us sit in jail a long time before he decides to visit. He doesn't even know what's happening."

"Actually, he does." Blaze lifted his head and turned to face the other direction. Marco's shoulder was a decimeter from his nose. "Whether he does anythin' about it is anybody's guess."

After a few minutes, one of the CIPs with a gas mask came over to them, took the antique off his face, and bellowed something at them.

Ting grunted, replied, and translated for the English speakers. "He wants to know how long they'll be unconscious."

"Tell them we don't know," Vipul said.

"I can't tell him that. They're angry enough as it is."

"Then make somethin' up!" Blaze rested his chin on the rough cement and closed his eyes. "Tell them ISPP's on the way, and Captain York'll be *very* unhappy if he finds we've been mistreated."

"Oh yes, *very* unhappy—as if he has any other expression." Vipul started to laugh.

Blaze tried to resist, but couldn't hold back. He laughed until his sides ached.

"I work with idiots," Ting muttered.

TWENTY-FIVE
WHITE VAPOR

AN ANGRY MAN waving a military-grade rifle threw open the door to the office and shouted at Shima and Danae in Mandarin. They scrambled to their feet and put their hands in the air.

Axe opened her eyes and attempted to sit up. She said something to their captor but her voice was weak.

"What's he saying?" Danae took a step back to put some space between herself and the gun, but the desk barred her way.

Axe managed to sit upright. "He wants me to go with him."

"Why?" Danae felt a jolt of fear. "What does he want?"

"Help me up." Axe didn't answer the question. She said something to the man, and he gave a curt nod. "Just one of you, please help me up."

"I will do it." Shima kept her eyes on the weapon as she moved around behind Axe and crouched down. She wrapped her arms around the engineer's waist and stood slowly, using her legs as leverage to lift Axe to her unsteady feet.

"What's he going to do with you?" Danae repeated.

"He didn't say." Axe groaned, unable to find a way to support her damaged right arm.

The captain had an idea. "Tell him I'm going to make a sling for you." She took off her belt and tried not to add to Axe's pain as she improvised a support for the arm.

"Thanks." Axe looked as if she was in too much agony to worry about being taken away at gunpoint. She shot Danae a resigned look as their captor rushed her out of the office and slammed the door behind them.

"We must do something!" Shima said, "They might kill her!"

"They might just want information." Danae thought being interrogated by slavers might be worse than being murdered, but she tried to put on a brave face for Shima's sake, just as Shima had done for her right after Erik was shot. "Calm down. We'll find a way out of here. Maybe you should meditate."

Shima nodded, although she didn't look convinced. She sat on the floor in the lotus position and closed her eyes. Danae envied her ability to turn off the stress so easily, if only for a few minutes.

The captain sat on top of the desk and drew her knees up to her chin, burying her face in her arms. She couldn't stop thinking about Erik. *Is he alive? Is he dead?* She wiped her eyes on the back of her arm and tried to put everything and everyone out of her mind. She wanted to feel numb. *It hurts too much to care.*

Moments later, an explosion shook the building. Both women jumped to their feet.

"What was that?" Shima shrilled.

"I don't know." Danae was tempted to try the door and peer into the hallway, but something odd about the noises outside made her hesitate. The shouts and run-ning footsteps abruptly faded and stopped. The silence worried her more than the shouting.

"What is that?" Shima gestured at the door, where curls of white vapor were seeping through the cracks.

Danae moved fast. "Help me!" She grabbed the paper shredder and dumped the basket out onto the floor. She seized two handfuls of shreds and crammed them into the space at the bottom of the door, trying to seal out the fumes. "Hold your breath!"

Shima grabbed more shreds and started plugging gaps.

"Keep going!" Danae began to feel light-headed, but she kept packing the edges of the doorframe anywhere she saw the vapor trying to get in.

"What is it? Is it poison?"

The captain didn't think White Swan would poison their own people, but she didn't intend to find out if her theory was correct. They finished stuffing the edges of the door with paper shreds, but the air inside the office was still growing hazy.

"The vent!" Shima pointed at the ceiling.

Danae shoved the chair across the room so it was right beneath the air-conditioning duct. "Hand me more shreds!" She held her breath as she stepped onto the seat and stuffed a few handfuls into the slots of the vent cover.

Shima handed a large bundle up to her, but when Danae reached down to grab it, her vision blurred. Her ears filled with a rushing sound like the howl of a gale-force wind, and she felt herself falling down a long, dark tunnel.

***

The sound of wood splintering pulled Danae back up, out of the darkness. She tried to focus her vision, but her eyes wouldn't cooperate.

"I found them!" a familiar, booming female voice announced.

Danae became aware of a sharp throbbing in her left shoulder. Someone tried to help her sit up, but she shrieked at the pain that shot through her shoulder, back, and arm, all the way down to her elbow.

"Dislocated shoulder," said another familiar voice, this one male with a Thai accent. "Looks like she fell off the chair. Hold on, Captain Shepherd, this is going to hurt."

Before she could protest, the speaker raised her elbow, turned her arm to the side, and pulled it straight up over her head. Danae screamed like a banshee, but she felt the bone slip back into the shoulder socket, halting most of the pain. She was able to open her eyes and bring her vision into focus.

Wisdom Moniesa was standing over her, supporting a woozy Shima with one muscular arm around her tiny waist. Dusit Jiang was crouched on the floor beside Danae. The smug look on his face needed no explanation.

"Thanks for giving me a painkiller first." Danae was too angry to suppress the sarcasm. "Where did you come from?"

The medic helped Danae to her unsteady feet. "Bangkok."

"No, I mean when did ISPP get here?"

"About thirty minutes ago," Moniesa said. "We received the transmission from Smith, requesting assistance, and lifted immediately for Guangzhou."

"Blaze sent a transmission?" Danae was having a hard time organizing her thoughts. "What was in the vapor that knocked us out?"

"It was a fast-acting gas anesthesia," Moniesa said, "delivered by an explosive device, courtesy of your clever navigator."

"Vipul bombed the hotel?" Shima's jaw dropped.

"Yes, he was able to knock out everyone inside so no more lives were lost." Moniesa grinned. "Shall we go now?"

"But where is Axe?" Shima asked. "Is she all right?"

"She is fine. She is on her way to the *Liberty*'s infirmary." Moniesa steered the first officer to the open doorway, or what was left of it. The shattered door was hanging off a single hinge.

Frantic awareness cut a path through Danae's muddled thoughts. "Where's Erik?"

"Dr. Sorensen is with our senior medic right now," Moniesa said. "He is going to be all right."

Danae's knees buckled, and she had to lean against the desk for support.

"Captain?" Moniesa paused in the doorway, glancing over at her with concern.

"I'm fine." Danae assumed she didn't look fine because she was shaking and tears were beginning to streak her face.

The ISPP officers gave her a minute to pull herself together. As relief flooded her senses, Danae thought of something else. "Tell Cade he needs all the information in this filing cabinet." She extracted the folded papers from the pockets she could reach with her right hand. "Make sure he gets these." She pushed them into Jiang's hands. "I'm ready to get out of here."

"Right this way." Moniesa slipped her free arm around Danae's waist and escorted her and Shima out of the hotel, into the warm night air.

Danae blinked at the glare of CIP patrol car headlights, which illuminated the entire street as if it were midday. Dozens of men and a few women sat on the curb in front of the hotel, their arms behind their backs in handcuffs.

"Captain!" Blaze and Vipul rushed over to greet her and Shima. The engineer started to give her a hug, but Danae shook her head to ward him off.

"Dislocated my shoulder so no hugs right now." She mustered a smile and scouted the crowd of CIPs, ISPPs, and assorted bystanders. "Where's Cade?"

"Captain York said he would meet with your crew in the morning." Moniesa looked as if she wanted to say more but had orders not to. She released Danae and Shima, made sure they were steady on their feet, and took a step back so the *Alex*'s crew could talk.

Jiang reappeared. He slipped a sling over Danae's head, adjusted it around her left arm, and wrapped a huge ice pack around her shoulder area. He also pressed a patch to the skin behind her right ear. "That'll help your muscles regrow."

"Thank you," Danae said, although she was still annoyed at the medic for popping her shoulder back into place without numbing the area first. *Masochist,* she thought as he walked away.

Danae was amazed to see Ting join the huddle. "Is everyone here?"

"Except Lorina, who went back to the ship to be with Niyati, and Phailin, who rode with Erik to the hospital," Blaze said.

"Want to give me a report, gentlemen?"

"I'll give you the super-short version," Vipul offered. "After you were taken captive, Phailin and Lorina were able to give Erik first aid and get him in a taxi to take him to the nearest hospital."

A taxi? Though it was tempting to start firing off questions, Danae vowed not to interrupt.

"Blaze came up with the idea of a prisoner exchange—"

A what? She had to bite her tongue to keep her mouth shut.

"—Cai for the three of you, but the White Swan representative she spoke to on the com would only agree to one prisoner, so we asked for Axe."

Danae glanced over at the lineup of prisoners sitting on the curb and spotted Cai wedged between two scowling men. The slaver had her head down, staring at the road. The arrogant smirk was gone.

After everything that happened, Danae's desire to exact some type of vengeance on Cai had faded. *If I'm ever going to have closure, I need to let it go.* It seemed like an impossible goal, so she set the thought aside and turned back to her crew, focusing on what Vipul was saying.

"Blaze sedated Cai so he and Ting could get her here, and I had him bring several items from the spare-parts workshop to construct a bomb."

"It was a tear-gas type of explosive." Blaze grinned, eager to elaborate. "Filled with anesthesia."

"Yes, Moniesa told us about it," Danae said. "Remind me to give you a raise, Mr. Ganguli. Your brilliant idea saved our lives."

The navigator appeared embarrassed by the praise. "I couldn't have pulled it together without Blaze's assistance."

"And none of this would've worked without my translation services," Ting said. "So I deserve a raise too."

Danae shot her helmsman a look of astonishment. "You actually helped?"

Blaze glared at Ting. "It took some persuasion."

"What happened after everyone was unconscious?" Shima asked.

"Well, the CIPs came and arrested us—" Vipul said.

"*What?*" Shima gasped.

"—then York and company showed up half an hour later, so we didn't have to lie on the ground in handcuffs for too long. ISPP searched the building, and what's left of White Swan is sitting here on the sidewalk."

"Were there any other prisoners inside?" Danae asked.

Moniesa spoke up. "Fortunately, no. Captain York believes the hotel was used as White Swan's living quarters and corporate office. If you are ready, Captain Shepherd, I should escort your crew back to your ship."

Danae nodded. "Let's go."

The weapons officer herded the *Alex*'s crewmembers to the tramstop on Canal Street. The captain sat in silence during the hour-long ride back to the spaceport. There were so many thoughts swirling through her mind, she couldn't focus on a single one. She leaned her head on Shima's shoulder, grateful for the dim overhead lights of the tram so no one would notice an occasional tear slide down her face.

Shima gave her right arm a squeeze and whispered, "It is over, *rafiki*. We can go home."

TWENTY-SIX
REBOUNDING

ERIK WAS AWARE of conversations he couldn't follow in Chinese and English, needles from IVs, the hum of medical scanners, and the strange tickling sensation of probe androids moving around inside the gaping hole that used to be his right shoulder. At one point he was aware of bright lights overhead and the scent of antiseptic air, but he couldn't pull himself free of the persistent fog which blurred the passage of time.

He awoke clearheaded and opened his eyes. He was astonished to find Cade York standing at his bedside.

"Welcome back," York said in his gruff, unwelcoming way.

Erik glanced around, startled to see he was in a high-tech infirmary instead of a Chinese hospital. It wasn't the *Alex*'s infirmary. This one was bigger and sleeker, the furnishings and fabrics all olive green. "This is your ship?"

"Yes, we moved you here three days ago. My medics took care of your shoulder reconstruction."

I've been out of it for three days? Erik knew the polite thing to do would be to thank him, but he didn't—since York was the reason he needed reconstructive surgery in the first place. Another thought took precedence over diplomacy. "Where's Danae?"

York hesitated long enough to make Erik worry. "She's aboard her ship."

The doctor blew out a long breath, and his relief morphed into rage. "You almost got us all killed!"

"I realize now I underestimated the risk." York didn't make eye contact. "I assumed Tse could handle any security problems."

"Well, obviously she couldn't!" Erik was annoyed York didn't bother to apologize. "Do you want to give me an update or should I wait to talk to Danae?"

York grimaced but gave him a synopsis. "I received Smith's transmission five minutes after he sent it, and we lifted immediately for Guangzhou. We were able to arrive in time to extract Danae and Oryang from White Swan's headquarters. Neither was seriously injured, thanks to Ganguli's ingenuity."

"They were taken prisoner!" It was worse than Erik imagined. "You mean someone *was* injured, and it was probably Danae—am I right?"

York shifted his stance but didn't answer the question—which was an answer in itself.

"How thoughtful of you to send in the Marines *after* it was all over!" *I hope he realizes how lucky he is I can't get up!*

York carried on as if Erik hadn't said a word. "No one else on your crew was injured. Tse has recovered from her gunshot wound, and I'll leave her and several of my senior officers here to sort out the mess with the

Guangzhou authorities while I return to Bangkok to finish sorting out the mess there."

"You seem to create more messes than you sort out."

York frowned and looked away. "I'll let Danae fill you in on the details. My senior medic Yamato said you can get up in two hours. I'll have Moniesa escort you back to your ship."

The captain turned to leave but paused a moment, squared his shoulders, and turned back to look Erik in the eye. "Investigating Shamian Island should've been our responsibility, and I can assure you I'll never recruit civilians to work for ISPP again."

"Good," was the only thing Erik could think to say.

"Your crew's efforts have been invaluable." York broke eye contact, evidence that praise was a foreign concept to him. "Thanks to your investigative work and courageous efforts, ISPP has been able to liberate many slave factories and brothels, and we were able to locate White Swan's headquarters. We have enough information now to free millions of trafficked children, and hopefully put an end to the galaxy's child-slave trade."

Nice speech. Erik was unmoved. "It's Danae you need to thank. She has more courage than both of us combined."

York nodded. "She's a remarkable woman." He shifted his stance, his expression reminiscent of someone forced to swallow a live toad. "I wish you the best with Captain Shepherd. You seem . . . well suited for each other."

Erik was impressed York didn't choke on those words. This time he did manage a quiet "thank you."

The ISPP captain turned on his heel and walked out of the infirmary, leaving Erik alone with his thoughts.

It's over. He felt fatigue down to his bones, and it was much more than physical exhaustion. *If I feel wiped out, emotionally, I can't imagine how Danae must feel.* Two hours felt like an eternity. He couldn't wait to see her again.

If she still wants to see me after all this.

So much for trying to shelter her emotions. Erik wouldn't be surprised if Danae's wall was back up and she didn't want anything more to do with him. *She's suffered enough these past few months. I should've stayed on Mars—stayed out of her life until she had sufficient time to grieve.*

He found himself wondering about Alex Shepherd. *Am I even in the same league with the guy?* He set the depressing thought aside. It was impossible to compete with a ghost.

Erik turned his head to examine his bare right shoulder. The darker pink synthflesh was sculpted to replace what the bullet destroyed. He felt the back of his shoulder with his left hand and found it equally smooth. His shoulder blade, collarbone, and ribs seemed properly restored.

He flexed his pectorals and was pleased to see they moved incrementally. He tried his deltoids but was rewarded with no movement and a dull pain. He knew intensive physical therapy would be the next step to full mobility. *Ting'll be sure to gloat.*

The doctor realized his reconstructed shoulder matched Danae's reconstructed left side. It struck him as morbid, but he couldn't help it—he started to laugh.

***

It took some effort to get out of bed, but Erik wasn't surprised his muscles were so stiff. "What day is it, anyway?" he asked Moniesa, who was ready to assist him into the wheelchair, if necessary.

She grinned. "December eleventh."

"What happened to the eighth, ninth, and tenth?" Erik adjusted the hospital gown he wore toga-style to accommodate the sling. He was grateful his backside wasn't feeling a breeze because someone put boxer shorts on him while he was unconscious.

This realization triggered an uncomfortable thought. "Do I have on York's underwear?"

Moniesa chuckled. "Of course. No one else wears your size, except perhaps me, although Dr. Yamato did not think you wanted to wear my panties."

Erik pursed his lips, trying not to picture that image in his mind. "Thanks for that. I don't suppose York could loan me a shirt too?"

The big woman shrugged, still grinning mischievously. "Your ship is only two levels below the *Liberty*. In five minutes you can put on your own clothing."

"Right." Erik managed to settle himself into the wheelchair without assistance. "Tell York thanks for the embarrassing souvenir."

Moniesa laughed and pushed him out of the infirmary. It took only a few minutes to reach the *Liberty*'s airlock with its loading ramp to the landing platform, the spaceport lift, and the collapsible staircase leading to the *Alex*'s airlock.

"Permission to come aboard," Moniesa called up to the open, round doorway.

The staircase took a moment to flatten into a loading ramp, and the weapons officer pushed Erik's chair up the steep incline, into the airlock antechamber.

The entire crew was waiting for Erik in the entryway of *Alex's Legacy*, standing in a line like an informal honor guard.

"Goodbye, Dr. Sorensen. You can keep the chair— and the undershorts." Moniesa laughed, nodded to the crew, then turned and descended the ramp.

"Welcome back!" Blaze was careful to pat Erik on his left shoulder. He cycled the airlock shut and headed up the ladder without another word.

"You look well, mate." Vipul shook his left hand and promptly followed Blaze.

Lorina and Phailin swooped down on Erik at the same time, each planting a kiss on his forehead.

"Thank you for saving my life." He didn't know what else to say to them. Words seemed inadequate.

"Thank *you* for not dying," Lorina said. "Jake would've never forgiven me."

Phailin gave his hand an extra squeeze. The young women moved to the ladder as Shima approached him next.

"You were very brave," she said.

Erik shook his head. "I was stupid to walk out in the open and get myself shot."

"You are a doctor, not a soldier, so you cannot be expected to know combat strategy—none of us knew what we were doing. It was a miracle none of us were killed. I still think you were very brave."

Shima added another kiss to his forehead but paused a moment while her mouth was near his ear to whisper, "Danae cares for you. I hope you are smart enough *not* to break her heart." She straightened, flashed him a stern look, and moved to the ladder before he could respond.

Erik realized his mouth was hanging open and shut it.

"You had us worried for a few minutes," Ting said with uncharacteristic sincerity, although he made it a point not to touch Erik.

"Thanks for your translation services. I'll be sure to ask the boss to give you a raise." The doctor winked at Danae, who was last in line behind the helmsman.

"Whatever." Ting was already scrambling up the ladder behind the rest of the crew, leaving him alone in the entryway with Captain Shepherd.

Erik felt his heart skip a beat as Danae approached him. She was wearing her poker face so he didn't know what to expect.

She studied his exposed right shoulder. He waited for her to say something as she reached over and traced the synthflesh with an index finger. Although the nerve endings in the repair site were less sensitive than undamaged nerves, her touch still sent a shiver up his spine.

Danae raised her eyes to his face. "If you'd been shot on the left side, near the heart, you wouldn't have survived."

"That's true." Erik wondered where she was going with this. "And if you'd been shot a few centimeters closer to the spine, you wouldn't have survived."

"I guess we've both been given a second chance at life."

He didn't know how to respond to this philosophical remark, so he tried to get her to focus on current events. "York said you and Shima were taken prisoner?"

"I don't want to talk about that right now."

He was startled at the brisk response but assumed she had something else on her mind. "Well, what do you want to talk about?"

Danae just stared at him with the calm look he found disconcerting because it masked her real thoughts.

He tried again to draw her out. "Do you remember what I said when I was laid up in the infirmary a few weeks ago?"

"No. Why don't you refresh my memory?"

"I said we've been through so much together that it's natural to feel an attraction." He hesitated a moment, searching her face for a flicker of emotion, but she wasn't giving anything away. "But if we acted on these feelings, we might regret it."

Her poker face broke—into a scowl. "You're saying you regret our relationship?"

Erik wanted to bite his tongue. The words hadn't come out the way he intended. "I'm saying I regret putting you through the emotional wringer again. If I'd had the sense to keep my distance and give you time—"

"Time to do *what*, exactly?" The color rose in her cheeks. "Time to mourn until I'd lost the will to live? Because that's the point I was at before I met you!"

Danae's hands moved to rest on her hips, and Erik decided it might be wise to shut his mouth and let her say what she needed to say, even at full volume.

"You still think you can shelter my emotions? Every relationship involves some level of risk. Without ex-periencing hurt or disappointment or grief, we'd never know what real joy feels like. Without risk, we'd never make friends or"—she stammered—"or fall in love. Shima advised me to stop putting up walls to keep people out, but you're telling me I'd be happier behind those walls because I should've kept you out?"

"I just didn't want to add to your pain," Erik tried to explain. He hated seeing her so upset and knowing he was the reason for it.

"Is this your way of saying you'd prefer some distance? We should quit while we're ahead so it won't hurt as much? Is that what you want?" She turned her back to him and moved a few steps away, fists clenched at her side.

"No! That's not what I want!" Erik made a grab for Danae, but she was just out of reach. Summoning his last reserves of strength, he gripped the arm of the wheelchair with his left hand and pushed himself up.

He lurched forward on unsteady feet and caught hold of her arm. He pulled her back, expecting some resistance, but was nearly bowled over as she threw her arms around him and buried her face in his chest, shaking with gut-wrenching sobs.

"I thought I lost you! I thought you were dead! And it was my fault for being so stubborn and not listening to your advice! I was so obsessed with the Baronowskis I put everyone's lives in danger! It would've been *my fault* if you'd died!"

Erik tried to get her to calm down, stroking her back with his left hand and whispering, "Shhhh—" but she was inconsolable. His leg muscles quivered from the strain of being on his feet and supporting her weight, so he slowly backed up with her until he reached the wheelchair and could sit down again. He drew Danae onto his lap and held her as she sobbed.

Even though he still considered himself a novice at understanding females, Erik knew most women needed to cry once in a while. His sister and former girlfriends had bawled on his shoulder many times, and Danae had plenty of reasons to lose her composure. He suspected she stored it up until there was no more room to contain it. The front of his gown was getting soaked, but she had an endless reservoir of tears.

"Did you cry this much after losing Alex?" Erik knew it wasn't wise to put this thought into words, but he couldn't help himself. He needed to know if she was projecting her grief onto him. Had the shock of his near death brought back a flood of emotions for her late husband?

"What?" She paused to listen, her sobs subsiding into sniffles.

"Are you this upset about what happened to me, or are these tears for Alex?"

She looked at him in shock with red-rimmed eyes, her face blotchy-pink from the extended cry. Her mouth opened and closed a few times but couldn't formulate an answer.

"That's what I thought." He shut his eyes so he could say what he needed to say without the guilty conscience her expression was sure to trigger. "I guess I don't mind being his replacement if it means I can still be close to you."

"*What?*"

Erik noted the sharp edge in her tone. He was afraid to open his eyes so he pressed on with what he hoped was a reassuring explanation. "It's my fault. I told you to take all the time you needed, but then I didn't follow my own advice. I knew I was taking a huge risk by not giving you enough time to grieve and that you might come to view me as a temporary source of comfort." He took a deep breath, determined to get it all out in the open. "But I didn't care because I'd hoped it would lead to something serious—something that would last long after the grief was over."

He paused to collect his stray thoughts. "Everything I've ever read about rebound relationships states that they rarely work out. One day you wake up and say, 'What was I thinking? This person can never replace who I lost.' Trying to get close to you while you're still in pain is wrong, and I should've known better. I've experienced enough grief to know it's not a one-time event. It's a process—it can't be turned on and off like a faucet. I was wrong to rush you into a relationship you weren't ready for, and you deserve better than someone as selfish as me."

Danae stopped crying and sat still for a few minutes. He waited for her to draw her own conclusions, vowing to be patient—for a change.

Erik felt her hand on his cheek and cautiously opened his eyes. Her piercing gaze once again gave him the impression that she could read his thoughts.

"I want you to listen carefully because I'm only going to say this once: What you and I have isn't a rebound relationship. Alex will always be a part of me and giving me more time to grieve isn't going to make me miss him any less. I can't replace him . . . and I don't want to replace him. I made a conscious decision the morning you picked me up during Marco's physical therapy."

He was afraid to ask. "What . . . did you decide?"

"I decided I wanted to let down my wall for you. You're not a replacement or a temporary source of comfort, and if you've been wondering whether I compare you to Alex in my mind—I don't. I never have, and I never will."

For the first time in weeks, Erik felt a glimmer of confidence that his instincts about Danae were right. It was irrational to tell her on the tram filled with orphans on their way to the Mars Station spaceport—on the run from Acheron—that he wanted to see her again. It was premature to tell her after spending a month in Acheron's prison—and under the influence of painkillers—that he wanted to be more than friends. And it was insane to demonstrate his feelings for her after witnessing the kiss with York. He expected rejection with every risky step, but his worries hadn't come to fruition.

"Alex is gone"—her voice cracked, and it took her a moment to continue—"he's dead. But you're here, you're alive, and you are *very* important to me. I don't want to lose you again."

"You'll never lose me." What Erik wanted to say was, "I love you," but thought he had put too much pressure on her already. *I'll wait. I'll let her take the lead—whether this leads to love or not will be her choice, not mine.* He pulled her close but realized this romantic moment was doomed to fail.

"I'd kiss you, but I haven't brushed my teeth in three days."

***

After showering, shaving, a thorough tooth-cleaning, and struggling into his own set of clothes, Erik put the sling back on and strapped himself into one of the post-op beds in the infirmary for the three-hour flight to Maui.

He couldn't believe how tired he was after Danae's emotional breakdown. *I wasn't the one who did all the crying!*

It seemed as if he just closed his eyes when the captain announced over the com, "Strap down for landing. Local time is 6:15 p.m.," she added, no doubt for Erik's benefit.

The ship had set down with only a few bumps. Erik re-leased the straps and used his left arm to raise himself to a seated position. He sat on the edge of the bed and thought about mustering the strength to get up and move around.

"Good evening." Danae breezed into the room. "Are you hungry?"

Erik's stomach answered for him with a loud gurgle. "Yes."

"Let's see what Jake has to say about what you're allowed to eat."

"I'm the medic on this ship." Erik pretended to be offended. "And I say I can eat whatever I want."

"One cup of vegetable broth, coming right up." Jake O'Brien poked his head in the doorway and shot Erik a mischievous grin. "As the acting medic on this ship, I'll let you have some gelatin too, if you behave."

Danae gave Jake a big hug when he reached Erik's bedside. The apprentice medic shot Erik an apologetic look over her shoulder, as if he committed an unforgivable indiscretion.

Erik wondered what prompted this reaction, but he grinned and said, "That's enough fraternizing with the crew, Captain."

"Well, I guess I'm in big trouble because I've been doing a lot of fraternizing lately." She winked at Erik and turned back to Jake. "It's good to see you. Thanks for holding down the fort."

Shima, Blaze, Niyati, Phailin, and Vipul showed up one at a time and greeted Jake. Niyati hugged his leg and wouldn't let go until Blaze threatened to tickle her.

"Jake!" Lorina joined the crowd, giving her cousin a bear hug. "I missed you!"

"Not much, I'll bet." Jake winked at Blaze. "I'm sure we have plenty to talk about. Why don't we head over to The Lost Sheep? Paul Ly has prepared a sumptuous welcome-home feast for the crew, although Erik will have to put his dinner through the blender."

"What? I don't think so!"

Zuri and Ekaterina came to see what all the excitement was about, and Shima introduced them to Jake. Ting arrived last, ignored Jake's greeting, and followed the crew to the starboard lift.

Without asking, Danae moved to Erik's left side and slipped her arm around his waist to support him as he got to his feet. He didn't need assistance to get around, but he shamelessly took advantage of the opportunity to be close to her. He rested his good arm on her shoulders and took his time walking, savoring the fact that they were back on Maui with no more dangerous missions on the agenda.

At the airlock doorway, Erik paused to look over Danae's beautiful sugarcane plantation. The ship set down in a rolling field of tropical grasses, dotted with an occasional coconut palm. There were lush green hills in the distance, just beyond the abandoned sugar processing plant, which stood about one hundred meters away from the ship. A large white, Victorian-style farmhouse was past the plant, facing the main road. He could just make out the chicken coop in the backyard and the kids playing soccer in the mowed field beyond the house. The warm breeze carried the fragrance of salt water, palm trees, and hibiscus blossoms.

The rest of the crew was already halfway across the field, walking toward the house, but Danae wasn't in a hurry to catch up. She and Erik descended the collapsible staircase and followed the group at a slower pace.

"Am I going too fast?" She glanced at his face with earnest concern.

Erik didn't have the heart to tell her his leg muscles were stiff but worked just fine. "No, this pace is perfect." He took a good look around. "This is the ideal place to rest and heal. I hope we plan to stay for a long time."

Danae made an impatient noise. "My bank account says otherwise. I should meet with the crew and see who wants to get back into the passenger transport business."

He sighed. "Well, let's take a few weeks off, at least."

"I figure we can afford ten days. After that we're officially back in the red."

Ten days, huh? Recalling Lorina's advice, Erik wondered how much romance he could squeeze into ten days.

***

His shoulder wasn't cooperating. Erik couldn't believe how hard it was to lift ten kilos over his head. Sweating as if he were outside in Bangkok at midday, he set the weight on the floor and flopped down beside it, disgusted with himself. "Even Ting bounced back faster than this."

"You're pushing yourself too hard." Jake was sitting cross-legged on a post-op bed, playing with his medical scanner, although he was supposed to be supervising Erik's physical therapy session. "You have a replacement shoulder to break in. Give it time."

"Danae wants to lift off in six days. I can't let her down."

"Judging by the dreamy look on her face whenever she sees you, I think she'll understand if you need more time to recuperate."

"She doesn't look at me like that." Erik stretched his right arm across his chest, grimacing as he held it in place with his left hand for a few seconds. "Owww!"

Jake snorted with laughter. "Well, since your eyes are closed whenever she's in the same room with you, I guess you haven't noticed."

"My eyes are closed?" Erik was confused.

Vipul stuck his head in the doorway. "He means you're usually *snogging* when you're in the same room with the captain. That's why your eyes are closed."

Erik felt his face turn red as Jake roared with laughter. "Something you need, Vipul?"

The navigator grinned. "Captain Shepherd requests that you do the next interview at 1600. She would've called you personally, but she's currently interviewing a Dr. Johnson from Hana."

"Isn't Johnson an old guy with a scruffy beard?" Jake asked.

"I don't think *Nora* Johnson has a beard." Vipul laughed.

The medical apprentice grinned. "I guess I didn't look close enough at the holograms on the résumés."

Erik glanced at the time and got to his feet. "I need to shower. Please tell Danae I'll be a few minutes late."

"Need me to give you a piggyback ride to the house?" Jake asked.

"Not unless you want to give yourself a hernia, little man."

Ten minutes later, Erik climbed the steps to the wide front porch of The Lost Sheep. He smiled at Danae, who was leaning back in one of the rocking chairs, looking frustrated. He sat in the rocker next to hers. "Any prospects?"

She shook her head. "I didn't think it would be this hard to hire a medic for the orphanage. I haven't spoken to anyone with a medical license. Three nurses, one EMT, and—I'm not making this up—Dr. Johnson turned out to be a chiropractor."

Erik chuckled. "Are you sure you don't want to extend our dirtside vacation a few weeks—or months—or maybe years? Long enough for Jake to finish his training?"

"I can't expect Phailin to run the orphanage without any money." Danae reached for his hand. "Do you want to interview the last candidate together or would you mind handling it solo?"

"Anything you need, sugar," Erik purred.

"I can tell you've been hanging around Blaze." Danae handed him a datapad and got to her feet. "Let's hope Dr. Perry isn't a podiatrist or a dentist—or a veterinarian."

Erik wanted to hold on to her hand a little longer, but it turned out to be a mistake. As she stepped away, a shockwave of pain traveled up his extended arm, into his shoulder. He gasped and snatched his hand back.

Alarmed, Danae crouched beside his chair. "What's wrong?"

"It's nothing." Embarrassed, he rubbed his shoulder with his other hand.

She took over the shoulder rub. "Let me help. You need to give yourself more time to recover."

"You sound like Jake."

"Well, he did learn from the best." She flashed a coy smile. "Seriously, why don't you head back to the ship?"

"I can handle the next interview, Danae."

She was skeptical. "You're planning to shake his hand?"

Erik hated feeling so helpless, *so handicapped*, he thought. "I'll work harder at my physical therapy. I promise you I'll be one hundred percent by the time we lift."

"Don't push it. Don't do what I did. I learned the hard way not to make unreasonable demands on my body to try and save time. It's not worth it."

"Sounds like good advice." He glanced past her and saw a portly black man walking up the driveway. "Dr. Perry is here. Let me take care of this for you."

Danae's frown was thoughtful. "Fine, but I want to have a long talk with you sometime about your recovery."

Erik grinned. "Yes, ma'am."

She gave him a mysterious look and a kiss on the cheek before going inside the house.

***

It was 2230 when Erik found Danae alone in the galley, sipping her evening cup of chamomile tea. "So pediatrician Dr. Winston Perry is all moved into the orphanage infirmary, although we need to get him a bigger bed. Is now a good time for that long talk?" He sat across from her and tried not to jump to conclusions about the strange look on her face. "Danae?"

"So I was thinking . . ." She tried to sound casual, but he could tell she was nervous. She cleared her throat and tried again. "I was thinking you might be more comfortable recuperating in my cabin."

Erik stopped breathing. This was the last thing he expected her to say. Apparently this long talk was going to be short, depending on his answer. He closed his eyes, his mind in a whirl as he half listened to her ramble on awkwardly about how her cabin would be quieter than the infirmary and how it had custom-built features for a larger-than-average occupant. She was referring to Alex, of course, but his name was never mentioned.

"Erik?" Danae's hesitant whisper reminded him to start breathing again. "Did you hear me?"

He forced himself to focus on forming a response with a mouth that felt frozen. *I said I'd let her take the lead, but that was only a few days ago!* Although they never had a where-do-we-go-from-here discussion, with her suggestion to cohabitate, Erik could tell he and Danae weren't on the same page about how a serious relationship should progress. He also knew he would be taking a huge risk by suggesting they try it *his* way instead of hers. He had a nagging thought what he needed to say wouldn't go over well—and he was right.

"I don't want to be your roommate, Danae."

"You don't?" Her cheeks turned pink, and she shifted her gaze from his face to the bulkhead behind him. "Well, this is awkward. I thought I was ready . . . but maybe it's premature, and I guess I'm the one rushing you. I know it's a big step, and I shouldn't have assumed . . ." She couldn't seem to articulate a complete thought, so she improvised an excuse to slip away. "You know, I'm really tired. Maybe we should talk later . . . excuse me."

Danae got to her feet and turned to leave, but Erik popped up out of his chair and hooked her arm, turning her to face him. "Let me explain—"

"You don't have to explain anything." She flashed him a halfhearted smile, trying to hide her disappointment. "You're allowed to change your mind. I can't say I blame you. You've certainly seen me at my worst."

"But I love you at your worst and your best and every stage in between. Now let me explain."

She stiffened when Erik mentioned the *L* word, but waited for him to continue.

"I haven't changed my mind. I'm ready to get *very* serious, but I have a better idea." He noticed her hands moving down to her hip pockets and captured her right hand before she managed to tuck it away. She attempted to pull it free, but he bent down and brought the back of her trembling hand up to his lips for a kiss.

He grinned at her thunderstruck expression as he kept hold of her hand and got down on one knee. "I don't want to be your roommate, Danae Shepherd. I want to be your husband, if you'll have me."

The rosy hue drained from her face so fast, he thought she might faint, but she took some deep breaths and regained her composure. He felt his own heart hammering against his ribs as he waited for her reply.

Erik was accustomed to making instant decisions—his profession required it—but this impulsive choice was borderline crazy, and he knew it. But he didn't care. He knew he was risking devastating rejection and heartache, but he also knew how he felt about the woman standing in front of him with her mouth hanging open in shock.

In his mind, the relationship wouldn't survive if the commitment didn't come first. He knew this wasn't the way most people viewed serious relationships, but he'd observed that the happiest people—the people who felt the most joy and security in their relationships—were those who were willing to take the extra step to make it official. Marriage was more than a verbal agreement to cohabitate. It was a binding commitment to work together so the relationship would last, ideally, forever. There was no room for trial runs, in his opinion. It was all or nothing.

Lorina had advised him to drop the logic and take a leap of faith. *But will Danae do the same?* Since he had no idea how she made the decision to marry Alex Shepherd, he could only go by what he observed: she made choices based on her gut feelings, her intuition, her conscience, *and maybe her heart?*

Danae took a long time to think it over. Her eyes were squeezed shut, and she was gnawing her lower lip. Erik was determined to wait as long as it took, but the extended silence invited doubts to creep in. His knee on the floor was starting to ache, and the hand holding hers was getting sweaty, but he didn't budge.

After what felt like a long time, Danae managed to find her voice. She opened her big blue eyes and stared into his, but her face revealed nothing. "Didn't you tell me I should take all the time I needed?"

"You need more time . . . to think about it?" When she didn't reply, Erik's doubts began to gather momentum. "Maybe we could discuss this again . . . in a few months?"

She shook her head, her face unchanged.

His heart sank. "Maybe . . . a year from now?"

She shook her head again.

Erik let go of her hand and got to his feet. It was his turn to hide the disappointment. "I guess I should . . . well, goodnight . . . Captain." He retreated a few steps and turned to leave the galley.

"Are you so impatient you can't wait a minute to hear what I have to say?"

Erik paused and slowly rotated to face her again. Danae's hands were on her hips, and she looked as angry as she sounded.

"Don't you want to hear my answer?"

He felt a stirring of impatience. "Do you think hearing the word *no* will somehow make it hurt less?"

"Yes," she said.

"Well, it doesn't—"

"Yes!" she interrupted, her anger turning to exasperation. "As in 'yes, I'll marry you'!"

Erik was so shocked, his brain stopped working for a minute.

Danae smiled at his dumbstruck expression. "I don't need more time to think about it."

"Are . . . you sure?" Relief flooded him, but a glimmer of doubt remained.

"Well, I thought about it logically—"

Erik tried not to flinch.

Danae continued. "I made you an offer, and you topped it with a better offer—one that's been in the back of my mind under the let's-see-how-things-go category."

"You'd already given it some thought?"

He moved a few steps closer to her but stopped short when she said, "Sure, I weighed the pros and cons—"

Erik flinched.

"And your pros well outweighed your cons—too many to list, really."

He didn't want to ask what was listed under his cons. "You make it sound like a science experiment."

"I'm not finished." She arched an eyebrow at him. "For a man who claims to be an expert in patience, you need a refresher course."

"I never said I was an expert, and I actually flunked that class."

Danae was grinning, enjoying the banter. "So after you passed the objectivity test, I examined my feelings."

Erik's concern turned to relief. "That's better. So how did I measure up in that category?"

He took another step closer but stopped again when she said, "First I had to separate any potential contributing factors—"

"And we're back to the science experiment."

"As I was saying . . ." Danae narrowed her eyes at him, though her grin remained. "I had to consider if my feelings were generated by all the emotionally charged misadventures, or if I needed comfort and you just happened to be available, or if I was lonely and, again, you happened to be available, or if I felt guilty for saying yes to the mission, which was the reason you were shot and almost died."

Erik nodded. He'd wrestled with these thoughts himself, many times. "So aside from excitement, comfort, loneliness, or guilt, how do you feel?"

"Truthfully, they all contributed to my feelings, but I tried to focus on what was in my heart."

"And—?" He was nearly exhausted from the emotional back-and-forth but hoped she saved the best for last.

Danae closed the space between them and wrapped her arms around his waist. "I realized I love you—for you, just the way you are. I never dreamed I'd be lucky enough to find a perfect man *twice* in my life."

"I'm nowhere near perfect, Danae."

"I meant perfect, for me. I think I could be very happy as Mrs. Sorensen."

"That's good because my plan is to make sure you're very happy." He leaned down, and she went up on tiptoes, their mouths meeting halfway in a kiss which left no doubt in his mind she accepted his proposal.

Danae broke off the steamy kiss. "Do you think Kirsten can afford shuttle fare?"

Erik laughed at how quickly she switched her focus to practical matters. "Kirsten won't leave Mars."

"Maybe we should get married on the station?"

"That's sweet of you to want to include her, but I think she'd understand if we stayed here where the setting is much more attractive."

"The setting doesn't matter. I don't want a fancy wedding."

"That's good because I don't either." Erik flashed a mischievous grin. "Shall we visit the Lahaina Town Hall?"

Danae's stunned look almost made him laugh again. "Elope? Um, sounds good, but when?"

"How about tomorrow morning?"

She hesitated for a moment and then broke into a big smile. "We'll need two witnesses. I'll ask Shima."

Erik nodded. "I'll ask Jake."

TWENTY-SEVEN
PLAN C

"THEY'RE PLANNIN' TO *what*?" Blaze dropped his spoon, splattering oatmeal across the table.

Shima nodded and wiped a dab of oatmeal off the back of her hand with a napkin. "They have decided to elope."

"When?" Lorina asked.

"As soon as the town hall opens at 0900." Shima glanced back and forth between Lorina's and Blaze's stunned faces, and smirked. "I do not know why you two are surprised, considering how fast you made the decision to marry."

"Yes, but we're young and restless. They're older—" Blaze began.

"*Older*?" Shima snorted with laughter. "You say it like they are elderly and senile! Yes, it was an impulsive decision, but it is one they are comfortable with."

"Sure, why not jump in with both feet? Marriage is an adventure." Blaze winked at his bride.

Lorina rolled her eyes back at him. "Well, good for Erik for taking my advice."

"I'm afraid to ask," Blaze said, "but what advice was that?"

"Good advice," she said evasively. "I think they'll be happy together. They're compatible." She smirked. "And they obviously have chemistry."

Lorina got to her feet. "We should get moving; it's already 0830. Where's Niyati?"

Hearing her name, their daughter emerged from the kitchen pantry holding a giant wedge of cheddar. "Hungry!"

"You're not eating that." Lorina made Niyati put the cheese back and shooed her out of the galley. "Hurry up, Blaze," she called over her shoulder. "We need to get dressed for the wedding."

"I thought they were elopin'. Doesn't that mean they want to be alone?" Blaze glanced at Shima, who was holding her sides from laughing. "I guess we'll meet you dirtside in a few minutes."

Half an hour later, Danae, in the curve-hugging pink and green muumuu she wore at Blaze and Lorina's wedding, climbed into the driver's seat of the solar van. Erik, in a dark gray suit and a blue tie which matched his sling, sat in the passenger's seat. They were joined by the entire crew of *Alex's Legacy*, plus Niyati, Zuri, Ekaterina, and Gordon and Olivia Grey.

Shima assembled a bouquet of pink hibiscus blossoms on the short drive into Lahaina. "I did not have time to find more flowers," she grumbled, working with scissors and floral wire.

"It looks good to me," Blaze said.

"It looks beautiful." Danae glanced at Shima in the rearview mirror. "Thank you."

"And thank you all for coming on such short notice," Erik said.

"I would not miss it." Shima's eyes sparkled with tears.

The *I-do*'s at the town hall took five minutes. After a few holograms on the beach and some congratulatory hugs all around, the crew left Danae and Erik at the Whalesong Bed and Breakfast Inn on Front Street in Lahaina.

Déjà vu, Blaze thought.

"Wonderful place; you'll love it," Lorina assured them, shooting Blaze a mischievous grin as the van pulled away from the curb.

"I thought the captain wanted to lift in five days," Vipul said from the driver's seat.

"I think there'll be a slight delay," Blaze said. "Although she did cut our honeymoon short, so you never know."

"What a honeymoon?" Niyati looked confused when the adults burst into laughter.

"Yes, explain that to her, *baba*," Jake said.

***

Blaze had plenty of work to keep him busy over the next five days. He inspected and tested each of the engines to make sure the ship was ready for space flight. He had the *Alex* fueled with the last of Captain Shepherd's savings. He also enjoyed some time off, exploring some of Maui's scenic spots with Lorina and Niyati, although they chose not to visit the beach where Lorina's mother drowned.

"She seems less clingy, doesn't she?" he asked his wife over dinner on the fifth day, casting a meaningful glance at Niyati, who already cleaned her plate and was eyeing her mother's spaghetti with interest.

Lorina batted her eyelashes. "Do you think she's ready to stay in her own bed at night?"

"I hope so." Blaze laughed.

"All crewmembers please meet in the galley at 1800." The captain's voice came over the shipboard com.

"I guess they're back." Jake sauntered into the galley and settled into the fourth chair at their table. "Good, I'm ready to go to Waikiki."

"Send us a transmission once in a while and let us know how you're doing," Lorina said.

"You can count on it, cousin."

The rest of the *Alex*'s crew trickled in, along with Zuri and Ekaterina. Blaze thought of the two teens as ship's mascots. The girls offered to assist Lorina with the cooking, although he doubted they had Phailin's culinary skills.

The Thai cook had been promoted to orphanage director for The Lost Sheep. It was a dramatic career shift for her, but one she was eager to accept. *Plus it gives her a good reason to get away from Ting*, Blaze thought.

The helmsman had demonstrated to Vipul and Captain Shepherd that he was ready to fly the ship again, so it appeared everything was in order for a return to the passenger transport business.

Or so he thought.

Danae Sorensen was the last to enter the galley. She walked over to the counter and turned to face the crew, who were scattered around the dining area. She exchanged a warm smile with her new husband before addressing the group.

"So this is the game plan: we'll begin advertising for passengers to shuttle between the stations. We'll return to Maui at least once a month. When our bank account improves, we can discuss assisting ISPP with the task of returning ex-slaves to their homes, just like we did in China." She glanced at Ekaterina. "I already know we'll be taking a side trip to Romania at some point."

"But we can't leave." Instant silence followed Ting's matter-of-fact comment.

The captain glanced at him with a suspicious frown. "What are you talking about?"

"We can't go into space until after you have the baby."

A chorus of gasps followed this announcement. Captain Sorensen leaned back against the counter for support. She was wide-eyed and speechless.

"That's not funny, Marco." Erik moved to the captain's side and put a comforting arm around her.

"I'm not trying to be funny. I'm sharing a premonition." Ting shrugged. "I know you ordered me not to tell you about any more of my visions, Captain, but I thought you'd want to make an exception for this one."

"Hold on a minute," Jake said. "When did we start believing Ting's premonitions?"

"When it became obvious they were all accurate," the helmsman said. "Do you want me to compile a list to jog your memory?"

Jake scowled back at him. "I thought you were the one with memory problems. Don't you have brain damage or something?"

Ting shot Jake a frosty look but didn't respond.

The Sorensens stared at each other, their faces a mixture of shock and disbelief—and hope.

"It's a girl," Erik whispered, but the whole room heard.

"How could you possibly know that?" Captain Sorensen's jaw dropped.

"I had a dream . . . twice . . . about a little girl who looked like a smaller version of you."

"How is this even possible, assuming it's true?" Jake asked. "Erik, you know better than anyone the fertility rates of Earth-born couples—"

"Danae was born on Mars," Erik spoke over him. "She's been pregnant before—" He glanced at the captain for her consent to share more. She nodded, somber. "But she had a miscarriage."

"I'm sorry." Jake appeared mortified. "I didn't know. I didn't mean to embarrass you, Captain."

"You didn't, Jake." There was a gleam in her eyes. "But we don't need to stand here and speculate. Everyone, stay put." She grabbed Erik's hand and they rushed to the door. "We're going to the infirmary for just a minute. Don't move."

"You know, the new medical scanners are very accurate," Jake announced to the remaining crewmembers.

"How accurate?" Blaze asked.

They had the answer in ten seconds. Captain Sorensen's happy shriek was amplified over the shipboard com. *"I'm having a baby!"*

The crew applauded and cheered. Even Ting managed a grin.

Blaze exchanged a smile with Lorina. "I guess this changes all our plans."

"I think we'll all get to enjoy a nine-month vacation in paradise," Vipul said.

***

"Transmission for Captain Shep—I mean, Captain Sorensen," Shima announced over the com. "Please come to the bridge."

It had only been a few days since Ting's stunning premonition, but the Sorensens were still in a dither, trying to come up with a new plan to generate income until after their baby was born. The crew met several times to brainstorm. Shuttling ex-slaves to their homes around the globe was the most popular suggestion, but only if ISPP was willing to help with expenses. Going into space was out of the question, due to the high risk of miscarriage.

It was obvious Danae Sorensen was thrilled to be expecting. After all the hardship and heartache she endured, Blaze was glad to see her enjoying double blessings: a loving, supportive husband and a baby she had longed for.

Blaze's curiosity was piqued by Shima's announcement. *Who could be sending the captain a message?* On impulse, he decided to eavesdrop while the Sorensens and Shima viewed the transmission. He took the lift up to the top level and stayed out of sight near the doorway to the bridge.

"This transmission is intended for Captain Danae Shepherd—"

"Sorensen," Erik said.

"—of the passenger ship *Alex's Legacy*, docked at Lahaina, Maui, and was recorded on December twenty-fourth." Cade York's voice sounded uncharacteristically upbeat. "Merry Christmas, Danae. I wanted to share a surprise with you today."

"That's his son!" Captain Sorensen gasped. "He found Linc!"

"Thanks to the information you uncovered in the White Swan's hotel office—"

"Don't forget she was being held prisoner there—no thanks to you!" Erik snarled.

"Shush," the captain said. "I want to hear the rest."

"—I was able to determine that Lincoln was relocated to a shoe factory in Taipei before Hat Yai was bombed. We liberated his factory, along with several others, and now I'll need another ocean liner to house twenty-five hundred children from Taipei. Please let Murphy know the cruise ship idea was brilliant."

I'll be sure to tell her, Blaze thought.

"This is the first time I have seen him look happy," Shima said.

"That's not a real smile," the doctor said, "he looks like he's constipated."

"Erik!"

The transmission continued. "Thank you for your courage and determination. I'm grateful for everything you've done. Without your assistance, I might never have found Lincoln. I wish you all the best. If you ever get bored—"

"Not likely."

"Erik, hush."

"—I hope you'll consider helping ISPP return more children to their homes. We have a lot of work ahead of us. I wish I had a dozen more like you on my crew. Merry Christmas and happy star trails. York out."

Blaze slipped away before anyone caught him lurking outside the bridge. As he descended the ladder to return to the engine room, he couldn't help thinking about the people in his life who were orphans, either literally or figuratively, but the ship brought them all together. He had a family of his own, and he considered his shipmates his extended family.

Except for Ting, Blaze thought, laughing to himself. *I guess he'll always be the weird cousin at the family gatherin' no one wants to sit near.*

I guess I'm fine with him too.

Author's Note

Child slavery is a heartbreaking, brutal business, and my books have presented you with a sanitized version of this global travesty. Victims of human trafficking don't come through it without permanent damage, if they're fortunate enough to be liberated—most aren't. The insidious plague of pornography fuels the multibillion-dollar trafficking industry.

Vipul told Danae, "You've helped me realize how much one courageous person can accomplish." Imagine how much good many courageous people can accomplish.

Please consider donating or volunteering to assist an organization that is working to reverse the misery of human trafficking. I personally recommend Operation Underground Railroad www.ourrescue.com, but there are many others.

SterlingRWalker.com

Acknowledgments

Thanks to my loving and patient family on both sides of the country who have supported me in my hobby-turned-career of writing. In North Carolina: Glen, Davis, Nathaniel, Braden, Meilin, and Malani, and in California: Harrison, Lizbeth, and my grandson Alex.

Huge thanks to my cover artists, Jessica Bartlett and my son Nathaniel Walker, and to Kelly Furr who makes an awesome model for Danae.

Thank you to my cousin, author Lisa Rector, for the updated editing and formatting of my books and ebooks for publication.

What's In a Name?

Although some of the names I used in *The Orphan Ship* trilogy are symbolic of what's taking place in the story (Mother Teresa's and Lincoln are two examples), here are a few you may not have recognized.

Heshima—Swahili for "respect"
Zuri—Uzuri is Swahili for "beauty"
Elmina—The name of the infamous 15th century castle in Ghana where Africans were imprisoned before being shipped abroad as slaves.
Thanatos—Greek god of death
Acheron—From Dante's *Inferno*, Acheron was the name of the last river a soul had to cross to reach hell.
Forsetti—Forseti was the Norse god of justice